"I lack nothing, sir!" said Anne, furious at her new husband . . .

"But you do, Anne," he replied. "You lack the power to lure a man to your bed, to make him feel he'd be welcomed in your arms. You're as cold as a trout out of a Colorado stream."

"Cold because I don't ignite for a price? I think not. I explained to you once, sir, that love cannot be bought."

"Yes, I do remember that. How *does* one earn such a commodity?"

When she didn't answer right away, Jude got up to leave. He stopped when she whispered, "I don't know."

He sauntered to the window, casually telling her, "Be sure your husband isn't the last to know if you give your love away, ma'am."

Under her breath, Anne whispered, "Fool," but she didn't know if she meant Eastman—or herself . . .

Forever Yesterday

Forever Yesterday

JAN LESOING

PAGEANT BOOKS

PAGEANT BOOKS
225 Park Avenue South
New York, New York 10003

Cover artwork by Pino Daeni

Printed in the U.S.A.

First Pageant Books printing: July, 1988

10 9 8 7 6 5 4 3 2 1

To my children, who never doubted;
and my husband, who did;
and Nan Neal, who erased my own doubts.

Forever Yesterday

Chapter One

✦ ✦ ✦ ✦

A LADY'S MAID?" Annie Ellis hated to reject the only job offer she had had in the two long months since she had arrived in America, but this was unthinkable. "I'm not qualified! I know nothing about being a lady's maid!"

"Nonsense," her guardian, Mr. Charles Barrister, declared. "Your mum was Countess Rossington's lady's maid for years before she became the housekeeper for their London residence, and a most expert one she was, too."

"You know I was never allowed in the wing of the castle where Mum worked. I grew up in Grandfather's cottage, helping him train and care for horses. I'm an experienced groom and horse trainer, not a maid!"

"Yes, but unfortunately, child, there are no

1

jobs for females working with horses, and you have found nothing suitable in your rounds of the factories nor at the employment office. Your grandfather entrusted your care to me and I won't let him down. This is a most desirable position," Mr. Barrister insisted.

"The Armstrongs are a very wealthy family, lovey," Mrs. Barrister added, backing up her husband. "They pay Charles an excellent wage—and they *did* pay your fare to America—"

"Only because you were kind enough to let me pretend to be your niece. You know I'd do anything to repay you, but I don't know how to do the things Mum did, like dressing the countess's hair—"

"You can practice on me," Mrs. Barrister interrupted.

"Or seaming in stylish clothes for a perfect fit—"

"You've done a little sewing. I'm sure that won't be hard to learn."

"Nor cleaning and pressing gowns of fine fabrics. All I've ever cared for is wool and flax-weave cotton." To this Mrs. Barrister was silent. Her own family's wardrobes were made of similar materials.

"You can ask their washwoman, or we will find you a book about such things," Mr. Barrister argued. "We can't let trivialities keep you from taking this well-salaried offer, now can we? There may not be another."

Annie bit back her frustration. She did not want to be a burden to the Barristers, who had to provide for four children of their own, and would soon be moving into the Armstrongs' carriage house, but what they were asking was impossible. Mum had reproached her many times about her "lack of the feminine skills." She should have listened, but she had been blind to the world beyond her beloved grandfather's stables. Training horses for fox hunts and steeplechases was as natural to her as eating food, and she had never wanted any other life. Yet Grandfather had persuaded her to leave England, and it had been easy to leave after . . . well, that no longer mattered. But a lady's maid!

"I just don't know," she said desperately. "I will feel very foolish being so inept, but—," she added hopefully, "—if you think I can do it, I'll try."

"Good girl!" Charles exclaimed as he put his tall coachman's hat back onto his head. "Come along. I shall drive you over there straightaway."

"Keep your chin up," Mrs. Barrister added cheerfully. "I know you'll do fine. You're a plucky little thing and sometimes that's all it takes."

Annie was afraid it would take considerably more, but she grabbed her shawl and followed Mr. Barrister to the carriage.

"This is it, Miss," Charles Barrister announced as he opened the carriage door for her after a short drive. "I'll take you around to the servants' entrance myself and introduce you to the housekeeper, Mrs. Dorn. She's boss of the house and the good soul who told me about Mr. Armstrong wanting a lady's maid for his motherless daughter. Since Miss Daphne is young too, maybe she won't expect you to be an expert. Come now, step down. Don't look so glum. Why, I like it here. I never had it so good in my life."

Charles Barrister had the enviable position of being Mr. William Armstrong's status symbol, as it had become the fashion among nouveau-riche Chicago aristocrats to have an impeccably attired, formally correct English coachman. Since William Armstrong's meat-packing plant had become a most lucrative venture, he followed the custom.

"Good day to you, ma'am. Fine, bright morning, is it not?" Mr. Barrister remarked to the tallest, most dour-faced woman Annie had ever seen. The dark-skinned giantess was dressed completely in black.

"That it is, Mr. Barrister. Is this that niece of yours you were telling me about?"

"Yes, Mrs. Dorn, this is Miss Ellis." He sounded proud to introduce her. The woman's eyes ran briefly over Annie.

"Hmpfh! She's just a scrap of a little thing, isn't she? But I don't reckon that matters for the job they'll be hiring her for. I'd make short shrift of her if it was me needin' house help!"

Annie felt obliged to defend herself. "I'm very strong, ma'am. I'm used to hard work."

Mrs. Dorn stared at her as if she could not believe Annie had spoken. "Like I say, it's of no import. Follow me, I'll take you up to meet Lady Armstrong. She'll be the one decidin' if you'll serve the purpose or not. I'll send a message out to you when she's ready to go home," she added, dismissing Mr. Barrister.

Annie suddenly felt fainthearted as she followed the housekeeper up a narrow, closed stairway at the rear of the house. She considered turning and fleeing down the stairs, but resisted the impulse as Mrs. Dorn stopped before the last door in the hallway. At the first slight rap, a voice with a hint of a British accent questioned, "Yes? Who is it? What may I do for you?"

"Lady Armstrong, I have the English girl with me that Barrister brought around."

"Do show her in, Mrs. Dorn."

An elderly lady was seated in a rocker near the window of the graciously furnished room. She was dressed in a ruffled morning jacket of pale blue over a striped gown of soft muslin. Her gray-green eyes were mild as she smiled eagerly. Not waiting for an introduction, she began to question Annie. It was so good to hear an English voice that Annie relaxed, easily answering all the questions the fleshy, white-haired matron asked, until she quizzed, "How old are you?"

"Twenty," Annie replied as the Barristers had instructed her to do when applying for work.

"How old?"

Annie gulped and admitted, "Past seventeen."

"Um-hum, and why did you think you needed to be older? You *are* experienced, aren't you?"

"Not exactly, but my mother was Countess

Rossington's personal maid for many years and—"

"A *real* countess?" Lady Armstrong interrupted excitedly.

Hesitantly Annie nodded, surprised at the woman's obvious awe, for she was a titled lady herself!

"I know what you're thinking," Lady Armstrong confided like a guilty schoolgirl. "Why would a lady be impressed by a countess? Well, I grew up in England, all right, but in a small fishing village. I was about your age when I came here, and lucky because my Willy made a fortune and bought me the title; loved to indulge me, my Willy did, but back to you. If Barrister says you'll do, you'll do nicely, I'm sure. Why did you come to America with your aunt and uncle?"

Annie felt uncomfortable being dishonest, but she could not bring herself to say she had been jilted. No, not even jilted—disillusioned by Dev, her oldest friend and the man she loved. The old lady seemed to read her discomfort and went on, not waiting for an answer. "You'll never be sorry. I can vouch for that. Not a pretty little thing like you!"

Annie didn't know what to say. She was unaware she was beautiful; no one had ever told her that her thick, blue-black hair and snapping deep brown eyes were ravishing. She didn't know her slightly tilted nose was the perfect foil for a square chin that foretold her stubbornness or that, at seventeen, her body had blossomed to mature perfection. She blushed at Lady Armstrong's compliment, making the old woman chuckle as she announced, "I like you, Annie Ellis. You remind me of m'self when I came here—a wide-eyed innocent. You'll be good for my granddaughter. I shall go and bring her here to be introduced to her new maid."

Does this mean I have the job? Annie wondered hopefully as she watched the lady walk slowly from the room. Evidently not, she decided as she tried not to listen to the shouting match down the hall.

"I don't want a personal attendant, Grandma," a voice screeched. "This is the 1880s, not the 1820s, and it's Chicago, not London. None of my friends are saddled with a watchdog!"

"You have it all wrong, Daphne, dearest, the idea is to have someone who will assist you with your hair and wardrobe."

"The upstairs girls do that for me!"

"Then perhaps as a companion—"

"That's it, isn't it, Grandma? Nanny no longer is here to smother me, so you want to replace her with someone who will keep track of me every minute—like they did in that jail of an academy you sent me to."

"Daphne," Lady Armstrong said, sounding hurt, "Sherwood Seminary is an exclusive school, reputed to turn out young ladies for the finest of society circles. That's why your papa sent you there. He wanted the best for you. The same reason he wants you to have your own lady's maid!"

"Papa doesn't want what's best for me, or he would consent to Geoffrey's suit—"

"We don't have time to go into that disagreeable subject at the moment, Daphne." Lady Armstrong's voice took on a new firmness. "Your father says we are to hire Barrister's niece, and hire her we will. You know how important it is to him to keep the man happy in his employ."

"La, yes! We must keep that snooty, high-toned coachman satisfied, mustn't we? Papa should put the man in his place instead of remodeling the upper level of the carriage house for him and his brood. After all, they are mere servants, and I don't want an old—"

"That is quite enough. If you aren't careful, she'll hear you. Come along. It's your father's order—"

The rest of the conversation could not be overheard, but Annie was afraid her fiercely grinding teeth might be. Who did this obnoxious creature think she was, insulting Mr. Barrister, and Annie, too? Gritting her teeth to keep them still, she angrily awaited the two ladies' entrance. It would only take her a minute to tell them they couldn't pay her enough to take this job!

Or could they? Where could she go? She had no money, no other job. She couldn't live alone in that sordid ghetto for penniless immigrants.

Mrs. Armstrong smiled sweetly at her as she returned to the room, acting as if nothing had happened. "This is my granddaughter, Daphne

Armstrong—Miss Daphne, that is, Annie. You will be entirely in her employ. I shall leave the two of you here in my sitting room to become acquainted. I have some things to take care of."

Annie speculatively eyed her sulky new employer. She was no beauty, but she was striking in her expensive clothing.

"That's a boner!" Daphne remarked after the door had closed. "Grandma's fleeing from an unpleasant scene. She always does."

Annie wished she dared rebuke this unpleasant creature.

Not expecting an answer, Daphne went on, "You aren't nearly as old as I expected. How old are you?"

"Seventeen."

"Seventeen! You must have learned your duties at a young age! When did you first go into service?"

"I haven't—I mean, I've never been a—a—lady's maid before."

"You haven't? Oh, this is rich! Papa paying you a handsome salary and you're not even experienced!" she said, smirking.

"Lady Armstrong knows—"

"She's softhearted. She won't tell him. He's become such an ogre these days, no one can please him, with the possible exception of your Mr. Barrister. And as long as you understand my terms, I'll not tattle on you. Let him waste his precious money. He's becoming a tightwad anyway. All our wealth is just for show of late—at home we are enduring stringent poverty."

Annie looked around at the lavish room, then sized up Daphne's taffeta and lace gown and wondered how the girl could call her life-style impoverished. "I'll be glad to learn to do everything you need me to do," she promised, feeling more guilty than ever. She was taking a job she was unqualified to do and they couldn't even afford her salary.

"Pish posh! Don't sound so sanctimonious. You don't have to learn much of anything to please me, and you can forget what I said about money. Papa can afford anything he wants. This stinginess is just a whim of his, probably to discourage me from marrying Geoffrey Beaumont. The Beaumont family has been experiencing a difficult time, so Papa thinks it's his duty to impress on me how miserable my life with Geoffrey would be. Papa wants me to marry someone richer—but I won't. I love Geoff and he loves me. Besides, their financial downturn is only temporary. Geoff told me so. Yes, I'll keep you—it serves Papa right!"

Without another word Daphne turned and sailed out of the room, leaving a bewildered Annie behind. When no one came to dismiss her, she went back downstairs in search of Mrs. Dorn. It was Mrs. Dorn who found her, almost as if she had been waiting for her.

"Hired you, did they?"

"I believe so."

"Well, remember this, little gal. You can fool some people sometimes, but you can't fool Lilah Dorn never, so don't try! You just consider who pays your salary and do right by *him*, not that spoiled daughter of his, or you'll have me to answer to."

"I'll try hard to please," Annie managed to stutter as the woman's hard-eyed scrutiny continued.

"All right. So be it. You can work here as long as you remember who you're to please. That girl will be after you to help her deceive her papa, mark my words. If you help her, I'll personally see you regret it."

At this, Annie's back stiffened and she ventured, "Lady Armstrong hired me. She says I am Miss Daphne's own maid. I will do as *she* tells me!" With this bit of defiance Annie stalked out the side door and down the veranda steps, determined to find Mr. Barrister herself. What kind of a household was this? A "lady" who wasn't an aristocrat, a rebellious daughter who wanted a maid only to spite her tightfisted father, and a threatening housekeeper. It was most confusing, but it was a real job with a real salary, and Annie knew she had to accept it—at least temporarily.

"Please let me ride up on the seat with you," Annie begged Charles when she found him at the rear of the circling driveway.

One look at her distraught face and he agreed. "You can probably see more of the town from here, anyway." More quietly he asked, "Did it go badly for you in there? Didn't you get the job?"

"I got it," Annie told him, "but I don't think I

want it. Oh—don't worry, I'm going to take it for now. They're a strange lot, aren't they?"

Mr. Barrister chuckled. "Not like our titled peers back in England, you mean? That's true enough. Here, lines between classes haven't been drawn for centuries on end. They're making their own rules."

"They're making some strange ones. That housekeeper thinks she has more say-so than Lady Armstrong herself."

"Mrs. Dorn? Mr. Armstrong relies heavily on her to keep his household running smoothly— and economically."

"They are hard-pressed for funds, then?"

"Perhaps. Nothing has ever been said, of course. Only innuendos."

"Then why are they hiring me? Did you ask them to?"

He looked insulted. "I should say not! Mrs. Dorn mentioned finding the daughter a personal attendant who would be cognizant of her whereabouts. It seems the girl is prone to leave the house without a proper chaperone. Naturally her father wants someone with her. I immediately suggested you."

"I *am* to be a watchdog!"

"Not at all. I would think what she needs is a friend. She probably misses her classmates."

"Mr. Barrister, she's twenty-five if she's a day, and she wants to marry someone named Geoff!"

"So that's it!"

"And that housekeeper is positively threatening with her gothic ways."

"She means well, but I don't believe any threats she makes would be idle ones. I'd stay on the good side of her, if I were you."

"That may not be easy."

To allay her worries, Mr. Barrister suggested, "Look around you. This is Prairie Avenue, better known as Millionaires' Row to the rest of Chicago. Isn't it something?"

Prairie Avenue was a misnomer, Annie decided. A street lined with towered mansions could not be remotely related to a prairie, could it? Each house sat in the midst of a landscaped lawn. All were ornamented with bay windows, verandas, or balconies. Some even had stained glass windows, and most were adorned with works of granite and marble. The ostentatious homes were impressive, even to a girl who had lived her life in the shadows of a castle. There was something overwhelming about so many people with so much money in such a small area.

After she had worked for the Armstrongs for six weeks, Annie believed that it *was* millionaires' row! Never in her life had she dreamed of such luxuries as the people on this side of Chicago took for granted: gaslights, closed carriages, power-driven trolley cars, even some indoor plumbing! And the houses were as richly adorned inside as outside, if the William Armstrong mansion was any indication.

After a lifetime of living in a small, sparsely

furnished three-room cottage, Annie felt as if she should tiptoe among such priceless furnishings. She tried to express her feelings to Daphne, but she only laughed at Annie.

"This house is nothing compared to some of my school friends' homes in New York or on the Hudson. It's small by comparison, but I admit Papa buys the most elaborate furnishings he can find. Impressions are important, you know. I like it better in the East; I hate it here. Now that I am engaged to dear Geoff, I'll stay here to plan my wedding, but we won't live in this burg. He doesn't want to, either."

"Then your father has consented to your marriage?" Annie had to ask. She'd found her job to be quite simple and the salary was excellent. She was even able to save a considerable sum. Not enough, however, to go out on her own yet.

"No, he's still being stubborn, but he will give in to me any day now. He always does. He's always been strict with my brother, Carter, but he can't refuse my sulks for long. Don't worry. I've grown to like having you around to wait on me. When I get married, I shall tell Geoffrey I want to hire you."

Annie wondered how Daphne would manage if she really did marry a poverty-stricken gentleman. Daphne complained constantly about how frugally she was being forced to live now. To Annie, a big house full of servants, with lavish meals cooked by a French chef, was not the impoverished life Daphne insisted it was. A personal maid who was only someone for Daphne to voice her complaints to was not an essential expense.

"The Beaumonts' carriage just pulled into the drive," Daphne announced, interrupting Annie's musings. "Be sure you find lots of excuses for leaving Geoffrey and me alone for a change."

"Every time I leave the room, Mrs. Dorn glowers at me."

"Ignore the witch. You're to do as *I* say, just remember that."

Annie also remembered Mrs. Dorn's threats. She felt in a real dilemma every time Mr. Geoffrey Beaumont came to call. Personally she saw no reason not to leave the pair alone in the parlor. Of course they did not want their every word overheard. Did Geoffrey say the same things to Daphne that Dev had said to her, she wondered? Or kiss her with such passion? Considering the haughty Daphne and the milksop Geoffrey, Annie doubted it, but she was still glad for days like today when Lady Armstrong joined the couple in the parlor. It cleared her own conscience.

Annie eagerly anticipated her day off each week. All day was set aside to explore the wonders of Chicago—to ride the trolleys and take in the sights from the six-story music hall to the edge of town, where one could look out on acres of farmland. Today she had gone shopping with Mrs. Barrister at the big Marshall Field

Store, and it was here Annie purchased her first store-bought dress.

It was the first dress she'd ever owned that had not been cut down from one of Mum's dark-colored ones, and she bought the brightest gown she could find: a heavy cotton chintz in red and black stripes with a white lace collar and jabot. The skirt fell into pleats in front and had an overlayer of pleats in back to give it a bustle-like fullness. It was perfect for Annie's petite figure.

As soon as they returned home she put it on, and she was trying to see herself in the cheval mirror in her room when little Margaret Barrister came running in all atwitter. "Annie! Annie! It's Miss Daphne. She sent Bixby, the tweeny, to say she wants you at once."

"Are you sure, little one? This is Tuesday, my free day."

"I know that!" Margaret's voice was childishly miffed. "She still wants you. Bixby said so."

Thinking there might be an emergency, Annie did not take time to change. She ran from the upper level of the carriage house the Barristers had recently moved into and flew up the back stairs of the mansion two at a time and was headed pell-mell down the hall just as Carter Armstrong stepped into the corridor. Taken by surprise, she tried to stop herself from crashing into him and in the process lost her balance. Reacting quickly, he held out his arms to break her fall and Annie found herself toppled against his chest.

Mortified, she expected an irritated rebuke from Daphne's older brother. Instead, he laughed as he helped her to stand. "Well, well, what have we here? A fiery comet streaking through our hallway?"

"I'm so very sorry, sir. I didn't see you, sir. I didn't mean to run into you at all, sir." She started to back away from him, but he continued to hold her upper arms firmly where he had grasped them to keep her from falling, eyeing her approvingly as he did so.

"And a fiery comet you are, I see. You blush very becomingly. Please accept my apologies. It was I who stepped into your path. I've never been 'sir'd' so delightfully, but please, call me Carter!"

"Yes, Mr. Carter, I shall if you wish."

"Not *Mr*. Carter. Carter!"

"Sir, I don't believe you recognize me. I am Miss Daphne's maid."

"Miss Daphne, is it? Daffy is coming up in the world. However, I very definitely recognized you, Annie, and when I asked you to call me Carter, I meant it. This isn't England, you know. We aren't nobility here. Haven't you heard our motto, 'All men are created equal'? Why, my family arrived in Chicago a generation or two ago with all their belongings in a covered wagon. Fortunately the land they settled was later purchased by the railroads for an astronomical sum. My father used the money to install feed lots for incoming cattle and later built a packing plant . . . and here we are today."

Smiling at his narrative, Annie looked up at him. He was only a few inches taller than his sister, but he was stockily built. His hair was medium-brown, which matched his medium-brown eyes. The combination would have been very plain if it hadn't been for the sparkle in his eyes and his pleasant smile.

He seemed to be waiting for her to say something. Should she continue to act the servant, or should she accept the friendship he seemed to offer? She tried to adopt a middle ground.

"That is the kind of tale they tell us of America back in England, but I suspect there are many more incidences of 'a penny the wiser' than fabulous riches such as your family has amassed."

Carter laughed. "Yes, a penny the wiser does describe most who come here expecting wealth to fall into their laps. 'A penny the wiser.' I like that, Annie." He smiled again, looking deeply into her eyes.

Annie suddenly recalled Daphne's unusual summons. "Excuse me, I must hurry. Your sister needs me immediately."

"I can't imagine any need for haste," he said as he reluctantly dropped his hands from her shoulders.

A chill replaced the warmth of his hands, and Annie felt a slight flutter of her long-still heart as she turned away. Don't be silly! she told herself. He is just being kind!

Yet his next words implied more. "You are the most beautiful comet we've ever had in our house—perhaps the only comet—but still very beautiful. I'll not wait to just run into you again; I shall make a point of it."

Flustered, she could only stammer, "Good day, sir—I mean Carter."

"You made it a good day, Annie," Carter called back as he bounded down the wide front staircase that wound gracefully to the marble-tiled vestibule below.

"Whatever took you so long?" Daphne asked as soon as Annie had stepped into the bed-chamber.

Not daring to reply with the truth, Annie murmured, "I was getting dressed, Miss Daphne."

"So I see. For once you don't look like a mousy little sparrow, or do I mean a wren? Indeed," she said speculatively, "with decent clothes you could accompany me when I need—a companion. Do you have more such gowns?"

"No," Annie admitted, hurt by Daphne's description of her.

"No matter. I have innumerable old ones. I'm sure you can hem them up to fit you."

Annie was befuddled by this. She still felt insulted, yet it sounded as if she should be thanking Daphne for the proffered kindness.

Daphne rushed on, "Annie, I am in a real brier patch this evening and you must help me. I am going out without Grandma's permission. I have told her I am ill and am going to bed, but you will get into bed in my place. With a nightcap on and the covers pulled snugly about you, Grandma won't be wise to anything. She's getting very nearsighted and if you mumble something about just wanting to sleep, she'll go away."

"You want me to deceive your grandmother? And Mrs. Dorn? While you sneak out?" Annie gasped.

"Stop being such a pious puss! It won't hurt you, you know. You get paid well enough for what little you do. I should think you'd want to earn your wages."

"Of course I do, Miss Daphne, but I was hired as a lady's maid. I shall willingly do all the duties—"

"Then, Annie, I'd suggest you consider this a duty. Otherwise, I shall tell Papa you are most unsatisfactory!"

Annie fell silent. There was no choice. She knew that she did little enough for her salary. Daphne *did* have the right to complain. Still, she cringed at the thought of being caught by the stern Mrs. Dorn.

"I hope your silence means you are reconsidering," Daphne remarked crossly. Then she wheedled, "Oh please, Annie! It is *so* important to me. Geoff is taking me to a small party at a private club he belongs to; it will just be a few people playing some card games. I only want to try my luck! He says it's great sport."

"It does sound as if it might be fun. I always liked playing cards," Annie admitted, wondering why it had to be such a secret. "Can't you just tell your father?"

"Tell Papa? Merciful saints, no! He hates Geoffrey, and he's an old-fashioned fuddy-duddy. He plays faro or monte all the time at Chapin & Gore's, but he thinks it unseemly for women to do so. If he had his way, the only thing I'd be allowed to do is sit in the parlor and visit with crusty old ladies and the drabs I went to school with."

"It does sound exceedingly dull. If I were you, I'd be out riding your beautiful horse, jumping hurdles and—" Annie's voice became dreamy as she thought of Daphne's well-trained Arabian.

"Jumping hurdles? That certainly sounds more exciting than the staid riding I do. Do you know how? Could you teach me?"

"Oh, yes!"

"Good! It will be an excellent excuse for just the two of us to leave the house sometimes. Now, I must go. I'm so glad you understand—and I wasn't really going to tell Papa, Annie."

That last Annie doubted. She felt certain Daphne would sharply retaliate if ever crossed.

After Daphne left, Annie took off her new dress and slipped into Daphne's voluminous nightdress and eyelet-ruffled sleeping cap. She carefully tucked her hair up and climbed into the high four-poster bed.

An hour later Bixby knocked to ask if she was coming down to dinner. Annie muttered that she was not feeling well enough. After dinner Daphne's grandmother looked in on her, and once again Annie choked, "Not feeling well—

just want to sleep." Lady Armstrong went away, too.

After the fear of discovery subsided, Annie relaxed, only to find it most boring to lie in the dark. For a while she thought of the friendly Carter Armstrong who seemed so different from his father. Mr. Armstrong always acted toplofty and put on pretentious airs, while his son claimed their family was rich only by chance and disclaimed social barriers. Before tonight, Annie would have said Daphne was like her father, but now she was not sure.

Hours later she was awakened by Daphne's voice ordering, "Move over, Annie, I must have room to sleep, too."

"Oh, Miss Daphne, I'm sorry I fell asleep. I'll dress now and hang up your things, then go to my quarters," Annie whispered as she scurried from the bed.

"Don't be silly!" Daphne shushed her. "It's two A.M. Barrister would have a dozen questions for you, and he's such a stickler for propriety he might tell Papa. Tomorrow I shall have the room next to mine prepared for you to use permanently. Go to sleep; I'm exhausted."

Annie wasn't certain she wanted to move away from the Barrister family, even to sleep. The Barristers were one of the last ties she had to England and her grandfather . . . and Dev. It was a long time before she fell asleep.

Chapter Two

✦ ✦ ✦ ✦ ✦

THE NEXT DAY, true to her promise, Daphne gave
Annie dozens of dresses, coats, and riding ensembles she claimed were too out of style for
her. To Annie, all of them were beautiful. Several
days later, Annie learned the reason her mistress
had been so generous.

"Annie," the older girl confided, "we are
going to tell everyone you are my cousin visiting
from England. Everyone except the family and
servants, of course. They must not hear of our
ruse."

"Why, Miss Daphne?" Annie asked seriously.

"Stop calling me 'Miss' Daphne at once,
Annie," Daphne ordered, then asked, "Annie
. . . don't you have a real name?"

"That *is* my real name!"

"It's too plain. We shall call you Anna—Anna
Marie. That sounds like gentry, doesn't it?"

"I suppose, but you still haven't told me the
reason."

"Yes I did. I told you I am secretly engaged to
Geoffrey, but I can't permit my family or friends
to find out. They must think I am out with you
whenever I meet with him."

"Why?" Annie remembered Carter saying
there were no class restrictions in America.

"He's older, that's why," Daphne told
her firmly. Then she added slowly, "Well,
that's part of the reason. The real reason is

23

because he has taken up gambling in order to recoup his family's fortune. Can you imagine anything more romantic, Annie? We'll be traveling on luxury steamers that cross the ocean as well as on excursion boats, and we'll attend all the race meets. We'll go to casinos in Paris and to clubs in New Orleans or New York. Fancy it!"

"Where will you live?" Annie could not envision such a life; it sounded terrible to her, always to be surrounded by people, traveling constantly.

"Eventually we'll have a palatial home on New York City's fabulous Fifth Avenue, but for now we'll be staying in the finest hotels wherever we go."

"But Daphne, you won't be able to take your horse with you," Annie warned.

"My horse! Whatever would I want with *it?* One horse is much like another. We can hire some if we wish to ride.

"That reminds me. You were going to teach me to ride like an English lady. I need to learn because I might be invited to a fox hunt. Geoff's friends in England are of the nobility," she added loftily.

"I'll start teaching you any time. I'd love to."

"That settles it, we'll ride this afternoon." She crossed the room and tugged on the bellpull. A shy young chambermaid was instantly at the door. "Have the grooms saddle my horse and Carter's at once."

"Carter's horse?" Annie asked hesitantly.

"You've led me to believe you're an expert

rider. Don't tell me you're worried you can't handle a Thoroughbred stallion?"

"Oh, I'm sure I can handle the horse, but won't your brother mind?"

"He'll never know. He's at the plant every day until six. We'll be back before then."

"But . . ."

"Annie, you just have to stop acting so nicey-nice. It's vexing to my constitution."

Nothing Annie had felt since she came to America compared with her joy that afternoon. Carter's horse was a superbly trained jumper, a beautiful gray stallion that tossed his mane and pranced proudly to the park as if he were as pleased as his young rider by this event. As soon as they reached the area of the park where the course had been set up, Annie gave the horse free rein. He eagerly began to pace himself and took each of the jumps with ease. Pure pleasure filled Annie's heart.

Carter Armstrong and his longtime friend, Nathaniel Ryan, were leisurely riding back from a late lunch when Nathaniel exclaimed, "Say, Carter, that horse is almost identical to that gray of yours. It is more fortunate, though; it's being ridden by a beautiful nymph instead of a clumsy oaf like you."

Carter didn't even wait to rap properly on the roof of the carriage. He stuck his head out of the window, shouting, "Barrister, stop at once."

"Yes, sir." Even Barrister's voice seemed to frown at such uncouth behavior. His frown soon turned to alarm as he saw what the two men had jumped out to watch—Annie Ellis. What was she doing out there? Even so, he admitted to himself, she had the horsemanship of her grandfather, old Clarence, all right. She was an eyeful as she gracefully took one jump after another and then trotted back to where Daphne waited, demanding, "Teach me this minute! Oh, it looks like great sport! I can't wait to learn!"

Carter had run over to the two riders with Nathaniel close on his heels. When she spied him, Annie began to blush with shame for being caught. Even Daphne looked flustered as she challenged, "What are you doing here? You're supposed to be at the plant."

Her brother ignored her. He only had eyes for Annie. Today his eyes were bright with admiration and his smile was one of pride, but Annie did not look up from where her fingers were nervously knotting the reins as she apologized. "I'm very sorry to have ridden your horse without permission, sir—"

"Carter! Remember, Annie, it's Carter! Don't apologize for riding my horse—I know whose doing *that* was." He glanced at Daphne, then his eyes immediately returned to Annie. "I thank you for showing my friend here what a truly splendid mount I own. My horse thanks you for letting him show off his abilities, and Nathaniel and I thank you for being a beautiful vision as you so skillfully took those jumps."

"You were really magnificent, Miss—"

"Ellis," Daphne supplied. "My cousin." She glared down at Carter, daring him to defy her. "Miss Anna Marie Ellis, who is visiting us from England."

"So *this* is why you take your meals at home each night, instead of joining us as you used to, Carter. I can't say that I blame you, but aren't you being a little selfish? Shouldn't you introduce her to your friends?"

Annie stood mute. Would Carter expose Daphne's silly ruse? To her relief, he didn't seem to mind going along with his sister's prank; in fact, he seemed to be enjoying it. Smiling at Annie, he agreed, "You're right, Nathaniel. I have been very remiss in my duties to my— cousin. I shall begin to rectify them by taking her to Knisley's for dinner this very evening. You and Daphne may join us."

Daphne was ecstatic. "Carter, that is a splendid idea. I haven't eaten there since my birthday. Can we eat in the French dining room?"

"We'll leave that up to our—cousin, Daffy. Do you prefer German or French cuisine? The chefs at Knisley's are experts in both."

Dumbfounded, Annie just stared at him. It was rare enough for a lady's maid to eat at the same table at home, but to go out to dine was unheard of! She decided that Carter probably wanted to play a trick on his friend, and that he would explain the joke later so she gallantly joined the merriment, saying, "Since I have never tasted German food, I shall choose that."

"The French is better," was Daphne's comment, but Carter said, "Wise girl," and his friend seemed to agree.

Lying in bed that night, Annie remembered the warmth and strength of Carter's hands as he had helped her in and out of the carriage. He had not taken his hand from her arm even when they had entered the vestibule of the house on their return from dinner. Instead, he had led her to the drawing room, where his father and grandmother were sitting.

Daphne had preceded them and perched herself on her father's knee. She was pouting. "Papa, next time *you* take me to Knisley's instead of Carter. I wanted French cuisine and we had to eat that heavy German food instead. Please, Papa."

He answered distractedly, "Yes, I shall. One of these days soon. Carter!" He looked up at his son, a worried frown marring his usually vague, full face. He rubbed his muttonchop whiskers with one hand as he continued, "I found out tonight that the Omaha stockyards of Paxton-McShane are going to build and lease a large packing plant to the Omaha Stock Company. You know what this means, don't you? The Union Pacific will be shipping even fewer herds straight through from Ogallala, Nebraska, to Chicago than they have been. Our beef supply has been halved and then halved again."

Carter led Annie to a velvet settee, then sat

down beside her. "Perhaps this is the time to sell the business, Papa."

"Sell! I wouldn't get enough now to half pay the mortgage I took on the plant—and this house, too—to build the new addition to the slaughter rooms and packing department. Why, I'd be ruined, Carter. Ruined, do you hear me?"

"Dammit!" Carter burst out. "Why in God's name did you take out a mortgage? You told me you were using surplus capital! Everyone saw the writing on the wall last year—our Chicago stockyards were sadly depleted by the Omaha opening."

"I thought it was a temporary setback. The overseas market is bigger than ever, and I wanted to be ready to meet demands for American beef around the world!"

"You should have cut back. You know my law practice is growing; I can't continue to help you at the plant and establish myself, too."

"Ingrate!" his father shouted. "I pay for your education so you can help me in the business, and I get a lawyer instead."

"William!" Lady Armstrong intervened, speaking sharply to her son. "Give the boy his due. You were proud enough of him when he graduated from law school with honors. You never once mentioned wanting him to come into the business. In fact, you were like a shark, wanting the waters all to yourself."

"Yes! Yes! Don't remind me of all that now, Mama. Things have changed. Money is scarce; I've put in place extreme economies at the plant, cut the labor force way back, and as you know, I'm holding a tight lid on our budget here at the house, but it's not enough. Unless I can get Gil Eastman's backing, I'll be broke before the year is out."

"Then that is your solution. Is there no way to get him into your pocket?" Carter asked.

"He's his own man, strong and tough as they come, but . . . there may be one way." William Armstrong stroked his whiskers even more determinedly, then ordered, "All of you, out! I have thinking to do and plans to make!"

"Now you sound like my son," Lady Armstrong pronounced as she gathered up her knitting.

Annie was relieved that they had all been dismissed. She had felt awkward sitting in on what should have been a private family matter. She had tried to leave the room, but Carter had restrained her. Now he turned to her, saying, "I wanted you to stay so you would feel a part of the family."

"That was kind of you, but I felt *de trop*."

"There you go again," Daphne rebuked, "trying to impress everyone with your meager French vocabulary."

"Daffy," Carter scolded, "remember yourself. Stop acting like an ill-mannered hoyden."

"I'll act however I please, Carter Armstrong, and I'll thank you to remember Annie is *my* maid. Just because we've been playacting that she's my English cousin is—"

"What's this?" Mr. Armstrong asked quickly

as Lady Armstrong turned from where she'd
started up the stairs.

"Nothing, Papa, I misspoke," Daphne assured him as she gave him a peck on the cheek
and scurried from the room. Before she reached
the door she remembered she did not want
Annie cross-examined by her father, so she ran
back and grabbed the younger girl's hand. Practically pulling Annie along, she told her, "I'll
need your help with all these buttons, Annie.
Why, I don't know how I ever got along before.
Papa was so sweet to hire you to attend me." As
an afterthought she called back over her shoulder, "You were right about getting Barrister to
recommend someone, Papa. Annie is indispens-
able."

If only that were true, Annie thought, she
might not be so disconcerted when she felt Mrs.
Dorn's eyes following her, as they were now.
She did not have to turn and look back down the
steps to know that the woman was lurking in the
shadows, watching.

America is so different from England, Annie
thought as she lay awake in her room. Who back
in England would give a maid a room like this
one, with a separate chamber for dressing and
bathing? Annie knew, of course, that this room
was hers only because Daphne was using her to
cover her absences. Still, it was remarkable:
taking her meals with her employers and wearing Daphne's elegant hand-me-downs.

All these things were hard to believe, but the most amazing was the way Carter Armstrong treated her. Taking her arm as they walked out from Knisley's, continuing to hold it as he spoke to acquaintances or greeted friends in the dining room and foyer. Even more important, he had held her arm and walked her right into the room where his father and grandmother sat. He made her feel special.

When Dev had cast her aside to marry the wealthy Lady Estelle, Annie's pride had been smashed. He had deluded her, saying they'd marry someday, but when the time came, he followed his parents' dictates to marry in his own class—or be disinherited. Her beloved Dev had chosen Estelle—for her money. How could she have been so innocent? Annie berated herself. Even now, his thick blond hair and his ocean-blue eyes haunted her dreams. . . .

She tried to think of Carter, whose attentions flattered her. He was kind and he certainly didn't try to hide his interest in her. But what was the meaning behind his actions? She could not deny that her heart beat just a little faster when he was around. Perhaps she didn't get those hot and cold tremors in his presence as she had when Dev had touched her, but . . . that was good. No one was ever going to have enough power over her to hurt her again. What would it take to evict him from her dreams?

Chapter Three

❖ ❖ ❖ ❖ ❖

ANNIE! ANNIE, WAKE UP." Mrs. Barrister shook her slightly to awaken her the next morning.

Sleepily Annie started to ask from old habit, "Is it time to—," then suddenly she sprang wide awake. "Mrs. Barrister! What are you doing here? Is anything wrong?"

"There is a letter to you from England in the post today. I brought it up to you as soon as it arrived. Perhaps it is from your grandfather."

Annie eagerly took the letter and examined it. A chill swept over her when she saw the writing. "It's from Mr. Burr, Grandfather's solicitor," she whispered.

Mrs. Barrister must have felt the same cold chill. "Shall I read it for you?"

Annie's eyes were filling fast with tears of premonition so she silently handed it back to Mrs. Barrister to read aloud:

> *I have been entrusted by your mother, Miss Clare Ellis, to inform you of the death of your grandfather, Clarence Ellis. He was fortunate in that he died in his sleep with no preceding illness. I sincerely wish you well, little Annie, and I know how happy your journey to America made my client. The last time I visited with him, he assured me you had found a splendid opportunity there already. He was most pleased. I am sorry I had to give you this sad news. Respectfully yours, M. Burr.*

Mrs. Barrister threw down the letter and hastily sat on the edge of the bed to take the sobbing girl into her arms. "Now, now, lovey, he died happy. That is all we can ask. He would not want you to weep like this, child. He always told us how proud he was of your strength and courage."

"What's going on?" Daphne entered the room, sleepily tying the belt of her wrapper.

"It's Annie's grandfather, Miss Daphne. She just received word he passed away."

"That's very sad for you, Annie. You may go with Mrs. Barrister for the day."

"Thank you, Miss Daphne," Annie managed between sniffles. For the first time, Annie was thankful Grandfather had sent her to America. How empty her world would have been there with him gone! Yes, Grandfather had been right—as always.

That afternoon, as she sat alone in her room mourning her grandfather, she sadly recalled the circumstances that had made her agree to leave him. Age had forced him to stop training horses, so she had gone to Birmingham to live with her aunt and work at a woolen mill. How she had hated it there! The mill had been closed down by a strike, so she'd used her savings for a round-trip fare back to her grandfather's cottage.

"Strikes! Strikes! Picketing! What does it all accomplish, I ask you?" Clarence Ellis asked as he pounded on the small table in the center of the kitchen.

"Ever since that despicable Disraeli was in favor and had the Queen's ear, we've had this unrest. Poor P.M. Blackstone will have his problems getting the country back to law and order now that he's in power again. In my day, we worked without feeling sorry for ourselves. We didn't demand this and that. We were glad for a job!"

Then his voice softened. "Don't worry, I have better plans for you, wonderful ones. I've found a way to send you to America! It's a land of golden opportunities, Annie. Once there, I know you'll make the most of them."

Disheartened, Annie scolded, "Grandfather! You're dreaming. It's much too expensive! It would take all your savings from selling the farm . . . and I'd not want to go alone . . . I'd loathe being away from you. Besides—" She started to mention Dev, but he cut her off.

"You won't be going alone and it's not costing us a farthing. Charles Barrister, the Earl's coachman, is emigrating to Chicago to become a chauffeur for a wealthy gentleman who is arranging all travel accommodations for the Barrister family. His niece, Phyllis, married Sam Rolfe's boy, Andrew, last month, so she'll not be needing her passage. Charles has agreed to take you in her place."

Annie knew he wanted her to be excited, so she tried not to sound as disheartened as she felt. "I don't know what to say, Grandfather.

This is so unexpected. I do love you so for trying to help me, but I don't think I could bear to go so far away. I'd miss you too much. And—and—" She debated explaining to him that she could never move away from Dev and Castle Cloud. Never!

He began speaking again, this time softly and sincerely. "You're trying to tell me about young Rossington, girl, but there is naught to tell. If he hadn't been as a brother to you all these years, I'd have chased the lad away a long time ago. He'll never be man enough for you, Annie Ellis. I never interfered with your friendship, but I never want to see you hurt by it, either. I want you away from here before that happens."

How can Grandfather say such a thing, she thought to herself. Grandfather just didn't understand Dev. She would have to prove to him that Devbridge Rossington truly loved her as much as she loved him. Grandfather was waiting for her to answer but there was nothing to say, not until she talked to Dev and they set a betrothal date. All she had to do was tell him of this and he would marry her at once. He would never risk having her sent off to America.

"We'll talk of this later," she promised, stalling for time. "I just can't wait to ride Star, it's been so long . . . do you mind?"

"No, no, run along with you. I'll just snooze a little, then Andrew Rolfe's coming to talk crops. Just remember, I'm right about this, my girl. I've thought it all through again and again and it's for the best. You'll like Barrister's missus, Annie.

They'll keep you company on shipboard and on the train to Chicago, and they insist you're to live with 'em until you make a place for yourself there. You'll do that soon enough—Chicago's in the middle of farmland, child. A handsome young farmer will snatch you up on sight. On a farm—that's where you belong. Mark my words!"

"I—I—don't know, Grandfather. I promise I'll think on it." She kissed his weathered cheek and hurried out to the shed to saddle her mare. Grandfather was going to be very stubborn about this America thing, she was afraid. Hopefully she could make him understand why she'd never go to America. She was going to marry Dev and live at Castle Cloud forever!

They had planned it for so long. The two had been friends since childhood, children whose parents had left them behind. As soon as Dev had learned to elude his tutor, he had found his way to the small horse farm and had spent all his free time there. Annie supposed she had loved him forever.

As she rode her mare into the glade where she was to meet Dev, she smiled dreamily to herself, recalling their last visit here. They had tied their horses to a low-hanging limb and walked together to an old fallen tree where they often sat.

At last Dev had spoken. "This place is special, you know."

Annie had answered glibly, "Very special.

Remember when we played shipwreck and the log was our survival raft in the middle of rough seas?"

"I was not thinking of our games when I said the glade is special to me. I was remembering the day you first gave your promise to marry me, Annie."

Quickly Annie had turned to him. Was he teasing her about their childhood vow? Did he love her as she loved him? Hesitantly she had answered, "I remember that too, Dev."

"I'm glad, for it makes the asking much easier. Did you mean it? You will marry me?"

For her answer, Annie had thrown her arms around his neck and flung herself against him. His arms had quickly encircled her and grasped her closer still when she tossed back her hair and looked eagerly up into his face, asking, "How could you doubt it, Dev?"

Then they had shared a kiss that was very different from those they had experimented with as children. It was a kiss of promise, followed by another even more passionate. And then another.

Dev had wanted to go on kissing her, but Annie drew back, for she sensed Dev's desire and feared her own might betray her. At first he had seemed disgusted with her for refusing him and had pushed her away roughly, but after a few minutes of sulking he'd promised, "I guess we'd better get married soon. I want you, Annie—all of you."

"Forever, Dev?" she'd asked, feeling as if the

sun had suddenly come out during the black of night.

"Forever, Annie, I promise you. Nothing can change it. I give you my solemn word!"

Elated, she had pressed, "Will you tell your parents tomorrow when they arrive? Will they let you marry an illegitimate commoner like me?"

Angrily he had retorted, "Never say anything like that again, Annie Ellis. You can't help your birth, and it does not matter to me. As for my parents, they won't give a damn one way or the other since I'm not their firstborn, their precious heir." His voice reeked of bitterness, but Annie teased him out of his dark humor with another kiss.

She had not seen Dev since that day. His father, the earl of Exbridge, had whisked him off to London, and she'd been sent to the factory in Birmingham by her irate mother. "Foolish wench! Gentry don't marry the likes of us! All you've done with your talk of betrothal to the Earl's son is fix it so they won't hire you for kitchen or dairy help. Now who's to care for the old man?"

Grandfather had assured his daughter that he could still care for himself and Annie, too, but all three knew how meager his savings were without the income from his stables. The following day Mum had purchased Annie a one-way ticket and warned, "This be the last time I'll spend m'own funds on you, girl. You're sixteen and long past the age when you should have been self-supporting, thanks to your indolent Grandfather, but no more. You're on your own now."

Coming out of her reverie, Annie wondered if it was eleven o'clock yet. She had left early; still, it must be eleven by now. Where was Dev when she needed him so desperately? He must come, she simply could not go to America.

As if in answer, he rode into the clearing. At the sight of Annie he galloped his horse over to her and jumped from the saddle, barely taking time to loop his horse's reins around a split tree trunk.

"Oh, my love," he said as he gathered her close to him, "how I've missed you these months." The kiss he gave her was an eager one boiling over with pent-up desires. It tore into the core of her being with its pulsating intensity. Dev was declaring himself to her, and Annie responded wholeheartedly.

Breathlessly he began kissing her eyes, her nose, her cheeks, her ears, saying between kisses, "There is going to be one kiss for each day—no, one for each hour—we were apart. Here you were, enjoying riding on the moors, while I was in the confines of my parents and their dullard friends. . . ."

The words brought Annie from her passionate trance, and she interrupted, "When you left with the Earl, my mum sent me off to her sister in Birmingham to work in the mill because Grandfather had to give up the stables."

"My poor Annie! How terrible it must have been for you. First your grandfather sells your lifeblood, the training stable, then to be chained indoors in a manufactory. Is there no way your grandfather can provide for you? Not even temporarily?"

"Oh, yes! I'm sure I can stay with him until we are wed! Has—has your father given his consent to our marriage?"

"Not exactly." Dev gently removed her arms from about his shoulders. Then he turned and walked silently to the log. Abruptly he sat down, still silent. Surprised, Annie stood as he had left her, but finally she, too, scuffed through the leaves to sit beside him.

Dev had been sure he had his future all settled when he rode into the glade today to meet Annie. When he'd announced his intentions to marry the girl six months ago, his irate father had immediately cut off all his funds, saying they would not be resumed until he consented to wed their neighbor, a titled young heiress. Dev was attached to Annie, but found he loathed being penniless. He had easily won the affections of the rich Lady Estelle Trenton, and she had promised to marry him in six months, as soon as she could plan a wedding and purchase a trousseau. But Dev still wanted Annie. He had planned to spend the next six months with her, convincing her of the necessity of his marriage to Estelle. Dev was determined to lure the beautiful girl into becoming his mistress. However, he had known he would need some time to accomplish this. Now it seemed he would only have a few minutes to win her over.

There was nothing more beautiful in the world than Annie Ellis mounted sidesaddle on a pure-bred stallion, jumping one of the high hurdles in the paddock. She was the essence of grace, leaning forward at just the right angle, her coal-black hair flying out from under the bowler riding hat she always wore, and that rapt look of pleasure on her face. The sight was always there when he closed his eyes, even when he was in other women's arms. His body craved Annie's so much it became a physical pain. How to tell her all of this? Her face was becoming more and more perplexed.

At last she asked, "What do you mean by, 'not exactly'? Haven't you told them you wish to marry me?"

"Not exactly," he repeated, then hung his head and continued, "Annie, if I was to try to beat around the bush, you would read right through me. You know me too well. In all fairness to you, my love, we can't be married. For economy, the drafty old castle is being closed; only the lands will be worked. If they do not pay better within a year or two, Father is going to sell."

"Sell—the castle?" Annie could not believe her ears. There must be some mistake. No Earl of Exbridge at Castle Cloud? No home for her and Dev? It was unthinkable.

"Yes. Also, instead of getting an increase in my allowance as I'd anticipated, it was cut off completely."

"Oh, my poor Dev." Annie moved closer and put her hand over his. "Did they do this because of me?"

"No, it is all because of economies. The family fortune is dwindling and their firstborn, dear big brother Darren"—he spit the name out viciously—"must be properly provided for, as one would expect a Viscount to be."

"Well!" Anger and determination fired Annie's words. "So much for your parents! This is once I shan't defend them. They are unfair, thoughtless, hateful things and we shall have nothing at all to do with them. The two of us will start Grandfather's training stables up again. We can make it profitable between the two of us, with Grandfather's advice. Why, we can take in twice as many horses as he did! We'll pay off the mortgage and then start a stud farm. He'll be so happy! I'm so—"

"Always my optimistic Annie. I am no farmer, nor have I any desire to be one, love."

Crestfallen, she asked, "Then what are we to do?"

"Pet, I have to marry Estelle. She is very wealthy; we'll never have to worry about money again."

Annie's face turned pasty-white and tears began streaming down her face. Dev quickly tried to console her.

"My darling, when I said we'll never have to

worry about money again, I was referring to you and me. Marriage will give me control of all Estelle's lands and funds. I will *buy* a stud farm and you can raise horses to your heart's content. I'll be with you every minute that I possibly can."

"What are you saying?" Annie's voice was an awful whisper.

"Annie," Dev tried to cushion the blow by taking her into his arms, but she pulled away. "You know I love you. I can't give you up. There's only one way."

"I'm to be your *mistress?*" The word hung between them like a death knell.

"Don't say it like that," Dev begged. "It's not that way at all."

But she knew it was just that way. Mistress. The word implied everything Annie had been raised in the midst of, all her mother's shame. She had been a burden to her mother, a reminder of a mistake. That was why she had gone to live with her grandfather at an early age, and had seldom seen her mother. Still, he could not shield her from the gossip of the villagers, or the taunts of other children. She was determined that no child of hers should know the sting of illegitimacy. She had felt so secure, so protected by the dreams that she and Dev had shared! But now Dev was asking her to condemn their children to the same fate. Her shock gave way to sobs.

Dev pleaded helplessly, "Annie, Annie, please stop crying. You'll still have everything you want—you'll never have to go back to the manufactory. Here—I'll give you a few pounds now to buy yourself some new things. As soon as I'm married, there will be lots more money for you—for us."

He held out the coins, but she did not touch them. She rasped, "Estelle's money."

"Darling, this isn't the way I dreamed of my homecoming. Come, let me kiss you."

"No!" Annie jumped from the log and ran to her horse. With shaking fingers she began to untie the reins from the limb.

Dev was beside her now. "Please don't leave like this. We have to talk." As Annie ignored him, he conceded, "No, you are right, love. Go home now and think about all this. In a day or two we'll talk again." With the choice of a life in the mills or being his mistress, Dev had no doubt about what her choice would be. She loved him. "Don't return to Birmingham. Promise me that."

Her voice was wooden. "I promise."

"Then you'll be back tomorrow."

"No." She sounded as one in a stupor. "This time, a week from today."

"If you insist, darling, but I don't want to wait that long for you. I'll be here every day at this time. Come to me sooner, please!" They both knew he would not come to the farm. He would not be able to face her grandfather.

Dev watched Annie ride away, pale and stiff, but he did not go after her.

*   *   *

The moment Devbridge Rossington announced his intention to marry Lady Estelle Trenton, Annie was pitched into a black abyss. At first she had suspected it was a terrible joke, but one look into Dev's eyes told her it wasn't. He did not even have to say the word "mistress." His desire for her, regardless of his marriage, was plain. How could this be happening! Dev, her own true love! Her whole world was crashing to a blinding end. Crushed by his betrayal and his assumption that she would eventually agree to his proposition, she retreated to an inner place where nothing could touch her.

Rushing from the glade was a natural survival instinct, but as soon as she had left she no longer cared if she survived. She jumped her little mare over barriers much too high and creek beds much too wide. Only the animal's determination to please her mistress and Annie's natural riding ability brought them safely to the paddock at her grandfather's farm. Annie was ashamed of her treatment of the mare and rubbed her down with extra care.

In a daze, she walked to the back door of the house. Andrew Rolfe was still there talking to her grandfather. Both men looked up as she entered, as if they had been eagerly anticipating her arrival.

"Young Rolfe has brought us very good news, Annie. The Chicago man was able to book passage on a ship leaving sooner than we thought. The packet sails from Liverpool on Sunday, and the Barristers will leave for Liverpool tomorrow. It's fortunate you are here—I would have been downhearted if all my dreams and hopes for you had failed because you were still in Birmingham." He hesitated. "You *will* be ready to leave, won't you?"

"Yes, Grandfather," Annie calmly assured him, "I'll be ready to leave."

At this he visibly relaxed as he pronounced, "Aye, it was a bird of good omen that brought you back for a visit right at this time, Annie."

If her grandfather had guessed that anything was wrong, he had wisely said nothing. He seemed pleased when she promised she would be ready to leave for Liverpool the next day. Like a child, he stood by her side as she packed, enthusiastically telling her of the wonders she could expect to find in America.

"Someday you will see it as I see it now, child. In America you will have the opportunity to become rich."

"When I'm rich, I'll send for you and take care of you," she'd promised.

"There is no need. I can take care of myself. Just knowing you have opportunities open to you is all I ask of you. Make the most of them— there is another drawer there to pack, my child."

"Thank you for reminding me," she had answered, trying to maintain her composure. Then suddenly it broke as she cried, "Oh, Grandfather!" and threw her arms around him. "I'm going to miss you so—and Star, and riding the moors, and the farm, but you are right. I have to go."

"My love for you, child, can be held in the palm of your hand. It will go where you go. You will never be without it, and when you run up against all the fates life may stack against you, don't throw up your hands to the winds, but instead, clench your fist. Fight through it all, for in that clenched fist will be all I've taught you and all the love I have to give. It will be all you ever need, Annie, for you're a born fighter. No obstacle will ever keep you down for long."

His words had not penetrated her apathy the day he had spoken them, but now, in Chicago, they were a lifeline back to reality. She knew she had to make her own future.

When put to the test, Devbridge Rossington had failed to take the jump; he'd turned tail and run for the easiest way out of the ring. Grandfather had a term for horses who did this: gutless bastards. "Gutless bastard" seemed appropriate now in thinking of Dev.

Annie was disgusted with herself for allowing Dev's actions to hurt her so badly. But Annie Ellis wasn't gutless—she was made of the same stiff fiber as her grandfather. Now she recalled his words and clenched her fist tightly. She had weathered a severe blow to her pride and her heart, but be damned if it would keep her down any longer. Hell's bells! She'd already wasted enough time on this self-pity. Her grandfather was gone, but his presence would always be with her and she'd make something of her life to honor his memory.

Chapter Four

✦✦✦✦✦

ONE DAY WHEN Daphne said she was shopping with Annie but was really spending the beautiful early spring afternoon strolling in the park with Geoffrey, Annie mistook the meeting place and was left to find her way back to the Armstrong mansion alone. It was easy enough to make her way through the area of familiar stores, but beyond the business district she had to walk past some unsavory neighborhoods of rough saloons and houses of ill repute. Along here, Mr. Barrister usually cracked the whip and trotted the horses briskly. Annie wished she, too, could hurry by, but she was afraid of calling attention by running, so she just walked as fast as she could, looking straight ahead. The area frightened her, but not half as much as the fear of being dismissed by Mrs. Dorn when she found out about this escapade.

Just as Annie thought she was safely to the end of the district, a man stumbled from one of the house doors and called, "Hey, girlie! Looking for a little sport? This here's the place. Why, old Madam will hire you on in full sail. She'll give me money for bringin' y'in. Come on back here!" He lurched awkwardly down the steps and when she neither stopped nor turned around, he started to pursue her.

Running was something Annie could do well, even handicapped with packages and a long, full skirt with a train. She had run alongside horses time and again while teaching them to circle the ring. Hastily she gathered up her skirt with one hand and clasped her purchases tightly with the other as she ran with the long stride of the horses she'd trained. For a while the man clumsily trailed her, but she could hear him breathing harder and heavier as she left him farther and farther behind. At last she heard him curse profanely in a breathless, rasping voice, as he gave up and turned back.

It was now completely dark. Too frightened to retrace her steps for fear her pursuer was still lurking in the shadows, Annie kept walking, hoping to see a house she remembered.

She heard a buggy approaching and decided that if it was a couple or some women she would ask directions. But the passenger was a lone man, so instead she tried to fall back behind the bushes growing near the boardwalk. She hoped he would not see her, for she was too tired to outrun anyone else.

She was too late. The man had seen her and the buggy sped up. Just as she turned to run again, she heard a familiar voice calling out, "Annie! Annie Ellis! Is that you? Annie, it's me, Carter!"

For the first time in her life, Annie Ellis ran into the path of approaching horses. She fell back, dropping her packages, just as Carter managed to stop the horses. He hooked the reins around the brake as he jumped down from the seat.

"My poor girl, oh my poor sweet girl!" he

repeated while she stood shaking in his arms, clinging to him desperately. He pulled her tightly against his broad chest, and she felt the comfort of his strength as he held her firmly.

She began to cry softly as she tried to tell him, "Daphne and I became separated from one another in the store and I waited and waited but I never found her. Did she arrive home safely, Carter? I have been so worried about her."

"For once in her life my sister is a little worried herself. She came home in the carriage, saying that she had had a headache and you had wanted to shop longer, and were to take a hack home when you finished. It didn't take many of my legal skills to break down her story once I got her alone. I left Daphne in tears after she admitted deserting you."

"Carter, you must not tell your father or Mrs. Dorn. Why, it was accidental that we were separated—"

"Annie, don't lie to me, please. I know you are only trying to protect Daffy's trysts with Geoff, but it is very important for you and me to build an honest relationship with one another."

"Does your father know? Or Mrs. Dorn?"

"Papa suspects. We just wish we knew why she's become so enamored with a notorious fortune hunter. As for Mrs. Dorn, I've already made it clear to her where the blame lies. But enough about Daf. Are you all right? Why didn't you take a hack?"

"I was so foolish, Carter." Her tears had

turned to thankful sniffles. Daphne was safe, and she was, too. "I saw a multicolored beaded bag for myself that I could not resist. It took all of the money I had with me. I only had two cents left, not even enough for trolley fare. When I saw how late it was, I knew I must hurry and walk home, but—oh, Carter," she began to tremble slightly, "a man came out of one of those houses of—those awful houses next to the taverns and he made a lewd remark, and then began to pursue me. He was big and lumbersome so I was able to elude him by running my fastest, but by then I was lost!"

"Good God, Annie!" Now it was Carter who shuddered at the thought of such a man attacking the English girl or forcing her into a brothel. They might never have found her. He tightened his arms as he asked, "Why, Annie, why didn't you just telephone?"

"Telephone!" She had been so ridiculously naive! Of course she should have telephoned, but telephones were so new to her, she had not even thought of it.

She hated herself for being so stupid and said so, to which Carter replied, "Never say that, Annie. Don't ever hate yourself for anything. Being stupid least of all, for you are one of the most intelligent girls I've ever met. It's a native intelligence that has nothing to do with the knowledge of telephones or the ways of our city."

Annie was still clinging to him, and at these words she raised her face from his chest. He was looking down at her and his eyes were filled

with kindness and something more—a special
kind of caring.

"I am so thankful to have you safe in my arms.
May I kiss you, Annie Ellis?" Carter's voice was
a whisper.

"I like feeling safe in your arms," she answered him softly, "and I think I would like it if
you were to kiss me."

Tenderly he brought his lips down to meet
hers. For a moment his mustache tickled, but
then as he began to deepen the kiss she liked the
soft, sensuous feel of it brushing above her lips.
It was not a long kiss, but it was a meaningful
one. When he raised his lips a few inches above
hers, he asked, "And did you like it, my dear?"

"Yes," she admitted, taking a breath of the air
they shared in the small space between their
faces, "after I got used to the tickle of your
mustache."

Carter chuckled at her honesty and asked,
"Would you like to have me shave it off for
you?"

"Goodness, no! It matches your hair and your
eyes," she exclaimed.

At this he had to laugh outright. "Annie," he
claimed when he had recovered, "you are a
breath of spring, so young and fresh and beautiful." He wanted to continue, but he knew it
was too soon. They would have time later.
Presently, he must get her home. Everyone
there was worried.

"Come, Annie." He turned her toward the
waiting buggy. "We must get you home. Are
you hungry?"

"I've always wondered why you have four or even five courses of food at every meal, Carter. Now I know! Being on your own in Chicago makes one famished! You and your father have to brave it every day. As for myself, I may never go past the wrought iron gates again!"

A week later Daphne grumbled, "I am sick to death of being restricted to the grounds just because you didn't take a hack home, or at least ring up for Barrister to come back for you. We could have covered up the whole thing if only you had used your head. Instead, I'm stuck in this wretched room for two weeks as punishment. And it's all your fault!"

She was interrupted by a knock on the door. Carter stood there, looking over her shoulder at Annie.

"What do *you* want?" Daphne snarled. "To spy on me some more? You may think you are clever because you forced me to admit that I met Geoffrey the day Annie got herself lost, but I warn you, if you breathe a word about it to Papa—"

"Calm your ruffled feathers, Daf. Father is much too busy worrying about his plant to concern himself with you. He wants to see us downstairs at once."

"What now? Why do *I* have to come? I don't know anything about solving the problems of his silly old plant!"

"Regardless, he wants to see you. You come along too, Annie."

Annie protested, "Thank you for asking me, but—"

"—but you are going to say this is a family matter. Well, you are practically family, 'cousin.' " He shot a meaningful glance at Daphne. "And I want you to come down." Not giving her a chance to decline, he led her down to the family drawing room where his father was waiting.

When everyone was seated, Mr. Armstrong cleared his throat once or twice, as if he didn't quite know how to begin.

"What was it you wanted us for, Papa?" Daphne asked impatiently. She planned to slip out that night to a private club where Geoffrey would be playing monte. She was muddling over where to lay her hands on some coins to take for herself to join the game, for Papa had not given her any funds lately. Annie was building a fair accumulation in that old sock under the mattress she laughingly called her bank, and Daphne decided she could borrow from Annie and pay her back when she got money from Papa, if she didn't win tonight. Actually, she decided, if she just took it without asking it would save the embarrassment of having to borrow from a servant, and since Annie would not be paid her salary to add to it for two more weeks, she wouldn't miss it.

William Armstrong cleared his throat one more time and then commenced. "I've talked to several of my friends and none of them are worried about the Omaha opening. Their yards are on the Chicago-Northwestern or the Burling-

ton, tracks that don't unload in Omaha. Only
the Union Pacific, which also unloads at our
yards, will be going into Omaha. Now they'll be
bringing fewer head than ever to Chicago—only
those herds that the owners specify are not to be
sold at the Omaha stockyards. This makes it
imperative I have some big cattlemen shipping
directly to me. I told you if I could convince Gil
Eastman, I'd be set.

"Well, I've done it! Done it in such an indirect
way he doesn't even suspect! Who would have
ever thought I could be so shrewd? Pulling the
wool over Gil Eastman's eyes for once in my
life!"

"So, Papa, now that you have us all in sus-
pense, tell us your plan," Carter suggested,
curious at his father's roundabout method of
telling the outcome of a business transaction.

"Well, it's a miracle, that's what it is! I called in
a bargain we made a long time ago. I'd almost
forgotten about it, and so had he, but he didn't
renege. Not Gil Eastman! In fact, I think he's
much in favor of the plan."

"Plan?"

"Yes. You see, Gil and I used to get together
when I went to Texas to purchase cattle for the
plant. We saw one another often when we were
young bucks. He ranched down in Texas, then.
After he got married and had twin boys, I didn't
see him for awhile. He always sent his foreman.
Then just before the war he started trailbossing
his herds himself and I was a beef buyer for the
Union Army, so I saw him a lot.

"We were both in Fort Worth the night I got

word that Daphne was born. Well, naturally we were drinking a lot of toasts to my new baby daughter and both of us were pretty far into our cups when one of us, I can't even recall which, decided one of his boys should marry my little girl. We drank on it! I completely forgot about it until the other day. I ask you, was ever a solution more tailor-made for my problems? No man would send his cattle elsewhere if his daughter-in-law's father owned a meat packing plant—"

"Wait a damn minute, Papa," Carter interrupted. "You aren't really going to write to him about a ludicrous notion you had twenty-six years ago when you were both drunk! He'd think you insane!"

"Nope, he likes the idea. Why, those twins of his are both over thirty now, and neither one's shown any interest at all in getting married and settling down. Gil's built a new ranch up in the Nebraska Sandhills, and he wants one of them to take a bride and move up there. He's fixed the place up and he wants a gracious hostess for it. He's sending a lawyer over Monday, some attorney who represents him here in Chicago. Gil's rich as Midas, interests all over. This lawyer of his, a Mr. Henry Fellman, will stand up for one of Gil's boys in a proxy marriage to Daphne."

"*What!*" Daphne screeched. "You *are* joking! This isn't humorous! You're just pretending this to make my punishment more humiliating to me, insulting me with such nonsense."

"It's not nonsense, daughter. It is a fact. A completed deed. You're twenty-six; it's far past time you were married, and you'll only be happy married to a rich man. Why, I was talking to Marshall Field the other day, and he said his niece went out there and married a Colonel Bratt or Pratt or some such name. They're in ranching and she loves it. If it's good enough for a Field, it's sure as hell good enough for you."

"I'll have you know I am of age, Papa. I can marry whom I please, and I certainly don't plan to marry a stranger and be stuck out in the middle of hayseed country. I'd be bored in a day."

"The West is an exciting place. You'll learn to like it—but no matter. One way or the other, Daphne, you are going to marry the lad. For one reason: I don't think you would want to see me lose my business. It would mean the loss of your folderols and doodads that you don't think you can live without. Nor would you want to see your grandma have to move from this house, for I will lose our home if I can't keep the plant operating at full capacity until the improvements are paid for.

"However, if you are so callous as to let those things happen, there is another reason. I have illegal gambling charges against Geoffrey Beaumont. I have evidence enough to convict him, and I will turn it over to the attorney general if you are not on that train to Nebraska on Monday afternoon once the marriage ceremony takes place. I don't believe you'd want to see that fellow jailed."

"You did this, Carter! Trumping up false

charges! This is your doing!'' Daphne shrieked.

Carter was quickly across the room. ''I swear to God, Daffy, I knew nothing of this!'' he said, but Daphne pulled away from him and ran up the stairs, sobbing.

Lady Armstrong started to rush after her, but Carter said, ''Let Annie go, Grandma. The three of us have to sort through all this. I'm sure we can find another way. Assure her of that, Annie. My God! This is 1885, not 1785! No one can be forced to marry anyone they don't want to!''

Those words echoed in Annie's ears as she thought of Dev. Of course he didn't have to marry Estelle, he wanted to—for money. She hurried up the stairs after Daphne, hoping she could convince her that what Carter said was true.

Before she reached the top, she heard Mr. Armstrong whine pathetically, ''She *has* to do it, Carter. If I am ruined, I shall take my own life!'' Annie knew Daphne had heard him, too, because her hand paused a moment on the doorknob. Then she opened it and flung herself into her room and onto her bed. She was no longer crying, and as Annie stepped through the door she commanded, in much the same tone of voice her father had used, ''Go away! I have to think!''

Annie had just finished putting on her nightdress when she heard soft tapping on the wall—Daphne's signal for her. Relieved, Annie rushed into the next room to console her.

She was appalled when she entered Daphne's room and found her dressed in one of her most stylish evening frocks. She was wearing a heavy diamond necklace and bracelet, and her hair was piled high in back, while in front her bangs emphasized eyes that looked as if they'd never seen anxiety or tears.

"I'm going out, Annie, so I want you to sleep in my bed. I doubt if anyone will have the courage to disturb me after my ordeal this evening, but just in case, be here.

"Right now, I am very thirsty. I want a glass of water before I leave." Annie stepped to the washstand to pour one from the embossed blue lusterware pitcher, but Daphne stopped her with a harsh reprimand. "This is stale; no one has refilled it this evening. Go to the kitchen and pump me a cold one."

Without argument Annie sped out of the room and down the back stairs to the kitchen. The chambermaid had filled the pitcher while Annie was in the room; it had been filled, in fact, just minutes before Carter knocked on the door, but it was understandable that Daphne might forget after tonight's tragedy. Annie might be poor and Daphne rich, but it was very likely they were going to share the same fate: *not* marrying the men they loved.

Daphne seldom thought of others. Was she sneaking out to elope with her Geoffrey tonight? Even a spoiled, selfish girl could not devastate her father and grandmother that way, could she? Returning with the cold water, Annie took

it to the walnut commode and refilled the glass
to give it to Daphne.

Daphne was stuffing silver coins into her
drawstring purse when Annie handed her the
glass. She seemed to have forgotten she was
thirsty for she barely sipped the water. "Put on
my new lace nightcap now and turn out the
lamp. Papa may feel a twinge of conscience later,
so pretend you are asleep."

Annie lay awake long into the night, thinking
of Daphne's problem. If Carter could not come
up with another plan, the girl would have no
choice but to marry the unknown rancher's son.
Yes, Daphne might well have to be married by
proxy on Monday. What a barbaric way to take
such sacred vows!

Drifting into sleep with these thoughts, Annie
suddenly arrived at a very rude awakening. If
Daphne married and moved away, what would
become of her? Alone in Chicago! Having to
work in a factory or packing plant! Living in a
cheap boardinghouse! These thoughts were un-
bearable.

Annie knew she was not a qualified lady's
maid. Never would she find another such position. And even though she would have preferred
to live in the country, she had been relatively
happy at the Armstrongs' mansion.

But the saddest part of leaving was how much
she was going to miss Carter Armstrong. While
she didn't love him, she was becoming very

fond of him, and he seemed to enjoy her company, too. Hadn't he said so last night? She permitted herself to dream. *What if he was to fall in love with her?* He was such a kind man that in time she would undoubtedly grow to love him, too. *Wouldn't she?*

Carter made her feel secure and protected. His kiss certainly had left her heart racing, if not exactly trip-hammer pounding.

Then her common sense took over. Why was she permitting herself to fantasize about someone who had only been kind to his sister's maid? She must accept her fate and make realistic plans.

She was still wide awake when Daphne tiptoed into the room. Daylight was just breaking and Annie could see plainly. Daphne's hair was disheveled, her dress no longer looked stylish and fresh, and her beautiful diamond set was gone.

"Daphne," Annie whispered, aghast, "did you put your jewels in your evening bag for some reason? You didn't lose them, did you?"

"Sh-h-h! You'll wake someone. Slip into your own room quickly. Tell everyone I didn't sleep well and am not to be disturbed for breakfast!"

Daphne did not seem the least disturbed about her missing jewels, so Annie fled silently to her room and got into bed. She was still very curious about Daphne's disheveled appearance. To be honest, Miss Armstrong looked as if she'd been attacked by thieves or pickpockets! But waspish Daphne hadn't been at all distressed; in fact, in the soft gray light of dawn, she had almost appeared pleased with herself. Very pleased indeed.

Chapter Five

✦ ✦ ✦ ✦ ✦

AT THE BREAKFAST table that morning Lady Armstrong broke the uneasy silence, asking, "William, Carter—have you found a way to save the plant that does not involve such a marriage for my granddaughter?"

"You'd rather have her string along with that impoverished gambler than married to a respectable rancher, Mama?" her son asked bluntly.

"He showed me the evidence, Grandma," said Carter. "Geoffrey Beaumont is deep in debt from his gambling. After reading the letter from Eastman, I'm not convinced that Papa's idea is all bad. We all know she will not be happy without a lot of money. These Eastmans have it, whereas Beaumont is so far in debt that the professional gamblers have a personal guard discreetly attached to him to make sure he does not leave town. Daf has flatly dismissed all other eligible men as insipid bores—to their faces, I fear."

"I'll grant you that, Carter," Lady Armstrong

said, nodding as she gingerly buttered a roll, "yet I can't believe the girl will find the excitement she craves in the country."

"Mischief, you mean, Mama," said William. "She'll soon get such nonsense out of her head with a house of her own and then a child. I'm not a cold-blooded bastard, for God's sake! I've always pampered and spoiled my baby girl; I admit it. I'm now doing what I think is best for her, not just for the business. You're damn right I want to save the business, but not enough to make the child miserable. I honestly believe life with that no-good Beaumont would bring her more misery than this proxy marriage.

"I did promise Carter I would not force her. I'll ask her, plead with her, even beg her, but if she refuses, then that's it. I won't end my own life over a failing business, either, as I threatened. Carter made me see how foolhardy that would be."

"Well, son, you've relieved my mind considerably," Lady Armstrong said. "I even have to agree it might work out. There's one thing, though—what of Annie? I'm sure they don't have lady's maids out West."

The question had been asked of Mr. Armstrong, but it was Carter who quickly responded, looking directly into Annie's eyes as he did. "You needn't worry about Annie, Grandma. She won't be leaving us. I intend to beg her to stay and eventually—well, eventually I think she will have a very special place here, if she is agreeable."

Annie thought her heart must have accelerated a hundredfold, for it was thumping and clubbing the walls of her chest so rapidly it nearly took her breath away. Her long night of worries had dissipated with Carter's words. She smiled at him gratefully.

"I do thank you for inviting me to stay. I was so frightened I would have to find a factory job and live in a flat somewhere. You can't believe how much it means to be allowed to stay here!"

At this, Lady Armstrong cried, "Annie! You poor child! No wonder you looked so fatigued this morning. Goodness gracious! I'd decide I needed a lady's maid m'self before I'd see you go to the ghetto. No, as Carter says, you are staying here, in one position—or another." She turned and gave her grandson a knowing wink.

He winked back, causing the girl's face to betray her feelings. It was a very happy pink.

Both Mr. Armstrong and Carter returned from the plant early that day. Everyone was seated at the table as the tall pendulum clock chimed seven times—everyone but Daphne. They all looked at one another, but no one mentioned her. Dinner had already started when she arrived in the room five minutes later. Daphne's hair hung down her back youthfully, and the dress she wore was one she had cast aside as "too babyish" the day she sorted out clothing for Annie. She gave her father a quick kiss on the cheek and smiled even more simperingly at

Carter. Mr. Armstrong broke the silence. "Have you reached a decision for me, Baby?"

"Why Papa, of course I shall do as you ask. Did you expect otherwise?" Her voice was guileless.

"Daf," Carter interrupted, "you don't have to. If you heard the remark about Papa taking drastic measures if you refused, I think it only fair you know he has rescinded it. Things will be very difficult, though, and I've come to the conclusion myself it might be for the best all around."

"Of course, Carter dear. You've always wanted the best for me, as has Papa. What an ungrateful girl I would be not to appreciate everything the two of you are trying to do for me!"

"You've forgotten all about Mr. Beaumont then? The man you were so sure you loved?" her grandmother asked incredulously.

"I never want to see him again." Daphne's voice was hard and firm.

"Thank God," Mr. Armstrong said in relief.

Carter added softly, "Good girl, Daffy."

Lady Armstrong announced, "I was right all along. The girl has Rowan blood in her. I knew in the end she'd make a good match."

Annie was stunned by this turnabout. Had Daphne learned some truth about Geoffrey Beaumont last night? Was she planning to marry this Eastman twin on the rebound, or had she tearfully bade her love farewell and determined to graciously help her father? This pattern just did not fit with the Daphne Annie had thought she knew. She might marry Eastman under dire circumstances, yes, but so willingly? Procrastinating, screaming, and rebelling all the way to Nebraska would have been more in character for Miss Armstrong.

"Tomorrow," Carter proclaimed, "we are going to celebrate. We shall all go to the Chicago Driving Club races and then have dinner at Knisley's."

"Races?" Annie exclaimed excitedly. "Do you have a steeplechase race course here?"

"No, it'll be harness races."

"Oh." Annie couldn't hide her disappointment.

"Don't look so crestfallen, my sweet. You will find it much more exciting than you imagine. I shall have Barrister take the carriage over early so we will have a good view."

My sweet. Lady Armstrong heard the words with pleasure. He *was* going to marry the girl. She'd suspected it this morning when he'd said Annie would have a very special place here.

My sweet. William Armstrong grinned. So that's the way the land lies!

My sweet. Annie was so happy she thought her heart might burst. He had called her "my sweet" in front of his entire family.

My sweet. Daphne was mad as hell. This would never do. Never! It would spoil everything!

* * *

After the races, Carter and Mr. Armstrong went to congratulate or commiserate with their friends. Daphne hurried off to see a school friend sitting in a nearby carriage, while Lady Armstrong and Annie remained in the open landau.

"You know how fond I am of you, don't you, Annie?" Lady Armstrong asked as soon as the others were out of hearing range. "And you know what a good boy our Carter is. You couldn't do better. He's like my own Lord Armstrong—" She did not get a chance to finish before they were interrupted by an old acquaintance who stepped up to the carriage for a brief chat.

Daphne, in the meantime, had found her prey, her old schoolmate Maybelle Meyers. In a dripping voice she gushed, "Why, Maybelle Meyers. You awful thing! Where have you been keeping yourself, you naughty girl? I haven't seen you in an age!"

"You can stop the gimcrack, Daffy, it's me— Maybelle. Of course you never see me! You are never 'at home,' nor do you return my calls. What do you want of me?"

"Well, Miss Snip! I wanted to do you a very, very big favor, but since you have become a cynic, I shall forget it. You'll live your life to regret it, too. Good day, now." Daphne turned to walk away.

"I'm sorry, Daphne." Maybelle ran after her. "Please tell me. Please!"

Since there was nothing she wanted more

than to tell her, Daphne was easily persuaded. "Oh, all right. I will tell you, but only because it's so important to you. It means nothing to me—or almost nothing. I do like you, Maybelle, in fact I like you so much I always wanted to have you for a sister-in-law!"

"You know I have always loved your brother," Maybelle murmured.

"Then it seems rather absurd that you are letting my English cousin walk off with him right under your nose."

"She's so pretty, Daffy, and I've seen how he looks at her. It hurts, but there is nothing I can do."

"Fiddle! If you want someone or something, you have to make every effort to obtain it. I have a perfect plan that will send Anna Marie willy-nilly back to England. I shall introduce you to her as Carter's fiancée."

"But I'm not!"

"Of course you're not, and you never will be if you don't do as I say. Just follow my lead. I'll go get her."

As she started away from the landau with Annie in tow, Carter called out, "Remember, we have a dinner reservation!"

"I'm not likely to forget when you've promised French cuisine for my prenuptial dinner. It's so nice to be having an engagement party with no bridegroom present."

"I know! I'm going to speak to Papa. You are being such a good sport, I think he should let you wait until young Eastman comes. You can have a proper ceremony after you've at least met your groom. What difference can a week or two make?"

"No! Don't you dare interfere, Carter," she snapped, then added more sweetly, "I just mean, I want to get it over with. My way! Please understand." Whereupon she rushed Annie over to where Maybelle Meyers stood waiting.

"I was so anxious for you to meet Carter's intended," Daphne eagerly informed Annie. "Maybelle, meet Anna Marie Ellis, my cousin from England. Anna Marie, Maybelle Meyers, my brother's fiancée."

"What!" The sound echoed from Annie's insides.

"You know, Carter's bride-to-be. They've been engaged ever so long—or at least planning to be married."

"Planning to be . . . married?" Annie whispered unbelievingly.

Then Maybelle spoke and Annie was no longer disbelieving. If ever words rang as true declarations of love from the bottom of the heart, these did. The girl said softly, "I suppose I've loved Daphne's brother since the first day I saw him. I've never thought or dreamed of another. All my life I've wanted to be his wife, his love, his companion. If he were to marry someone else, I don't believe I could stand the pain."

Annie turned without speaking and walked back to the carriage.

Daphne whispered, "You did wonderfully. I couldn't have done better myself."

Maybelle looked strangely at her old schoolmate and said simply, "I spoke only the truth."

"This time I will not permit myself to grieve," Annie swore to herself. "This was no childhood sweetheart, no lifelong love. I have simply allowed my imagination to run wild—but the things he said! The things his grandmother said!"

Despite her determination not to be upset, her eyes were so full of unshed tears she could hardly see to take the hem up on the last of the garments she had to alter. Annie did not know what she would do with all these fancy dresses now that she would no longer be going places as Daphne's "cousin," but she had to have something to keep her busy. The question once again was, what was to become of her? She could not stay here and be a servant for Carter and Maybelle. That must have been what he had meant when he said there would be a special place here for her.

It was a relief to have her thoughts interrupted when Daphne popped into the room without knocking. She was beautifully dressed in a black velvet traveling suit with a gold and black checkered satin shirtwaist. Her hair was piled high under a tiny velvet hat with matching checkered ribbon. Annie thought it was too bad the groom could not see his expensively gowned bride in person.

Daphne began speaking without any saluta-
tion or greeting. "You had a strange look on
your face when I introduced you to Maybelle
yesterday. You didn't believe Carter had anything serious on his mind where you were
concerned, did you? You weren't *that* foolish?"

When there was no answer, Daphne patron-
ized, "Oh, no! I see you *were* deluded. Oh, dear,
and you only an inexperienced lady's maid!
Hardly in his class, Annie. Maybelle's father is a
banker—much more appropriate for the wife of
a lawyer, don't you think?"

Oh, yes, Annie thought. Much more appropriate! If only he hadn't called her "my sweet" in
front of his family.

Daphne continued, "He likes you, that's true
enough. The whole family knows he has selected
you as his—what is that French word that is so
appropriate—his *chère amie?* Yes! That is one I'll
wager you know, coming from your station—
mistress!"

"Mistress!"

"Why, yes. Carter would be very good to you,
until he tired of you."

"Your family knows this?"

"He's made no secret he likes you, has he?
Isn't that what you want?" Daphne feigned
innocence. "I thought all servants and factory
girls were looking for a rich man to take care of
them."

Slap! The hard swing of Annie's open palm
made Daphne's ear ring. Annie was small, but
she had a lot of strength. It was exactly the

reaction Daphne was hoping for. Rubbing her red cheek, she glared venomously at her attacker.

"How dare you!"

"I dare because I am no longer in your employ, nor in the employ of anyone in this household. That you could all approve of such—" She turned to run from the room as the tears streamed down her cheeks.

Before she reached the door, Daphne began to shout, "Annie, wait! If you hate this degradation as you say you do, we can help each other. Please! Listen to me!"

Annie turned skeptically, her hand still on the doorknob, ready to run. Would no man ever want to *marry* her?

"In two hours, Annie, I am supposed to wed Jude Eastman by proxy. Only a pastor and Eastman's attorney are to be present—I've forbidden my family to attend. *You* can be wed in my place. The lawyer doesn't know me, neither do the Eastmans. Then, Annie, I can leave Chicago with Geoff. I gave him my diamonds to sell, for he has had a run of bad luck. The diamonds will pay off his debts here and stake him in New York. We will marry later. I have a good friend at Saratoga who will not tell Papa I am staying with her.

"Oh, Annie, just think! You'd have a rich husband. A *husband*. Surely that would be better than working in a factory or being a kept woman. Why, you say you love the country—and you know I'd hate every minute of it."

"I don't know! I don't know! I don't know what to do or think! Maybe I should talk to Carter. I have to—"

"No! You can't do that! His engagement isn't official. He'd know I told you—and you know as well as I do we shouldn't be talking about such things as . . . his mistress! You mustn't talk to him except to tell him you want to go with me," Daphne pleaded.

"I've already convinced Papa it is best if I take my lady's maid along," she went on. "I told him we would act as if it had been expected. He won't deny me anything since I've saved his precious packing plant. That will give both of us a reason for leaving. I shall leave on the eastbound with Geoff, and you'll be on the westbound to join your husband."

"Husband!" Annie voiced the word aloud, but in hushed awe. A husband. Husbands weren't supposed to be men you didn't love, didn't even know! He might not even *like* her! Even a horrid factory job would be preferable to such a fate. "I can't do it, Daphne. I'd like to help you, but you see, all my life I've dreamed of marrying for love. It's a dream I can't forfeit. I'll find some job—don't worry about me."

"Oh, I'm not, but you should be, for I'll tell Mrs. Dorn how you deceived her. She has friends and kinfolk all over Chicago. You'll never find employment or lodgings if she blacklists you!"

"I'm not frightened of her," Annie insisted, but she was. Ever since the day Carter had found her lost in the streets, Mrs. Dorn had been giving her evil looks.

Daphne watched as Annie set her jaw with rigid determination and turned to leave the room again. This time she called her back with a new urgency. "Annie, oh Annie, I am so sorry I told you about Carter and Maybelle, and I swear I never considered telling Mrs. Dorn. I want you to go for your own sake. I truly think you will find the love you are seeking. A marriage will make it happen, won't it? Out west they all love horses, just as you do. Why, on a ranch you'll have so many horses you'll think you've arrived in paradise! This fellow will probably worship you. You know women are scarce out there; why, there are thirty or forty single men for every woman—"

"There are?" Annie hesitantly turned back into the room again.

"Oh, yes, at least. Think of how much it will mean to this Jude Eastman to have a wife at last! It will be a dream come true for him."

"Do you really think so?"

"You know it's true. Papa said his friend Gil telegraphed that Jude is so anxious he can't wait for me to arrive. Why, I'd go in a minute if it weren't for Geoffrey. I've loved Geoff ever since I was in grammar school. Can you imagine how devastated I am at even the idea of giving him up?"

Annie didn't have to imagine it. The pain from losing Dev was still very real, and Carter's perfidy hurt, too. Could Daphne be right about this proxy husband? Would he be a man who would love and respect her, a man she could in turn care for? If he wanted a wife badly enough to marry by proxy—

"Are you considering it, Annie?" Daphne asked pointedly.

"Maybe," Annie confessed. "If I thought he would love and care for me as a man should his wife—"

"He will, Annie. It's the code of the West. They practically revere women out there, especially their wives. You could make him the happiest of men, and at the same time you'd be helping me and Geoff—and yourself too, of course. You could ride horseback all the time."

Ride horseback all the time. The thought was like a glimpse through a door she'd thought forever closed to her. A weak smile crossed her face. "I would like that part."

"Say you'll do it. There's very little time—we have to pack your things. I'll order down your trunk and a chambermaid to help us." Not waiting for an answer she went flying out, leaving a confused Annie standing in the middle of the room.

She was still rooted there when Carter pushed the door open and entered. He put his hands on her shoulders and commanded, "Look at me, Annie."

She did, then quickly looked away again. She didn't trust her control over her tears.

"What is this Papa tells me about Daf taking you with her? I don't want you to go. You don't

want to go. Why, Annie, why are you doing
this?"

"She will be all alone. She will need someone." Annie heard her voice coming from far
away.

"She'll have her husband, Annie."

"A stranger."

"I see she's used some persuasive means to
convince your soft heart, darling." He sounded
upset but resigned. "All right. Go with her for a
month or two, but then I'm coming after 'you.
I'm bringing you back here to—"

"No, Carter! Don't say it to me! Don't say it to
me!" Her voice had risen to a near-hysterical
shriek.

Carter was honestly puzzled by her words, so
he asked, "Say what? That I think I'm falling in
love with you? That I want to get to know you
better, sweetheart? That I suspect there might be
something very special between us? Why would
you beg me not to tell you these things?"'

"You know you already belong to someone
else, Carter, someone who loves you very much,
has always loved you."

"What—? Who—? You surely don't mean
Maybelle Meyers? It's a schoolgirl crush, one
she's just taking longer to outgrow than most
girls do. She's nice enough, but I'm not—"

Just then Daphne dashed into the room and
inquired testily, "What are you doing in here,
Carter? Trying to dissuade Annie, I'll wager.
Papa says she's to go with me! I leave for my
wedding ceremony in less than an hour. I have

made my farewells to everyone else. Now I'll tell you good-bye, for I'll have none of you at this sham ceremony, nor anyone to tearfully bid me good-bye at the depot. Whoever thought Daphne would sacrifice herself to save the family? Aren't you shocked, dear brother?"

"Shocked, but very proud. It's the first selfless thing you've ever done in your whole life, and although you may not believe it, it is what is best for you. If you want my good-bye now, then you have it . . . but Annie, I want time for a private farewell with you. We must talk!"

"No. It has all been said except that I thank you for being so kind to me, and I regret—"

"Get out, Carter! You are upsetting her and we have much to do. Out!" Daphne began to shout to drown out Annie's words.

"I'm going, but I will write to you, Annie. I don't know what Daphne has said, but I suspect there is something—"

"*Out*, Carter. Now! Papa and Grandma won't like it if you upset me and make me cry. They, too, are very proud of me, going so willingly to my vile wedding by proxy to live in the big bad West with a total stranger!"

Dear God! What have I let myself in for? thought Annie Ellis as Daphne's words pierced her very soul.

Annie put on one of her old gray merino dresses with its slightly shabby matching coat. She was to appear in the guise of Daphne's lady's maid so the Armstrong family would not be suspicious. Daphne warned her repeatedly that they must believe she was traveling out west with Daphne after the marriage, to which she was to be a witness. No one must suspect their real plan. Annie was beginning to have a great many reservations about this scheme of Daphne's.

How had Daphne been able to work out so many details on such short notice? She must have already made her plans to elope with Geoffrey Beaumont. But until Annie's own unhappiness had surfaced, evidently no one had been going to take Daphne's place at the proxy wedding. Hadn't Daphne ever considered how soon she would be missed? Hadn't it occurred to her that, angered, her father might very well have turned his charges over to the authorities? Geoffrey would have been brought back to stand trial and Daphne returned to a very irate father— returned to the impending loss of home and status. All the things money could buy were very important to Daphne Armstrong. The girl must have been so torn by the thought of not seeing her lover again that she had been heedless of all these consequences. If nothing else, Annie's trip west would enable Daphne to get far away before the impersonation was discovered, for discovered it surely would be.

As soon as her things were packed, Annie reached under the mattress for her money, knowing how badly she would need it when this ruse was found out.

Her stocking was gone!

Frantically she tore the bed apart, then got down and looked beneath it. Finally she pulled all the coverlets and pads off the bed, shaking each one as she did. She was trying to push the mattress off to see if the stocking was stuck in one of the crevices when Daphne appeared at her doorway.

"Annie! The hired coach has arrived. We have to go. The ceremony and train departure are scheduled very closely. Come along now!"

"No! I can't leave until I find my money. You know, the stocking I always kept hidden here. It's gone!" Annie was almost hysterical. With a last hard shove she managed to push the mattress onto the floor.

"You were foolhardy to hide it there. Didn't I tell you it was unwise? Some chambermaid probably took it when she changed your linens. Now come along. You won't need it. Money is one thing the Eastmans have—in quantity. It was the one temptation to tie myself to such boredom."

She took Annie's arm and pulled her out of the room and down the stairs, wishing she had won at faro that night at Geoff's club so she could have put the silver coins back into Annie's old sock. Carter would interrogate the servants if Annie complained to him, and there was no time. They had to be on their way immediately or Geoffrey might think she had changed her mind, and all her carefully laid plans would fall apart.

Carter was dejectedly leaning against the

newel post at the foot of the stair banister. When he looked up and saw the expression on Annie's face, he bounded up the stairs and roughly took his sister's arm from Annie's.

"It is obvious you have browbeaten Annie into going with you, Daf. She's caring and sensitive and you took advantage of her. We both know she will be happier here. Do one more unselfish thing, little sister. Let her stay."

"No!" Daphne refused stoutly. "I need her!"

Just then Daphne saw her father and grandmother enter the hall. "Papa! Tell him to leave Annie alone!"

"Annie, my child," Lady Armstrong said sympathetically as she came forward, "you don't have to go if you don't want to, no matter what Daphne has told you."

"Papa!" Daphne pleaded for his intervention, knowing if they didn't get out of here soon, Carter might propose to Annie and that would ruin everything.

"Carter! Mama!" Mr. Armstrong rebuked. "We all have agreed it is better for the child not to travel alone. The attorney is very pleased with this arrangement. He thinks the Eastmans will approve of Daphne traveling chaperoned by a maid, and it will help her when she gets there to have someone her own age to talk to. As I understand, the only women on the ranch are an older housekeeper and the foreman's wife, who's older, too.

"Once our little girl is busy with her home and husband, she will be glad enough to part with

Annie. Until that time, in all fairness to me as well as Daphne, I think the two of you should encourage the plan."

Even Carter could not argue. He put his arm tightly around Annie as they proceeded down the steps and tried to look into her eyes, but she kept her head bowed. How he wished he had had an opportunity to be alone with Annie to find out her true feelings. No matter. He would write all his thoughts and feelings to her in a letter that would reach her shortly after her arrival in Nebraska. He was confident he could convince her to come back and marry him. He knew she was starting to return his affections. He just had to be patient and tolerate this separation. What the two of them would have was worth any amount of waiting.

The rented victoria was already loaded with baggage which was piled carelessly on the top and back. Mr. Barrister was obviously out of sorts because he was not in charge of this expedition. The hackman was waiting impatiently for his passengers so the farewells had to be brief.

Before the carriage exited the Armstrong gates, Annie pressed, "Daphne, now that we are alone we must talk about all this. How can you be sure your Mr. Beaumont will be waiting to elope with you today?"

"I'm not a complete idiot, Annie. I ensured he would have to marry me the other night. Not that he isn't eager to, of course. He was hoping for Papa's blessings, naturally, but when I told him the plant is in dire straits right now, he agreed to take my marriage settlement and go to New York. We shall return for Papa's blessings when business improves. By then, Geoff will have recouped his own fortune and everything will have worked out."

"For you, maybe, but what about me? The Eastmans are bound to discover they've been deceived before long. They want someone elegant and elite to give their ranch a dignified air. Mr. Eastman said that in his letter. I've never supervised a household or gone about in polite society."

"Neither have I—supervised a house, that is. You can fake that as well as I could. As for polite society—fah! You can fake that, too. Why, even with your mispronounced French words and meager knowledge of the nobility in England, I'll wager you can make a real impression on those hayseeds. Just act uppity-up. Don't be interested in business or politics. Never act as if you're enjoying yourself. Whatever you do, don't act knowledgeable about horses or farming! Most important, make up some excuse for that awful British accent of yours!"

"I just don't know! I'm afraid. I'm not sure I can live a lie."

"Of course you can. Or is it that you've decided you'd rather be Carter's mistress? I saw that good-bye kiss!" She pulled back as Annie started to bring back her hand, shouting, "Don't you dare hit me or I'll put you out right in the middle of the street. Then where would you be? Who'd believe *you*?"

"Daphne, please, I have no money now. What if they do turn me out?"

"They won't, but to make you feel better I'll send you some as soon as I cash Papa's generous wedding draft."

"Are you sure about your Geoffrey? What of the charges . . ."

"All false. Geoffrey felt badly that Papa would stoop to such a thing to prevent our marriage. Hush now. We are approaching the office where you're to be married."

Once again, Annie thought what a heathenish way this was to take such sacred vows, but now it was she and not Daphne taking them. Only one word forced her to step down from the coach. *Husband*. A man who would love and cherish her forever. A man who wanted a wife so much that he had agreed to a proxy wedding sight unseen. It gave her gooseflesh to think of it. "Oh, Grandfather," her heart cried, "I'm to be the beloved bride of a farmer, just as you predicted!"

Chapter Six

+ + + + +

THE TOWN OF Cattle Creek was a wide place along the trail close to the water, where herds camped for the night. It had been established to supply necessities and restock chuck wagons. It also allowed the drovers a little diversion while on the trail to the Ogallala railhead from the east.

The creek and the town were always referred to by the same term, hence the name. The town's general store was aptly called "Wheeler's Cattleman's Supply Co. and General Store," and the one combination hotel-saloon had a sign hanging crookedly from its shabby frame porch that promised "Cattleman's Haven." Another sign by the rickety front door proclaimed, "Whiskey, 10¢." All the cattlemen and drovers knew the place offered a great deal more than was advertised.

The Haven was practically empty tonight, for no herds were camped on the creek bank. Only two riders from the nearby Double Tree Ranch stood at the bar. When customers saw the pair, they often wondered if they'd drunk enough to see double. Both men were six feet tall, and both of them had powerful, broad shoulders that tapered to slim waists and hips. Their shotgun chaps, rich leather holsters, and highly polished six-guns were identical. Their well-worn boots even rapped the same staccato on the plank

85

floor. Both had dark unruly cowlicks that escaped their broad-brimmed hats and waved across their foreheads.

Only a close inspection of facial features could distinguish Jude Eastman from his twin brother Jules. Both of them had craggy, rawboned faces which somehow managed to be handsome. Jude's eyes were gray, bright gray, like the clouds after a rain had passed by, while Jules's were almost green. Although both of them had wide, masculine noses, Jules's was slightly crooked from being broken, while Jude's was perfectly straight and ended just short of being patrician. He had been fortunate, too, that his mouth had escaped the narrow upper lip of his brother and had turned out perfectly proportioned. Not that Jules's nose or mouth detracted much from his own good looks; in fact, they gave him a charmingly impish expression which competed well with his twin's rugged handsomeness.

"To your nuptials, brother mine!" Jules held up a full shot glass of whiskey in a mock salute to his twin, who looked as if he was in a black rage.

"Rein it in, Jules, or I'll flatten you. In fact, right now I'd be obliged for an excuse to knock somebody flat."

"You know you're always welcome to try, Little Brother!" Jules continued, undaunted. "Perhaps your new bride will be a big woman with strong muscles and a barrel-like body and you can fight it out with her."

"Damn it! It's obvious you think this is all one big joke. You're not the one who's leg-shackled. What if you were in my place? Tied by a god-damned proxy marriage to some—some—hell, I don't even know what! But I do know exactly why her daddy sold her—he's scared shitless about that Omaha beef-packing plant they're building. Even the old man knew that, but he still made the bargain and forced it on me! What I don't know is why any sane woman would ever agree to it!"

"She's twenty-six and isn't married. Probably a bull-shy heifer."

"Maybe. Or maybe she's so ugly no bull ever came sniffing around. Then there's the possibility there's dirty linen to wash, and her daddy found out about it. What the hell do I do if she's pregnant?"

"Jesus! I never thought of that! I don't think Pa did, either. He's so danged determined to have a woman like Ma was out on that ranch that he's gone loco."

"It still burns my ass to think the Old Man would use me this way. He knew I wanted to take over the Sandhills ranch; making it contingent on me being saddled with the daughter of his old drinkin' partner was just plain under-handed."

"He's a desperate man, Jude," Jules tried to explain. "Has been ever since Ma left. He's got some kind of guilt he can't quite shake. He wanted to give her everything, and she took off before he could afford to give her much of anything. She sure kept reminding him of it, too. I think building that big house up in the Sandhills and furnishing it with all those fancy gewgaws he had shipped out here was just a penance to ease his old soul. But what is the point if there's no hoity-toity woman like Ma in it? He's never been inclined to remarry. What I couldn't believe was that you agreed! I knew you were tired of trail drives and runnin' off nesters, but to give up your freedom! I swear, I didn't believe it when Pa told me."

"Believe me! Our old man is a stubborn old cuss when he sets his mind to something. It was the only way to get him to let me take over the Sandhills ranch and run it my way. I know you feel like me about going against him since he's had the heart attack. It's pitiful to see him in bed when he's always been so damn healthy. That and my determination to set up the Twin Trails Ranch finally got him his goal—to get one of us married.

"I've got a few notions about some changes ranchers are going to have to make," Jude went on, "and I can make them there. Free government range isn't always going to be here for us. The damn foreigners and Easterners are already overstocking it. They don't know buffalo chips from cow manure but here they are in our midst, buying spreads right and left with imported money.

"The pesky nesters won't continue to be so easily frightened off in the future either. They used to run if you waved a six-gun under their noses. Now there's more of 'em; they're bandin' together. This land's worth fighting for, and they know it.

"Jules, I want to ranch a new way. I'm gonna cut grass for winter feed for my own herd. I can even see a reason for the damned barbed wire everybody is cussin'. If you fence in your own water and range, nobody else can overstock it or waste your water, or worse yet, squat in the middle of your land and plow up a couple hundred acres."

"You do have your mind set, don't you? I agree with most of your notions, but—man! You must really be dead set on trying them if you're willing to be hog-tied for life to that highbrow old maid Pa's having sent out here!"

"Hell, I"m not about to be!" Jude exploded. "I have a foolproof strategy that's gonna make her do an about-face and run back to her daddy faster'n you can say skat! Pa won't know, but instead of taking her straight to that fancy house he built, I'll drag her along with the herd I'm moving up there. The rigors of a trail drive are bound to be too rugged for her nicey-nice city notions. No place to wash her homely face. No sunshaded buggy to ride in. No potty. If that don't work, I'll take her to that god-awful soddy we found built into the side of that hill last winter and tell her it's her new home! The rodents'n filth there'll send her hightailin' it back to Chicago for sure. 'Eeek—a mouse! Ten, twenty mice! Oh dear me!' Hell, she'll probably swoon at the sight!"

Jules was laughing so hard that he was practically doubled over. At the thought of an upper crust Chicago spinster in these situations, Jude began to roar with laughter, too.

The brothers finished their drinks and then Jules left for home, reminding Jude to meet his "sweet lil wifey" in North Platte in the morning and hurry'n bring her to Double Tree. He could hardly wait to meet the "victim."

Jude went upstairs to Rose O'Mara's room. Rosie had married Old Man O'Mara, the owner of the Cattlemen's Haven, when she was only fifteen. By the time she was twenty-four, he was dead and the place was hers. She'd hired a good bartender to replace her husband and borrowed enough money from Jude Eastman to go back east and find some saloon girls well qualified both in looks and experience. It had been a good investment.

Rose had wanted Jude from the first time she saw him. They had had a marvelous relationship for several years, especially since her husband died and they no longer had to sneak away to enjoy one another's company.

Her bedroom was done in red flocked French wallpaper because Jude once said red was his favorite color. She hoped it was his favorite because of her bright red hair. Rose loved the room and was positive Jude did, too, for, when he was in town, he spent many nights in it with her. Lately, though, he'd been talking about moving to the Sandhills, and she fully expected him to ask her to marry him and go along. He wouldn't want to be up there in that desolate country all alone. Not Jude!

The minute she recognized his footsteps in the hallway, she flung open her bedroom door and threw herself into his arms. Rose was an armful of woman. Her brassy red hair should have looked gaudy, but it didn't; it had enough gold highlights in it to blend with her creamy white skin. She had calculating blue eyes and a full, sensuous mouth. Her large, full breasts were equally tempting, as were her buxom, rounded hips. That she wanted Jude Eastman for a husband was a well-known fact; that he was off-limits to her girls was an even better known one.

"You rode up to the hitchin' rail an hour ago, Jude darlin', and you're just now coming upstairs? Don't I appeal to you anymore?" she pouted.

"Rosie, sweetings, don't scold me tonight. If you saw me ride up, you also saw my brother. We had some talking to do. In fact, I can only stay a few hours; I have to be in North Platte very early in the morning."

"What are you goin' there for?"

"Nothin' of importance." He bent to kiss her, but she pulled away.

"Tell me! It *is* something if you had to discuss it for so long."

"No. It's nothing to concern your pretty head with. Concern yourself with me. Kiss me properly."

Rosie gladly complied, opening her mouth as soon as he began to move his lips upon hers. He immediately plunged his tongue into it and plundered within until her desire matched his. One of his hands began to manipulate the heavy fullness of her breast, which he easily freed from her thin, loose red lace nightgown. His other hand pressed on her buttocks to pull her firmly against him, while her hands raced from his hair to his hips and back again, over and over. Jude's kiss ignited Rosie's own needs, and she began to tug off his vest and unbutton his shirt. He helped her by undoing his belt and the buttons on his bulging pants. She pushed him down onto the bed and tugged off his spurs and boots, then untied his chaps and flung them to the floor with his shirt and vest.

Jude pulled her down on top of him and suckled one of her hard, excited nipples, then the other. As he did this, Rose began to sensuously stroke his hardened manhood. They were familiar, well-matched partners with years of practice, and within minutes they brought each other to a relaxing climax.

It had been awhile, Jude thought, and was exactly what he needed so badly tonight. He'd stayed out at the ranch wrangling with his father about the damn Chicago ceremony. He should have come to Rosie's warm bed last night, his wedding night! He couldn't think of it as a wedding but as a loathsome burden, an encumbrance he had to get rid of. It wasn't that Jude was contemptuous of marriage; he just liked the arrangement he had with Rosie better than a wife who would always be around to nag him. That sort of thing wasn't for him! He knew Rosie wasn't faithful—hell, he wasn't! When he needed a woman, she was here for him; the rest of the time he was free to do the ranching he loved.

Jude enjoyed the comforts of a home and knew he was going to enjoy the new house up in the Sandhills, but the last thing he wanted was for some society dame to move in and turn it into a highfalutin' showplace for his father's guests to envy.

It was strange Pa had any hankerin' for this kind of house or a fancy hostess to go with it. It didn't fit at all with the common sense, down-to-earth rancher Jude knew his father to be.

"Jude, darlin'!" Rosie's voice interrupted his thoughts. "Somethin' is botherin' you. You're too quiet and immune to my charms!"

"Never that, Rosie my sweet. I just reckoned you'd fallen asleep, you were so still lying there with your head on my chest."

"I was waitin' for you to talk or—whatever else you might wanta do."

"Again? Already! You are a horny little thing tonight, aren't you? Never let it be said I can't keep my woman satisfied." He started to rise up, but she pushed him back down and rose up on her elbow so she could look into his face.

"Am I your woman, Jude?"

"You know you are, sweetings."

"I don't mean your mistress. I mean your woman. For always! Your wife one day?" she asked pointedly.

For this one moment in time, Jude Eastman was actually glad he was married. "I seem to be married already, sweetings, married to one

Daphne Armstrong from Chicago," he tried to say nonchalantly.

Nonchalant it was *not* going to be!

Rosie sprang off the bed and stood beside it, naked. It was hard for Jude to ignore her because her large breasts were heaving up and down rapidly from her breathless anger. "You liar! Telling me this damn trash to avoid marrying me! I thought you loved me!"

She looked furiously around for a weapon. The closest thing at hand was a pillow, which she grabbed and used to pummel him, releasing some of her anger.

Jude protected his face with one arm and wrestled her down onto the bed beside him with the other. As soon as he had her arms pinned and his leg across her kicking ones, he pushed the pillow onto the floor, then continued his explanation.

He drew a deep breath before promising, "It's no lie, but it's not what you think. This female has nothing to do with you and me. She's one of Pa's whims. He knew I wanted to take over the Sandhills ranch so he made it depend on me marrying the daughter of his old friend in Chicago. Hell, Rosie, it was only a proxy marriage! I never went to Chicago; some lawyer stood up with her in my place. She's an old maid."

"How old?"

"Twenty-six."

"I'm twenty-six! So now you think that's old?"

"You're not a maid, sweetings, very definitely not." He tried to take her in his arms, since she seemed to be calmer, but she pushed him away.

"She'll just stay in Chicago? It was like a business arrangement?"

"Yeah, sort of a business merger, you might say, but she'll come out here—for a while. Then she'll return to Chicago and stay put!"

"To have your child?" Rosie asked bitterly, thinking an heir might be what Gil Eastman had in mind.

"Hell, no! I'm not going to *sleep* with her, for God's sake! Then I'd really be saddled with her." An untouched old maid bride could be returned to her daddy, but not a woman he actually took to wife. "Nope, she'll soon be packing up and going back East, I guarantee. She won't interfere with our lives. I'll be here as much as ever— except, of course, when I go up to Twin Trails."

"Will she be going *there* with you?"

"Yes—and no. She'll start the journey up there, but I doubt very much if she'll have the grit to finish it. I'm takin' her along on the drive with the herd. She'll sleep in the chuck wagon— alone—but that will be the only consideration she'll receive. It'll be a rough trip for a city gal—" He began to chuckle.

Rosie nuzzled into his arms, satisfied that this female would not be a permanent impediment to her plans. "You're a devil, Jude Eastman. Prove to me you love me like the devil!"

"Gladly, Rosie. Gladly!" Jude was relieved this had gone so well. He would have to pretend to stay married or Rosie would be after him to marry her.

Jude loved Rosie's body but he didn't love *her* anymore, and he knew he'd never want to marry her. Maybe this Chicago deal wouldn't be too bad after all, if the woman just ran quietly back to Daddy and didn't get a divorce. Pa was going to be hurt that Jude hadn't been able to persuade her to stay, but Pa knew what it was like to live with a dissatisfied woman. Jude sure as sin wasn't going to. He'd never buckle under to it. He hated to deceive his pa this way, but he hated worse the idea of living with a woman like his ma—the ma he'd missed like hell and then learned to hate. Pa claimed she was dead, but his sons knew better. She'd broken their pa's heart by running out on him. No woman was going to do that to Jude Eastman, not on your life!

He'd made one fool mistake in caring too much for Rosie when she'd first come to him. All she'd ever wanted was to use him. He'd learned that lesson soon enough. The first time he'd learned she was sharing her bed with others for profit had hit him hard. It wouldn't ever happen again. He had his heart wrapped in steel now. No woman was going to touch it.

Chapter Seven

+ + + + +

THE BRIEF CEREMONY was over in a few minutes.
The kindly attorney, Mr. Fellman, assured Annie that he knew her new groom was going to be
well-pleased with his bride and her new father-in-law would be ecstatic. He had very tenderly
placed on her finger a gold ring encrusted with
rubies and gently kissed her on the cheek when
the minister said, "I now pronounce Jude East-man and Daphne Armstrong man and wife."
Daphne had assured Annie the name on the
certificate and used in the ceremony meant
nothing; it was the actual *living* with a man that
made a marriage legal. Annie had earnestly
taken her vows, sincerely saying "I do" when
the minister asked her if she took this man to
love and to cherish. She'd said "I will" even
more firmly when he'd asked her to promise to
love him "until death should part you."

The overloaded buggy with its disagreeable
driver had taken them straight from the little
church to the train depot. When they had arrived
at the busy station, Daphne imperiously ordered
the hackman, "Set off all those unmatched pieces
of luggage onto the platform and see that they
are tagged for the baggage car. They are to be
sent direct to the Gil Eastman ranch at Little
Creek, Nebraska."

"*Cattle* Creek," Annie corrected as she grabbed Grandpa's pigskin holdall before it was roughly tossed to the ground with everything else. It held the dress she'd chosen to wear when her groom first saw her. It was so important to have him love her from the start. The beautiful green dress was perfect for the occasion, she'd decided.

Daphne did not get out of the hack to bid Annie farewell. "I mustn't be late to meet dear Geoff. You are a lucky girl, Annie, to have landed yourself in such a prosperous situation. Remember, I'm the one who deserves your gratitude for making all this happen, and someday you'll realize how fortunate you are, if you don't already." She did not wait to hear if Annie thanked her or not. Loftily she ordered the driver, "Proceed to the Richelieu Hotel," briefly nodding good-bye as the carriage pulled away. Daphne did not once turn and wave in answer to Annie's upraised hand.

Annie looked forlornly about her. How could anyone feel as completely alone as she did in the midst of so many people? They were huddled on the platform or busily rushing to and fro. There were hawkers selling all sorts of things to eat; since she was feeling a nervous hunger, Annie decided to eat something. It was then she remembered she had no money with her.

The big black engine hissed and whistled and chugged its way up to the platform, stopping at last with a metallic grinding of brakes. Now the milling throngs whirled into action, and Annie found herself being shoved further and further along the crowded platform. She tried to show her ticket to a train conductor standing at the number three passenger loading door, but he only looked disdainfully at her well-worn coat and scratched satchel and motioned her to keep moving on down the platform. When she reached the next-to-last car she was pushed aboard by a mass of eager humanity. No one was even there to take her ticket.

This car was very different from the one in which she had traveled with the Barristers from New York to Chicago. That one had aisles and cushioned seats in rows where passengers rode and slept. This car was completely open. Wooden benches were nailed to the floor in the middle, while stacks of baskets, bedrolls, and luggage were piled everywhere. There was a black potbellied heating stove set up in the center with its chimney pipe vented through the roof. All the benches seemed to be filled.

Annie looked around, not quite knowing what to do. On the trains she had ridden in England, each ticket had a seat number on it, as well as the car number. There must have been a mix-up. Perhaps if she could get off and go báck to No. 3, they could straighten out the problem for her. Unfortunately, by the time she pushed through the standing crowd, the outside door was closed and the train had started to strain forward. The movement jolted her, and she nearly fell onto the lap of a middle-aged woman sitting on a bench, holding a sleeping child.

"I'm so sorry," Annie stammered in apology.

"Think nothing of it, dearie. My, but it's good to hear an honest-to-goodness English voice again! All the way from New York town, our own family be the only English-speaking homesteaders in this car. You could set here aside me if you'd like!

"You, Willie," she looked down at a small boy in the seat beside her, "set on the floor. Let the lady be havin' your seat."

She turned back to Annie. "Where's your man? Where are you goin' to homestead? Maybe Nebraska?"

By this time Annie had guessed she was on one of the emigrant cars the railroad furnished free or at low fares to prospective land buyers. In return for building railroads through treacherous mountains and unsafe Indian territories, the United States government had reimbursed the railroad companies with many acres of land. To make their lines prosper, it was important these lands be sold to settlers who would then use the railroads' services for transporting produce and people.

The woman's little boy slid off the seat, and Annie quickly turned her holdall onto its side for him to sit on. She was glad she did not have to remain standing as the train began to pick up speed. Others were evidently afraid of losing their balance, too, for if they had not found seats they sat on the floor on bedrolls.

The woman was obviously waiting for answers to her questions, so Annie hastened to explain.

"My—man is meeting me at North Platte, Nebraska. He is a cattleman out there, along with his father and brother. I will live up in the Sandhills, I believe."

Disappointment was obvious in the older woman's voice as she lamented, "I be hoping you'd live down along the Platte River where me and my man hope to homestead. I think the Sandhills be north from there. M'sister says they ben't no use for farmin'. When the soil's tilled it causes big blowouts in the land, just sandy holes left. M'kinfolk lost everthin' they had because this happened to them. They're gonna join us now to help out at our place. We be needin' all the help we kin git to put up a soddy and git a crop in."

"A soddy?"

This was a new word to Annie and she must have looked perplexed, for the woman laughed and nudged the man sitting on the other side of her, saying, "Edwin, here's a willin' listener for you. Someone you kin tell all about the sod house you're gonna build us."

It must have been a favorite topic of the man's, for he spent the next two hours telling Annie in detail how they would cut thick slabs of sod and lay it and then make a ridge-pole roof for the house. Annie was glad to have something to think about besides Jude Eastman.

Late the following day, Annie sat holding Willie while he slept. She needed to relieve herself but she did not wish to wake the boy, nor did she want to use the little boarded-off corner where every sound from within echoed into the rest of the car. Willie must have felt equally shy about the makeshift toilet, for in his slumbers he had wet his pants. Annie felt the warm liquid seep through the folds of her cloak and dress. She almost cried out and dropped the child, but, not wishing to embarrass these people who had been so kind to her, she sat for another hour in miserable discomfort. Her legs fell asleep from the weight of the boy, while the dampness of her clothing chafed her skin.

At long last the train pulled into Lincoln, Nebraska, for a two-hour layover. When the English immigrant woman saw the stain on Annie's dress, she apologized profusely and then scolded the half-asleep child, lightly boxing his ears.

"Please," Annie tried to assure her, "it was nothing."

The woman insisted. "No, no! It was a turrible thing. Our brochure said there's an immigrant house here that serves hot food 'n you can bathe 'n such. You come on over there with me. We'll sponge out that spot."

"There's no need for that. I have another dress in my bag—if I could just go there and change . . ."

"Well, of course you can, and you can join us for some of that free food, too!"

"Perhaps I can check with someone about my ticket. I really think I'm in the wrong car." Annie was positive of this. There was no way on God's

Green Earth that Daphne would have traveled with less than first class accommodations. She almost giggled aloud at the idea of the pampered Daphne Armstrong sleeping on a plank floor with only a thin comforter, as she had last night.

"The other cars are expensive, we were told. Unless your man's a rich bloke, you're probably to ride the Zulu car."

"I believe he is fairly well to do."

"You don't know?"

"No, I'm afraid I don't."

The Englishwoman kept looking at her, obviously waiting for more of an answer, so Annie admitted, "It was an arranged marriage."

"Oh." The woman seemed willing to accept this, but she did add skeptically, "I always thought those were more for the nobility or uncommonly homely maids. Since you're a sightly lass, does this mean you're of the gentry?"

"My father was a baron," Annie told her, hoping that would satisfy, for she knew no more about him than she did about the man she was married to. Annie only knew that the baron had brought a horse to her grandfather to train and had begun taking long walks with Mum. When he left with his well-trained horse, he'd promised to return soon. But they had never heard from him again.

"My, my! A baron's daughter! One down on his luck, no doubt," she remarked candidly, eyeing Annie's dress. "A lot of gentry swells are nowadays, so don't fret about it none. You're better off in America, dearie. A whole lot better off. Come along now."

The immigrant house was a big wooden structure painted boxcar red. It had eating and sleeping accommodations for the immigrants detraining at Lincoln while they chose farms in this area. It also had a large dining room for the travelers. Annie found a chamber with a latrine, a big wooden tub, and several buckets of water. She had never before realized what privileges the necessities of life could be.

Clean once again and wearing the beautiful green traveling dress Daphne had given her, she went out to the big dining room. People glanced crossly at her as she filled her plate from the huge kettle of food and went to sit with the English family. Her emerald green dress with the tiny black beads embroidered around the hem and sleeves looked out of place among the calico and homespun of these travelers. She wanted to shout at the ones who looked askance at her, "Yes, I've a fancy dress, but it was given to me. I haven't a farthing to my name and my man is someone I've never met. I'm going west as you are, with dreams and hopes pinned in my empty pockets."

But of course she didn't. She self-consciously gulped down the food and hurried out of the room. Her parting with the kind family was hasty as the train whistle blew its first warning. They would surely meet again in western Nebraska, she and the woman promised each other.

Seated in her own private compartment, Annie was almost glad for the error yesterday. This evening the conductor had taken one appreciative glance at the wealthy-looking lady and, carrying her worn bag, had escorted her to this walled-in chamber of loneliness. Here there was too much time to think. Even after they came and turned the seats into a bed, she still could not sleep. Her thoughts were in England with Dev at one moment and then drifting back to Carter in Chicago, but mostly they were on her future.

Who was this man who had married her sight unseen? He was over thirty years old and much under his father's thumb, evidently, to agree to this proxy wedding. He must be very shy and easily manipulated. Maybe a good, hard-working man who loved horses and whom she could love and respect. She would try to be a good wife, as well as the Chicago socialite Daphne had instructed her to be, for she wanted to please this son and his father. Hopefully they would never learn she was an imposter.

Mrs. Jude Eastman. She was married! Never would she be confronted with the ugly word "mistress" again!

Chapter Eight

✦✦✦✦✦

FOR A THIRD time since her arrival at North Platte, Nebraska, two hours ago, Annie reluctantly went to the ticket seller's window. He and she were still the only two people in the depot. As soon as the train had pulled out to continue its westward journey, the crowd of gaping towns-folk who had filled the small wooden platform outside had dissipated.

The disembarking immigrants had been met by a land agent who had hustled them off in three wagons he'd had waiting at one end of the platform. Annie had not even had a chance to say good-bye to the kind family she had spent the day with yesterday. It was as if they were her final link to reality; now she was a part of these unfamiliar surroundings. All she had seen from her train window this morning was flat, green grassland. Occasionally there was a glimpse of water or a sod house, and one or two of the soddies had had windmills beside them. It was rare to see one with a shed or barn, although some seemed to have a lean-to attached to protect a horse or a cow or a wire-fronted crate of chickens. Annie could not envision the primitive living these places must provide. Would she ever get used to the barrenness of the Nebraska prairie?

"Sir," Annie interrupted the depot agent one more time, hating to be such a nuisance, "I believe there has been some misunderstanding about my time of arrival." She was beginning to feel like the victim of a cruel hoax. The train had been an hour late, which meant three hours ago someone should have been here. No one could be *that* late!

For the first hour she had sat, primly sedate, on a green wooden bench, with what she hoped was a pleasant expression pressed firmly on her face. Each minute she had held her breath, waiting for her first sight of Jude Eastman. Now that expression had changed to a frightened frown and the expectancy had given way to despondency.

The little man glowered at her from under his green-visored shade. He lay down the stack of coins he was counting and told her the same thing he had an hour ago.

"Nope, no misunderstanding. The Double Tree foreman come in and purchased the tickets and I wired 'em to some Chicago lawyer m'self— two of 'em," he looked at her suspiciously. "He tol' me Jude would be here. The way Jude rides that black stallion of his like a bat outta hell, he more'n likely broke his neck! Of course that would be his fault, not the railroad's. The Union Pacific don't make mistakes." Once again he peered out around her and frowned at the pile of luggage. "He's gonna have to rent a spring wagon instead of a buggy to carry all those big ol' trunks."

At this moment Annie wished all she had to concern herself with was the easy-to-carry holdall. When she remembered how the dress that was presently stuffed into it smelled, she decided it might be preferable to have no luggage at all, for she would have to walk up and down the short North Platte main street and hope to find a paying job of some sort. Her aunt employed girls to cook and clean at her boarding and lodging house in Birmingham; Annie was sure she could handle a similar chore if a town this small even had rooming houses. Perhaps the ticket agent would know. Before she had a chance to ask him, though, he suggested an alternative.

"Bert will be leavin' here in a few minutes on his freight wagon. You could hitch a ride with him as fer as Cattle Crick. Somebody there could take you on out to Double Tree, or git word to one of the Eastmans to pick you up there."

"I don't know! Maybe they don't want me," Annie was so upset she spoke without thinking.

The agent gave her an even stranger look. "If they paid for your ticket out here, now why wouldn't they want you, lady? It don't make sense!"

"No, certainly not. I misspoke. Of course they want me. You are right—something unforeseen must have happened to Mr. Eastman." She hoped he hadn't broken his neck. She wasn't prepared to be a widow any more than a bride.

"Where can I find this van boy?"

"Van boy? Don't know no Vans around here."

"You know, the one who drives the freight wagon."

"He's an old man."

"A 'van boy' does not refer to age, but to one who drives a—" She realized her explanation of the English term was only confusing the man, so she lamely finished, "—where would I find him?"

"I'll go hunt him up, soon's I lock this money up in the safe." He was giving her that suspicious look again.

Riding on a freight wagon was quite an experience. It was loaded with hundreds of blocks of salt licks for the cattle and two dozen twenty- to thirty-foot pine ridgepoles for barns and soddies. Annie rode on a high seat with Bert, the bewhiskered old driver who told her not to fret if he used muleskinners' language on his horses. He said he used to drive supply wagons pulled by mules for the Union Army during the war.

His language Annie could suffer, but not his use of the whip on his poor horses. She bit her lip several times to keep from berating him for it. She knew she shouldn't get cross with this man who had been good enough to make room for her and one of her trunks on his already overloaded wagon. It lurched from side to side and Annie was positive the double trees were pounding the horses' legs until they were raw. The six-horse team was hitched with a heavy harness that jangled constantly. If they came to a ravine or creek bank, the horses had to pull against the screech of the post brakes going downhill and with the crack of the whip on their limbs going up the other side. She welcomed the sight when the wagon finally rumbled and clattered into Cattle Creek.

Annie might not have recognized it as a town if a sign had not stated its name and the population of 33 on a post. There were only three houses, two of them soddies, the other of rough-hewn lumber. "Blacksmith" was carved onto the porch rail of the latter. There were two other weathered frame buildings; one was two stories tall and the other had a sign on top that said "Wheeler's Cattleman's Supply Co. and General Store."

Bert stopped in front of the store with a last jingling of the chain harness. As she climbed down, Annie tried to be gracious to this man whom she privately considered a cruel master.

"No trouble a'tall, ma'am," he declared. "Enytime! I make th' trip once't, maybe twice't a week. Allus glad for a purty lady to ride along, even if she don't say much. Reckon my language kinda shocked ya. Sorry 'bout that, but those hosses only understand two things: me yellin' at 'em like mules and that whip.

"There you go again, ma'am, bitin' that lip. You must be powerful determined not to holler at me 'bout somethin'."

"Well, Mr. Bert . . ."

"Jist Bert."

"Yes—as I was starting to say, whips are to be used on horses lightly, sparingly, and only on very rare occasions."

"Yes, ma'am! I sure agree with you there! I'm mighty careful not to use the whip on m'horses like I did on those goldern army mules. No, sir! I use it sparingly, as you prob'ly noticed."

Annie looked at the man to see if he was jesting, but he was dead serious. She thanked Bert once again, picked up the slight train of her dress to keep it from dragging in the dust, and walked carefully up the wooden planks that served as a sidewalk to the porch of the general store.

Three grizzled old men were whittling sticks as they perched on benches made of split logs. All three stopped talking and stared at her as she came up the steps, but none of them acted as if he wanted to help her or even speak to her, so she hurried inside the building, hoping there was a friendly shopkeeper on duty.

There was no one. She looked around for a doorway to another room, but there wasn't any, just one large room that seemed to stock about everything from foodstuffs to shovels.

Beside a large wooden pickle barrel was a chair, so Annie apprehensively sat down to wait for the shopkeeper's return. The three men on the porch turned every once in a while to peer in at her through the narrow front window, but made no effort to come inside and offer any assistance. After overhearing part of their conversation, Annie was too embarrassed to think of going out to question them about the missing storekeeper.

"Gawd a'mighty! Where'd she come from?"

"Bert brought her in. Hope she belongs over at the Haven; I'd sure spend m' last dime to spend tonight with her!"

"Hell, Gordy, you spent your last dime years ago. If it weren't for Herm, you wouldn't even have chewin' tobacky. Him 'n his missus was damn fine to take y' in."

"He's m'son, ain't he? Oughta."

"Naw! He shouldn't oughta! You shoulda saved like I did. You spent too much on drinkin' 'n women already."

"So sez you!"

"So I say!"

"Wanta make somethin' of it?"

"Shaddup, you two ornery old coots! That little tootsie in there's a gonna hear you. She ain't one of Rosie's bawds. Ol' Rose'd never pick one better lookin' than herself! Naw, she's somebody's woman, but damned if I know whose!"

"Maybe she's one of them mail-order brides?"

"Not a looker like her. Nobody could git that lucky, gittin' that little tootsie sight unseen!"

They all guffawed loudly at this notion. If they only knew, Annie thought.

Jude Eastman was in an even blacker rage today than he had been yesterday. To fuel the coals, Rosie had let him oversleep by several hours this morning. Then she'd acted out a clinging sob scene, costumed in the buff, while he tried to put on his clothes. She wanted him to let his bride think no one was going to meet her, and then she would turn heel and run back to

Chicago. That wasn't such a bad idea, Jude had to concede, except that Pa was bedfast and patiently waiting at the ranch to meet his arranged-for daughter-in-law.

Jude had cut across country on horseback, so he'd arrived at North Platte only three and a half hours late to meet his proxy bride. By then, the fool woman had already inveigled a ride for herself on Bert's freight wagon. Worst of all, she'd left her trunks behind so he still had to rent a surrey at the livery stable. Pa was going to be mad enough Jude had not met her train; if the old hen complained about not having her "necessities" on top of it, he'd be angrier still. Jude couldn't imagine what trappings anyone would need that would take up this many boxes, in addition to a satchel and a big trunk.

With the loaded buggy he couldn't cut across country, so he had to return by way of the deeply rutted road. All the while he kept hoping to overtake the freight wagon, but the team they'd rented him couldn't overtake their own shadows.

Consequently, Jude was in one hell of a mood by the time he finally reached Cattle Creek. Bert was still unloading salt blocks, so the freight wagon must have just arrived. That eased his temper a bit. Hopefully the woman was still here and hadn't sent word to the ranch yet. He automatically started to tie the team he'd rented to the hitching post at the Haven before it occurred to him a lady wouldn't set foot in that place. If she were here, she'd be at the store.

*   *   *

At the sound of steps on the wooden porch, Annie jumped in anxious anticipation and started toward the door, relieved that at last the proprietor had returned. It was strange he would leave his store unattended for so long, but perhaps he'd had to make a delivery or some such thing.

The man who came through the door did not look at all like a merchant. In fact, he looked like an advertisement for Buffalo Bill's Wild West Show. He even had those clunking metal things on the heels of his boots, as well as silly-looking pieces of cowhide tied over his dungarees. It looked as if he'd cut another piece of leather into a vest. With all the cattle they had out here, she supposed it was natural they'd make use of the hides instead of cloth. Obviously this man was no storekeeper.

At second glance, Annie realized this particular cowboy would be quite handsome in a rugged sort of way if he weren't scowling so ferociously. He was certainly rude, not bothering to remove his hat in her presence; he just shoved it onto the back of his head and stood staring at her.

Belatedly she remembered she was the elegant Mrs. Jude Eastman, just arrived from Chicago. Daphne would not speak to a stranger of this caliber, so neither did Annie. She walked haughtily away from him.

It did not diminish Jude's hostility to find his

new bride was already in a snit and giving him the frost treatment for not meeting her train. Ignoring him, she snootily turned and walked back to the chair and sat down, waiting for him to crawl to her on hands and knees, begging her royal forgiveness. Well, she could sit there 'til hell froze over if that was what she was waiting for. Right from the start she'd better get used to the idea that Jude Eastman didn't crawl. Not for anyone—especially not for a pretentious old maid!

Not that she looked her age. In fact, she didn't look too bad at all. He wondered why she'd ever agreed to come out here. What was the reason a handsome filly like her had agreed to something like this?

He took out his tobacco pouch and cigarette paper and rolled a smoke. His back was to her, but he could see her in the mirror by the dry-goods shelf. Nose up in the air, hands in black silk gloves neatly folded in her lap, not so much as twitching a muscle.

He licked the edge of the paper, put it into his mouth, and reached for a match. When he discovered he didn't have one, he went behind the counter and bent underneath the low shelf for a new box. After lighting his cigarette, he wrote "Sulfur matches—1 box" on the Double Tree slip tacked on the wall.

Out of the corner of her eye Annie watched his actions. Maybe this insolent fellow *was* the storekeeper, getting merchandise from under counters and writing on store slips of paper. Mr.

Barrister had said all the ranch owners and cowboys dressed the same out here; perhaps store proprietors did, too. This town was so small he probably could not make enough money running a general store and had to farm or raise cattle as well. Wouldn't a storekeeper greet a customer or offer to wait on her, though? Perhaps gentlemen always waited for ladies to speak first. Was it part of the code of the West Daphne had mentioned? At least he might be able to give her some information about this thoughtless man she'd married.

"Sir," she said, breaking the lengthy silence, "are you perchance the proprietor of this establishment?"

Jude whirled around to face her. Did she really not suspect who he was, or was this a game to put him in his place? He decided to play along and find out.

"Nope."

"But you got a box of matches from under the counter and wrote on a sales ticket."

So she *had* been watching him from under those alluring long lashes of hers. "That's what everybody does when Wheeler's gone home to lunch or out for some reason—makes their purchase and writes it up."

"He's certainly a trusting man!" she exclaimed and then remembered to act more dignified. "My good man," she felt certain this was a directive a Chicago matron would use, "would you be so kind as to tell me when he will return, or better still, how I may contact someone from the Eastman family?"

"Why would you want to contact them?" he asked innocently, enjoying this game.

"I do not see that that is any concern of yours. Can't you answer a civil question?"

"Maybe."

"What kind of answer is that?" Annie was becoming riled and forgetting her stately demeanor.

"What was the question?"

"I need to contact someone from the Eastman ranch. It is quite near here, I believe. Can you or can't you tell me if it is possible?"

"It's possible."

"Will the shopkeeper be coming back soon? I'd prefer to deal with him, I believe," she announced.

"He's got a spell of ague. He may not be here for a couple of days." This statement was made in a tone more delighted than sympathetic.

"Oh, dear!" She was genuinely upset. The three old whittlers on the porch were gone now and the storekeeper might not return for a day or two. There was only this aggravating cowboy to help her, and he seemed inclined only to antagonize her. His expressive gray eyes told her he was impudently assessing her—or were they undressing her? A shiver of apprehension ran through her.

There was nothing else to do. She would have to explain her bizarre circumstances and hope he would be understanding enough to help her. She keyed up her voice and imitated Daphne's brusque demeanor. "I shall be quite frank with you, sir, I find myself in a rather unique situation. I was to have been met in North Platte by my new husband. Perhaps you know him? He's an older, rather shy type who follows his father's dictates religiously. I fear he is a somewhat forgetful fellow, or perhaps he was so involved in work that meeting me slipped his mind.

"It is only one of a number of misfortunes which have befallen me of late. At the train station in Chicago I was mistakenly shoved by the rushing crowd into an emigrant car and had to ride in it all the way to Lincoln." Her voice became more plaintive as she continued, "Now, here I am in this forsaken store with no transportation to the Double Tree ranch. I do not even know which direction it is from here, nor how far. I have no way to send word to my errant husband or his family. I must put myself at your mercy, sir, for as you can see, I do need your cooperation to help me locate my husband, Mr. Jude Eastman."

Jude was speechless. From "shy older man under his father's dictates" on through "forgetful, careless, errant husband," he'd been whisked from humor to anger to pity to guilt and back again. *This old maid thought she'd married a hard-working, forgetful old fellow dominated by his father!* When she found out how wrong she was, she would hightail it back to her daddy in a hurry! He was determined to set her straight at once.

"Sorry to disillusion you, Lady, but you have a few mistaken thoughts about me. I'm Jude Eastman."

"You're—"

He didn't give her a chance to finish. "As you can see, I am neither old, shy, nor senile! Nor am I under my pa's thumb. Far from it! If it was these qualities you had in mind, you have had bad luck once again, haven't you?" He watched her striking brown eyes with interest as they appeared to grow larger in her suddenly colorless face.

"You are not what I expected, but that is not important," she ventured, trying to sound haughty.

"Just what *is* important? I know why your daddy sold you, I just don't know why you were for sale."

Annie was hurt and angry now, and all thought of acting like a Chicago socialite flew from her mind. Hurt for hurt she retaliated, "Three little words brought me."

"I sure as hell never said I love you!"

"No—the preacher said, 'man and wife.' *Man and wife.* That is all I wanted."

"It's a damn good thing that's all, for you'll never hear me say the other three!"

It was not going to be easy to love and cherish this man, Annie realized, but deep inside a determination surged through her. She *would* have a love-filled marriage as she had dreamed of so long ago. Then she realized, no, this was better. She could never be hurt again if there were no love involved. Love wasn't real, but marriage could mean lifelong security.

To cover her dismay, Annie taunted, "If you

are not under your father's thumb, then why did you marry me? You were 'sold' just as I was. What was *your* price?"

She had hit close to the truth, but Jude wasn't about to admit anything. Besides, he didn't think she was being honest. With her exceptional looks, she would have had no trouble getting a husband if marriage was all she wanted. Perhaps she was in the family way and they had shipped her out here in disgrace.

He lied. "Pa wanted my twin or me to get married. The old man's sick, so we agreed to it to make him happy. We flipped a coin."

"You *won* me on the toss of a coin?!"

"Nope," Jude told her flatly. "I lost."

Masking her shock, she turned back to him, announcing, "So. You have signed the vows that purchased me. What now?"

"My pa bought you. I already have a woman—bought and paid for!"

"You're already married?!?"

"I said a woman, not a wife. A real woman!"

"A—mistress?" Annie wailed without thinking.

"Why yes! To put it in a blunt, most unladylike way. But perhaps your other ladylike sensibilities will prefer the idea, for it means I'll never bed you."

"Never?"

"Never!"

"Do you give me your word? Is that a promise? You *swear* it?"

"You're damn right I do, lady. You can depend on it!"

"Oh, thank God!" she proclaimed with relief and smiled the most devastating smile Jude had ever seen in his life. What a beauty she was when she smiled! More important, why did this vow he'd intended as an insult please her so much? She must not be carrying another man's bastard, or she'd be eager enough to get him into bed so she could foist it off as his. She didn't have the appearance of a cold, frigid type, that was for sure. Probably just overly modest. No wonder she'd never married, if sleeping with a man was abhorrent to her. Jude didn't take it personally; too many women had wanted him to jangle his spurs under their quilts over the years.

Once more Annie's nose was up in the air and she was the prim miss. She would remember that all they wanted her to be was a glorified housekeeper. This obnoxious man would not make her forget her position again, she determined as she ordered haughtily, "Please load my trunk, which is on the store platform. I wish to be taken to my new home. I am most anxious to see it."

"The Double Tree is Pa's ranch. You'll only be visitin' there. He wants to meet you. I'll be leaving you there while I spend a few weeks helping with the cattle roundup. You can keep Pa company."

"Splendid," she informed him stonily. He didn't know if she meant splendid because she could keep Pa company or because he'd be gone a few weeks. He suspected the latter.

Wordlessly he strode out onto the porch and hoisted up another big trunk to tie on with the rest of her belongings. If her trunks were any indication, she had come for good. His plot would change that; once roundup was over and the trail drive begun, she'd soon tire of following a slow-moving, dust-raising herd and then she'd pack up all this paraphernalia and go back. In the meantime, Pa could have the company of the highfalutin' lady he thought he wanted. Pa would be glad enough to have just Maudie after a few weeks of this snob treatment. He climbed up into the buggy seat while she remained standing in the road.

"Aren't you forgetting yourself, sir?"

He wanted to tell her to get up the best way she knew how, but instead he got down and went around to help her up. He needed to get into her good graces before they got to the ranch if he were to skillfully deceive the old man about how things really were.

"Allow me to assist you, *Mrs.* Eastman."

Until he helped her in, he hadn't really noticed what a little thing she was—little but shapely. When he turned to go back to his own side of the surrey, his eyes were drawn to the doorway of the Haven—there was Rosie, glowering at him. He'd convinced her his proxy bride would change nothing, but that had not been true. He wouldn't be going to the Haven for awhile; it wouldn't look right. Especially not to Pa. No, he'd have to pretend to be the smitten bridegroom around the old man, day—and night.

As she sat perched stiffly beside him on the high front seat of the surrey, Annie's insides began to turn. Once again the enormity of what she had done swept over her.

Without turning her head she sneaked a look in Jude's direction. It was apparent he was deep in thought, and whatever those thoughts were, they were making him clench his jaw and grit his teeth. In silent retaliation she firmly locked her own jaw and thrust her chin up stiffly. Neither broke the silence for several miles.

Finally, knowing this would be his only chance to explain, Jude spoke. "Did you know when you came out here that my pa had had a heart attack?"

"No! How dreadful! When did it happen? Is he all right?"

At least, Jude surmised, she hadn't come hoping the old man would pass on and she'd stand to inherit. "A few months back. He's bedfast now, but he's going to be okay."

"That's good. Then he'd already had this attack before he heard from M—my father."

"Yep! Deranged his thinking a little, I guess." Jude forced himself to sound derogatory.

"Yes," Annie agreed, remembering her precarious position again, "it would seem it did. If only mine had had such a reason," she added wistfully.

Jude bristled at this. "Come now, we all know your daddy had good reasons for his devious ploy, so let's get serious. You play the role that's expected of you and I'll do my part. We'll act like syrupy newlyweds in front of Pa, is that agreed? I don't want him to suspect we're not. If he gets agitated it might give him a setback."

"I'll agree up to a point. It's that 'syrupy' that puzzles me. What did you have in mind?"

The question was innocently asked, but Jude couldn't resist turning it against her. "What do you think I mean? What sickly-sweet sort of things do newlyweds do?"

Annie floundered for an answer. He'd told her he didn't want her, wouldn't bed her. He surely didn't plan to submit her to hugs and kisses just for the benefit of his father, did he? "I guess you could say a honeyed word to me now and again," she finally answered.

"Just a word?" One of those arched eyebrows of his went higher still above imperiously twinkling eyes.

"That would convince him," Annie persisted.

"I rather think not."

"Then what?" She was still very skeptical. While animosity was rife between them, she also felt something else, something unnerving.

"There'll have to be an occasional touch, a brief kiss now and then."

"*Mr. Eastman!* You promised me!"

"Oh, don't worry, there's no danger whatsoever I won't keep my promise." Jude had no intention of breaking it, but he was rather galled by her insistence. He began to wonder if he *did* repulse her. Well, she wasn't his type, either. A little thing like her couldn't measure up to Rosie's ample charms. "All I was considering was looks."

Annie coldly agreed. "Well, as long as they're only for appearance's sake," she said, which caused Jude to clam up again.

He wondered what this nellie-blue-nose was going to think of the house on the home ranch at Double Tree. It was run by his Aunt Maudie. There was nothing fancy about the house, but there were always good vittles and a clean bed to sleep in. It had originally been built of sod, then a log addition had been added, and finally the frame dwelling across the front. The log addition was now the bunkhouse and the original soddy was used for storage. Everything from canned food to extra tack was stashed in there. It would not meet her nicey-nice notions, he suspected, but that was good. The sooner she was disillusioned, the better.

They traveled a few more miles in silence. Maybe, Jude thought hopefully, she was already reconsidering staying. "Look, Daphne—"

"My name isn't Daphne!"

"But the letter said—"

"Said Daphne, but I go by *Anne*. My middle name."

"I see. I agree, it's a much more tolerable name. As I started to say, *Anne*, you've had a lot of unfortunate experiences on your way here. It's only a sampling of the raw life you can expect to find out west. Why don't I just turn around and take you back to North Platte? I'll buy your ticket and make certain you are installed in a private compartment all the way back to Chicago. You can just tell your daddy—"

"No!"

"What do you mean, no? You've liked your beginnings here so much?"

"They were mistakes."

"It was no mistake that your bridegroom overslept this morning in the arms of his mistress and failed to meet you—intentionally!" Jude hated to be so cruel, but he didn't want Pa to see this girl. She was exactly what Pa wanted. He'd never be able to accept Jude's inability to make her happy and get her to stay out west. Hell, he didn't want to put this innocent-looking female through the rigors he'd planned!

Annie raised her chin higher and clenched her fist tightly. She was a fighter, not a quitter! This man could be made to see that. She'd work so hard he'd have to respect her. She amended that to "tolerate her" when she glimpsed his stern countenance.

Determined not to be quelled, Annie informed her new husband, "I detest you, Mr. Eastman. I'm glad you have a mistress. Glad! But sir, I *am* your wife. My role is to be the lady of the house, and I *will* be! Do you hear me? I *am* your wife until death do us part!"

All right! She asked for it! Trail drive, line soddy, and all! Whatever it took! No woman told Jude Eastman how things were going to be!

Chapter Nine

✦✦✦✦✦

It WAS NEARLY dusk when the buggy passed under
the arch of rough poles with an equally rough
sign nailed to it. Even falling darkness could not
disguise the ugliness of the place. Mr. Armstrong had implied Gil Eastman was an affluent
rancher. If this home was any indication, Mr.
Armstrong had had the wool pulled over his
eyes. One part of the house seemed to be tacked
to another with no thought for appearances. It
had barns and sheds, but they, too, were crudely
built. One looked as if it might originally have
been built of hay reinforced by poles. Since it
was partially disintegrated, it was hard to tell.
Chickens scattered every which way when the
buggy drove into the yard, and a couple of
scrappy dogs barked ferociously until Jude
hushed them.

A short, plump, gray-haired woman stepped
from the house, wiping her hands on a tea towel
apron, and a tall man came from the area of the
sheds, looking like an exact replica of Jude. Two
or three other men appeared outside the buildings, but they did not come forward, just stood
where they were, curiously watching the arrival
of the new Mrs. Eastman.

Jude's twin brother surprised Annie by giving
her a broad, friendly smile when the buggy
stopped at the door of the house. He was much
the handsomer of the brothers, she decided,

with his flashing white teeth in his sun-bronzed face. His green eyes sparkled as he came forward, removing his hat as he did.

"Welcome to Double Tree, little sister. We expected you three or four hours ago. In fact, Pa suggested we go in search of you. He was sure you'd had a mishap with the rented buggy. We were just saddling up."

"Train was late," Jude growled and looked at Annie, daring her to contradict him.

Smiling sweetly as she held out her hand to Jude's friendly twin, she agreed, "The train *was* late, but not nearly as late as my new husband. It seems he had problems with his filly—or was it a stallion? Nonetheless, we are safely here now and I am so delighted to make your acquaintance."

Jules looked questioningly over her head at his scowling brother but made no comment. He lifted Annie to the ground, remarking, "You're as light as a feather, but in my entire life I have never seen a feather that compares to you in beauty."

"Thank you, I think." Annie smiled. "I've never carefully observed many feathers." Then she turned to hold her hand out to the older woman who stepped up with a warm smile when Jules released his new sister-in-law.

"She is a lovely little thing!" the friendly-looking lady said in a surprised, pleased tone of voice. "That green dress just suits you to a 'T.' I'm Maudie, your husband's aunt. I cook and clean around here. My, but I'm pleased to meet you, Daphne."

"It's Anne. She wants to be called Anne. Better than some silly, citified name like Daphne," Jude remarked.

"Yeah, it suits you better—Anne," said Jules. "Anyway, Maudie doesn't just cook and clean. She runs this house with an iron hand. She practically raised us boys—and you must admit, she did an admirable job of it!"

Jules was smiling broadly at her again and she wished for a fleeting moment this had been the twin who had acquired her on the toss of the coin. Then she recalled that he had *won*. Of course he was happy and could pretend to be welcoming.

Annie found herself in the warm arms of Maudie, who was not much taller than she was herself. "Oh, girl, you're gonna make my brother Gil the happiest man alive."

The voice that boomed from within the house sounded anything but happy. "Maudie! Jules! What in tarnation is going on out there? I saw Jude drive in, what are you doin' standin' outside when I'm lyin' in here waitin'?"

"The voice of command has spoken, Mrs. Eastman. I shall convey you to be appraised by your pur—new father-in-law," Jude said snidely, looking at Annie with attempted disdain.

Equally disdainful, she answered, "I hope he'll be pleased with his bargain. It would be nice if someone was." She put her little nose in the air and started to the door with Jude at her heels until Maudie stopped him.

"Let me take her in, Jude. I want to see the

look on his face. You and Jules unload your bride's things and put them in your room. I've spiffed it up as best I could."

Annie flashed Jude a warning look, then agreeably took Maudie's arm.

Jude and Jules stood staring at one another, Jude still looking disgruntled while Jules looked awestruck. "You have to be the luckiest son-of-a-buck in this whole world. Imagine getting a little beauty like her from a mere business transaction. Why, she's sensational. You can tell just by looking at her that she's warmhearted and loving."

"Looks can be very deceiving, little brother. She is anything but a loving, biddable, docile wife."

"I did notice the two of you seem to have put some burrs under each other's saddles. What trouble did old Rocky give you?"

"That horse never gave me a minute's trouble, and contrary to what everyone thinks, he never will."

"Then what—"

"I just told her that because I accidentally overslept."

Jules read his brother much too well to believe this. "Never say she found out about Rosie."

"Hell, yes, she did. I told her and she doesn't give a damn. In fact, she's glad I have a mistress! Glad!"

"No kidding! She said that! In those words?"

"I told you, looks are deceiving. She's hard as nails. All she wanted was my name in marriage."

"Well, in spite of all you say, I'll gladly give her mine. You can still run the ranch up there. I'll live in the house with her and be your assistant. We'll tell Pa—"

"What? What could you possibly say to him that wouldn't put me in his black book permanently? No, there's nothing but to go on with this farce. When you get to know this uppity, snobby old maid better, you're going to be glad I didn't take you up on your ill-considered offer. Why, just now during this act she's putting on is the first time she's smiled all day." *If you discount the one she gave me when I promised she didn't have to sleep with me*, he thought. Now he was going to be evicted from his own bed. Since Maudie had put them in his room he'd have to sneak into the bunkhouse to sleep.

"I still think you're misreading your new wife, Jude. You were probably in a rage when you met her, and she's too spunky to cosset you."

That fact was true enough. Jude thought amusedly of the way she'd announced she hoped "someone" was pleased with this bargain.

Gil Eastman looked over William Armstrong's daughter from head to toe and drew one immediate conclusion: this comely lass was no relative of his chubby friend, nor his horse-faced wife. There was not one trace of either of them in her attractive features nor her petite body. He didn't know what was going on, but this might be an unexpected blessing. He'd had severe misgivings about saddling Jude with an offspring of Armstrong's, but it had been the only way to get one of those consarned stubborn sons of his to take a wife. Gil wanted a gracious hostess up at the new ranch house he'd built, and he'd thought at least in that respect the socially-prominent Armstrong's daughter would fill the bill. Now he understood the brief telegram he'd received yesterday from Chicago. "All went well, but not as planned. You can be glad. Be assured that it's all right and that I'll take care of everything." Since he had complete confidence in his Chicago attorney, Hank Fellman, Gil knew he didn't have to worry about this turn-about.

"So you're Willie Armstrong's daughter?" he asked to open the conversation.

"Yes."

So she was pretending to be Daphne, Gil thought to himself. Well, so be it. He didn't care who she pretended to be so long as she was poised and dignified, which she seemed to be.

"I'm pleased to meet you, Daphne."

"I go by my middle name, sir. Anne. Mr.—my papa always calls me Daphne, but no one else does. I'm very pleased to make your acquaintance, too. Jude told me a great deal about you."

"None of it good, I'll wager."

"He spoke most respectfully of you, Mr. Eastman."

"Don't spread the butter on too thick, girl. I know the boys respect their old man down deep, but they don't go around saying so!"

Annie chuckled, "All right, I'll confess. He

tried to give me a fright of you, but I suspect you are as blustery as my grandfather. All bark and only a bite when needed."

Gil laughed uproariously at this and Maudie stood there beaming. It was so good to have Gil happy again.

"Your grandfather, you say? Willie's pa, or his Mrs.'?"

Annie had to think fast. "It was my mother's. As you know, she passed away a few months after I was born, so I was sent to England to live with her parents. I spent my childhood with them." There, Annie thought, that will account for my accent and any slips I may make about England. However, she was not to be let off that easily by this man with the knowing look in his eyes.

"Strange. I would have thought Willie's ma would have taken charge of you, living there in Chicago and all."

"Grandma did for a while, but then she wanted to travel, and as you probably know, the great fire of 1871 took her home. I've been in her charge more recently." Annie did not feel comfortable lying to this man; she had liked him on sight. "You'll not believe this, Mr. Eastman, but the story of my entire life does not measure up to the tale of my adventures coming here," she promised, hoping to change the subject.

"Sit down, Annie, right here on the edge of my bed, and tell me all about your trip. And stop calling me 'sir' or 'Mr. Eastman,' child. I'm your new pa, even if by marriage only. I always wanted a little girl. Why, I was so jealous of your daddy the night we went out drinkin' to celebrate your birth, I reckon that's why I pledged you'd marry one of my boys. It was a way of gettin' something he had that I wanted."

He tentatively reached out a gnarled but powerful hand, and Annie eagerly grasped it with both hers, wishing she could tell this man how much she'd always wanted a father. But she only said, "I could never call you 'Pa,' sir. I respect you too much, but I'd love to call you 'Father,' if I may."

Annie saw a slow smile creep across Gil Eastman's face. He had the craggy bone structure of his sons, and it had aged well. She wondered if his sons would be as handsome when their hair grayed and their sun-browned complexions paled. Even bedridden, this new father of hers had an aura of strength, vitality, and steadfastness.

Father! Gil liked the sound. High class. Dignified. Caring.

"You certainly may," he told her readily. "Now get on with the telling of this adventure."

When Jude and Jules came in somewhat later, they could not believe the sight. Maudie was not bustling about as usual, but sitting in the old oak rocker wiping tears of laughter on the tail of her apron, and their pa was actually raised up off the flat of his back, propped on one elbow, insisting excitedly, "Go on, what happened next?"

Annie was perched on the edge of Gil's bed, her fur-lined cape flung over the foot of it, fancy satin bonnet hanging down her back by its strings, animatedly saying, "The van boy was just as dense as the suspicious little man at the North Platte Depot. When I tried to explain to him he could get more cooperation from his horses by kindness than he ever could from that whip, why he actually said," and her voice dropped down to the gravelly one of Bert, "I shore do agree with you, Ma'am. Why, I'd never take the whip to m'horses the way I did to those goldern Army mules. Why, you prob'ly noticed how sparin' I was with it."

Maudie was wiping more tears away from her face, and Gil had to lie flat again, he was laughing so hard, for they knew Bert well. Jules and Jude had only heard the end of the story, but they had to chuckle too, especially when Annie added pugnaciously, "Can you believe it? He actually thought he was being sparing, when in truth he used the whip much too frequently. Why, if he used it more on his poor Army mules, they probably had no hide left on them!"

"Take heed, Pa," Jules warned. "You're pretty handy with a whip yourself."

"Only on those half-broke horses he always insists on driving," Maudie interceded.

"So go on with the story," Gil urged impatiently. "You said you got to the store and it was forsaken."

Jude certainly didn't want this part related, so he sauntered over and put his arm possessively around his bride's shoulders, under the soft fullness of her luxuriant black hair. The hair softly brushed against his hand and for a brief second he forgot why he had interrupted. Remembering, he lazily commented, "I'm half-starved. Maudie, when's chow?"

"It's ready, I'll dish it up. You just go right on visitin'."

"That's really about all. Jude finally caught up with me and set everything straight—and here we are." Annie looked up at him with what she hoped was a sweetly shy look.

"Now, if you will tell me where you keep the linens, Mrs.—ma'am, I'll be glad to dress the table for dinner." Annie wanted to get away from the heat of Jude's arm across her shoulders. She tried to shrug it off without being noticed, but he had it firmly anchored.

"Maudie, dear, just call me Maudie . . . but there's no linens, we just eat on the oilcloth," the older woman apologized.

Gil hurried to add, "Your new house is well-stocked with them. Mrs. Danvers, my cousin who has gone on ahead to set up the house for you, well she said she would tat or crochet or some dang thing any she couldn't purchase through them mail-order wishbooks."

Annie felt badly that she had made such a faux pas. Her discomfort from it and from Jude's arm made her answer hoarsely, "How very wise of you, Maudie, to use oilcloth. In this house full of men, I suspect you have enough to do without laboring over linens the men wouldn't appreci-

ate anyway. I shall set the dishes on for you."
With this offer she jerked from Jude's leisurely
hold and practically ran to follow Maudie to the
kitchen.

She's a lady, all right, Gil determined. Used to
linens, unfailingly polite, and making others feel
at ease no matter what. He lay back on his pillow
and took his first completely contented breath in
a long, long time.

Jude did not like the way things were going at
all. While his new bride showed every air of
dignity and grace one could ask for, she still
seemed to temper it with a certain charm that
did not make her appear uppity and snobbish at
all. He had to find a way to discredit her in his
pa's esteem. Maudie's, too! Even his brother was
fawning over her like a lovesick calf tonight.
Jules and Annie were playing a game of domi-
noes beside the bed so Pa could watch. Even
Maudie found time to sit in the leather-padded
oak rocker and do some mending since, with
Annie's help, she had finished the dishes so
quickly.

As he looked around the room despondently,
Jude's eyes suddenly lit on the dusty old piano
in the corner. It hadn't been touched since Ma
left. Ma used to play high-class opera and con-
cert pieces on it, but she'd lacked talent and
none of them had liked her choice of music.

If this girl didn't play, Pa would be sure to
think she wasn't cultured enough; and if she did

play, she probably only knew that concert-opera stuff they taught rich little girls to play. Pa and Maudie and Jules would be stuck here listening to music they hated. Jude didn't relish submitting himself to listening, but it would be worth it if it made everyone less comfortable with Anne. It would serve Pa right. He needed to be reminded of the unpleasant side of having a woman like Ma around again.

"Jules. Don't deal another game. I've a splendid suggestion." Jude tried to make his voice at least sound enthusiastic. "I bet Anne can play the piano. Of course she can, her parents would have insisted on piano lessons. Why, culture demands it." From the glowering look he was getting from his wife, he guessed she'd never had a lesson in her life. Very pleased with himself, he continued, "Please play for us. We haven't had such a treat in a long time."

Jules laid down a domino disgustedly, wondering whatever possessed his twin. They were too old to be rude and sneak out. What was he thinking of, wishing this fate on them?

Even Pa said, "It's not necessary tonight if you're tired, Annie. Of course, I'll admit, I'd like it if you could play. It's one of the more refined amenities we don't often find out here. *Do* you play the piano?"

Annie knew she should say no, for she did not know any of the concertos a piano teacher would have taught her. She could only play by ear. However, when she saw the smirk on her new husband's face, she was determined to wipe it off. Resolutely she stood and walked to the piano. As she reached down to raise the seat on the stool, she said, "Piano lessons were never one of my favorite pastimes. I hated them and I was very careful not to pack any sheet music. However, I shall play you a few little songs I know by heart that my grandfather always enjoyed." Once Annie figured out the off-key notes to avoid, she managed to play rather well on the long-neglected piano.

Even Jude was content as he listened to the medley of English ballads, Irish ditties, sea chanties, and folk songs she played with ability and flair. When Jules wanted a cattle-lulling tune, she told him if he could sing it, she would be able to catch on. Soon he was teaching her the words of the song as she played it, and the two of them sang in harmony. Jude's ire nearly choked him as he got up and stomped from the room. Pa, Jules, and Maudie were so entranced with the music that they didn't even notice, but he heard his wife give the piano an extra hard "plink, plink, plink" in farewell.

Later Maudie took Annie to her new room, assuring her that Jude would be back before long. He just wanted to give his bride a little time to be alone before he joined her to spend their belated wedding night. Maude had given her a sweet, knowing smile and hurried out.

Annie looked around at Jude's bedroom. Even with Maudie's "spiffing up," it left a lot to be desired, such as curtains or shades at the window. It had no commode, but there was an unmatched porcelain pitcher and washbowl on a table in the corner. She draped an extra quilt that was on the back of a chair over the window and began to undress. There was no clothes press and the few hooks in the corner were filled with Jude's clothes.

She casually examined his wardrobe. More leather things—a heavy leather coat that looked as if it might be lined with sheepskin, and another one trimmed with fringe. There were several shirts hanging one on top of another and possibly a wool suit on the end hook, but it was covered by a couple of pairs of long union suits.

Annie felt pinpricks of embarrassment for staring at Jude's underwear. She had frequently washed her grandfather's, but this was quite different. She quickly looked away and continued her appraisal of the room. It was very simply furnished—no books, no bric-a-brac. Perhaps Maudie had packed his personal things away.

Annie wished that Maudie had packed that dratted underwear out of sight, too. Her eyes kept darting back to it. Did it stretch enough to cover the width of his broad shoulders, or did he have to leave the buttons undone to accommodate his chest? If the buttons were left undone, what would they reveal? Annie had never seen a man's bare chest. Those buttons went below his waist, she surmised, and found herself discomfitted at such a wayward thought. She pulled her eyes away from the long, dangling legs and rebuked herself for being a ninny.

The door to the bedroom opened silently, and Annie almost screamed before Jude ordered "Shh-h-h!"

He stood silently leaning against the door, his expressive gray eyes staring intimately at her until she hissed, "What are you doing in here? You promised me! Get out!"

Ignoring her, he went to the hooks and took down a couple of clean shirts and a pair of his union suits, as well as the heavy coat. He muttered, "I had to come in. They were all waiting in anticipation for my romantic entrance to my new bride's boudoir. Besides, I need my duds. I'll be ridin' out to join the roundup before anyone's up. Be so kind as to tell Pa you insisted I go, because you knew how guilty I felt about not being there when they needed me. Can you handle that?"

"Of course. Now go!"

Instead of leaving, he came across the room to where she stood and put a hand brazenly on her shoulder. He could feel her warmth through the nightie; she seemed to be shivering a little, causing him to hesitate before he asked insolently, "Not even a good-bye kiss or a wifely 'I'll miss you, dear'?"

In that moment of hesitation Annie had been tempted to put her head against his shirt just to feel the security such a broad, muscular chest might provide. His words brought her back to reality and she rebuked cattily, "I'll leave those for your mistress to tell you when you 'over-sleep' in her arms tomorrow morning."

"You're so sure that's where I'll be sleeping?" he snapped.

"Of course."

"And you don't mind?"

"Not in the least."

"Well, wifey mine, Pa would. Were I to saddle up and ride out tonight, I'd never hear the end of it. Thanks to you sleeping in my comfortable bed, I'll have to bed down on a cot in the bunkhouse for the night."

"If you are seeking sympathy from me, sir, you are wasting your breath." Annie wished he would just get his things and leave, for his presence was too intense in this small room. The height of him and the breadth of those strong shoulders bothered her, made it hard to remember her role as a prim miss.

Jude finished pulling a few more things from a drawer and then rolled everything up in his coat. He glanced over at her as she stood with her arms primly crossed in front of her. She might be an uppity, prudish old maid, but her looks denied it. Her eyes were too soft a brown and her cute little nose was too tilted . . . and that mouth of hers just begged to be kissed. He couldn't help being curious about what that big flannel nightdress covered. With her face scrubbed till it shone and that long jet-black hair in braids, she looked about sixteen years old. In fact, she looked like a lonely and forlorn kitten someone had abandoned.

He lay his things on the foot of the bed and started toward her, wanting to do something to erase that lost look on her face. Before he reached her, he roughly reminded himself she was twenty-six years old and tougher than leather. She'd told him she detested him, but she'd proceeded to try and wrap Pa and Jules around her little finger, just like Ma always had when she'd been in one of her flamboyant moods. They couldn't see Anne for the shrewd money-grabber she was, which surprised him. They both knew she was nothing but William Armstrong's olive branch to keep the Double Tree and Twin Trails' herds coming to Chicago.

Oh, she might be refined all right, and he admitted she was a dazzler, but she was still cheap. Any woman who could be bought wasn't worth marriage vows. Maybe after having her here a few weeks, Pa would read her true character and be glad to be rid of her. Within days, Anne herself would probably be unhappy, stuck way out here in the middle of a boring cattle range. Maybe he'd get lucky and she'd leave before he came back.

Jude took some gold coins from his pocket and threw them on the bed, forcing himself to say rudely, "Pa put up the money to bring you out here. I'm willing to put out my own coins to send you back. You'll tire of it here soon enough. When you do, just go on back. Don't think you need to wait until I return to tell me good-bye. I'll understand."

"No, Mr. Eastman, you don't understand. In

fact, you are the densest man I've ever met! Haven't you ever heard the marriage vows? For better, for worse, for richer, for poorer, til death us do part—man and wife forever and all the rest of it? Well, I took those oaths and it has turned out to be for the worse, not for the better, but all the same, I said 'I do' and so help me, I *will*."

"Well, I never said it."

"No, like everything else, you paid someone else to. It's your way. If you don't pay, then your father does! You even have to pay a woman to sleep with you! You think you can buy anything with money, but someday there's going to be something you'll want that you can't buy for any price."

"I can't imagine what it would be. You Armstrongs rate yourselves pretty high, but you were purchased. Any woman who can be bought isn't worth her salt, and I've never run across one who wasn't for sale if the price was right. All any of you want is to be a kept woman, mistress of the house, mistress to sleep with. What the hell's the difference?"

His arrogant tone angered Annie as much as his words did. She was furious, and worst of all, he was right! To find security, she had sold herself. She had refused Dev and Carter's love because she wanted marriage. Now all this man she'd married wanted was to make her miserable.

"Oh, yes. Some women sell their bodies, others are forced to do such things as marry against their wills. As you say, it can all be accomplished for a price. But there's one thing you can't buy, and that's a woman's true love, her heart, her soul—and her respect. You're like the horses my grandfather trained. You run contentedly around and around the ring, happily jumping the little hurdles, but when you come upon a real obstacle that demands a real effort or commitment you break stride and run for the paddock. Grandfather had a name for such horses—gutless bastards! It describes you perfectly. Fortunately, you are not the first one I have known, so your pettifogging demands do not upset me."

"Pettifogging! What the hell kind of word is that?" Jude snarled.

"It means childish. Spoiled. Always wanting your own way. Trying to weasel out when you lose the flip of a coin. Trying to make your father's commitments meaningless and the words you gave a lawyer your signature to vow in your name null and void. A pettifogging, gutless bastard, Mr. Eastman, does not receive love, nor heart, nor soul, nor respect no matter what price he pays. I thought until tonight that love was for sale, but it's not. Love can't be bought at any price. Wives, husbands, mistresses, marriages. You are right, they can all be purchased, but true love, never."

"I don't know about this 'true love' crap, but I know a woman's loving arms can be had, with or without the purchase price. Would you like to have me prove it to you, Mrs. Eastman?"

Annie quickly backed away, thinking maybe

she had gone a little too far, but she refused to
back down. "Force doesn't prove anything, *sir!*
May I remind you of our deal. You will be
getting all you paid for. A mistress for Twin
Trails. Now do try to grow up before you return
so you can at least attempt to hold up your end
of the bargain!"

"You bet, lady! I'll return to hold up my end.
By God, it's you who will take the gate not the
obstacles, wait and see!" He yanked the quilt off
the window, pushed it open and climbed out
leaving a very mixed-up new bride behind.

It was a long time before Annie fell asleep that
night. Her mind kept reviewing the incidents of
today and last week and last year. Had it really
been a year since Dev had asked her to keep her
childhood vow and marry him? How innocently
happy she had been then. Even those terrible
months in Birmingham working in the manufactory had been bearable because she had been
sure of Dev's love, sure her world would be
blissful as soon as he returned. Even a simple-
minded child should have known no earl would
allow his son to marry his wife's maid's illegitimate daughter.

And Carter Armstrong! Annie had felt secure
with him, as if a bond was developing between
them; yet Carter was engaged to Maybelle Meyers. He himself had tried to tell Annie he did not
love Maybelle, but as Daphne had said, it was a
suitable match. Both of these men had loved her

in their way, but both had only wanted her for a mistress, and she could not make that much of a sacrifice, even for a man she loved.

This brought her thoughts up to the present. She might not have sold her love, but she had sold herself to Jude Eastman. How ironic. Now she was the unloved bride of a man who loved and wanted his mistress.

Annie was convinced she could endure any amount of Jude's hostility if she were allowed to remain here in the country. Horses seemed to be a very big part of life in these wide-open prairie grasslands, and from the little she had learned about ranching this evening, Annie determined Jude would be gone a great deal—perhaps months at a time. Hopefully their relationship would become one of polite aloofness. She had to admit she wished she *felt* more aloof to him. His mere presence sparked something indefinable within her that was frightening, because she knew it was not reciprocated in any way.

When she had stolen a few peeks in his direction tonight, she had discovered her new husband truly was a handsome man when he was not scowling and looking ferocious. The smiles he gave Maudie when he teased her were endearing, the smiles he gave his brother were fun-loving, and those special smiles he saved for his pa were smiles of deep caring. The closest he had come to smiling at her was the smirk he had given her when he'd suggested she play the piano. The curmudgeon had hoped she couldn't play a note. It was written all over his face!

What if he found out she was not Daphne Armstrong? Annie shuddered at the thought of how fast he would return her to North Platte, probably without even giving her train fare. She was glad she had gathered up the coins he had thrown on the bed. After he'd left, she'd rammed them in her multicolored beaded purse, thankful that she was no longer completely destitute. He had sworn as he left she'd be the one to run for the paddock gate. Well, Annie Ellis Eastman would show him what well-trained thoroughbreds were made of. He'd never be able to put up an obstacle she would turn away from. Never! With this sincere vow she finally fell asleep, alone in her bridegroom's bed.

Jude had never spent such a miserable night, and it wasn't because the cot was uncomfortable. No, it was the words of his wife that kept him wide awake and restless. "Pettifogging, gutless bastard." That phrase rang over and over again in his ears as well as her barbs about paying a woman to sleep with him and a man to take his wedding vows for him! Wedding vows! He felt like storming back in there and making her keep those vows—he wouldn't have to use force either. She might be a prudish old maid, but he didn't think she'd be entirely immune to his practiced charms. He actually sat up on the cot and reached down on the floor to find his trousers when he remembered her taunt implying he'd attempted to make his father's bargain worthless. The vixen had a sharp tongue, all right. Just like Ma had when Pa didn't please her. Imagine living with that the rest of his life! Not that he would, of course. But still, he swore vehemently, she could flaunt the biggest, highest obstacles in the world in front of him and he'd take them in stride to prove how wrong she was about him. Jude Eastman might be a lot of things, but he wasn't gutless, nor was he "pettifogging."

He lay down again. It would be Anne who turned and ran, probably after only a day or two on the trail drive. If she was stubborn enough to hang on clear through it, then the cavelike soddy would be the final straw. One look at that and at the complete isolation up there, and she'd be back on that train to Chicago like a shot. He'd better start thinking up a good, plausible story for Pa. The way the old man was acting tonight, you'd think an angel had descended on them from heaven. He'd have to contrive a damn good story for her departure.

The first hint of light at dawn found him in the barn, saddling up. He was almost ready to ride out before Jules came in carrying his own blanket and clothing roll on his shoulder.

Jules was incredulous. "That isn't you, is it, Jude?"

"Who else could get close enough to Rocky to saddle him?"

"What are you doing here?"

"I'm riding out with you, little brother. I told you I was going to."

"But that was before you saw your bride. Before you spent the night in her bed. You don't have to go. Barnes and I can handle the Double Tree's end of this roundup. Why, even Pa expects you to stay here."

"Well, my wife prefers I don't! I spent my first 'love-filled' night with her alone in the bunkhouse! Let's ride."

"I never thought I'd live to see the day I was related to a damn fool! My own kin and he's skinning out on a dead run."

Jude was suddenly furious with Jules. This remark was too close to what Anne had said to him. It felt good to Jude to double up his fist as he had as a kid, ready to bust his brother a good one, but Jules had turned his back to him and was now tying his bedroll behind his saddle. Jude knew Anne was the one he should be angry with, or maybe himself for landing in the cactus this way. It was too late for recriminations now. With any luck, she'd be gone before he got back.

No, he amended, with the old man doting on her and Maudie catering to her and that stubbornness of her own, she would still be here. Hell, it might just be rather interesting to get her on that trail drive. Yeah, damn interesting. He began to whistle as he swung up onto Rocky.

"For a thwarted groom you sound damn chipper!" Jules told him.

"I told you my plans, Jules. The last thing I needed was to bed her. What if I'd got her pregnant? Then I'd really be some kind of an ass to make her ride drag day after day when we take the cattle to the Sandhills."

"You're not still planning that jackass scheme, are you? Not after seeing her?"

"I told you, her personality is a hundred miles apart from her looks!"

"What about Pa, Jude? He seems mighty taken with her. If she goes, he could have a relapse."

"Let me worry about that, dammit. I'll take care of it. You know I won't hurt Pa. He'll see it's for the best by then, I'll wager."

Chapter Ten

✦✦✦✦✦

GIL HAD JUST dozed off for his habitual midmorning snooze in the front room when the back door banged and his new daughter-in-law came rushing in. One half-awake glance told him Annie was in an agitated frenzy, and he immediately pulled himself into an upright position.

"Father!" she cried, "I cannot believe you condone such a barbaric way to break horses here at the ranch! The method your men are using is positively brutal!"

The distress in Annie's voice twinged Gil's conscience as he tried to explain the western method of topping off a bronc fresh from winter range to a girl who had helped to gently nurture horses to accept a saddle and rider. "I'd be the first to admit it's primitive, Annie, but you see it's mostly a matter of time. The men need another eighteen or twenty horses for the roundup in a hurry. Some of these critters are mighty stubborn about giving up their freedom to lead the hard life of a cow pony. Broncbusting is the fastest way we've found to convince those critters they have to go to work. Put 'em in the corral, slap a saddle on their backs and a steel bit in their mouths, and hope some cowpoke has enough guts to climb aboard. The important thing is if he'll climb back up after the second and third times he gets tossed off.''

"Do your sons?" Annie asked, thinking of Jude. She had implied to her insolent husband that he'd pay another to do things for him, but she had an inkling that when it came to his ranch duties, he wouldn't take the easy way.

"The twins? They ride broncs with the best of 'em. 'Fact, they probably get tossed off fewer times'n any hand I've got, unless it's Curly Reiley. He's a born broncbuster.

"Like I was sayin', every man I've got out there helping with this roundup has to have a string of at least five or six horses. They're in the saddle sixteen, sometimes eighteen hours a day by the time they take their turn night-herding. On a no-grain, grass-only diet, a horse can't work too many hours. Especially if it's being used for cutting. That's a mean job for a horse.

"When my ramrod—that's another name for a foreman—sends word he needs horses, it means he needs them now. He's probably had to hire on another wrangler or two, had a horse go lame, go loco, or get rattler-bit. Nope, it's the only way. These horses are mostly wild mustangs. They'd never take to friendly ways."

"Am I to have a horse of my own someday?" Annie pleaded, her dark eyes wistful.

"A horse of your own! Why, girl, you can have a half-dozen of your own if you want 'em," Gil offered, glad she had temporarily forgotten about the men breaking broncs out in the corral.

Annie laughed, "I don't want but one horse for my very own and I want to train it myself."

"Train it, yes, after one of the boys breaks it in for you."

"No, I want to choose one and break it myself. Oh, please, Father!"

How could he refuse this sweet girl?

"If it was possible, you know I would agree, don't you? But it's not, Annie. These animals were born wild, not in a warm stable. You may have any four- or five-year-old you choose. You can even have Reiley ride the meanness out of it for you today."

Annie hated to argue, but this issue was too important not to try to win him over to her point of view. "I'll pick an intelligent one with nice eyes! I don't want Reiley nor anyone else to ride him for me. I must gain his complete confidence right from the start if I'm to turn him into a jumper. All of my life I've dreamed of having a stallion of my own. In England I had a beautifully trained little mare, but I've graduated to a bigger horse now!"

"A bigger horse! A stallion! No, no! Pick a nice mare or one of the geldings. Not a stallion, even if he does have 'nice eyes.' "

"Then you forbid it, Father?"

He knew he couldn't forbid her; he would do whatever he could to make her happy. And he knew from previous conversations that Annie did have experience with stallions, so he consented.

"No, I don't. It'll probably be okay." Gil's voice revealed doubt and concern. "Pick one out and have it put in the back corral. One thing, though. I must have your word you won't try to ride it until I give the go ahead. We'll see whether it is you or Curly or one of the twins who rides this horse when the time comes. Or have you already picked one out? I saw you standing and staring into their pasture this morning."

"Then you know which horse I've chosen, for Maudie tells me you are an excellent judge of horseflesh."

"Not the chestnut!"

"I was sure I had picked out the best! Now you've confirmed it!" She gave him a solid smack on the cheek. Gil was pleased beyond words, but he remained concerned.

"I'll grant you he's a royal beauty, but he's a wild horse, never been broke to bridle. We managed to bring him in off the range, but I refused to let them break him for just another cow pony. If I was younger, I would have picked him too, but I was a tough hombre then, Annie. I could have handled him. You can't!"

"Wait and see!" She quickly turned and rushed from the room before he could change his mind. "I'll keep my word not to ride without your approval, and thank you! Thank you with all my heart!" she called over her shoulder.

For Jude Eastman, four weeks of rounding up strays had seemed more like four months this spring. Back and forth, back and forth across the hundreds of miles of flat green rangeland to gather the herd for the tally branding. Then they'd have to brand the spring calves and castrate most of the bulls.

It was going to be June, maybe July, before the Double Tree's herd was separated into three divisions. One herd was to be returned to this free government range, one was going to be moved to the Twin Trails ranch up in the Sand-hills, and the balance was to be trailed on to Ogallala and shipped to Chicago. Jude had enjoyed these tasks in the past, especially taking the herd on to Ogallala. That was one wild town! It had almost as many brothels as saloons.

Jude fondly recalled some of the lusty bawds he'd spent the night with at Dusty Preston's Hotel or Ma Banner's Boarding House. That was what was wrong this spring, what made the weeks seem like months. He wasn't going to Ogallala. Jules was. *He* was taking the herd up to Twin Trails. While Jude was eager to move the cattle to the new ranch, he was not eager to live chastely for at least the summer.

Even when he got to Cattle Creek, he wouldn't

be able to spend his nights at the Cattleman's Haven as he always had. Pa would know when this herd got near enough to ride in nights, and ride in he would expect Jude to do, too—ride in to the home place where his bride was. Damn it to hell! Curly had told him when he brought back the string of horses that he'd never seen the boss happier in his life. "That bride of yours is sure something special, Jude, and your pa thinks the sun rises and sets on her raven black hair," had been Curly's precise words. Raven black hair! That was all Jude had seen in his restless dreams lately. Raven black hair softly touching his hand, raven black hair pristinely braided. Untouchable raven black hair! He'd tried to think of wrapping his fingers in long red hair, and pulling Rosie's nude body down on top of him, but the vision always faded, blotted out by the unwanted vision of Anne. Rosie was going to be mad as a redheaded hornet when he didn't come to her nights, but Jude knew he couldn't while he had a wife in residence. It was against the way he'd been raised, against his own standards. The irony was that his prissy wife would be glad if he spent his nights in town with Rosie! Glad! He recalled how she had stressed that fact to him. What a mess!

He was still trying to untangle it in his mind when young Rawlings, the son of their home-place manager, came riding into camp from the home place. Cripes, they must be even closer than he had thought! When Rawlings spotted Jude, he trotted over, eager to give him the message he'd been sent to deliver.

"Jude, your pa wants you and Jules to ride in to the place day after tomorrow. He says you'll be close enough by then so there won't be any question about your making it in by noon and back out here by nightfall. You're to bring five or six drovers with you including Curly."

"Whatever for? If there's an emergency at home, we aren't waiting a day or two. I don't care how hard we have to ride!"

"There's no emergency. I'd know if there was."

"Then why?"

"See, I don't know! That's why it can't be an emergency. He just said for you to be there, that's all!"

"Okay, tell him he can count on us. Get yourself some chow and one of the spare horses from the remuda, then head out, boy. I want you back there before dark."

"I was hopin' I could sort of stay and just go in with you."

"Sorry, kid. Pa wouldn't know if we got the message that way. Besides, he's liable to stew and fret for fear you'd get lost or hurt. If you want to herd cattle so bad, I'll take you up to the Sandhills with me later this season."

"For sure? Hey, that's great! I can't hardly wait!"

"Neither can I," Jude told him flatly, knowing each of them had different reasons for the same wish.

* * *

Jude and Jules were leading the band of galloping riders into the gate as Annie stood in the yard watching. She wondered why they had returned so quickly. It was obvious the horses had been ridden hard, for she could see their lathered flanks, flaring nostrils, and the foam around their mouths. Had there been an Indian attack? Maybe rustlers had stolen the herd!

Eager to learn what had happened, she rushed toward the barnyard where the men were dismounting, but before she could reach the gate she heard the back door of the house snap open and turned to see what the men were staring at.

It was Gil Eastman being carried outside by young Rawlings, his father and Pecos the stablehand as he sat upright in the big oak rocker. Maudie was holding open the door, trying to tuck a quilt across her patient's lap at the same time. Annie quickly turned from the men and ran to Gil, as did both Jude and Jules.

"Father!" Annie cried. "What are you doing out of bed? You know the doctor ordered one more week's bed rest for you. You must return at once!"

"Pa!" Jules' breathlessness indicated how hurriedly he'd jumped the fence and come running. "Oh, Pa, you old rascal! Can't we even turn our backs on you and trust you to listen to Maudie and Anne? Damn it all, we've got to get you back to bed."

"Not on your tintype, Jules," his pa told him firmly.

"At least tell us the meaning of this foolishness, Pa," Jude insisted. "It must be something important for you to call us home and get out of bed when you know you're not fit to be up yet."

Gil looked around at all the anxious faces, but did not know how to tell them his reasons in front of Annie, so he ordered, "Annie, girl, you help Maudie fix the boys all a bite to eat and a good hot cup of coffee. They'll be in in a minute."

"Of course, Father, but I still think it unwise for you to be out here."

"I just need to talk with the boys here about a few things. I'll take it easy," he promised her.

Jude listened to this conversation as he carefully kept his eyes glued on his pa and avoided looking at his bride. Curly had been right. The old man thought too highly of her, and she knew it. She had him buffaloed, all right. He looked up to see if she was gloating, but she was not even looking at him, only at his father, her eyes were full of worry and solicitude.

Jules chided, "I think we have all spoiled the groom's homecoming. Go ahead, little sister. Welcome him as you should. We'll all pretend we're not here. In fact, if you choose to kiss him, we'll just look the other way."

Annie wished she could kick her husband's brother right in the shins, but of course he didn't know how it was between the newlyweds. Now Gil was smiling, too. "I plumb forgot it's been a month since the two of you have seen one another. If only time weren't so dang short, maybe we could—"

Annie hastily stepped forward. "Don't worry. We both understand the importance of business. Why, we'll have the rest of our lives to make up for the time this roundup has stolen from us, won't we, Jude?" she asked sweetly.

"The rest of our days," Jude agreed, thinking silently, *and they are numbered.*

Annie guessed his thought and determined to embarrass him for it as he so fittingly deserved. Throwing her arms around his neck, she murmured falsely, "Welcome back, Jude, darling," then stood on tiptoe and kissed him full on the lips in front of everyone.

Jude's first thought was one of disgust that she would go to such lengths to impress Pa, but something inside said this kiss was not to impress Pa. She didn't need to impress him. No! This was strictly a kiss to embarrass Jude Eastman because she'd suspected what he'd implied by "days." Well, he wasn't going to be embarrassed, she was! He pulled her tightly into his arms to roughly return her kiss. His scheme backfired, for as soon as he began to kiss her, he found himself pouring into it all his pent-up passion. It didn't matter who she was—she was soft and warm and feminine and she smelled of lilacs. Her lips tasted sweet. He couldn't get enough of her. He pulled her more firmly against him and began to gently pry her lips apart with his seeking tongue. Only Pa, clearing his throat, returned him to the time and the place.

As he drew himself away from Annie, she positively glowered at him. The second he released her, she turned and practically ran into the house.

Jules was standing next to him and said in such a low undertone no one else could hear, "Ah, yes, the cold bride for whom you feel nothing."

"Shut up, dammit!" Jude swore almost under his breath, too.

Slam! The back door reverberated with the anger and frustration of Annie Ellis Eastman.

By the time Jude and Jules turned back to their pa, he was already speaking. "I know it was a bad time to pull so many of you off the crew, but it's an emergency. Annie is determined she's going to ride the chestnut today, and I wanted every man here to make her ride as safe as can be."

The number of indrawn breaths and near-silent exclamations denoted the shock of the men standing there.

Jude was the first to rally. "The hell she is!" he exploded.

"Pa," Jules added, "you're not serious. This is some kind of joke."

Even Curly Reiley defied his boss. "That's one mean horse, that chestnut. He don't allow no-body even close to him."

"There's nothing to discuss here. She can ride Maudie's mare. Maudie never rides anymore, and Tiny is strictly a woman's horse," Jude stated, trying to close the subject.

However, his father was adamant. "Let's get one thing straight here," he announced sharply.

"I may be as worthless as the tits on a boar, lying in that bed day after day, but I am still the owner and head ramrod of this outfit and what I say still goes!"

In a somewhat gentler voice he added, "Jude, I know how you feel about your wife taking such a risk. I'd feel exactly the same way if I hadn't watched her gentle that wild chestnut down these past weeks. She's got him eating out of her hand—literally."

The stallion's not the only one, Jude thought.

"Annie's not new to horses, boy," Gil continued. "She asked if she could have her pick of my horses, and by Jove, she picked the best. She wouldn't let me have the meanness bucked out of him. She don't go for it. Every day she's worked with that horse. Gave me her word she wouldn't ride him until I'd okayed it. Sunday she brought him out in front of my window and saddled and bridled him and led him around a few times to prove he was ready. I told her today was the day."

"Okay, Pa. I see she has you in a bind. You know and I know even the wildest horses will follow you around if you can get close enough to feed them a few sugar lumps. Keep her in the house serving lunch. I'll go ride the damn thing until he's worn out past that rank savage stage. Eating lumps of sugar and being ridden are two different things to a half-wild stallion. By the time she comes down to the corral, just maybe she can handle him. I doubt it."

"You got the right idea, Jude, risking your

own neck to protect your wife's. I'm right proud of you, but you can't do it. She don't want that fierce pride bucked out of that horse. I gave her my word, son. A man's word has to mean something or he's no man at all.

"I wouldn't let her do this if I thought she'd get bad hurt! I've got a plan all figured out. Everyone will be in strategic positions to get her out of there safely, just in case. That's why I made her wait till you boys could ride in."

"Come and git it!" Maudie called out the back screen door, interrupting his words.

"I'll explain my plan after lunch. You go on in and eat now," Gil told them. "I'll just sit here in the sun and enjoy being outside till you get done."

Annie hoped she was not blushing when her eyes met her husband's as she handed him a plate of food. She was sincerely afraid she was. She was still angry at the way he had taken advantage of her kiss, but most of all, she was angry at her own body's miserable betrayal. Crushed against his hard muscular chest, the nipples on her breasts had begun to harden and her heart had started beating much, much too fast. Even her arms and legs felt weak.

Whatever was the matter with her? She had responded to Dev's advances because she had loved him, and Carter's kiss had been comforting. Responding to such kisses was natural.

But this! This was beyond belief! That she

could be anything but repulsed by a kiss from her mistress-loving husband was ridiculous. She handed him his plate and pulled her hand back quickly, as if in fear of getting burned.

Jude smiled sarcastically and said in a low voice, "Next time, don't start anything you aren't prepared to finish, little wife. You'll soon learn I never back down!"

"Nor did I!" she reminded him heatedly, looking him right in the eye.

He couldn't deny that. She hadn't tried to push him away when he kissed her so passionately. Only her eyes revealed her disgust. Taking his plate, he turned sharply away from her to go to the table.

"I'd sure like to know what Gil's got the boys in here for," Maudie remarked as she handed Annie another plate to dry. "He usually mentions if something comes up. It must be important or he'd never pull this many off the roundup at one time!"

"I even eavesdropped while they ate lunch," Annie admitted, "but I didn't hear a thing, either." She dried another plate and set it on top of the pile.

"They all scurried out of here fast enough after lunch. Why, I thought sure Jude would hang around the kitchen for a spell."

"If Father needed him for something important, he wouldn't." Annie hoped her comment would fool Maudie. It was becoming increasingly difficult to keep Father, Maudie, and Jules convinced she was a happy newlywed.

Young Rawlings came busting into the kitchen door just then without remembering to knock. It was obvious he was too excited to recall any manners.

"Ma'am! Mrs. Eastman! You're to come ride the chestnut now!"

"What!" Maudie ejaculated. "Why, she'll do nothing of the kind! What nonsense is this?"

"I am going to ride him, Maudie, but not today." She turned to the freckle-faced youth and smilingly told him, "Thank your boss for remembering that today was the day I was to try my luck, but since he has other important business, I'll wait until another day."

"But ma'am—you are the important business—the reason he had the men ride in. So's they could watch you."

Annie was too stunned to even answer. She knew Gil considered it farfetched for a woman to break a horse, but she thought she had convinced him she knew what she was doing. Why would he ridicule her this way? Were they so short on amusements out here that this would be entertainment? Their own little Wild, Wild West Show! She, too, was a little afraid Pegasus would toss her off, but she was determined to be like the others and get on again.

Pegasus was now tame and gentle enough that if he did unseat her, he would not viciously trample her. In fact, Annie was positive that her horse liked her well enough that once he was used to the weight on his back, he would be content to let her ride him.

She was sure all these men were waiting to laugh at her newfangled, gentle way of training horses, and that made her angrier by the minute. She was going to go out there and tell every one of them they had wasted their time, for they'd get no laughs at her expense! Then she was going to tell Gil Eastman—tears came to her eyes at this trick he had played on her. Never had she been so disappointed by anyone's deceit.

Furiously she started to pull open the door just as Jude pushed it open from the outside and stormed in. He looked her up and down insultingly and asked, "Now, tell me, what is all this hullabaloo really about? It's obvious you have no intention of trying to ride that horse. Not that I ever thought you did. Were you just trying to put a little excitement in your life? Did you miss me so much you contrived such a bold-faced scheme to bring me back?"

Maudie and young Rawlings didn't know whether to stay to defend Annie or to run from this obviously personal conflict.

Annie didn't need anyone to protect her. She could face anyone or anything, even her arrogant husband and his equally provoking father . . . and yes, a half-wild stallion, too!

"I have to change into a riding skirt, sir! Just as soon as I do, I will be out to ride my horse. He's beautifully trained and won't give me a minute's trouble," she said brazenly. "In fact," she added, "you will see just how unnecessary those silly spurs you wear are!"

Annie glanced defiantly at Jude, then haughtily marched out of the kitchen to change. Jude shook his head in exasperation and went back outside.

When Annie got to the corral, she saw that the men were not just there to watch her ride; each one of them had been carefully stationed a few feet apart inside the pen, and not sitting on the top rail, as they usually did when spectating. Glancing at Gil, she saw the concern in his face and regretted that she had worried him to this degree. He was so concerned for her welfare he'd pulled his men off the roundup! For his sake she might have backed down—if she didn't want to ride Pegasus so very much, and if her insolent husband wasn't standing there watching. Instead, she bent low to go under the bar and into the pen.

Bravely, without saying a word to anyone, she walked through the corral. Gill called out, "There's plenty of time to change your mind, Annie girl. Any one of the men here will break that horse for you."

"No! I'll not have his spirit broken! Truly, Father, there is nothing to worry about."

"Do you want us to run him into the corral, Anne, or to help rig him out?" Jules asked her.

"No, I'll manage," she assured him as she walked on through the corral to the fenced-in pasture and called, "Pegasus, come, boy." Unobtrusively she took down the bridle she'd left hanging on the fence early this morning.

The horse nickered, pawed the ground once or twice, and then slowly, shyly, came over to her. She petted his back and nuzzled her face against his neck, saying, "Remember we're good, good friends, Pegasus. Don't let me down now." She reached the hand she had been patting him with on across his neck and grabbed the other side of the bridle to force the bit gently into his mouth as she brought it up with her other hand. Surprisingly, he permitted this maneuver with only a fraction of his usual sidestepping, and she was able to easily get the leather straps over his ears and bridle into place.

Once more she patted him and talked softly to him, then slowly led him to the corral gate. However, he was intelligent enough to sense something unpalatable about the pen and the humans standing around it. At the gate he reared back with unexpected force. Grabbing the reins with both hands, Annie dug her booted heels into the ground and pulled with all her might while constantly soothing Pegasus with her calm, "Come on, boy. It's all right, Pegasus. Come on. In, boy." With his mistress' tugging and her calming words, Pegasus finally decided to venture into the corral. His gentle eyes, which had so appealed to Annie, looked rather wicked as they rolled this way and that, taking in the position of each bronc rider. He lunged back once more when Jules closed the gate behind him, but this time Annie was ready for it and had a firm hold.

With more coaxing, she got him to stand close

to the rail where she had put the saddle. Annie found it easier to bring the horse to the rail than to carry the heavy saddle to the horse. She was used to saddling horses, but not with these heavy western-style saddles.

None of the men made a move or a whisper while she was between the horse and the bars where she could easily be crushed. Hastily she threw the saddle onto Pegasus, then quickly went to his nose to rub it softly before she cinched the saddle into place and led him to the center of the corral. Pegasus was still nervously eyeing his audience, but Annie's voice kept him from crow-hopping or rearing back away from them.

When she stepped beside the horse, Mr. Rawlings got her attention and then grasped his ear with his finger and thumb. Annie knew what he meant; it was customary here to grasp the horse's ear painfully so it would not move while a rider mounted. Appalled by the thought, she shook her head no.

Annie knew it was now or never. She had to put her foot into that stirrup and swing up into the saddle. There wouldn't be any difficulty, she told herself, for she trusted Pegasus—almost. With only a brief, "Steady now, old Peg," she was on his back and behold, he only looked back over his shoulder to see what his little friend was up to. Relieved, Annie bent forward and scratched his neck for him. With a slight nudge of her heels and a tug on his rein she actually had him walking in a circle just as he had walked following her lead.

There were obvious sighs of relief all around
and visible relaxation of tensed positions too
long held. Some of the men were shaking their
heads in awe, and Annie was gleefully giving
Pegasus a pat on his hip, saying "Oh, good
boy," to him.

When she was able to rein him to a stop and
nudge him to walk somberly again, one of the
men sputtered, "Well, I'll be a damned horned
toad!"

Young Rawlings was so excited that he threw
his hat into the air and yelled, "Wa-hooo! She
did it!"

That was all it took to turn Pegasus into a
whirling dynamo and send his hooves several
feet into the air with his body arched high in the
middle. Annie grabbed for the pommel and tried
to grip with her legs, but too late. She had been
unprepared and was ignominiously thrown to
the ground, landing on her arm and hip.

For one second she lay there wondering if she
was dead or alive or if she might possibly have
one bone that wasn't broken. If pain was any
indication, she doubted it. The corral was pan-
demonium. Her horse was immediately block-
aded several feet from her by human bodies
while Jude, Jules, and Mr. Rawlings were all on
their knees leaning over her, their eyes filled
with anxiety.

Annie's only thought was Pegasus. He must
not get the best of her now, not after all the
hours she'd painstakingly worked with him. He
had to know who his mistress was, or she would

never have the kind of control she wanted. She tried stretching her arms and legs, and when everything seemed to move, she scrambled rapidly to her feet, pushing back the outstretched hands that tried to stop her. Once on her feet, she ran between two men and yanked the reins out of Curly Reiley's hands as he stood there holding Pegasus with a tight fist. Annie looked her horse in the eye with a determined glare and swore to him, "Hear me, Pegasus, I will ride you! I will!" Then without another word or so much as a pat she went to his side again and painfully hoisted herself back into the saddle.

It was almost as if the horse was sorry for misbehaving, he handled so well for her. She rode around the corral several times and then back to the rail, where she unsaddled him before taking him out to the pasture. Then she unbridled him while scratching his ears and rubbing his nose profusely to show that she was pleased with him.

The sound of a voice startled her, and she turned to look into the ferocious face of her husband. "Proud of yourself, aren't you? You really showed everybody, didn't you? From now on they'll all bow low to the imperial Mrs. Eastman who accomplished the impossible. Oh, yes, you should be patting your own back instead of the horse's, but was all the glory really worth risking death for?"

"I wasn't even hurt! You're just mad because I rode him, and without using saw-rowled spurs, either! Pegasus is gentle. I didn't risk my neck!"

Annie lashed back, hurt by his belittling words.

"Who gives a damn about your neck?" he continued. "It nearly killed Pa when you got throwed. He could have had another heart attack!" Angrily he turned and strode away, leaving Annie hanging onto Pegasus' mane while she sobbed brokenly, her face pressed against his soft neck. Why had she been so stubborn about riding, and why hadn't she immediately thought of Gil and run to let him know she was all right? Instead, all she had thought of was her horse. Not pride or glory, as Jude had implied, but a horse. Yes, he was just a horse, but at this moment, he was probably the only friend she had in the world.

Jules tucked a quilt over Pa after the others left the room. They'd easily carried his chair back into the house and helped him into bed.

"It wasn't too much for you, was it, Pa?" Jules asked as his father lay back on his pillow with a deep sigh.

"Too much? In one way it was, Jules. It was too much and more. More than I ever dared to hope and dream for. You have to know I've had my reservations about making Jude marry that girl to get his hands on the Sandhills place; I knew how bad he wanted it and I put the pressure on.

"But my scheme! It's working, Jules! I did right! That girl's got spunk. Why, Annie'll tame your brother just like she did that horse. Give

her a little time and she'll have that wild bucka-
roo just as gentle and loyal as that stallion. Mark
my words, son'"

Chapter Eleven

✦ ✦ ✦ ✦ ✦

THE FOLLOWING WEEKS were the busiest Annie had
ever known. She could not begin to imagine
how Maud ie had managed alone. Once the herd
was stationary at the Cattle Creek crossing, the
ranch had two or three tablefuls of men to feed
nearly every meal. First it was the owners of
neighboring ranches who came to visit Gil and
always ended up staying for a meal or two. It
was hard to believe some of these "neighboring"
ranches were over a hundred miles away! Every
one of them ran herds on the same massive
range south of the Platte River. At this time of
year they joined forces to gather the half-wild
animals that had grazed all winter on the unbroken prairie. When the roundup was completed,
the cattle were divided into each owner's herd
by brand. Spring calves went with their mothers
and all strays were divided among the ranches
equally.

Gil seemed proud to introduce Annie to everyone as his new daughter-in-law, and the tale

of her breaking of Pegasus was told and retold. With each telling Pegasus became wilder and her defiance at climbing back on again after her vicious bucking off was raised to a higher level of courage.

Her husband never mentioned the incident. He continued to act like a happy newlywed when they were in front of others, but both of them avoided any opportunity to be alone or to have a private conversation. At night he still went through her bedroom to sleep in the empty bunkhouse, but she was often so exhausted that she was asleep before he crept through to the window.

Twice he had opened the door to come through before she was tucked primly into bed. The first time he'd quickly closed it and gone away for another half hour, but the second time he came on into the room where she sat on the side of the bed, putting in her nighttime braids. Seeing him standing there with the lamplight casting a rich bronze to his skin started Annie's heart flailing. Angry that the virile handsomeness of this cowboy husband of hers could disturb her so, she hissed, "If you please!"

"If I please?" He cocked his eyebrows and continued to watch her, his gray eyes amused, a smile playing across his lips. "Please what? Please sleep in my own comfortable bed? Please get the hell out of here? Please act like the husband I supposedly am, or please get myself conveniently trampled and killed? Just what is your meaning, Mrs. Eastman? You are usually more explicit."

Taken aback, Annie quickly corrected, "I certainly don't want you killed! Your family—"

"Ah, yes, always thinking of my family."

Ignoring his sarcasm, she went on, "Nor do I have any intentions of giving up this bed. You yourself disabused me of any notions I'd had about a husband—"

For a moment Jude wondered exactly what this prudish old maid's notions had been about a husband. Perhaps he should try to dispel them? "That leaves 'get the hell out of here,' doesn't it, ma'am? Surely that isn't the meaning of such a sentence as 'If you please,' is it?"

Flustered, Annie could only nod.

"So that is my greeting from my bride? I should think, wifey mine, that you would be glad I slipped through here before you have to crawl under all those bedcovers for protection. Lord, you must nearly suffocate on these warm nights with the heap you draw around you. Actually, that bulky night thing you wear covers anything you might have that a man would want to see."

When this retort only caused her to drop the braid she was doing and clutch the unbuttoned top of her nightdress tightly, Jude knew he should go on to the window, but he found he really didn't want to. He was enjoying teasing her, watching her blush. He enjoyed making those beautiful black eyes of hers snap at him. Instead of going out the window, he perched on her big metal trunk, leaning back on one hand, a booted foot comfortably up on the edge of it. "You know, we're fortunate that Rawlings and his son have their own room at the rear of the barn and Pecos hates to sleep indoors except during the worst of the winter. Everyone else who uses the bunkhouse is on roundup and stays with the herd. Otherwise there'd be a lot of explanations necessary!"

All that Annie could think of were the nights he claimed he had to go back to the herd because it was his turn to night ride, or he thought it might storm. She suspected he went to spend the night with his mistress when he insisted he had to night herd.

Storms were something else. She learned from Gil that this was the beginning of the season of Nebraska's numerous thunderstorms and tornadoes. The heat of the large herds actually attracted lightning. It seemed the cattle sensed oncoming storms, for they became restless and the slightest thing could spook them to stampede.

Not wanting Jude to suspect she missed him the nights he wasn't in the adjoining bunkhouse, she commented lamely, "I rather think you would contrive some story to tell. You easily contrive night herding to see your—that bought and paid for 'real' woman of yours."

"Oh I do, do I? You're sure of that? Or is it that I sense a hint of jealousy, a sign that you do care whether or not I have a mistress? Maybe you're only complaining of your own lack."

"Lack! I lack nothing, sir!"

"But you do, Anne. You lack the power to lure a man to your bed, to make him feel he'd be welcomed in your arms. You're as cold as a trout out of a Colorado stream."

Jude was surprised to find he wasn't exactly teasing her just to make her blush. He really wanted to know why she had remained unmarried for twenty-six years. It certainly wasn't because she wasn't alluring! Seeing her sitting demurely, like she was tonight, would tempt a saint.

"Cold?" she flared back, stung by his insult. "Cold because I don't ignite for a price? I think not. I believe I explained to you once, sir, that love cannot be bought."

"Yes, I do remember that. 'It has to be earned,' I believe you said. How does one earn such a commodity?"

Was he serious? Did he really want an honest answer, or was he still insulting her? She wished she'd had more experience reading men.

When she didn't answer right away, Jude got up to leave. He stopped when she whispered, "I don't know."

It wasn't the sanctimonious answer he had expected from her. "Are you telling me you may not know when you have bestowed this valuable item?"

Her voice was still a near-whisper. "I'll know."

Jude thought of going over and sitting on the bed beside her and whispering, "How?" but she looked as if she was frightened by his presence. He sauntered to the window, casually telling her, "Be sure your husband isn't the last to know if you give your love away, ma'am."

Under her breath, Annie whispered, "fool," but she didn't know if she meant Jude—or herself.

The doctor had given his approval for Gil to be out of bed most of the time now, but his activities were still limited. It was a godsend that so many ranchers came to help him pass his long days. When she was free Annie sat with him, but she was seldom free.

In addition to helping Maudie with meals, she also helped plant a garden. Maudie thought they should plant a much larger one this year. "Knowing Gil's cousin Dannie, there won't probably be none at all planted at the Sandhills ranch. She's a house mouse if ever there was one. I'll send some of the produce and canned goods from here up to you at Twin Trails, for otherwise you'll survive the winter on beef and biscuits, as I did that first year I came here to live with my brother."

"Beef and biscuits?"

"Yep! Dried beans and soda biscuits along with fresh beef was our diet 'n it's still most ranchers' mainstay if they don't have a woman to plant a garden."

"Back in England any kind of meat was a rare treat to us, especially good beef. We ate a lot of dried foods in the winter, of course, but there were always eggs and cornmeal or ground wheat for hotcakes or mush. I could not believe the way they ate in Chicago!"

"Well, if you're not afraid of a little hard work

in the garden and kitchen, you can eat good out here too."

"I love working in the garden—but I've always hated preserve time. All the cooking and peeling and mincing! I didn't mind helping put up the few things in grandfather's garden, but I hated having to fill the big crocks when Mum sent me up to help at—" She caught herself before she added, "the castle." As her friendship grew with the Eastmans, it was getting harder and harder to remember she was the pampered Daphne Armstrong. Since there was no way to recall her words, she stammered, "to help at an elder friend's house."

She'd hoped Maudie was too busy hoeing to notice, but she was not that lucky. Maudie immediately quizzed, "Your 'mum'?"

"I—I called my grandmother that," she lied, adding, "and I must confess, I was very little help to her. I only did it when I was—bored for something to do."

Maudie doubted that. Annie was too willing to help her, too experienced in both the kitchen and the garden. Then there was the capable way she cared for her horse, currying him and rubbing him down herself. Gil had told Maudie that he suspected she was not the wealthy Armstrong heiress but he hadn't seemed disturbed, so Maudie didn't pry. She only wished Anne would have enough confidence in her to trust her with the truth. She'd grown to care for the girl, and she was glad Anne wasn't the citified girl she'd expected.

Maudie had dreaded the thought of playing

hostess to an uppity female like Gil's wife had been, a spoiled girl putting on airs, making her own and others' lives miserable. It had hurt to see the way she cajoled Gil one minute and then lashed out at him the next, but it had hurt worse to watch her play with her baby boys for a few minutes until she had them cuddly and laughing, only to ignore them for the rest of the day.

Annie decided to change the subject. "Dannie—Mrs. Danvers—is your cousin, isn't she?"

"Yes. She was left penniless in the world, and Gil feels responsible for her and her boy. You don't mind having them there at the house, do you?"

"Oh, not at all!" *Not in the least,* Annie almost cried out. She was fearful of the time she and Jude would leave here. Not that she was frightened he would physically harm her—quite the opposite. A woman would feel very safe within his protection. It was more that she feared herself.

Those silly notions had begun to creep back again. Dumb ideas, like having him fall in love with her and forget his mistress. It wasn't likely, but it wasn't impossible—was it? With other people around she wouldn't be apt to embarrass herself by trying to make him fall in love with her, when he'd blatantly stated he didn't want her. Yes, it was good Mrs. Danvers and her son would be there.

"I'm glad you don't mind," Maudie was saying. "Gil wanted you to have household help, but I told him you'd probably prefer to be alone, newly married and all. He just laughed at me and called me an old romantic. Said you were used to a houseful of servants."

"There were eighteen, including the coachman," Annie admitted.

"Eighteen! Goodness gracious me! How did you keep them all busy?"

"I really don't know," Annie confessed with a smile, "but Mrs. Dorn always seemed to have everyone doing something."

"Including you? You're such a big help to me, I can't believe you just sat prissy-like in a parlor." There, she had given Annie an opening—if the girl cared to talk about her past.

"I'm afraid I did—sit around, that is—or go shopping or socializing. If I'm of any help to you, it's things I learned to do at—at my grandparents' in England." To pad the lie she added, "They were gentry, of course, but with only two longtime retainers to serve them. Not of the wealthiest class, to be sure, nor of the nobility."

"Oh, I see," Maudie answered, but she didn't sound at all convinced to Annie.

No matter how many demands were made on her time, Annie always worked at least two hours a day with Pegasus. She made obstacles for him to jump with nail kegs or stray boards. Gil Eastman, Jules, and Maudie had become a dear family to her, and having her own beautiful stallion added to her happiness. She was quite content except when she thought of Jude Eastman and having to leave Double Tree.

After the other ranchers took their herds and started their treks home, the Eastmans' table was filled with Double Tree's own men at mealtimes. They no longer used a chuck wagon for preparing food; instead, they came to the ranch kitchen during the branding, castrating, and cutting of the herd.

Annie saw a great deal more of her errant husband than before. He was home for three meals a day and the men from his own crew seemed more interested in the newlyweds than the neighboring ranchers had been.

"Hey, Jude," one of the drovers asked one day, "how did you get so lucky as to get a pretty little thang like her?"

"Born lucky, I guess," he told them as he put an arm around her waist.

Privately Annie thought he overplayed his role, for he was always putting an arm possessively across the back of her chair, or twitching his fingers through her hair. To him it was all an act; to her it was becoming uncomfortable since his most casual touch caused a thousand unruly tremors to rampage through her.

She tried to step away as someone else guffawed, "Had to be more'n luck! You had to meet her somewhere. Where was that?" A silence fell around the table as they awaited his answer.

Jude held her tightly so she couldn't squirm loose and nonchalantly explained, "Remember a couple of years back when Jules and I went to Chicago to buy some new stock? While we were there, Pa had us look up an old drinkin' partner of his, Willy Armstrong, now Mr. William Armstrong, a big-shot meat packer. Well, I took one look at this daughter of his and I've been writin' to her ever since, hopin' to persuade her to marry me."

Annie was pleased with this thoughtful story until she heard the tag. "She finally got destitute and did it."

Jules was quick to jump to her defense. "Destitute? Any fool knows that's a lie by looking at her. No, you were right the first time. It was the luckiest day of your life when Anne said 'I do.' "

"As you say, little brother," Jude casually conceded. He walked to the elk antlers on the wall and took down his hat, ordering, "Come on you cowpokes, it's time we hit leather."

He didn't look back toward Annie as she stood watching him and the others leave. All of them said a pleasant, "Good morning, ma'am," as they filed out the door.

Jules stayed behind a moment. "It's me he's ticked at. Don't fret."

She wasn't actually fretting, but she did miss the quick good-bye kiss he usually planted on her cheek as he left the house. Disgusted with herself, she turned back to the table and started stacking dishes, thinking she hadn't realized before how many men worked for Gil.

The large crew made her wonder just how big a herd of cattle they were working with at Cattle Creek. The next time Gil watched her put Pegasus through his paces, she asked him while she rubbed down her horse and put the tack away.

"Close as we can tally, it's forty-three thousand, give or take a few head," he told her.

"No," Annie laughed, "I don't mean all of them you rounded up, Father. I just mean, how many cows are in your own herd."

"That *is* my own herd, Annie girl. Mine and the twins'. Tex Barnes and Rawlings and his boy run a few in with ours, but we try to subtract them off the tally."

"I can't even fathom how many that would be. It must be a gigantic herd."

"That's right, you haven't seen it yet, have you? Well, we'll remedy that this very day. I'd just decided this morning it was time I hitch up a team and drive the buckboard over there to see for myself how it's going."

"Are you sure it will be all right with your doctor?"

"Doc's pleased as punch he's managed to keep me down this long, girl. I guarantee you one thing: he never would have if you hadn't been around to keep me from getting too restless. Yep, it's okay for me to go. We'll leave as soon as we eat."

"I can't leave that soon. I have to help Maudie with the dishes."

"Nah! We'll get young Rawlings in to do that. He always did it before you came. Like I've tried to tell you time and again, we didn't expect you to come out here and work the way you do. Why, I meant for Jude's wife to have it soft up there at the new place, with Dannie to do the house and her son to be a gardener-chore boy.

"What with Jude tellin' young Rawlings he can trail the herd this summer and you doin' all his house and plantin' chores, he's gonna git too big for his britches. Like I say, he can help Maudie. It'll take him down to size."

"Don't I have you convinced yet?" Annie laughed. "Like I've tried to tell you time and again, I like to keep busy. I don't mind the work here at all; in fact, I love gardening. However, I'll certainly agree to go with you today, for I do want to see this sight—and my least favorite task is doing dishes."

Gil chortled at her honesty.

A patchwork quilt covering acres and acres of land—that was the only way Annie could describe the herd the first time she saw it. Dark red Herefords blended with the light reds of the polled breeds and piebald black and whites. Backing the entire pattern were the shaggy brown Texas Longhorns. Annie knew that originally most of the herd had consisted of Longhorns, but they had brought cattle from Scotland and England and the crossbred cows were most desirable for market. The Texas Longhorns had great, widespread horns and longer legs on their lean bodies, while such breeds as the Hereford were stocky and fat with short legs. This year they were shipping primarily Longhorns to Chicago to sell them off.

Annie was still enjoying the picturesque scene, when suddenly Gil, beside her in the buckboard, took such a deep gasping breath that it frightened her. When she looked toward him, his face was bright red and he was definitely breathing too rapidly. Alarmed, she reached for his hand, which had tightened to a clenched-fist on the reins.

"Father!" The words came out as a high-pitched squeak. "Father, are you all right? Here, let me take the reins. Sit back and try to relax." When he said nothing but continued to stare mutely at the corner of the pasture, Annie followed his gaze.

There stood her husband, his arm around the waist of a gorgeous redhead wearing a bright red dress. She had the most provocative curves imaginable. It was obvious they had not seen the buckboard coming, for her arms slid sensuously up around Jude's neck and their lips met in a brief kiss. The minute it ended, they pulled apart and the redhead turned toward a waiting buggy. Jude slapped her playfully on the bottom, causing her to turn and pretend to shake her finger at him, but she was laughing.

Gil did not move until she got into her buggy, gave her small gray and white horse a snap with her bright red whip, and drove away. He seemed to be breathing much too rapidly.

"All right, Father," she tried to keep her voice steady, "I have seen the herd and am awed by its size, but we must return now. You can't overdo on your first excursion. Give me the reins, I'll drive back." While she spoke, she tried to pry the reins from his grip.

At last he let go voluntarily, but before she could grab them and give the horses even a brief "get-up," he was climbing down and taking the buggy whip from its slot beside him, cussing a blue streak. "Damn his two-timing hide! That he could shame his vows with that rotten, no-good whore! I'll take every inch of his skin off! I should have done it long ago when he didn't settle down. He's got the worst morals in the country!"

By now the buckboard had been sighted by not only Jude but every other cowpuncher around. While they had all tried to politely turn their backs when Rosie O'Mara was here, this scene was something no one was about to miss. Work came to a standstill as they gawked. The old man looked fearsome as he strode across the ground that separated him from his son.

When Jules saw the coming confrontation he turned his horse and galloped in their direction, hoping he'd make it to Jude before Pa did. He himself had told Jude he was six kinds of fool for still wanting Rosie instead of his bride, but Jude was one stubborn ass. Still, this was no answer. It would cause a permanent break between Pa and Jude, and would only worsen the situation between Jude and his bride. Perhaps Pa never should have brought this Daphne Anne Armstrong out here and forced Jude to marry her to get the Sandhills place, if he was really in love with Rosie. Jules couldn't imagine one other reason why any man would be fool enough to want a strumpet like Rose O'Mara when he had a wife like Anne. Only love. Jules would never have believed his brother could love a woman like Rosie this much, a woman that he must know was unfaithful to him. That wasn't Jude's nature at all. Again, Jules sincerely wished, as he had so often in the last few weeks, that it had been he who had wed Anne Armstrong by proxy.

Annie caught her skirt on the hand brake as she tried to get down from the seat. It wouldn't come loose until she tugged hard enough on it to tear it free. Oh, what a terrible mess this was! While Annie had nothing but contempt for her husband, she could not let this happen because of her. She was able to catch Gil's arm just before he started to raise it with the whip clenched fiercely in his hand.

Jude stood there unmoving, a look of black rage and humiliation combined on his face. God! He'd warned Rosie never to come near the herd or the ranch. Whatever had possessed her to ride out today, trying to lure him into town tonight? He'd refused her, of course, which made her as angry as a volcano ready to erupt. He had avoided a scene only by reminding her of his plans to be rid of Anne in the near future.

"You sure you're still gonna do it?" she'd challenged. "I saw her, and Lord love us, I've heard enough about her to make me puke. She's all any of the men who stop at the Haven talk about."

"Hell, yes! Nothing's changed. Now for God's

sake, get on back to town and let me get back to work.''

Instead of leaving, she'd flattened herself against him and he'd put his arm about her from habit as she inflamed the old urges. Pleased by his response, she'd pleaded once more, ''You need me, Jude darlin'. Come in tonight and we'll get all these clothes from between us—'' Instead of finishing the sentence, she'd unexpectedly slid her arms about his neck and put her lips against his.

His prolonged abstinence had made it tempting to return the kiss, but his desire to be rid of her was stronger, and he'd quickly moved his face away. ''I mean it, Rosie, get going.''

''All right,'' she pouted. ''But promise to send her packing soon, or I'll take all m'clothes off here 'n now and we'll see how immune you are to me.''

He'd had to laugh at her audacity and give her a playful slap on the rear. ''You'd do it too, wouldn't you?''

She'd shaken her finger at him and warned, ''I mean soon, Jude!''

''Okay, okay,'' he'd agreed and turned away. That was when he'd seen the buckboard.

Jesus! What a fouled-up mess! Worst of all, he could only stand here and take whatever Pa dished out with that whip. He had it coming in one sense—but not in another. He knew Pa's standards for a married man. In that respect he'd played the fool—but what the hell! He wasn't married, except maybe on paper. Still, he couldn't fight back. This whole thing might cause Pa to have another heart attack as it was. Anything more Jude said or did to anger him would only increase the danger.

One lash was all he'd take. He glanced to where Rocky stood saddled nearby. He'd get on the horse and ride out and he'd never return. Jude knew himself. If Pa humiliated him this way, he wouldn't stay around. Thoughts of Pa and Jules and Maudie and the Sandhills place gave their own tiny tugs inside him, but he'd learn to live without any of it if he had to— especially that wife of his, who, he was sure, had caused all this. She had probably pointed out Rosie to Pa.

Rosie? He could get along nicely without her, too. She was getting too demanding and too damned possessive. Like coming out here today when he'd warned her not to! She was a good enough bed partner, but he didn't care much for her otherwise anymore. He should have told her so a few weeks back, then this never would have happened. He'd intended to ignore her today when she rode into camp until he thought of that little snip he was married to and the way she gave everybody but him those sickeningly sweet smiles. For him she always put on a fake one to go with that false tone she spoke to him in. "Did you have a good day?" "Is everything going well?" "How did the cattle tolerate the rainstorm last night?" "Do you care for more potatoes, Jude, dear?" "Would you like me to play the piano for you?"

He'd like to wrap that piano around her neck, and Jules', too. They sang duets almost every night while she played, and Pa and Maudie sat there and purred with pleasure like a couple of cream-fed cats.

Annie praised God she had reached Gil before he had actually pulled the whip back to lash out, but what should she do now? She had a firm hold on the older man's arm, and she'd been able to break his eye contact with Jude. Gil was now looking straight at her, and she read his terrible sorrow and disgrace on his face. Was there any way to come through this with both men's pride intact? Only she could make that happen.

"Let go my arm, Annie girl. This has to be done. I'll not tolerate having my own son behave so shamelessly."

"Father, this has to be between my husband and myself. You must see that, don't you? If you interfere, you will only lose both of us and we'll lose each other."

Gil searched her face, reading seriousness and concern. "What are you trying to say, girl?"

"We cannot talk about it here, but I guarantee you will regret it if we don't leave now and let this matter lie. There is more to this than you know. Oh please, please, for my sake, I beg of you! Let's go home. I just want to go home." Tears of distress were flooding her eyes and she was trying desperately not to cry in front of the men. They would all assume she was crying over her husband's infidelity, when all she could think of was preventing a breech between father and son.

When Gil saw the tears filling her eyes, he put his arm around her shoulder. "Buck up, girl! You're right, it's not my place."

Jules had ridden up and dismounted in the space between his pa and his brother. Jude was still standing stiffly, but it looked as if Anne was calming Pa down.

Jules stepped closer to Jude and muttered, "What the hell were you thinking of, you bastard? Entertaining the drovers with your trollop! I never dreamed I was twin to an addlepated nincompoop."

"Fire away, little brother! Nothing you can say will be as hard on me as I've been on myself these last few minutes. I should have ignored the bitch, ridden away. I honestly meant to. If—" He didn't get the chance to finish, for Pa was calling to him.

Gil made sure his voice carried to the nearby drovers. They would pass it around. "You and I both know, boy, what a disgraceful scene your wife just witnessed, am I right?"

"Yeah," Jude admitted gruffly.

"Then you'll want to make your apologies, I take it, and give your wife your word as an Eastman that nothing like this will ever happen again. She's willing to try to work things out, I take it. Are you?"

"Yeah."

His father looked at him in disgust and then turned Annie toward the buckboard.

Jules swore, "Apologize, little brother, or I'm gonna tromp you into the ground!"

Annie deserved his apology and Jude knew it. She had managed to forestall a bad confrontation when she could have pitched a tantrum, as most women would have done. Instead, she'd concerned herself with calming Pa. Of course, most women weren't glad their husbands had mistresses. Still, he'd been in the wrong, and she did deserve at least a begrudging thank you for her efforts.

Reluctantly he started to follow them, then stopped. He didn't want to get close enough to either of them for a conversation right now. Instead, he only called out, "I'm sorry, Anne. I give you my word as an Eastman, you won't be embarrassed this way by me again."

He thought he heard her say thank you, but he couldn't be sure, for everyone had resumed cutting out Longhorns for shipment and she neither stopped nor turned around. Nor did Pa.

The ride back to the ranch was silent as both Gil and Annie were deep in thought. Gil had been so sure when he first saw Annie that Jude would forget all about that O'Mara floozie. He had recently even seen a guarded look of pride in Jude's eyes when they were together, and when Annie had ridden that horse, Jude's fear had been real when she got pitched off. Yet afterward, Gil had noticed, he only looked angry.

In spite of Jude's dishonorable behavior where women were concerned, Gil was proud of his boys beyond measure. Gil had sown his own wild oats in his day, but not while he was married—and never in front of his men. Jude had some growing up to do, and he'd better do it in a hurry or he was going to lose the best woman he'd ever be likely to know.

"You're wondering why I didn't jump out and take the whip to him myself, aren't you?" Annie's soft, husky voice interrupted his train of thought. "Would it shock you to know the thought didn't even occur to me? While I was embarrassed, I was neither angered nor hurt. I'll never allow myself to love a man enough that I can be hurt again."

"Again?" Gil puzzled aloud. "So that's why a beautiful filly like you agreed to this bizarre plan. I've often wondered the reason. Deep inside I knew it had to be something other than to save the Armstrong Meat Packing plant from possible ruin. Were you hurt bad by some damned bounder, Annie girl?"

"Yes," she answered, "hurt enough that I accepted this marriage by proxy. It was probably foolish of me, but at the time it seemed my only way of escaping an intolerable situation." She wished she could tell him the truth, that her only alternatives had been a job in a dark, gloomy factory or life as a rich man's plaything. This life was preferable to her; in fact, she loved it here, even with a husband who disgraced her. "The first day I arrived here, Jude told me he'd been forced to marry me only because he lost the flip of the coin."

"What's this?"

"I shouldn't have told you he admitted it. They agreed to the toss to please you, you know.

They both love you very much, so please don't let Jude know I told you.

"Father, please don't worry about me. I am not foolish enough to expect loyalty in a situation like this, but I want you to know that I do have some pride. Jude has never been permitted in my bed. He goes through my room to the bunkhouse each night."

"He—*what?*"

"Yes. Our marriage is a sham. He's entitled to his mistress, I suppose one might say. He's gotten the worst of the bargain. I want you to be assured, though, that I'll attempt to be a fine hostess and help make the Sandhills ranch house one which will be inviting to you and your guests, if I possibly can."

"I don't believe any of this, girl. First off, let me tell you—there was no toss of a coin. Jude was no loser! He got exactly what he wanted by marrying you: complete control of the Twin Trails ranch and ownership of it when I die. Nope, he was well paid, I would say, and that he would tell you otherwise is shocking. Loser, indeed! I'm going to have more than a few words to say to him—a damn sight more!"

"No, please!" Annie implored. "That's exactly what you can't do. I don't want his love, but neither do I want to cause a rift in your family. I need a home, and I love it out here. I dearly love *you*, and I just can't part with Pegasus. Leave it alone, Father, just leave it alone—please."

He couldn't or wouldn't deny her. Both of them knew it without words.

*   *   *

Annie did not know exactly what she had expected Jude's mistress to look like. She should have been prepared for the woman's youth and beauty. Annie herself was young, wasn't she, and two men had wanted to make her their mistress? It had been easy to tell her arrogant husband that she was happy he had someone else, but it made her anything but happy to see him with that exotic redhead. As she had watched the woman move into Jude's arms, she had been jealous. And she had been angry and hurt. Annie hoped Gil believed that she was indifferent to her husband; heaven knew she wasn't! When Jude had smiled at that creature and slapped her behind, Annie had felt like pulling out every strand of that red hair.

But why was she jealous? She certainly didn't want his attentions. She tried to convince herself it was only because it was in front of everyone—but it wasn't. It was more, so much more. She would have to sort it all out someday, but not now. Not today. Now she was back at Double Tree and Pegasus was waiting for her. She knew this afternoon she'd not just put him through his paces, instead she'd take him for a long run across the grasslands. A run far enough and fast enough that all thoughts of today would be blotted out by the joy of the wind on her face and the speed of her horse. It would remind her of how lucky she was to be out here in these beautiful, wide-open spaces underneath such a tall, tall sky. Yes, she was sure such a ride would make her forget that scene between her husband and his mistress—wouldn't it?

Chapter Twelve

✦✦✦✦✦

THE SANDHILLS

A SIMPLE WORD like "sandhills" did not begin to describe the beauty of this glacial deposit of sand unique to Nebraska. "Sandhills" implied desert lands and sand dunes, bereft of water and vegetation, but the Sandhills were quite different from their name. Lush thick grasses covered the rolling hills and gentle valleys. Thickets of chokecherry, plum, and gooseberry dotted the edges of the small tree-lined streams and creeks that wound through the valleys.

However, they were as their named implied, Gil had told her. "Imagine, Annie girl, thousands of square miles of grass-covered sand dunes, so isolated and strange that for years they frightened away cattlemen and homesteaders alike, for they were known as a jinx. Those who were bold enough to venture into them were often never seen again, for even those familiar with the terrain can easily get confused and lose their way. Consequently, only the Indians and a few outlaws took the risks. The homesteaders who try to farm their outer perimeters find that once they've plowed up the grass, a windstorm or a twister may strike and leave a deep hole in the side of the hill where their crops were planted."

"Blowout," Annie had said knowingly, using the word the English immigrants on the train had used to describe it.

"Yes, happens to most who plow the soil there, but two or three years ago, some men from the Newman Ranch braved the hills to round up additional strays. Instead of finding the usual half-starved cows of an early spring roundup, they found the cattle were in better shape than other cows that had wintered on the open range. The hills had provided protection and more nourishing grasses."

"It sounds a bit eerie, like witchcraft or something."

Gil chuckled, "It does a bit, don't it? Well, eerie or not, I was convinced, and I bought thousands of acres from the Chicago, Northwestern Railroad. The CNW ran its line across the Missouri River at Omaha, just like the Union Pacific did. However, it laid its rails up along the Niobrara River instead of down through the Platte River valley, acquiring government lands along the north perimeter of the state. Lucky for us it sold its Sandhills acres much cheaper than it did the fertile ones down in the eastern part of the state near the Missouri River. Those are valuable corn- and wheat-growing lands. At the time I made the purchase, the Sandhills were still considered wastelands. The twins and I weren't the only ones to see the value of those hills. Ranches as well as towns are being established all over this newfound cattleman's oasis."

"I can't wait to see it," Annie cried, excited by Gil's description.

"I can't wait to have you see it. Wish I were gonna be there when you first lay eyes on it. You'll love it, Annie girl."

And he was right, Annie thought as she looked around her, breathing in the majestic splendor.

For days before arriving at this beautiful place, the herd had crossed the flat prairie of the Platte River valley. The venture had been uneventful except for the actual crossing of the Platte and several hard rainstorms. Since the Platte was not bank-full this year, the cattle only had to swim a short distance and not one had been lost, not even a calf. The men on horseback had had their biggest problem contending with the mud on the shallow river bed.

Then, last night, a hailstorm had hit. Seven calves and one horse were killed by the huge hailstones that had pounded down from the sky. Only the dropping temperature and the massive white clouds above the gray ones had given any warning of the impending storm. It had struck so swiftly while they were preparing the evening meal that Annie had barely had time to take cover under the chuck wagon with the cook, P.T. He'd been dubbed "P.T. O'Maine" after the first meal he cooked in camp and had gone by it ever since. They might imply his food was poison, but they all knew he was the best chuck wagon ramrod north of Texas.

The cows stampeded as soon as the first sharp thuds hit their bodies, and it took the men the rest of the night to bring the thundering herd under control. While they did this, Annie and P.T. tried to repair the damage to the tarp over the chuck wagon and attempted to dry out the food that could be saved.

"Even m'coffee pot's dented beyond repair by them dang hailstones," P.T. groaned. "Never saw such big'uns in all m'born days!"

"Me neither!" Annie concurred vigorously. "When I heard father—Gil, that is—and then the other ranchers talking of the dangers of hail and tornadoes and stampedes, I thought they were exaggerating."

"Nope, they're like all hell broke loose. Especially tornadoes. They're worse'n this was."

"Worse? They must be terrible!"

"Yep, shore are."

While they talked, Annie was in the wagon conscientiously wiping the puddles of water off storage barrels and crates. Just then, young Rawlings rode back into camp, yelling, "The herd's quieted now and all the stragglers they could find are finally rounded up, P.T., so you're s'posed to hurry and bring the chuck wagon and grub, cause everyone's near starvin'."

Knowing these men's appetites, Annie could believe that. The storm had denied them supper last night and breakfast this morning. "All right, all right, I'm comin'," the cook promised. Jude rode up to the wagon as soon as it rolled into the new campsite.

"What's the situation on supplies, P.T.?" he asked, with only a cursory glance at his wife to determine if she had come safely through the storm.

The small, square little man rubbed the graying bristle beard on his chin as he tried to calculate in his head what damage needed to be reported. "Wall—first there's the coffeepot, and I didn't git time to cover the flour. The sugar will be lumpy but edible. I already had a list of things for you to git in Cottonwood, so now I reckon you'd better plan on pullin' the wagon on in to restock. You won't git it all on even a couple pack horses, not if you plan to use the wagon and supplies onc't we get there, like y'said."

Tex Barnes had ridden up now. "Why would we use the chuck wagon once we get there? Why, there's a—"

Jude quickly interrupted before Tex could say more in front of Annie. He had no intention of letting his wife find out there was a house and even a bunkhouse with a kitchen built and waiting at Twin Trails. He was going to make her believe the line soddy was the only building for miles around. The line soddy was his last resort and he hoped it would accomplish his purpose, which was becoming harder and harder to carry out. He'd unwillingly begun to admire his wife's spunk and good nature, not to mention the tempting look of her. Several times he had almost succumbed to that innocent charm of hers before he reminded himself of her duplicity. Her daddy must have promised a little beauty like her a sizable fortune to go along with his scheme. Women! All of them would do anything for money, even leave two lonely little boys . . . he pushed thoughts of Ma away and returned his mind to his present plight.

Actually Jude had not thought he would ever have to use this last weapon. He had been positive that a trail drive would send his unwanted wife scampering back to Chicago. He'd been high in the clouds with anticipation of victory the day he and Annie joined the herd. The looks on his drovers' faces when the two of them rode into the camp were ones of amazement.

She had not been wearing one of her divided riding skirts, but instead a full-skirted satiny dress with a slight bustle and train. He'd allowed her—and Pa too, of course—to believe they were traveling to their new home by carriage. He had assumed she would refuse to ride in such a fancy gown without a sidesaddle. In fact, he had hoped she'd get angry enough at the mere suggestion that she would demand to return to her daddy's mansion where her life was one of pampered comfort. That would have saved him the embarrassment of facing his shocked crew.

Instead, she had surprised him by climbing down from the carriage when he informed her that he had to ramrod the cattle drive himself, and he insisted she join him. Only her eyes and her actions had spoken of her dismay. She had opened trunk lids to get out her needed clothing and then loudly slammed them shut. She took time to open a half-dozen shoe boxes before she found the boots she wanted.

In between each box opening and closing, she glared at him with contempt and indignation stamped plainly on her face. It had taken considerable effort to keep his poker face, for he'd wanted to chuckle at her inviting lips tightly puckered and her snub nose so impudently in the air. As soon as she had her clothing assembled, she had rolled it into a bundle as she had watched him do the first night she'd arrived at the Double Tree. This surprised Jude. He'd expected her to want to take several pieces of luggage, and he'd looked forward to autocratically refusing her request. He loved arguing with her, especially when he knew he would be the victor.

With one last glower in his direction she had grabbed a comforter from the stack of bedding they had loaded on the wagon to take to the Twin Trails ranch. She wound it tightly around the rest of her things.

"What do I do with this now that it's ready to go?"

"Tie it behind your saddle," he told her nonchalantly.

"With what, may I ask?"

"Oh, anything strong enough to hold it," he told her unhelpfully as he mounted his own horse.

Annie wondered if any other man in the world

was as aggravating as this cowboy. There was no rope or leather thongs in sight. She stormed back to the wagon that was hauling her trunks and unbuckled one of the leather straps on her steamer trunk, but she could not lift the heavy trunk to remove the strap. Her wretched husband ignored her plight, but both of the ranch hands who had been driving the wagon came rushing to her aid. Triumphantly she took the strap and walked back to her bedroll and efficiently tied it into place.

Jude remarked offhandedly, "If you're finally ready, let's ride out!" He wondered how she was going to get on her horse in that gown. To forestall any help she might receive from his men, he rode back to where they stood and engaged them in conversation as he curiously watched out of the corner of his eye.

Twice she tried to put her foot high up into the stirrup to mount Pegasus, but each time her leg got tangled in her full skirt. She glanced in the men's direction and must have determined no one was looking, for then she angrily hiked her skirt up and wrapped it around her legs above her knees. Jude was provoked with himself because he actually enjoyed seeing his wife's trim ankles and slender legs for the first time as she quickly climbed up and sat sidesaddle—only to practically slide back off again because of the slippery fabric of her dress. Hitching herself backwards, she finally managed to loop one leg around the pommel to keep herself in place. Once situated, she tried to smooth her skirt down over her legs as far as possible before she rode over as if nothing at all was amiss and chided, "If you are in such a hurry, I do believe we should ride out, *sir*."

Wordlessly Jude took off at a gallop, thinking he would soon outdistance her, but she kept up with him. When he realized he had to slow his pace for the sake of his horse, he turned and looked at Annie for the first time since they had started. He was prepared to see her disheveled and irate, but she looked exhilarated. All the combs and pins that had kept her hair piled fashionably up on her head had been lost, and it had fallen manelike, enhancing her beauty. What thick, luxuriant hair she had! The stylish hat she'd been wearing had been lost, too, but she didn't seem upset. Her cheeks were bright pink from the exercise, and her dark eyes had an irridescent sparkle he had never seen in them before. It was obvious she was trying hard not to smile, but she could not conceal her enjoyment.

Disgruntled, he turned away from her and rode on. He could have sworn he heard her trying to muffle a giggle and that annoyed him more. Well, a nice gallop on an excellent horse like Pegasus was one thing; riding a cow pony tomorrow would be the real test. He knew just the stubborn, mule-assed mustang he was going to assign to her. Now it was his turn to stifle a chuckle.

Jude thought highly of his crew of drovers. They were probably one of the best outfits anywhere in the country, but today he was thoroughly disgusted with every one of them. He'd counted on all of these tough wranglers resenting a woman along on the drive and showing it. He had smirked with pleasure at their surprised faces when he and Annie had ridden into camp. He could hardly wait for their snide insults and anti-female attitudes to pour forth.

He dismounted and handed his horse over to the Rawlings kid to rub down for him. Then he turned to help Annie down, for in front of his men he wanted to act the gentleman.

Curly Reiley had already held up his hands, and Anne unhooked her leg from the pommel and easily slipped down to be caught in his waiting arms. He swung her to the ground, telling everyone enthusiastically, "Didn't I tell you that was one beautiful horse she broke and that she had him trained perfectly already? Was I right or was I right? You sure did yourself proud, Mrs. Eastman."

"Can I wipe 'im down for you, Ma'am?" This from a confirmed woman-hater, Frank Trent, who also offered, "I'll just put your bedroll in the chuck wagon for you."

"Good to have you aboard, Annie girl," Tex Barnes told her. "Now you'll get the answers firsthand to all those questions you always had for Gil 'n me about the cattle and trail herdin'."

"I'll have you a cup of tea in no time, missy," the cook announced. "Lucky I keep it around for medicinal purposes. Maudie told me you're a little English gal and don't care much for coffee."

And so it went. Every last one of them sold

out Jude for a smile and a greeting from his
show-off wife. Even shy Lester Carter smiled a
little as he timidly said "H'lo, Miz Eastman. Nice
t'see ya."

Their welcome wasn't the only problem Jude
had with this bunch of turncoats. They all had
their own prized horses and none of them would
touch the stock in the remuda unless it was a
necessity. None of them would have considered
riding that no-good cayuse, but the minute Jude
gave the animal to Annie to ride the next morning, every single one of them offered to trade her
their own animals for that mulish critter. Even
Jude had to give his wife a little grudging
admiration when she refused to accept their
generous offers. The damn mustang was almost
as aggravating as his men; it wasn't half as
stubborn that morning as usual.

Annie was equally adamant about riding drag.
Jude explained to his men he was putting her
there because she lacked trail experience. She
insisted it was fine with her, but the looks and
remarks Jude got from his men told him the idea
was not acceptable at all. For drag was the most
unpleasant place on the drive. It meant riding at
the rear of the mile-long herd to prod stragglers
determined to stop and chew grass. At the end
of ten hours riding drag on cow ponies, he
expected Annie to come up to him in camp that
night and announce she wanted to leave. He
tried not to look relieved when he saw her
coming toward him as soon as she rubbed down
her horse and tied it to the picket line.

"Jude," she called out to get his attention as he pretended to walk away, "may I have a word with you?"

"Certainly, Anne, what is it?" He was careful to keep his expression blank.

"I just wanted to ask if you mind if I wear that western hat that's in the chuck wagon. I believe it belongs to you. This bowler that I always wore for riding in England is just not the protection over my eyes that one of your Texas-style hats would be. Spending all day outside on a horse is a real treat for me, and I want to do a good job. I think I could do better if I could keep more of the sun out of my eyes."

"The hat's yours if you want it. Take the damn thing," Jude told her as he turned and stomped away.

Holy hell! This contrary wife of his liked trail herdin'!

Day after day, Annie had ridden any old cow pony Jude gave her, no matter how stubborn or rough-gaited it was. She rode drag for so many days in a row without complaint that it had bothered his conscience and he'd pulled her off it. She'd be covered with the thin layer of dust that hung over the herd from the hoof-worn dirt after fifteen thousand head passed over it, and yet she always managed to look sparkling fresh when she helped P.T. dish up chow.

*   *   *

One evening as Annie handed him his gray enamelware pie tin of stew, she asked unexpectedly, "Jude, I noticed a stream just beyond that hill today when I was—what do you say—pushing steers? No . . . shoving cattle . . . no, wait, it's prodding strays!" Proud of her newly acquired trail lingo, she smiled and then went on, "I'd like to go back there but Tex and P.T. have given me such a fright of everything from wild animals to even wilder Indians that I'm afraid to go that far from camp alone. Will you walk back there with me? I'd love to bathe and wash my hair."

Too many of his men had heard her request for Jude to out and out refuse, but he had to try. "Water's too blamed cold."

"No t'ain't," young Rawlings interceded. "I dove in just 'fore supper. Felt fine to me."

"We're not talking tough hides here, kid, we're talking delicate skin," Jude argued.

Somebody guffawed, "That young tenderfoot's skin's still delicate, Jude. If the water's warm enough for him, I'll wager Mrs. Eastman kin tolerate it." Several men close enough to overhear chuckled while somebody else sniggered, "Aw, say yes, Jude, and get this line movin' again. I'm hungry as a bear in winter."

"All right," Jude conceded. "We'll go whenever you're ready." He grabbed his plate and went to sit against his saddle, thoroughly provoked with himself. He'd sworn to make this trip rough for her, no niceties like bathing and washing her hair, and here he was, pushed—

shoved—no, prodded into it. Damn! The last thing he wanted was to be alone with the scheming little temptress. Of course, he had to admit her schemes and machinations were not meant to tempt him! The chaste old maid was probably so innocent that she did not know she provoked his desire. He certainly couldn't accuse her of that! She didn't have to resort to the ruse most women used to defraud a man of his money. By marrying him in that damned proxy marriage she'd legally latched onto a chunk of his without even thinking of giving herself in return. Plus all her daddy had undoubtedly promised her for this fluke . . .

"I'm ready to go," her voice rang through his aggravated thoughts. "P.T. was kind enough to loan me his bar of castile soap and Tex gave me his flannel towel to use. Wasn't that sweet of them?"

"Sweet indeedy," Jude chirped, which made all his men laugh. To him it wasn't funny. He felt like a darn fool walking away from camp with her while they all watched enviously. Little did any of them know!

As soon as they were out of hearing, Annie explained, "I hated to ask this of you, but I feel I've an inch of grime clinging to my scalp. It's hard to wash up in a bucket, isn't it? Especially hair—well, maybe not short hair like yours, but—"

"Anne," Jude knew just the threat that would subdue her appreciation. "Don't apologize. I'm going to enjoy a bath as much as you."

"What!" She stopped walking.

Tongue in cheek, he went on, "Yep! I saw this stream today too, and my thoughts were the same as yours. Maybe we have more in common than we thought. Perhaps we should rethink things. A nice cold stream should clear our heads. Come on, what are you stopping for?"

"Jude, I meant for you to sit and guard the stream. That's all! I couldn't ask anyone else, could I?"

"Any one of them would gladly have obliged—except for one thing. They know they'd have me to answer to. You did the proper thing; don't worry, we'll be safe enough."

Safe? Annie didn't think she'd feel safe at all. Why, she'd probably shiver the whole time she bathed, even if the water wasn't cold. Just the idea of being naked in the water with Jude gave her goosebumps.

"I've changed my mind. I think I'll forgo a bath until we reach Twin Trails. The water is no doubt muddy."

"Muddy? Nope, not at all. Not here in the Sandhills. The streams are clear because of their sandy beds. Soft sandy beds," he added in a sensual tone, enjoying himself tremendously. Jude wished the moon was shining brighter, for he'd love to see how beet red her face was. Those dark eyes of hers were probably shooting sparks.

"The truth is," Annie tried to speak sharply to save face, "I will not feel safe unless you sit and guard the area."

"I can't guard it from your thoughts," he warned.

"What do you mean by that? Surely you aren't suggesting all my fears are imaginary."

"Not at all, they're quite factual."

"Then there *are* animals, or maybe Indians, about?"

"I didn't say that, nor were you thinking it. Face it, Anne, the idea of sharing even a long, wide stream with a man is abhorrent to you. It shocks your maidenly modesty."

If only that were my problem! Annie moaned to herself before challenging, "Thanks to my gallant husband, I can still cling to my virtue, can't I? You'll never know if I find sharing a stream with a man repulsive or not, will you? Maybe my objections are only because I'm repulsed by a mistress-loving husband!"

Jude wasn't prepared for his wife's candor. She'd made him feel guilty instead of victorious. To get even, he asked, "How much money is your daddy paying you for this escapade, anyhow? I must say, you got the best of it. He probably expected you to have to part with that virtue you prize so highly, and you got off scot-free. Will you give him a refund? After all, one way or another you're bound to end up with some of my old man's wealth, too."

"How dare you, Jude Eastman? Such implications are low and vile, even coming from a degenerate like you—"

"A degenerate?" Jude snarled, but Annie was too angry to curb her tongue.

"Yes, a degenerate, someone morally degrading! A throwback to an uncultured civilization! That's you! You may not believe it, but even William Armstrong's moral principles are notches above yours! Why, he thought he was sending his daughter into a marriage as much for *her* benefit as for the good of his company. There was never any talk of monetary reward. Never! It was you, not I, who chose to make our marriage a farce."

"Yeah, well what if I told you I'd changed my mind?" Jude growled.

"I'd say you were lying. I saw you with Miss—Mrs. O'Mara myself."

"Who told you her name?"

"I spent far too much time serving meals in the kitchen of your father's house for me not to discover the name of the brazen redheaded widow who owns the town's lone bar. It didn't take a lot of deep thinking for me to piece together everything." She took a deep breath.

"Please, this subject bores me. May we dismiss it?" Annie tried to calm herself. *Had any man in history ever had such power over a woman?* This husband of hers could ignite her passions while infuriating her beyond reason.

"Ah yes, no doubt any mention of anything related to lust or passion is a bore to you," Jude taunted, trying to salvage at least a partial victory for himself. He didn't have the satisfaction however, for Annie proceeded to stymie him once again.

"Lust and passion without real love would be

boring to me, I believe. Desires should have genuine emotions as a base. The passion that would spring from a loving relationship might not be boring at all." Whatever had prompted her to reveal herself so plainly? Her husband didn't care how she felt about such things; he was only trying to provoke her. Tartly she added, "If this obnoxious discussion is closed, I would like to proceed to the stream now. That is, if you will just watch?"

Angrily Jude took her innocent words and tossed out, "I'll gladly watch you!" He began walking with such long strides that Annie had to run to keep up.

Why is he so mad at me, she asked herself as she gingerly stepped behind a thicket to undress. *He is the one who dictated the terms of our marriage!* Before she scampered to the water she peeked in his direction, relieved to note he was sitting with his back to the lake, smoking a cigarette. He didn't glance her way once while she quickly bathed and washed her hair.

Jude knew better than to permit himself even a glimpse of the fiery maiden he'd so foolishly agreed to marry. One look and he was apt to forget his hard-won armor. He knew her for what she was. Still, he couldn't immunize himself from wanting her. Lord! He didn't need to see her without clothes to imagine how tempting she'd be to him.

Had Ma tempted Pa innocently, as Anne did, or had she set out to do it purposely, he wondered. He knew little of their courtship. If Ma had thought Pa's small Texas ranch and his growing herd of cattle meant he was a rich man, he figured she'd been the conniving one. She sure lit into Pa often enough because he wasn't rich. When he did come home with money after selling off some beef she sure was sweet until she wheedled all of it from him! He remembered it all too clearly.

He still recalled how empty the house had seemed when he and Jules returned home after a term at the Indian school and found her gone. Dead, Pa claimed, but he wouldn't talk about it. He just up and sold the ranch. Then he packed up his sons and his crew and drove the cattle to Nebraska. It had turned out to be a good life, especially after Aunt Maudie came.

The ache of missing her had vanished by the time he and Jules had run into Ma in Wichita, Kansas, three years ago.

"Can't be," Jules had insisted about the attractive, well-dressed store proprietress.

"Nope, you're wrong. That's Ma."

"What the hell—name of God! I can't believe it. Think maybe some renegade Indians stole her?"

"Nope; Pa would still be trackin' 'em."

"Then what? It *is* her."

"She must've run off—"

"She loved Pa—and us—too much to do that!"

"Did she?" Rosie had given Jude a much more cynical attitude about women. "Let's ask her." He strode purposefully across the room.

Jules whispered, "Be careful not to embarrass her."

Jude turned to ask, "Why not?"

When Jules saw the pain in his brother's eyes, he suggested, "Let's just leave. Who wants to—"

He hadn't finished when the woman turned toward them, an awful fear of recognition in her eyes. Jude said scathingly, "Hello, Ma. Here's your two darling little boys back from the school you insisted they go to. Aren't you glad to see us?" Before she had a chance to speak, he mocked, "Your loving husband sends his regards too—"

"Jude. Jules. It is you! Oh, it is! So often I've thought of the handsome men you'd probably turned out to be and now I'm actually seeing you!"

"Cut the bullshit! You didn't give a damn or you would have stuck around to see how we turned out."

"You have every right to say that to me, but I won't listen to it—not from you, not from anyone. You don't know what it's like for a woman alone in a cabin day after day during the long winter months—"

"I don't recall you being too busy with chickens or a garden the rest of the year, either. Aunt Maudie seemed to find plenty to do even in those long—"

"So he did persuade her to come live with you! I figured he would. She'd been raised on a ranch; her dead husband was a rancher. Maudie never lived in a town. I had, and I hated the country and worse, I hated being poor. Your pa kept promising me a fancy house and a housekeeper—oh, what's the use of trying to explain? A peddler with money enough to start his own store came along, and I accepted his offer. I've never been sorry—"

"Let's get the hell out of here," Jules had interrupted and Jude had agreed, commenting, "Jesus but this store has a stench to it. Nothin' stinks like a rotten woman."

"Jude." Annie spoke his name louder this second time. "I've finished. I need to get back and dry my hair over the fire."

Still stinging from his memories, Jude growled, "You'd like that, wouldn't you, madam? Putting on a show like that for all those men who are already eatin' their hearts out for a woman."

"I never thought anything of the sort," Annie cried, shamed by such an accusation.

"Don't you know anything about men, for god's sake?"

"No," Annie admitted, then added as a spinster should, "I'm a chaste maiden, remember? Such wants and needs as you refer to are totally foreign to me."

"I'm not so sure. If you're as pious as you claim, you'd be shocked by suggestive words like 'mistress' and 'lust'—and yeah, 'needs,' too."

"May I remind you, pious and ignorant are not synonymous, sir? And whether I am or am not shocked, I won't give you the satisfaction of knowing. I'll comb my hair in the wagon out of sight until it's dry, if that's agreeable with you."

"The men'll miss your company, not me." He stood up to follow her back to camp. Every cowpoke on the drive had told her his life story as they sat around the campfire at night and she always seemed totally absorbed, as if it was the most interesting story she'd ever heard. Instead of acting like a hoity-toity, snubnosed aristocrat as he'd expected her to, she had been a well-mannered, charming woman who made even the lowest drover feel important. They couldn't speak highly enough of her.

Well, playing cowgirl and being the darling of a dozen men might be exciting for a while, but living in an isolated soddy wouldn't. No! She'd want to go back soon enough then. That was why he was taking her into Cottonwood with him. Even a town that big might remind her of all the niceties she was missing in the sod house. It would only be three or four more days of trailing before they got there. If town life was fresh on her mind, maybe she'd leave sooner. Jude sensed that if this soddy life didn't decamp her he was apt to be stuck with her for the rest of his life.

God! Imagine living the rest of one's days with a sharp-tongued woman! And on top of that, a tight-laced old maid to boot! Hell and damnation! He had to get rid of her so he could return to his life of freedom. Worst of all, Pa had never realized what she was really like; she'd always kept that facade of hers in place around the Double Tree, just as she had on the trail drive.

None of them knew Anne Eastman the way he did.

Annie was dubious about going alone into Cottonwood with her husband. Yesterday, when he'd interrupted Tex to ask her to go, she'd thought it was just another way to belittle her, but this morning he'd told her to dress for the trip as soon as she finished eating so they'd have time to make it back before dark.

Sitting here beside him on the jolting wagon seat, she wished she knew his intentions. Did he have a scheme to ridicule her again? A mistress in this town? Or was he only making a good impression on his drovers? She wished she could believe that he was trying to foster a friendlier relationship between the two of them. He had given her his word she'd never be embarrassed by his mistress again and she wanted to believe that.

They had had few conversations since that agonizing day. They didn't even pretend in front of his family or the crew anymore that they were happy newlyweds; it was pointless when everyone knew they were not. Desperately she began to wish Jude would say something so that she knew what to expect and could plan accordingly. If he was to make a sincere effort to be polite to her, she would reciprocate in kind. However, if this was another of the obstacles he was building to try to dishearten her, well, she could handle that, too.

"I must confess I was surprised when you

asked me to come along with you today, sir."

"Why, Mrs. Eastman. Wouldn't it be improper for a husband to ride off and leave his wife alone with all those woman-hungry drovers?"

Annie hated his smug pretentiousness. "That's the silliest thing I've ever heard in my life! Why, every one of those men respect me. They'd never insult me nor harm me."

He was still using that sweet-sounding sneer as he answered, "Perhaps it is I who am trying to earn their respect by not insulting or harming *you*, as you know I am prone to do."

"That, sir, makes sense. You and that Mrs. O'Mara did make a deplorable exhibition in front of them at Cattle Creek. You should have been more discreet with your carryings-on!"

"Do I hear a note of jealousy?" he queried, one eyebrow cocked questioningly.

"Most certainly not. It was for your father's pride in you, not myself. I have found no reason whatsoever to take pride in my pettifogging husband." Annie knew that word bothered him, for he visibly clenched his jaw and set his lips in a hard line. Those gray eyes of his were icier than ever as they glanced piercingly in her direction. Defensively she jutted her chin up higher and clenched her fist tighter, hoping he couldn't read her inner thoughts.

Despite her words, she had found innumerable things to admire in this man she had married. She loved to watch him ride; he was an excellent horseman. If a steer ventured off from the herd, he would gallop after it, and his body moved

with the motions of the horse magnificently—
not in the stiff-backed style of English gentlemen, but more relaxed, as if he were part of the
horse.

Then there was his way with the men. Aside
from his strange behavior regarding his wife, it
was obvious they respected his judgment and
that he was fair in his dealings with them. Until
she came along, Annie suspected the rapport
between Jude and his wranglers had been excellent.

He also worked harder and with less rest than
anyone else. Where his work was concerned, he
didn't pay to have someone else do what he
considered was his place to do, nor ask others to
do more than he did himself.

As for the jealousy—of course that was only a
figment of his imagination. She didn't give a
pence if he had one mistress or a half dozen. Did
she?

"You've been quiet long enough," Jude interrupted sarcastically. "Haven't you thought of
anything malicious to say? You'll spoil your
notable record of insulting me at the rate of ten
words a minute."

"I've insulted you?" Annie roared in anything
but a well-bred Chicago socialite's voice. "Isn't it
enough that I have had to bear your malodorousness day in and day out?"

"Ah ha! It is vocabulary lesson time again!
And what do you mean by 'malodorousness'?"

"Just as it implies—a bad odor! Aye, it stinks,
sir! The way you have heaped unspeakably vile

insults and horrid contempt on me . . . right
from the first when you tried to humiliate me
because you thought I couldn't play that out-of-
tune piano, or when you displayed your love for
that harlot in public, and then putting me at the
rear of the herd in all the dust and the dung!"
Immediately Annie wished she could recall every word. This man had made her so angry
again, she had completely forgotten her socialite's demeanor and she'd retaliated like a Birmingham street urchin.

Instead of taking her to task for such unladylike language, Jude began to laugh uproariously.
When at last he could catch his breath enough to
speak again, he shook his head and said, "Oh
why, oh why, Anne Eastman, don't you reveal
this viperous tongue and rotten temper of yours
around my father and my twin, or even the
men—or Maudie? They won't ever believe their
'angel' is actually the devil incarnate."

Annie almost smiled at the resignation in his
voice, but she refused to apologize. After all, he
was the one who asked for it, wasn't he? "Only
you have the knack of aggravating me to the
point where I forget myself," she admitted. "If
you would be polite and dignified, then I would,
too."

"You would? No matter what?"

"No matter what," she promised.

Well, well, Jude thought to himself. We shall
see how polite and dignified she remains in a
sod hut.

Chapter Thirteen

❖❖❖❖❖

No ONE COULD have been a more polite and considerate husband than Jude Eastman that day in Cottonwood. Cottonwood, Nebraska, was obviously a new town, but it looked as if it were being built for permanence. Most of the buildings were freshly painted frame, but two or three were brick. Part of its wooden boardwalk had been replaced by cobblestones to help resist fires.

Two of the new houses had glazed tile roofs and several had large stables. Here the privies were discreetly concealed behind the houses, but garbage as well as offal was obviously flung in the alleys.

"Jude, look," Annie exclaimed excitedly, "the cornerstone on that building has Eastman State Bank of Cottonwood engraved on it. Does it belong to one of your relatives?"

It niggled Jude's conscience considerably to say, "Nope, I don't have any kin living here." The last part was true; before the bank had been completed, Pa had had his heart attack so a cashier he'd hired was running it for him. The bank was Pa's pride and joy. Jude wanted Annie to know it belonged to Pa, but that wouldn't fit at all with the story he himself planned to tell her.

"Is Eastman a common name in this country, then?"

"Not half so common as North or West. There's a bunch of 'em around. One of the biggest ranches down in the Platte valley belongs to a family of Norths. Funny you never hear of any Souths, isn't it?"

"Why are you trying to change the subject? Are the Eastmans that own the bank estranged from your part of the family or something? A longtime feud or . . . ?"

"Anne, are you accusing me of playing games when I promised to be on my best behavior if you would?"

"Oh, no, I didn't mean it like that. I was just curious."

Glad for a reason to dismiss the subject, Jude offered, "I'll tie the wagon and then help you down. Here's where we pick up the stuff on P.T.'s list."

The store was twice as big as the one at Cattle Creek, yet it seemed to be filled with the same items. The storekeeper greeted them as they walked in. "Jude, boy, good to see you. Heard you took yourself a purty wife, but purty ain't a strong enough word, is it, you lucky devil? She's a beauty."

"She sure is," Jude concurred before formally introducing her. "Mrs. Eastman, meet a real storekeeper, Albert Schoenard. I'm afraid my missus got a rather bad image of you fellas. Wheeler was out with one of his ailments the day she arrived."

"Is he still pullin' *that?*"

"More often than ever. Here's P.T.'s list.

Looks like we need everything from a few slabs of bacon to a couple hundred pound bags of flour." Then he casually added, "Honey, why don't you pick out a coffeepot and anything else we need?"

Honey? Annie almost preened until she realized he was only flattering her to impress the storekeeper. Darn him and his playacting! This time he'd pay for it. She picked out the most expensive coffeepot and held it up. "How's this one?"

"Fine." He didn't even look at the price, so Annie grabbed a nearby gray stoneware butter churn lettered in cobalt blue and commented, "Goodness, this was made in Birmingham. I think we'll take it as it will remind me of England."

"By all means, dear. Just hand it to me, it's too heavy for you."

A three-gallon churn heavy? He was going too far with this act of chivalry.

"I see you have a nice selection of baskets." She walked to a back step and picked up two big ones. "We'll take these. We need them for produce."

"We do?" Jude's attention was now on her purchases.

"Yes, we most certainly do," Annie insisted. "We need a new coffee grinder, too, and a tin to keep it fresh after it's ground, and here, put this in the box," she handed Mr. Schoenard an unusually fancy lamp.

Even the storekeeper was looking askance at

the growing pile of merchandise, for he'd visited the Eastmans' new place a few days ago with his wife, and it didn't look as if it lacked anything.

"What a dear little sewing box. We do need one badly. Here, put this pair of scissors and these spools of thread inside it, Mr. Schoenard, and a package of needles too, if you please."

Had his bride lost her sanity or did she suspect his plan? Only Jules knew his scheme. Jules and Rosie, and neither of them would have warned his wife, he could count on that. So why was she making all these purchases? Was she a spendthrift? He quickly took her arm and, leading her from the store, reminded, "We must hurry or the hotel's dining room will close for the afternoon before we get there. Pack our stuff up, Al. We'll pick it up in an hour or so," he called back to the storekeeper without stopping.

Once outside they were besieged by some friends of his wanting to meet his new wife, so he didn't get to question her until they were on their way back to camp. "What, may I ask, Mrs. Eastman, was that spending spree back at the store all about?"

Annie was feeling guilty for such extravagance. Her get-even scheme had backfired, for he hadn't refused her any of her foolish purchases. She could hardly admit now that she'd only wanted to act like a spendthrift bride to repay him for his too-noble role of a loving groom. How could she explain she'd wanted him to rebuke her so she could do likewise? When she thought she could trust her voice, she croaked, "All things we needed."

"A satin-lined sewing box?"

"I have some mending to do."

"That fancy lamp?"

"Why, to light and sit on a barrel in the chuck wagon so I can see to sew, of course."

"Oh, well, fine, if you needed them," was all he said.

Annie was astonished by Jude's behavior. All day he had been careful to properly take hold of her arm as they walked and to politely open doors for her and to graciously assist her up onto the wagon seat. If she hadn't known better, she might have thought he was proud to be seen with her. He almost seemed to be showing her off, he wore such a smug, arrogant air as he introduced her to his innumerable acquaintances. It seemed he knew most of the population of Cottonwood, and everyone pumped their hands and congratulated them. The men remarked Jude was a lucky devil, but Annie suspected the women thought she was the lucky one.

At lunch Jude had been the epitome of courtesy. As she had promised, Annie responded in kind, and they made it back to the camp and through the next three days with this new regimen intact.

The day for the primitive sod house scheme dawned startlingly clear with an unseasonable early morning chill. Jude and Annie headed east in the chuck wagon while the drovers and cattle continued to trail slowly on north. Jude felt a slight twinge of guilt, thinking of Pa back at

Double Tree relishing the thought of Annie installed in the new house. He tried to stifle these disquieting thoughts by reminding himself of the consequences. If he did not go ahead with his plan to install his shrewish bride in this crude sod house and convince her it was her new home, then he was going to find himself permanently astraddle a fence.

True, Annie had been very pleasant the last few days, but both of them knew it was only an act. If she wasn't that society-conscious Armstrong snob's daughter, he might even have suspected she was an actress, she was so expert at playing a role. The most disquieting thing was the way she'd set out to win everyone over. She knew just how to feign the airs that would ingratiate her to them.

The one thing Jude would not admit, not for a minute, was the gnawing jealousy deep in his innards when she laughed and sang with his twin, or gave Pa or one of the men that smile of hers, a smile that did something to cause a thumping heartbeat. Phony, well-rehearsed efforts on her part, he convinced himself, just to sweeten her image.

This charade of a marriage couldn't continue indefinitely, but Jude could not be the one to end it, for two good reasons. First, because he had accepted Pa's terms and he could not lower himself to renege, and second, he couldn't just outright hurt Pa.

No, his spitfire bride had to want to go back to Chicago. He was going to feel guilty as all hell around Pa as it was for taking Annie to the soddy. Pa was sure to hear all about it. The old man had a way of sniffing out everything. He'd just have to pretend to Pa—as he had to Tex, P.T., and all the others—that he'd thought it would be good for their marriage to have some time alone together. Then he could say Annie had decided she hated him and didn't want to go on living with him even after he told her about the big house. He'd tell everyone that once they were by themselves, she had turned into a cold-blooded, self-centered woman whom he could not please no matter how hard he tried. He'd tell Pa she had ranted and raved at him one minute, belittled him constantly, and intermixed it all with tears of self-pity. Strange, that sounded almost like a description of Ma. Yes, a description of a woman like that would reconcile Pa to the idea of her going back to Chicago. *If* she went back.

She would, he was sure of it. After a day or two in a sod-fronted hole. To ease his conscience, Jude decided he would try to cooperate in every way. Then he could look Pa right in the eye after she was gone (or at least he hoped he could). The old man was going to suspect the real reason was Rosie, but Jude planned to stay away from her permanently anyway, so that would soon dispel that notion. Hell and damnation! What a snarled ball of twine his formerly uncomplicated life had become! Now was the time to start getting it straightened out once and for all.

"Anne, there's something I think you should know," Jude began as they were jostled roughly over the unbroken prairie on the seat of the chuck wagon. He slowed down the team a little so that the wagon and its contents wouldn't rattle so loudly.

"When Pa first had that heart attack, he became—confused about things. It was almost like in his mind, some dreams became realities. While we're quite certain—as soon as he completely regains his health—that everything will be clear to him . . . well," he hedged, cautiously trying to give credibility to his prevarication, "in the meantime, we've all tried to humor him for fear the shock of cold truth might make his condition worse. Believing his fantasies seemed to help him recover his strength faster. You yourself have noted his improvements each day, haven't you?"

"Yes, of course I've noticed. He seems to be making excellent progress, but what is this about dreams and fantasies? I've never met a more down-to-earth man in my life." Annie wondered if her husband really knew his father. The man was no dreamer; he was an earthmover, the kind who made things happen.

"That's what makes it so heartbreaking. You're right, Pa's always been a very earth-bound fella, yet one who dreamed dreams and made them happen. Oh, and he will these, too, of course, with Jules's and my help. These dreams he has for a successful ranch up here in the Sandhills—he'll have it all someday. Not just in his mind, either, like now. His fantasies will be realized, but that is far in the future. Right now, the only dwellings on the place are a couple of sod houses—if you can call them houses—that were already built here when we bought the land. The men and P.T. will use the larger of the two for a bunkhouse and kitchen, and we're headed for the smaller. In fact, I'm afraid it's so small it's only a hole in a hillside."

"But I don't understand. Mrs. Danvers and her son are there—"

"Cousins of his, Anne. She's a widow and he'd like to provide for her to help her out. She lives in Omaha."

"But Maudie said Mrs. Danvers would probably sit around making useless frilly-dillies instead of planting a garden or piecing much-needed wool comforters!"

"I'll wager she also said it loud enough for Pa to overhear her! She dotes on her big brother and humors him even more than the rest of us."

Annie tried to recall if this had been true, but couldn't seem to remember, so she questioned, "The new carriage and the wagon full of supplies?"

"The supplies were for the bunkhouse. The carriage, of course, had to be returned to North Platte where it had been borrowed."

"Borrowed? Father said it was a wedding gift to us!"

"If he could have afforded it, I know he would have given us one, Anne. But the purchase of the land from the Chicago, Northwestern Railroad has put him too far into debt to buy anything now. However, he has blocked out his financial straits for the moment.''

Annie was mute and Jude knew she was trying to assess the truth of his story. He thought he had sounded very convincing. Glancing around him at the splendor of the land in its early summer bloom, he sighed contentedly. How he loved the Sandhills! He'd been fascinated by this part of the state since he and Pa had come north to look it over two summers ago; ever since, he'd planned and dreamed of ranching up here in the midst of such bounty. Thick lush grass grew on these sandy hills and loamy valleys.

Annie looked all about her at this place she had instantly fallen in love with. Much like her beloved moors back home in some respects, and not at all in others. This land had not been desecrated by hundreds of years of so-called civilization. The Sandhills still retained their wild charm. She could understand why Gil would have dreams and, yes, even hallucinations during his illness about such a place as this. Still, it was unbelievable that everything he had told her about the Twin Trails Ranch was only in his imagination, for he had sounded so sincere and so proud. Down inside, she expected to come over a hilltop at any moment and see the white, two-story house he had described to her so explicitly.

How could he have talked that way about a figment of his imagination? Yet why would Jude tell her such things otherwise? Only to test her? Did he still think she could be persuaded to go back to Chicago? Surely after all she had done to prove him wrong, he had that ridiculous notion out of his head. She had told him firmly she was here to stay! To stay forever in the midst of this beauty that surrounded her would be no problem—although living with Jude Eastman assuredly would.

Just sitting beside him like this on a wagon seat was a problem in itself. His mere presence had a torturous effect on her body. Her heart beat at a different rhythm when she was around Jude, and she had to draw deeper breaths than normal. Try as she might to tell herself it was hatred and disdain, she was not convincing. Nor could her love of the land account for the feelings within her heart. The last thing she needed was for her heart to become attached to this arrogant cowboy who would never return her feelings. No, she must keep the barriers firmly in place.

Chapter Fourteen

✦✦✦✦

THE SOD-FRONTED WALL of a hill with a rough wooden door and one dirty glass window convinced Annie that Jude's story was true. Next to this monstrosity, the Birmingham row houses were palaces. However, other things about this

place made it more palatable to her. It was
nestled snugly into the side of a canyon wall
overlooking a peaceful, grassy valley. The
unique blue haze of the Sandhills hung above it
and a rippling little stream flowed nearby.

The sod house had only a partial roof, from
which the chimney extended. The rest of the
roof was the hilltop. It was precisely as Jude had
described: only a dugout in the side of the hill.
He was trying to pry the door open, which was
stuck only from disuse, for there was no lock on
it, Annie noticed.

The air outside smelled fresh and clean, but
inside there was a damp, moldy odor that of-
fended even her city-toughened sense of smell.
The odor matched the rest of this filth-encrusted
place, which had been taken over by rodents
that lived in the ground nearby.

Jude watched Annie closely as she silently
looked about her, shock and dismay evident in
her grim expression. At any moment he expected her temper to break loose and he waited
for her to tell him there was no way she'd live in
this hole in the ground. He could agree with
that—he certainly did not want to have to live
here himself.

At last she spoke, but her voice was soft and
sad, not violent and angry. She said only, "Poor
Father."

How terrible, she thought, *for Gil to have had
such grand dreams when this house was the awful
reality.* But things could be wonderfully different. Her new father-in-law's dreams *would* come

true: Jude had said so. He and Jules were going to work to make it happen, and she would, too. Earnestly she turned and went back outside to the wagon.

Jude thought Annie was going to climb silently up onto the high spring seat, but instead she lowered the back gate of the wagon. Digging purposefully into one of the cupboards right inside it, she pulled out a much-washed muslin flour sack with its seams torn open. Annie tied it around her waist and proceeded to unbutton the tiny pearl loops at the wrists of her white voile blouse so she could push her sleeves up. Jude watched in amazement as she turned and went back into that putrid-smelling soddy. As he started to follow her in, *splat*, he was hit with a moldy, mouse-chewed blanket she had just thrown out the door.

"What the hell!" he exclaimed, dropping the half-rotten blanket to the ground with distaste. "What do you think you're doing, woman?"

"I think, Mr. Eastman, that I am going to clean our home. You should have cleaned out the debris and chinked the rodent holes when you bought this place intending to live here!"

"Threw out the debris? Chinked the holes?"

"Yes. You cannot call the contents here anything but debris," she informed him bluntly, adding, "which needs to be burned—and we need to make the house rodent-proof. We shall just fill in the holes as best we can, for I don't think we should even use the cave walls, do you? We can build out from the front wall."

"*Use the cave walls for what?*" Jude exclaimed. "Build what out from the front wall? Woman, this whole thing has deranged your mind! We'll get you back to North Platte; as soon as you are in a town again, things will be clearer to you. Once you're on the train back to Chicago—"

"My dear sir. You are the deranged one and your mind's the only thing that's on a train and I swear it's on the wrong track, for it only goes in circles. Did you truly think I would let your father down just because of a setback like this?

"It must be obvious even to a pettifogger like you what needs to be done here. A nice big sod house has to be built that Father can take pride in." Annie's voice was firm and convincing and she sounded bossy, Jude noted, as if she was explaining to a child. He became more irritated by the minute as she continued, "You and I will build it. That is, if you can handle the heavy work, for there is no one here you can hire to do it for you!" *Whish!* Another molding piece of bedding came spiraling through the air, forcing him to duck.

Damn her hide! The women was going to play her role to the final curtain. After a day or two of building a sod house, she'd find there was more to it than talk. Once she discovered it was hard, heavy work . . . Suddenly her belittling remark pierced and he growled inwardly. He'd show her who was afraid of hard work! He'd worked on the ranch his whole life, not lived a soft city life as she had.

Jude certainly couldn't admit there was really

a ranch house now. She would read his scheme then for sure, and no doubt expose it to Pa. No, there was nothing to do but follow her lead.

Pugnaciously he picked up the rough-hewn table to carry it outside. All four legs fell off, leaving only the rusted nails protruding from the top plank. He used it to start a fire down near the creek to burn the things she was slinging out the door. Hell and damnation! He'd thought he'd soon be ensconced in his comfortable new bedroom at Twin Trails—not spending the night here with her!

That was it! That would send his prudish wife packing fast enough!

Jude hurried back up to the doorway, cautiously peering inside before stepping in to avoid being hit again by the lice-infested bedclothes. Dirt was flying everywhere as Annie vigorously swished an old handmade rush broom. Casually, but loud enough she could hear him over the swoosh, swoosh of her broom, he asked, "Which corner shall I build our bed in? I am going to cut down one of the cottonwoods and I need to measure how much wood I'll need."

"*Our* bed?" The broom was instantly still.

"Why yes," he continued innocently, "I thought I should build the bed in time for tonight. I can work on the table and chairs tomorrow."

"You forget yourself, Mr. Eastman! You gave me your word! You swore ours would be a marriage in name only!"

"Anne!" Jude's voice fairly dripped with reproach. "You disappoint me. My, my, such base thoughts. I gave you my word and I shall certainly keep it. We merely have to have a place for the two of us to sleep. I had no intention of anything—but to sleep, of course."

"Oh," she replied softly, not knowing what else to say, and feeling ashamed that she had been the one to have such thoughts. After all, he'd made it clear he didn't want her in that way.

Could she honestly sleep in a bed with him and be expected to feel nothing? Not with this traitorous body of hers! Why, even the thought of him in those clinging union suits and her in her flannel nightie side by side in a narrow bed gave her the tingles. He might be able to "just sleep," but she wouldn't be able to sleep a minute!

Jude loved watching the red blush that stained Annie's face. Her cheeks had already been flushed from exertion, so the humiliation he had heaped on now made them fiery red. What fun to watch her eyes switch from anger to embarrassment to—to—what was it they were revealing now? Was it fear of a man? Somehow she didn't look fearful. Maybe a little worried. He could hardly wait to hear what excuse she would invent for why they had to leave at once. He knew it hadn't occurred to her she'd be alone with him for the night.

Annie tried to display an unconcern she was far from feeling. "For the present time we'll just continue our former sleeping arrangements: I'll sleep in the wagon and you can sleep underneath it. We'll not bother with building beds for this . . . this . . . this is just going to be our storage area, and we'll build our house with at least two bedrooms."

"No. It's the tornado season now as well as the time of year for hailstorms. You witnessed the damage they can do the other night. We can't constantly afford to replace our supplies. We have to get into shelter," Jude pressed.

Once again she murmured "Oh," and remained perfectly still. At last she told him, "It will take no more wood to build half-beds in each corner than to build one whole bed. I do believe that would be best under these circumstances."

"Then you don't trust me, Anne?" He pretended to be hurt.

She could hardly say she didn't trust him, for he had certainly never given her any reason to mistrust his intentions. Quite the opposite, in fact. Finally she admitted, "It would bother me to sleep with—someone. I've always slept alone, since I had no sisters, you see. I just wouldn't be able to sleep, that's all."

"With anyone, Anne, or just with me?" he asked as he stepped very close to her. Much too close. She could almost feel the warmth of his body through her thin voile blouse and knew she was quivering faintly from the heat he seemed to disperse. She did not trust her voice to answer him firmly.

Jude took his thumb and forefinger and turned

her face up to his so he could see her eyes. He didn't mean to kiss her, but her closeness was his undoing. Her big brown eyes were filled with questions he wanted to answer for her, and her full, slightly parted lips were irresistible. Slowly he lowered his face to hers. She was so tiny. His arms hungrily went around her to hold her closer to him and lift her up just a little to fit perfectly against his chest.

When their lips first touched, hers remained rigid, but only for a moment. He could almost feel their softening response. In fact, he was sure he felt just the tiniest pressure, then he was positive, for suddenly she was returning his kiss and with such sweetness he was overwhelmed. Her arms started to creep up the front of his chest, but they hesitated before they reached his shoulders. He tightened the hold he had on her and pressed his firm lips harder against her softness, demanding more of this honeyed nectar that sent his blood pulsing.

Annie wanted to clasp her arms around his neck and make him continue this kiss, but as her arms inched up she recalled the arms of his redheaded mistress slipping wantonly up around his neck and she quickly stilled her hands before they followed the same path. Yet she could not bring herself to push him away as she knew she should. His kiss felt too wonderful. Right now she needed to feel the strength of his body against hers. Every inch of her was responding to her previously unacknowledged needs.

Unfortunately, Jude's needs were soon just as

evident to her as her own, and she was frightened her passion would betray her and go beyond her control, as it nearly had that day in the glade with Dev. It would be much worse if it happened this time, for it was only another plot of his to humiliate and belittle her. He only wanted to make her body respond even though he did not desire her. She had to stop this degradation.

When Jude felt Annie grow cold and stiff in his arms, something unexpected happened. He discovered he did not want to stop kissing her. For a moment there had been a spark of warmth in this wife of his, and he wanted very much to try to ignite it so it would burn beyond mastering. Regaining his senses, he released her and stepped back to look at her. She was shaking slightly. Was it from fear? Anger? Surely not passion—not Daphne Anne Armstrong Eastman, the pious spitfire who was helping clean out a sod hut for them to live in only because she held his father in such high esteem.

Whatever had made him forget himself and kiss her? Had the only reason he hadn't wanted to stop been the thought of igniting her? Could it possibly be that his own body was in flames? Disgustedly he turned and tromped out the door, leaving Annie to wonder about his behavior as well as her own response.

They ate supper in complete silence. As soon as she cleaned up the plates, pans, and utensils, Annie went back to her task of putting rocks into the rodent holes and chinking around them with mud. When it became too dark to work inside, she went back out to where Jude was sawing up the big cottonwood tree he'd cut down today. He had cast off his shirt and thrown it over the stump where the tree had stood, and Annie watched the play of his arm and shoulder muscles. The sight of him made a funny prickling inside her as she watched him saw the wood into lengths. Her eyes were magnetically attracted to the ripples that moved across the broad expanse of his chest. Never had she been exposed to such masculine virility before.

During these hot summer months he had evidently discarded his union suits, for he was naked above the waist. Annie found herself wondering what he had on underneath those dungarees and nearly blushed at her thoughts. She shuddered even more at the thought of sleeping in her thin old flannel nightie next to his bare chest. She was relieved to see that the poles being formed and nailed together were for two narrow beds.

As she sat idly watching, it occurred to her that deep in her heart she wished he was her man, making their new bed. A bed in which they'd be sharing love. This afternoon's kiss had told her how much she desired him, and more important, he wanted her. Perhaps not in the way of real love, but he did want her. What was it he'd said about men craving a woman when they were forced into abstinence? Mrs. O'Mara had been left far behind. This might be her chance to make him fall in love with her.

Making Jude Eastman desire her, want her, love her, challenged Annie's spirit. She almost laughed aloud at the idea of felling his highness, having him need her as much as she needed him. She began to plot a strategy. Of course she'd continue to work hard so he'd admire her and she'd surmount any obstacle he cast her way to show she was a thoroughbred, but she would try other things, also.

Hurriedly, before she lost her nerve, Annie vaguely sketched her plans, wondering why she didn't have any woman's intuition to guide her. Well, even a novice seductress knew they'd have to talk to each other more. Biting the corner of her lip, she contemplated the two dresses she had with her. Neither of them struck her as the gown of a temptress. Besides, it would be too obvious if she changed dresses just to stroll down to where he was working. Unbuttoning the top of her blouse would have to suffice.

Annie smoothed back her hair, bit her lips hard to redden them, and pinched her cheeks. Then she walked toward him with what she hoped was a provocative gait. While she didn't have a conversation mapped out, there were two things she'd remember: first, not to lose her temper, for no man would fall in love with a shrew; second, not to use the imperious voice she used to imitate Daphne. Jude wasn't Geoffrey Beaumont.

"Lovely evening, isn't it?" she said in her most honeyed voice.

Jude glanced up at the threatening clouds before brusquely answering, "Looks like rain."

Then he went back to his sawing, leaving Annie to try to think of something else to say.

She wasn't prepared for his bare chest to be so close to her. It was covered with a thin sheen of perspiration, which made it glisten as his rope-taut muscles moved rhythmically. It completely unnerved her. Finally she managed, "You look like you're an old hand at sawing, yet I don't remember seeing trees around Double Tree. In fact, I often wondered how it got its name."

He didn't stop sawing, so his end of the conversation was as breathless as hers. "Pa had a wagonload of logs hauled in now and then for firewood, but we more or less just chopped that up with an axe. My expertise comes from several years back when we built the log part of the house and all the pens. The place got its name from the two lone trees that were close by the sod house we originally built. They both had to be cut down the first winter for firewood."

"So that's why the place looks hodgepodge. You've been adding on over the years."

"You didn't think we planned it that way, did you?"

"Goodness, I didn't know. Did all of you share that tiny sod house? I mean, you and the drovers?"

"Pa didn't have much of a crew then. To get ownership we had to build soddies on the other homesteads too. That's where Tex and his missus lived, as well as the few men he had. In the other soddies. The two men at the home place slept in that barn made of hay—"

"The one that's disintegrating?"

"Yeah, it was whole then, but not warm. As I recall, they slept on the floor of our place when the blizzards and cold snaps came."

"Blizzards? Cold snaps?"

"Blizzards are like that hard rainstorm the other day but with the rain turned to snow or sleet. You saw the winds that came with it . . . well, imagine them with below-zero temperatures thrown in."

"I can't."

"A cold snap out here is when it gets several degrees below zero and stays there day in and day out."

At least she had Jude talking to her. The only thing was, she'd been so interested in his answers she'd forgotten to use her sultry voice and to try to lure his attention. She certainly wasn't getting that; he was still sawing away.

Annie tried unobtrusively to step closer to him. It was a fatal move, for now his male scent assaulted her and she could almost feel the heat of his body. Instead of sounding sultry, her voice was a hoarse squeak. "Maudie said when she first came you lived on beef, biscuits, and beans."

"So we did. You notice that's still the mainstay for the chuck wagon, except that now we can buy smoked hams and slabs of bacon and some canned stuff like peaches and tomatoes to break the monotony."

"You're lucky she came here. You'd really be sick of such a diet if she hadn't."

"Reckon so. Might even have nudged me 'n Jules into taking wives."

"You had chances?"

"Quite a few."

"I thought single women were so scarce out here."

"We got around. There's always some matchmaker anxious to introduce a successful rancher's son to an unmarried female relative."

"Oh." So much for Daphne's argument! One look should have told her Jude had had his chances to marry, he just preferred not to. She muttered aloud, "Why?"

"Why, what?"

"Why didn't either of you marry if you had all those chances?"

For a minute he stopped sawing, but it was getting too dark to see his expression as he turned to her and mocked, "I must have been waiting for you."

"Why do you always tease me?"

"Am I teasing?"

"You weren't waiting for me, that's for certain. You didn't want a wife."

"There, you see, you answered your own question." He started to saw again.

Annie deemed it unwise to follow this topic to its conclusion. He didn't want a wife because he had a mistress. Why hadn't he married her? She caught herself just before she asked and quickly changed the subject. "How old were you when Maudie came to live with you?"

"Twelve, thirteen."

"That old? She said she came after your

mother died. I didn't realize you weren't little. Why, you must remember your mother quite well. What was she like? I never heard Father mention her. Did she come to Nebraska with you? How did she die?"

Jude's voice was cross as he accused, "Why all this sudden interest in me and my family, Anne? I can't believe you truly give a damn."

Taken aback by his sudden rudeness, Annie stammered, "But I do."

"Yeah, well I don't care to talk about it, okay? Why don't you run along and let me finish up here? Do whatever you have to do, then get yourself tied snugly in that wagon, 'cause I'm going to be turning in myself in a few minutes."

Without another word Annie turned and blindly stumbled back up to where the wagon was parked. Tears stung her eyes as she climbed into the wagon where her bed was built on a shelf above the supply barrels and boxes. Thank heaven tomorrow she could unload all these things and take them inside so she didn't have to crawl over everything. There would be room to walk on the floor.

Then she remembered that tomorrow night the new beds would be in that little house. There would only be six feet between their beds. Restlessly she fell asleep wondering if six feet would be enough.

Jude watched Annie until she reached the wagon, wondering what her friendliness was all about. She was acting about as coy as some of the husband-hunting females he'd been introduced to in the past. Almost as if she were trying to attract his attention. Only she wasn't. She already had a husband.

It was too dark to saw anymore, but by the light of the lantern he could drive the nails into these ridiculous beds, he decided. Maybe pounding a few would drive the questions Annie had asked about Ma from his mind. Did he remember his mother? Hell, yes, he remembered her. What was she like? A bitch.

Jude woke up with every kind of ache known to man. How many years had it been since he'd had to chop wood at home? Not since the Rawlings kid got big enough to do it. He should have brought the Rawlings kid along to do it here. With that mercenary idea came Annie's sharp words—"If you can stand the heavy work, for there'll be no one here you can hire." He opened one eye and peeked out at that awful sod house.

There was Annie, tugging the wagon seat into the door. The wagon seat? What was the woman up to now, and how had she managed to unbolt it without waking him? He was a light sleeper, always alert for any noise that might spook the herd. Rolling painfully out from under the wagon, he suspected he must have injured some muscles or ligaments to be in this much agony.

By now she had the seat shoved through the doorway and was coming back out again. When she saw him she smiled just as chipper as anything, and cried out eagerly, "Listen, Jude! Listen to that bird! That's a meadowlark, I'm sure, for P.T. said they sing a tuneful song at the break of day that sounds like someone whistling. Do you hear it? And I saw a doe with a fawn come right up to the creek to drink when I was bathing this morning.

"I'm so glad you're up, for I need you to help me carry in the cupboards and the tailgate from the chuck wagon. Those will work fine for a temporary kitchen cabinet and tabletop. Even with the cupboards on it, there will be room for the two of us to eat. We'll sit on the wagon seat."

Annie was so excited by everything this morning she just could not suppress her enthusiasm. "I thought if you did not have to build a table and chairs, we could start cutting sod today. I put the patched wagon tarp over the floor in there and it is much better. The rust came off the stove with sand. I was sure it would, for rust on cast iron could not be worse than the food P.T. burned onto the camp skillets and dutch oven. They were cast iron, too. He always carried some sand in a pail to clean them up with—oh, yes, I put your breakfast in the dutch oven to stay warm for you."

After this breathless rush of words she did not wait for an answer but went over to the side of the wagon to take down a coil of rope. She took it to the two beds he had finished and left sitting by the stream last night. While he watched in amazement, she knotted one end around a corner post seaman-style and then crisscrossed it back and forth over the side logs to make supports, cut it with a knife, and tied a sailor's knot on the post at the opposite end.

In awe, Jude went over to the coals and dug out the dutch oven with his breakfast in it. She'd even rigged up the metal bar they hung the coffeepot on all night long in camp so night riders could have a cup when they needed it. Jude needed a cup now—he needed several cups. He felt like he'd been hit by a twister. Annie had acted so angry when she turned and ran from him last night, he had figured she wouldn't deign to speak to him today, but there she was, back to being Miss Radiant Politeness. Or would that be Mrs.? He sipped the coffee. It was hot and strong, just the way he liked it. Maybe he'd be able to make it through the day.

When he looked at the topless, seatless wagon, he doubted it. God above! Now she wanted to dismantle the back end, too! He'd thought they'd be pulling out of here in that wagon today or tomorrow, but unfortunately it would take them a day to reassemble it before they could even leave!

"Are you ready to carry in the beds?" Annie called out to him with an airy lightness he didn't share. She'd impatiently waited until he finished eating his entire breakfast: fried bacon and mush with molasses and two cups of coffee.

"I can get them without any help," he told her churlishly. It was easy enough to carry the bed, but awkward to get it through the door and

turned so it was sitting in the corner. When he
went back to get the second one, she was
standing at one end of it. Wordlessly they each
picked up an end and easily carried it in and set
it in the corner.

"Shall we get the chuck wagon cupboard
next?" she questioned, hesitating a little.

"Why not?" he responded sullenly. "You
seem determined to demolish the Twin Trails'
only chuck wagon."

"It's only temporary, Jude. By roundup time
this fall we will have the sod house built, as well
as the furniture to put in it. We have to remove
everything from the wagon to transport the sod
over here from the valley, anyway."

"Transport the sod over here from what valley? We have no way to cut sod in the first place,
and in the second place, I'm not going to plow
up this grassland and risk a blowout. Don't you
realize it takes at least an acre of sod for a house,
woman?"

Undaunted, she answered, "Of course. I told
you I met some immigrants who told me how to
build a soddy. In the Platte valley they didn't
risk blowout, of course. Most of the ranch houses
P.T. and I saw here in the Sandhills were made
of valley sod and logs, and some with lumber or
stone. If only we were not so far in debt, we
would build him the frame house Gil dreamed
of."

Jude noted the way she said "we." He also
noticed how she accepted their "poverty" without complaint. She continued, "Since we have to

plow a six-foot windbreak against prairie fires all around the edge of our land, why can't we use some of that earth for sod?"

Jude was astonished both at her knowledge of the danger of prairie fires and at her ingenious idea for getting sod for a house without plowing up good acreage.

"We could, Anne. That's an excellent idea, in fact," he admitted. "But," he went on, hardly able to conceal his relief, "we have no plow."

"But we do, Jude. The trappers or settlers who built this must have intended to come back someday, for they left behind the grasshopper plow they used to cut the sod for the front of this house. I found it when I went behind the brushpile to dress after I bathed."

She'd bathed nude in the daylight! And he'd slept through that, too? Son-of-a-gun. He would have liked to have seen his own wife just one time when she wasn't all rigged out in clothes or that big flannel nightgown. What in tarnation was he thinking? Why, he'd seen Rosie wear "show-all gowns," so why were his loins inflamed over a prudish old maid with no curves in an old fashioned nightie? She did have *some* curves, he corrected himself, recalling the softness of her high, firm breasts when he'd lifted her up against his chest.

She stood waiting for him to share her excitement about the plow.

"It's probably rusted."

"You could clean it up with sand, as I did the stove."

"The grass up here is too thick. No plow will cut through it without extra weight. It takes one man to push and one to ride holding the plow down to cut straight rows."

"I'll ride."

"You're not heavy enough."

"Then you ride!"

"Woman, you'd drive a teetotaler to drink. You can't push the plow through the soil, let alone with my weight on it. We can't plow!"

"Yes we can! I'll sit on it on your saddle. Why, it must weigh forty pounds. That will make me as heavy as either of those Englishmen I watched. And the soil in the valley is loamy; it will be easier to cut."

"It won't work."

"It will!"

"It won't!"

"Prove it!"

It worked. They cut two long strips of soil, and Annie worked side by side with Jude to load it onto the wagon. He was surprised by her strength. When they got the sod back to the site, he pointedly asked, "Shouldn't we have done something about tamping down this grass where the floor is going to be?" He wasn't too concerned about making a proper house, but he couldn't let her know that. She had to see for herself how hard the work was. Maybe one more day of this backbreaking labor would do it. If *he* was dead tired, she must be exhausted! By tomorrow she'd ache so badly she'd be screaming to head for Chicago.

"Of course we have to do the floor first, silly, but we aren't building the cabin yet, just the privy."

"The privy! We're not wasting our time building an outhouse! You can go down the stream a ways like you did on the trail. Use a bucket at night if you're afraid of the dark."

Jude hadn't even thought of the close confines of that cabin when he spoke, not until the crimson began to crawl from her neck to the roots of her hair.

"Oh, all right," he conceded. "I'll dig a hole."

"I'll make supper while you do. Then after we eat, we can stack the blocks around the outside."

For the rest of his life Jude wondered if supper that night had been the best meal he'd ever eaten, or if he'd just never been hungrier. Annie had cooked on the little stove in the soddy for the first time, using the wood he'd splintered off from the bed rails the day before. She'd baked a large cut off the ham they had bought and flavored it with brown sugar, then served it with some fresh greens she'd found growing nearby. Best of all was the cobbler she'd made from a can of peach halves.

"This cobbler needs cream," she apologized. "We must get a cow, and some chickens, too, as soon as we build a pen. I'm so glad now that you bought me that churn. At the time I thought it was an extravagance, but it turns out to be a necessity. In England my grandfather bought butter, but when I worked at the castle as a dairymaid, I had to take my turn on the churn's stomper.''

"You worked as a dairymaid in a castle?''

It was too late to retract the statement. Annie almost giggled at the idea of Daphne Armstrong working as a dairymaid, but she refrained and hastily elaborated, "Yes, I did. You see, my grandfather was very well to do, but not of the nobility. In England there are very rigid class distinctions and they are seldom crossed.'' She thought of Dev with a twinge. "My friend and I wanted to visit a nearby castle, but we knew we would never be invited, so we posed as dairymaids and worked there in order to explore every nook and cranny. It was quite a lark.''

"So this playacting isn't new to you then, is it?''

Jude's question trapped her. "What playacting?''

"You know. The role of the prim, proper Chicago socialite you put on for Pa 'n everybody.''

Annie was appalled. How had he guessed? Had Gil guessed, too? No, he couldn't have. She'd been very careful around Gil not to lose her temper or use bad language. It had only been Jude who had brought out her true disposition, but how much did he suspect?

"Why do you imply being my true, even-tempered self is playing a role? Only *you* seem to make me forget myself. I never created scenes before I met you!"

"Well, you're a mighty fast learner!" he accused.

"You tried to put me in *my* place mighty fast!"

"No more so than you attempted to put me in mine!"

"And we both seem to have failed. I tried to place you in the role of husband, and you in turn tried to place me on the train back to Chicago."

Jude couldn't help laughing. "It's true! We have been at loggerheads from the beginning. Just supposing I had been the docile old gentleman you expected? How would things have been for us then? That first night, for instance, when I came to your room, I would not have gone out the window, you know."

"No, I suppose not. But then, you would not have had a mistress. You would have wanted *me*," she told him without thinking.

"And had I wanted you, Anne," he asked curiously, "what would I have said to you? What would your docile old fellow do to indicate he wished to make love to his new wife?"

This conversation had gotten out of hand, but she could not stop. She thought of how Dev had indicated to her he wished to make love. Was that what a husband would do? No, a husband would not treat a wife that passionately. He would be very respectful.

"Well," she finally stuttered, "a true husband probably would have gently taken me into his arms and kissed me softly—"

"Yes, go on," Jude's voice grew a little huskier.

"Then he'd—" Now it was Annie who was feeling a little overheated. She looked into Jude's eyes. They weren't icy at all and she felt as if she was being drawn into their spell.

Quickly she jumped up and started clearing the dishes. "We had better get back to work. The sod has to be laid the day it's cut or it will dry and crumble."

"But you didn't finish," Jude persisted. "What would your groom have said?"

Annie didn't know, but she'd just have to improvise. "He would have blown out the candle and then politely asked, 'Will you please lift your nightie, dear?' "

Jude laughed so hard he nearly fell off the wagon seat. His eyes were so full of tears he didn't even see Annie as she stormed from the house. My god! He was married to the most priggish of old maids!

Annie was furious with herself. Here he'd given her an opening to stage a seduction scene and she'd muffed it. Why couldn't she have thought of something sensual to say instead of something that branded her a pious spinster? Oh well, they'd be alone here from now on. She'd have plenty of chances, especially in beds only six feet apart.

Chapter Fifteen

✦✦✦✦✦

Six feet. Sixty feet. Six hundred feet. It made no difference to the two exhausted bodies crawling into the uncomfortable beds night after night. Grim determination kept each of them toiling at the task, but for different reasons. Jude's determination to win his battle for his lost freedom was beginning to wane. It was now July, and Nebraska's hot humid days and hot still nights had descended on them, but Annie still hadn't left. Why didn't this stubborn wife of his run from this primitive existence? Her wealthy father lived in a mansion in Chicago, so she had an alternative.

Annie didn't mind the hard work it took to build this house. Every day she could see progress, and it strengthened her determination to complete it. For the first time in months she was almost completely happy.

Almost. She still had not convinced Jude she'd be a good wife. She almost wished she *was* Jude's mistress, the woman he loved. They had established a spirited working relationship and that pleased her, but she knew now she wanted more. She *was* in love again, but this love was very different from her childhood crush on Dev or her comfortable caring for Carter. She realized she had not even known the meaning of love before.

Annie knew Jude would soon return to check

on his cattle. In fact, she was amazed he'd stayed here this long. As soon as he left, she would concentrate on a plan to win him over.

It came as no surprise when Jude announced one morning he had to ride over to inspect the herd and give a few orders. The only order he had to give, though, was for someone *not* to come searching for him.

"I'll go with you," Annie volunteered, "and we'll bring back a milk cow."

Jude couldn't possibly take Annie along, and he had no intention of herding a stubborn cow over here. He doubted if there even were any milkers this late in the season.

"I'll probably be taking you to Cottonwood— for supplies—soon. We'll at least get a case of eggs," he tried to make the lie plausible, "but it's too late to get a cow. There won't be any still fresh."

"Fresh?"

"Yes, you know. Once they don't have suckling calves their—well, they dry up if they're not milked," he finished lamely.

"Of course I know that! But two or three dropped calves on the trail to the new ranch. They'd still be giving milk."

"Hell's fire, woman! would you have me search through thousands of head of cattle to hopefully find one of those?"

"No, I suppose not. It is just hard to get used to cooking without milk, butter, or eggs."

This was the first real sign of discontent she'd shown, so Jude pressed his advantage. "You'll get used to it—and much worse things, too—if you insist on staying here in this godforsaken place!"

His words stung but Annie said nothing. Down deep, Jude knew she wasn't going back to Chicago. What was he going to do now? He needed to get on with his life, and he couldn't build up the ranch when he wasn't even there to oversee it. He'd have to think of something, but what, dammit?

Right then he almost told her about the Twin Trails house. He figured he might as well tell her and get it over with, then he remembered his deceit was going to make her hate him more than ever. He could imagine the tongue-lashing she'd give him. "Pettifogging, malodorous, gutless bastard" would only be for openers! Worst of all, once she was installed in that cozy house, there would be no hope she would ever leave. He'd be condemning himself to the life of a monk! He decided to stall for another day or two.

"Look, Anne, I'm sorry I blew up. We'll get a cow as soon as possible. We really need a shed for one first, you know, as well as for our horses. I'll ride over there—"

"Just go ahead and leave. I just thought you wanted a house with all the comforts of home as much as I did. I want to make a real home for Father."

"Pa! Always Pa!" Jude jumped on this as an excuse. "Don't you ever think of what *I* might think or feel? Don't you feel anything yourself?"

Annie wished she could tell him exactly what

her true feelings were, but she merely replied, "Of course I have feelings myself, but mine are very different from yours. I don't think this is a godforsaken place, I love it here. I thought we shared this feeling. I believed we were working together because building a house and a ranch here in the Sandhills was important to both of us.

"As for your—other feelings, I know well enough you feel trapped, but I cannot help that. You should never have signed the proxy marriage vows."

"I told you, I had no choice." Jude was feeling rotten, but he couldn't back down now.

"No choice!" Annie exploded.

"I told you, I lost when Jules and I tossed a coin to please Pa."

"Far from losing, Jude Eastman, you were paid handsomely for marrying me! You were bought and paid for just as I was! This ranch you wanted so much became yours permanently, just by signing your name. Oh, yes, you got what you wanted but now that's not enough. At my expense, you want more. You want all this *and* that mistress of yours, too! How convenient it would have been for you if I had gone scurrying back to Chicago after my first day of riding drag, or at my first sight of this hole! I, unlike you, sir, am not a 'pettifogging, gutless bastard.' If I take a vow for better or worse I stick to it! Do you hear me?" With each word she'd spoken her voice had risen, until now she was nearly shouting.

"Hell, yes, I hear you, woman. The whole

world can probably hear you!'' Angrily he stormed out and grabbed the saddle and bridle for Rocky. *Hell and damnation, this fool woman had read his every thought, action, and motive.* He rode away as fast as he could, not turning to look back. He hoped he could signal an outrider without going far. He had to tell them they'd be coming in tomorrow. He'd tell Anne about the Twin Trails house tonight. The farce was over. He'd lost.

Annie was thankful Jude had ridden out without looking back because she did not want him to see her cry. All these weeks she'd pretended she didn't know the truth about how Jude won Twin Trails. Now she had lost her wicked temper and spoiled everything. She had thought building a house and sharing a love of the land might make it possible for them to live together harmoniously—maybe even more than harmoniously—but now, thanks to her, that would never happen.

She pulled her chin up and tried to stop crying. Tears accomplished nothing. She swiped at her tears with her fists, thinking she should probably go in and pack a few things, then saddle Pegasus and leave. She did not want to be here tonight when Jude came back—if he came back. Then she remembered she had no place to go and would undoubtedly get lost in this labyrinth of hilly terrain. Instead, she decided to clean the house thoroughly today, since it was the first time she hadn't been busy laying sod.

*   *   *

It was while Annie was emptying a bucket of dirty scrub water down the privy that Pegasus began to nicker nervously. Cautiously she peeped around the corner, thinking the horse had heard Rocky's hoofbeats. Jude must be coming back early. Heaven forbid! She wasn't ready to face him yet!

It was not Jude. It was an Indian!

The only Indians Annie had ever seen in her life had been those in a Wild, Wild West show in Chicago. To her, this one looked as big and fierce as the leader of that ferocious band had been. Even more so. He was shirtless, and his bronzed skin seemed to stretch tightly over a brawny chest and bulging arm muscles. He appeared to be alone, but she feared his tribe might be hiding behind the hill.

With pounding heart she watched as he stealthily prowled into the soddy. Within minutes he came back out with a large chunk of their uncooked smoked ham. He was eating it, along with what appeared to be the remaining soda biscuits from last night's supper. He sat down by the tree stump and began to devour his loot, his bow and arrow beside him. When Pegasus nickered again, he got up and walked over to where the horse was tethered.

When Annie saw him take her bridle off the deer antlers over the door of the soddy, she knew he was planning to steal her horse.

Oh no! Not Pegasus!

Then she remembered his bow. If only she

could make it to the bow before he made it to the horse. If not for her bulky skirt, she might have a chance of running fast enough. Without hesitation, she stepped out of the skirt and petticoat and ran as fast as she could. Scooping up the bow, she grabbed an arrow from his pack just as he neared her horse. The heathen probably didn't understand English, but she could only think to yell stop.

"Stop! Thief!" The words echoed loudly through the valley and the Indian turned menacingly toward her. She was shaking violently but she managed to hold the bow up with the arrow aimed at him, just as she had always aimed at Dev's target board.

Upon discovering his adversary was a beautiful woman, the Indian smiled at her. *Lord! He had dimples!* Did Indians have nice smiles and dimples underneath their warpaint? This one didn't even have a painted face and he called out in English as he pointed toward the horse, "Squaw better watch out. Shoot horse!"

"No!" she warned him. "Squaw good shot. Shoot you, not horse!"

The heathen raised his bushy black eyebrows toward the line of his beaded leather headband. Annie was sure he was evaluating his chances of attacking and scalping her. She kept the arrow at a level aim on his heart as he moved a few inches one way and then the other. This maneuver must have caused him to take her seriously, for he dropped the bridle and put both hands up, saying, "I give up! Don't shoot by accident, okay, lady?"

His use of her language was still perplexing her when she heard galloping hoofbeats. For a second she was afraid it was another Indian, then with relief she recognized the resonance of Rocky's familiar gait. She never took her eyes or the bead of the arrow off the Indian. He might try to grab her and use her as a hostage against Jude if she let down her guard.

Jude barely waited for his horse to stop before he leaped off and wrestled the Indian to the ground. As soon as he had him on his back and was straddling his body, he pulled back his arm and doubled up his fist to slam the Indian in the face. The Indian wasn't fighting back at all. "Dammit, Jude, what the hell's wrong with you! I didn't do nothin'!"

"He was going to steal Pegasus!" Annie cried, not realizing the Indian had used her husband's given name.

"Borrow the stupid horse," the Indian corrected. "I left you a note in—"

Not letting him finish, Jude smashed his fist into the Indian's face, shouting, "Who gives a damn about the horse! I won't have my wife ravaged, you savage bastard!"

The Indian was using his tongue to inspect the inside of his mouth for broken teeth and trying to mutter at the same time, "No ravage your woman, Jude."

"You lying red devil, Rance! I have eyes! I can see what happened for myself." Jude glanced in Annie's direction and the Indian's eyes traveled that way in dismay. Annie looked down at herself and saw only a pair of very ruffled knee-length panties showing below her shirt-waist. She blacked out completely at the sight.

When Annie regained consciousness, Jude was carrying her toward the sod house. The Indian was walking close behind them, still explaining, "I swear I never touched your woman. Hell, I never noticed she was only wearin' her underbritches until you said so. God, man! She had a deadeye aim on me with my own bow and she was shakin' so I was 'fraid she was gonna let that arrow fly!"

"He didn't touch me . . . but he was stealing Pegasus . . . I was afraid he would scalp me and ra—violate me!" Annie's voice was broken. Some of her words were incoherent, but she had to convince Jude that the Indian was telling the truth.

"You'd better get out of here before you scare her any worse, Rance. You deserved that punch on the jaw for frightening Anne so badly."

"I told you! I didn't know she was even here. I never seen her until she yelled, 'Stop!' I just heard *you* lived here.

"Why are you living in this gopher hole, anyhow? I'll sell you an old tepee that's in better shape, White Man!"

"Shut up. I'm in no mood for your humor. Just ride on out. Take Rocky. Go to the home place and tell Tex I said to sell you a horse—and I said sell, Rance—not give or loan! Have Tex put Rocky in the barn. I'll be driving the team over tomorrow."

Annie's confused mind tried to make sense of

what Jude was saying. Where was he going to drive the team tomorrow? They had to lay sod! He seemed to know this Indian, and know him well. Weren't Indians savages who stole cattle and murdered people? How did Jude know one? How did the Indian know English? Her mind drifted in and out of the darkness.

Jude roughly kicked the door of the house open and took the few steps to his bed, where he turned and sat, still holding Annie in his arms. She was trembling with fright and crying softly with relief. Rocking her back and forth like a child, he crooned, "It's all right, Annie girl. You're okay now.

"Rance—that Indian—went to school at a Spanish mission with Jules and me. He's as civilized as most white people out here. Why, there haven't been any Indian uprisings in this area for years. They're all friendly enough if you overlook a stolen cow every once in a while. The few Indians that aren't living on reservations have to steal to survive since the buffalo are gone.

"Please don't cry. I'm sorry I left you alone. I just wanted to signal a Twin Trails rider. I wanted to tell them we'd be in tomorrow— Anne? Annie girl . . . ?"

Jude shook her gently, but she only nestled closer and did not respond.

Had she fallen asleep? Probably. It was a natural reaction. The poor girl had been afraid Rance was going to steal her horse and probably rape and scalp her, and yet she had stood bravely with Rance's own bow and arrow as her only protection. She was one in a million.

Surprisingly, he'd been thinking that about her all morning. At first he had been mad as hell because she had been able to guess his scheme to get her back to Chicago, but after he simmered down he saw how valiant she was. Jude had never considered himself a stupid man. Why had it taken him so long to see Annie as the beautiful, high-spirited, courageous woman she was?

Why? Because he'd been a stubborn ass, that's why! He had always resented following orders. That was why he'd been so indignant at Pa's insistence he marry William Armstrong's girl. If he were honest, he supposed he'd thought she'd be like Ma, but it hadn't taken highfalutin' things to satisfy Annie. She was happy just having a horse of her own to ride and the beauty of the Sandhills around her. More important, she was willing to work side by side with a man to build his dreams.

He gazed down at her sweet, gentle face as she slept in his arms. How right it felt to hold her like this. He should have held her that first night when she had looked like a forlorn kitten. How different things would be now if he hadn't been a fool. Would she ever forgive him? Especially after he told her about the ranch house? Dammit to hell! He realized that if she had gone back to Chicago he would have lost the only woman he had ever known that he could love, respect and admire—and—and—yes, want only her in his bed for the rest of his life.

He tightened his grip. The heat from her body penetrated the thin muslin of her ruffled bloomers and the sheer voile of her white blouse. Her lips looked so soft and inviting, but he didn't want to wake her.

He leaned back against the dirt wall and reminisced about their first day here, remembering how he'd kissed her. For a moment she'd responded to his searching lips, then she had tensed. Was it from fear, or was it from revulsion? God knew he'd given her every reason in the world to hate Jude Eastman's guts. How could he ever hope to win her love as she had won his, and how could he even dream she might someday accept him as a true husband? Well, he possessed the devil's own determination. He'd proved that by acting like an ignorant fool to make Annie hate him. He'd turn that same damn determination around to try to make her love him. He had to. His whole life depended on it.

Undoubtedly he would fare better if he could be alone with her a few more days. Unfortunately, he'd already sent the message he'd be bringing Annie to the ranch tomorrow.

Jude needed to find a way to cancel his orders, so the unexpected sight of a drover riding past the small window glass was a relief. Maybe he could send a rescinding message after all. Gently he lay Annie on his bed and went out to meet the rider.

It was Jules!

How could fate be doing this to him? The last

thing he needed was to have Jules here to rub salt in his wounds.

Jules was already dismounting and looking thunderstruck at the sight of the sod walls. Shaking his head, he exclaimed, "I don't believe my eyes!"

Jude motioned him away from the soddy before he told him, "Annie is asleep. I don't want her disturbed. Rance came in here while I was gone today and scared her pretty bad."

"Why would anybody be afraid of Rance? He's been one of our best friends for years."

"She's never seen a live Indian before. All she knows are the wild stories about Indian massacres they tell back east."

"What were you thinking of, leaving her alone here? There are a few of those redskins still roaming around who would debauch her, as well as some outlaws hiding out in these hills. Another of your damned plots to get rid of her? Frightening her to death? It looks like you've really gone all out with your ridiculous scheme!"

Jude couldn't admit to his brother that he *had* been a fool, just as Jules had said.

"This isn't what it looks like, little brother, in fact, quite the opposite. Annie has won me completely and believe it or not, now I'm trying to win her. This wall has been backbreaking labor, and chopping down trees is torture of the first degree, but it may just win me her esteem. Lord! I thought I was as tough as they come, but I've acquired a new respect for those nesters and sodbusters."

Jules chortled, "Sort of like the grasshopper

and the ant story Maudie used to read to us. Only instead of the grasshopper going vainly on his way all summer and depending on the hard-working little ant for winter sustenance, this ant put the grasshopper's nose to the grindstone, huh?"

Jude grimaced at his brother's ridicule but had to admit, "Something like that. I don't want her to see you, so just go on to the home place and tell Tex—just tell him I've changed my mind. I'll see him a few days from now."

"You're really serious? You're trying to win Anne's regard?"

"I've never been more serious in my life."

"But not serious enough to treat her right. I spent last night at Dusty's new place in Cottonwood. She says Rosie is coming up here to stay with her for awhile."

"Believe me, little brother, I didn't know Rosie was coming to Cottonwood, but even if she came to this very spot, it wouldn't mean beans to me. I don't ever want her again. I swear it! I've come to my senses about Annie."

"Thank God you did, or maybe I should admit I'm sorry you did, for if she'd gone back to Chicago I would have been on the next train. If you aren't good to her, Jude," he warned, "I'm right behind you, but for the first time in our lives, not on your side."

This disloyalty was deserved, but it still rankled. In the past, they'd always stood together.

"Don't make me remind you whose wife she is."

Jules grumbled, "You know better than to

think that. I swear, you've gone plumb loco!"

"Only where Annie's concerned." Jude had to snigger a little himself as he revealed, "She does have me plumb loco."

"Maybe we are twins after all, Jude." Jules gave him a hearty slap on the back as he left.

When she finally managed to open her eyelids the following morning, Annie wondered what she was doing in her husband's bed. Then the memory of the Indian came bounding back to her. Had she passed out and slept through the night? She couldn't remember anything clearly after seeing her embarrassing ruffled panties exposed to Jude and a savage. Vaguely she recalled her husband seemed to know the Indian, but she could not recollect any more.

At the sounds of Jude moving around in the room, Annie hurriedly glanced down. The offending bloomers were modestly covered by a quilt. She felt little pinpricks all over her legs thinking of Jude covering her up like this.

"So, sleepyhead," he was saying, "the aroma from this delicious breakfast I'm fixing finally roused you."

"You can cook?"

Her husband's high good humor continued as he told her, "That depends on how we are defining the word 'cook.' Can I prepare superb meals as you do? No. Can I fix edible chow to survive on? Yes. However, my specialty is ham and redeye gravy over biscuits, so that is what

I'm makin'. I thought we had some biscuits left, but I couldn't find them.''

"That Indian did. He ate them with raw ham.''

Amused, Jude explained, "Smoked is about as close as Indians come to cooking food. They eat meat either very, very rare or else so overdone you can't chew it. I've never eaten edible meat in an Indian camp.''

"You've eaten in an Indian camp?'' Annie was so surprised she started to get out of bed, but when she threw back the quilt, the sight of her bloomers made her quickly cover up again.

Jude noticed her dilemma and offered, "I'll tell you about it while we lay sod today. I'll also tell you about my good friend, Rance Whitebear, but right now I have to go to the stream and fill our water bucket. We seem to be about out.'' He hoped she didn't notice the water splashing over the top of the full bucket as he quickly carried it out the door. He wanted to stay inside and watch her blush, but he reminded himself he was on his best behavior today.

Immersed in thought, Annie took her clean skirt off the center support pole of the roof. Jude seemed to be trying to disregard the terrible things they had said to each other yesterday. Perhaps he, too, wanted to improve things between them. Hoping she was right, Annie eagerly put on her skirt and tried to smooth back her disheveled hair. For comfort she wore it twisted into a knot on top of her head in this hot weather, but flyaway tendrils always slipped loose and fell across her cheeks.

Most women looked like skinned onions when they pulled their hair back from their faces, but not Annie, Jude thought as he came back in the door. The smooth hairstyle added to her rare kind of beauty, for it made those dark eyes of hers seem even bigger and accented the cute little tilt at the tip of her nose. It also emphasized the sheen of her luxuriant, satiny smooth skin. Just thinking of her delectable little body made Jude excited. How could he ever have thought overly ample curves were preferable to Annie's petitely seductive body?

After plunking the water bucket back on the work bench, he dished up their breakfast, serving it with a flourish. "For you, Annie girl," he said, grinning as he sat down beside her.

To Annie, the wagon seat bench seemed narrower than ever today, but she was glad. Jude's mood made her heart soar. Smugly smiling, she realized that anything was possible.

"What's that smile for, wife?"

"Why, I was just thinking, sir, how nice it will be for us to take turns with the cooking. This breakfast is very good."

"You're just hungry because you didn't eat last night. These biscuits are flat, tasteless, and tough compared to yours."

"Really?"

"Really. By the way, where did you learn to cook? I can't believe you didn't have someone to do it for you back in Chicago."

"I—I—" For a brief moment Annie wanted to tell Jude the truth, but she resisted. She still wasn't sure he wouldn't send her away if he knew she wasn't Daphne. As soon as she seduced him, she would tell him, she vowed. She couldn't stand to live a lie much longer. "I learned from my grandmother—in England."

"I think it's lucky for me you spent so much time there."

"You do?"

"Yes, I do."

Annie turned to look at him. He was already looking at her, his eyes unreadable. *Here's your chance to inaugurate your campaign, Annie Ellis*, a little voice inside her prodded. *Yes, but how?* With a burst of bravery she leaned over and gave Jude a tiny peck on the cheek, then pulled back and jumped up so fast from the seat that the tins on the table clattered. "I'll pour the coffee," she stuttered breathlessly, shocked by her own audacity. "It seems I must teach you the finer details of serving a meal if you are to efficiently take your turn."

"I'm learning, Annie girl," he promised, so seriously that she sensed he was talking about more than pouring coffee. Annie was so distracted that she burned her finger on the coffeepot.

Jude thought the mist today was a brighter blue and the grass more fragrantly scented as they set out to cut more sod. Miraculously, Annie was not holding a grudge about his behavior yesterday. She seemed willing enough to let bygones be bygones and take up their task where they had left off. Then there was that unexpected, sweet little kiss. Jude smiled widely.

They hadn't even reached the end of the first plowed row when they saw Jules riding rapidly toward them, waving his hat, signaling for them to hold up. He was leading Rocky.

Jude knew Jules would never have come here today if it wasn't something urgent. Fearfully he dropped the plow handles and dashed in his brother's direction. Annie, too, suspected something was wrong. Normally Jules would be waving his hat in greeting, not like a red flag to halt their progress. *How did he happen to have Rocky with him?* she wondered as she jumped from her seat on the saddle and ran toward him.

Jules had already climbed off his horse and begun to speak by the time Annie reached the twins. His voice was not filled worry or anxiety, but consternation. "There's problems up at the place, Jude," he announced without preamble. "You and Anne have to come at once. Last night Pa pulled up in a carriage he rented at North Platte. It seems he made the long trip from the depot there, after he picked up a woman who says she's Daphne Armstrong. A few days ago she telegraphed him that she was finally well enough to make the trip out here and gave Pa the time of her train arrival. To solve the riddle, he brought her up here instead of taking her to

Double Tree. They're waiting for you at Twin Trails."

Both men looked at Annie, waiting anxiously for an explanation. Jules continued to look perplexed and Jude looked—looked angry? Sad? Relieved? Annie couldn't read his expression. All she could concentrate on was the unexpected arrival.

What was Daphne doing here after all this time? Where was Geoffrey? Annie didn't dare tell Jude or Jules anything until she talked to Daphne to find out why she had come to visit, and why she had telegraphed that she had been ill.

"Anne?" Jules questioned.

"Annie girl?" Jude pleaded.

She could only turn from them and attempt to saddle and bridle Pegasus with fumbling fingers. What had happened? Why would Daphne come for a visit?

As soon as she had her horse saddled, the brothers wordlessly mounted their own horses, then all three of them galloped away from the little sod house that was only a hole in the wall of a canyon.

Chapter Sixteen

✦ ✦ ✦ ✦ ✦

TWIN TRAILS RANCH

THE FIRST THING that surprised Annie was that they had not ridden many miles when they came upon the Double T herd's summer range. Outriders were keeping it stationary. She had thought they were much further away since they had not seen anyone since moving into the soddy.

The second thing that rocked Annie to the bottom of her heart was the sight that met her eyes as they crested a hill. There sat the white frame house with its cedar-shingled roof, just as Gil had described it. The little balcony over the front porch. The many bedroom windows, all with wire screens. Even the colored squares of leaded glass across the top of the window panes winked at her as they caught the reflection of the morning sunlight.

What was apparently Tex and his wife's small cottage sat nearby. Another building, probably the bunkhouse, sat behind the house, and there were several sheds and even a barn. A big windmill creaked above her as it turned in the stiff breeze. She reined her horse to a stop and stared at the panorama, a queasy feeling engulfing her.

Jude quickly rode back and pulled to a stop beside her, trying to think of something to say to erase the ghastly look from her face. The awful thing he had done so flippantly now wrenched at his soul. Finally Annie tore her eyes away from the house in anguish. "I never knew you hated me *this* much!" Then she nudged Pegasus and clicked her tongue to guide him in the direction of the fence where Jules was dismounting.

Gil Eastman sat in an overstuffed chair in the parlor and waited for Jude and Annie. He had seen them stop under the big Dempster windmill and wondered what was said between them. What was going on? He'd been in North Platte on his way to Cottonwood when the telegram came announcing this second girl's arrival. He knew before he ever laid eyes on her that the woman was not an imposter. Upon seeing her, even the most minuscule doubts had to be squelched; her limpid blue eyes were like Willie's, and her pointed nose exactly like her ma's. She was Daphne Armstrong, all right. Now that she had arrived, it brought back the question of who Annie was and why she was here. When Annie had arrived, he'd thought he had been duped by Wily Willie Armstrong, as they used to call him, but he was uncommonly pleased by the substitution. The real Daphne's arrival blew that theory.

Gil berated himself for being a stubborn old cuss. Hank had wired from Chicago that things weren't as they seemed. On sight Gil had known Annie wasn't an Armstrong, but Hank had said he was taking care of it. Gil had trusted his lawyer to take care of the details.

He'd also trusted his own instincts about the girl; he knew she was very special. He'd been waiting for her to confide in him, to tell him why she was here in place of Willy's daughter. When the letter from Hank had come he'd tossed it unopened onto his desk and dismissed it. Annie was exactly what he wanted, whatever her circumstances. Softhearted, Maudie would say. Softheaded was more likely to be Jude's reaction.

As if all that wasn't enough, when he'd arrived here late last night he'd discovered Jude and Annie hadn't been here yet. Tex and Jules had tried to give him some hogwash about Jude wanting to spend time alone with his bride. Hell's teeth! That was beyond credence. Gil couldn't even sleep last night, trying to make heads or tails out of any of this.

He looked Annie up and down with concern when she came into the room. She politely said, "Hello, Father. It's good to see you again," but her eyes were full of pain. Strangely enough, Jude's eyes were troubled, too, and he hardly took them off Annie.

Without preliminaries he asked, "Am I to be given any explanation for this strange journey of yours to a soddy, son?"

"There's nothing I can tell you, Pa, at least not until I have discussed it with my wife," Jude answered tersely.

Gil took notice of Jude's tone when he said

"my wife." Yes, things had changed considerably since they'd left Double Tree. If Annie didn't look so miserable, he might even have thought the stay at the soddy had been beneficial.

"Annie Ellis!" Daphne's clipped, impersonal voice grated from the doorway. "What are *you* doing here? When you ran away, we all assumed you had gone back to England. Why did you come out *here?*"

Annie stood mute as Daphne continued, "Annie was my lady's maid until I became ill and needed her desperately. Grandma said she probably did not like nursing duties or else she was afraid that I was contagious, and that was why she disappeared." She turned and looked disparagingly in Annie's direction. "It was not in the least contagious, Annie, and you put a heavy burden on Grandma's shoulders when you ran off the way you did. Papa finally had to hire a nurse before Grandma herself became ill. You still have not told me what you are doing here."

There was not a sound in the room as everyone held his breath waiting for Annie's answer, but she stood silently staring at Daphne. Gil encouraged, "Tell us, Annie girl, why did you come to us? You told me once you'd been deeply hurt by a man."

"Oh, Annie," Daphne chided insultingly, "what kind of tales have you been telling my new father-in-law? Surely the mere fact that my brother, Carter, wanted you for a—a *chère amie* instead of a wife as you had hoped did not upset you. You had to have known you were far beneath him. A mere maid! That still does not explain how you come to be here."

She appeared to ponder the matter, then exclaimed, "Oh, no! Was it you who took my tickets? I was sure a chambermaid had misplaced them. When I got well enough to travel, Papa had to buy me a second pair of tickets and hire a woman to escort me. Naturally he would not consider letting me come out here without a chaperone. Goodness knows the awful things that could happen to a female traveling all alone!"

Annie thought of her own eventful trip and wanted to cry, scream, or perhaps both. How could she contradict Daphne's story? Would anyone believe anything she said? She still did not understand Daphne's motives.

Jude, too, had been wordless. Annie was denying nothing, and he had to admit this other creature looked more like a twenty-six-year-old Chicago socialite. So who was his Annie and what was her story? Had she really run from a man who'd wanted to make her his mistress? No, that could not be it. But what had happened?

When Annie finally spoke, her voice was so soft they had to strain to hear her words. "It's true, I *am Annie Ellis*—or I was until my marriage—and I was Miss Daphne's maid—"

"Marriage? What marriage, Annie? When did you wed?" Daphne cried.

"Daphne, you know better than anyone it was

I who took the proxy vows in Chicago, for you yourself witnessed the ceremony."

"What nonsense. No one believes such rubbish." She turned to Gil, asking, "Weren't the papers sent to you? They will prove the girl is lying, for they will have *my* name on them."

"The certificate was undoubtedly mailed to me." Gil rubbed his chin as if in deep contemplation, then added slowly, "I tossed the unopened letter with some other papers I wanted to put in the vault in my bank at Cottonwood. They're still at the Cattle Creek ranch house. You say these papers are the legal proof that you are wed to my son and that this Annie Ellis is an imposter?"

Daphne smugly sneered, "Absolutely."

"Jules, first thing tomorrow I want you to go to Double Tree and get the letter from Hank that's inside the top right-hand drawer of my rolltop desk. On horseback you can make the trip in two days. We shall soon have this mess straightened out. I swear it is beyond me."

Jude spoke up firmly, his voice filled with authority. "It won't matter whose name is on the certificate, Pa, for it is Annie who has been living with me—"

"Illegally, in *sin*," Daphne reminded everyone in an indelicate voice. "How could you be so immoral, Annie Ellis?"

"Stop demeaning her!" Jude ordered icily. "I don't know her reasons, but I know one thing for damn sure. I've never seen *you*, and if there is a marriage between us, it can be annulled."

"Oh no it can't! Papa made certain it was legal and binding, even though it was only by proxy." Suddenly her voice changed as she pleaded, "Please, Jude Eastman, let's not quarrel. I've lain in that bed for weeks and weeks just dreaming of this day when I would be united with my bridegroom. Don't spoil it for me. You are every bit as handsome as the man of my dreams, and it is so wonderful to be here at last. Your father was telling me he's recently built a bank in Cottonwood; we can build a house and live there."

"What's wrong with this house?" Gil asked anxiously.

"Nothing in particular. It is just a little—" She looked around critically and finished lamely, "—old-fashioned."

Annie saw the hurt in Gil's face and cried, "It's not at all old-fashioned! It is the latest style! Why, I saw a lot of this very same furniture in the stores in Chicago. It's a beautiful house filled with lovely things!"

"The shops you saw this furniture in were probably the catalog mail-order stores. The mode now is to furnish one's home with imported furnishings and antiques from France and England, or at least the ornate Eastlake style, if one is going to use oak."

Annie could not keep silent at this. "Well, if your fancy house in Chicago was any indication of style, I'm sure none of the Eastmans would want it. While it was richly adorned, it was dark and dreary, like a mausoleum."

"You're just jealous of the lovely mansion I had in Chicago!"

Her haughty attitude propelled Annie into shouting, "I'm not! I just came from a cave that was more cheerful!" When she realized what she had said, Annie blushed furiously. Gil and Jules were looking at her questioningly, Daphne was glaring at her maliciously, and Jude's eyes had lightened considerably from their storm-cloud gray. She felt very foolish that she had just compared the Armstrongs' home unfavorably with a cave. It was only that Gil had planned this house so carefully, and was so proud of it. A twinge of conscience made her add truthfully, "Your house *was* magnificent, Daphne, a real mansion, but it would not suit in the country, for it took a large staff to maintain it. Life here is very different, and houses must be different, too."

"This just shows how naive and baseborn you are, Annie. Mr. Eastman wants me to give his house the elegance our home had in Chicago. We can build a house in town with adequate rooms for servants. I have already instructed Mrs. Danvers about changes she is to make in serving dinners and planning menus while we are here."

"There'll be no house built in town, woman," Jude practically hollered, "and until Pa or Jules or I give you leave to do so, you are not to instruct Dannie to do anything!"

"Now, Jude," his father tried to placate, "shouldn't we let the girl at least try to give this place some refinement? She's right. I said I wanted that. It was why I sent for her in the first place, to give the ranch a little class and dignity."

Jude glared at the older man but made no comment, just turned and left the room followed closely by Jules. After they left, Daphne cautiously asked, "Where are the servants' quarters that Mrs. Danvers and her son use? We can put my maid there, too."

"Dannie and her son have bedrooms upstairs with the family, for they *are* family, and it will be wise for you to remember it, Daphne," Gil told her crossly. Not at all in the same tone of voice he'd used while Jude was here, Annie noticed. "As for Annie, she will sleep in the big front room upstairs where her clothes were hung when her trunks arrived. My son's things in there—"

"Can be moved directly into my room," Daphne interrupted, "for this is practically our wedding night."

"His things will be moved to the bunkhouse until we know whose husband he is—legally. You've waited this long for him. A couple of days more can't hurt."

Father has already accepted the situation, Annie noticed, and felt the keenness of his rejection. Now that he knew she was only Annie Ellis, a maid, he had practically promised Daphne—the socialite he'd wanted from the start—that she could have her wedding night with Jude in two more days. Well, Annie thought belligerently, let her have the lying, mistress-loving, deceitful . . . why, even Gil's bank in Cottonwood was another lie. Jude had hated her so much he had not wanted to share any part of his life with her. He really had been trying to rid himself of her when he'd made her ride drag and taken her to the sod house, just as she had suspected. It was only that she had hoped he was starting to change his mind about her . . . this morning he had seemed almost like . . . a husband. A knife slashed through her sharply. He *was* a husband—Daphne's!

Annie looked around the room that had been meant for Jude and his bride, the room he had refused to bring her to see. It was beautiful. The big bed had a five-foot-high headboard carved with forget-me-nots. Two of the dressers in the room had beveled mirrors. One was a low commode with a wishbone holder for its adjustable mirror. A huge wardrobe press of dark walnut stood in the corner.

The curtains were lace panels to allow the light to enter the room, but there were heavy paper roller shades on the windows to keep out the heat of the sun or cold winter winds. Lace doilies were on all the dressers and a beautifully appliqued quilt adorned the bed. Its colors matched the flowers on the wallpaper, so someone must have made it especially for this room. Mrs. Danvers? Had she been the one who'd placed a welcoming bouquet of fresh-cut flowers on the marble-topped dresser?

Annie loved the room and wished it was hers. Painfully she wondered if Jude would give up his mistress for Daphne. She had been surprised at Daphne's eagerness to share his bed, but perhaps she shouldn't have been. He was handsome and any woman would want him for a husband. Would he have treated Daphne the way he had her, Annie wondered? She smiled at the thought of Daphne Armstrong on a freight wagon or in a country store that was missing its proprietor. She certainly wasn't a skilled enough rider to have handled the job of riding drag, and Daphne would most certainly not have stepped a foot inside that sod house!

But why was she here at all? Where was Geoffrey Beaumont? And most important of all—what was Annie Ellis going to do now?

There was a light tap on the door, and Annie opened it to a tall woman in a checked gingham dress. Her hair was streaked with gray and her face lined with years of hardship, yet there was a softness about her mouth and her blue eyes were kind. "I'm Mrs. Danvers, Gil's cousin Dannie, Mrs. Eastman. We've been expecting you for a long time now. Hope you find everything satisfactory."

"Please come in, Mrs. Danvers. The room is more than satisfactory—it is lovely. Did you make the beautiful quilt and doilies?"

"Yes. I love handwork and spend more time on it than I should, as Maudie probably told you. I'm not much for gardening, although I planted some flowers about the place and had my boy Shawn put in a few vegetables."

Annie wished she could assure this kindly woman that they would get along fine, because she disliked handwork immensely and loved gardening, but it did not really matter now. Instead she told her honestly, "Mrs. Danvers, I don't know if you have heard about the—the—mixup. I think it would be best if you just called me Annie, not Mrs. Eastman."

"I've heard nothing *but* the mixup, as you call it, since last night when that woman arrived. She has done nothing but belittle us and tell us how isolated it is here. She's relegated Tex Barnes' wife, Elmira, and myself to the lowest rung 'round here. However, her reign as queen will be short-lived; Gil will see to that. He holds you in high regard."

"There is really nothing Father—Mr. Eastman—can do, I'm afraid, and I'm sure he'll not want to. He thinks I am a scheming imposter and Daphne is everything he wanted the mistress of this house to be. She has the proper airs and manners."

"Now, now, don't fret, for Gil assures me all this will soon be swept under the rug and we'll hear no more of it. How would you like my boy Shawn to carry up the tub and some buckets of hot water so you could have a nice warm bath?"

Annie eagerly accepted, "I would love it. It has been so long since I've bathed, except in an icy cold stream, that it would be a real treat."

*   *   *

Jude and Jules got their chance to discuss the situation privately while they rubbed down the horses. Jude told his brother bluntly, "Break the seal on that letter from Pa's lawyer tomorrow and blot out that woman's name if it's on there. Put Annie's in place of it. I suspect that somehow it *is* Daphne Armstrong's name on the document, but for some reason it was like Annie said; it was she who took the vows. I just wish I knew the whole story, but chances are she won't confide in me."

"Can you blame her, little brother? God! The look on her face when she saw the house was frightening. For a moment there I thought she might pass out and fall off her horse."

"Jules, I'm begging you to help me out of this terrible coil I've gotten myself into. Believe me, I feel lousy about the whole rotten mess."

"Strangely enough, I do believe you, Jude, and I'll do what I can to help. But even you must know it would not solve anything to break that seal and put Annie's name on the certificate, for there's probably a copy on record in Chicago, as well as the witness of the pastor and Hank's word. There's got to be another way. Can't you devise one of your magnificent schemes and have this dame live in a sod house for a spell? I'll lay odds she'd run at the sight."

"If you're only going to rub it in what an ignorant ass I've been, then just shut up. I don't need your scorn."

"Scorn?" A guttural voice from the next stall interrupted them. "Let a red man tell you the meaning of that word."

"Rance! What the devil are you doing here and why are you lurking around in the barn?" Jules asked.

"I was asleep on a cot Tex let me make up back here. When I saw this spread, I decided it would be my permanent home. This place can use an expert wrangler."

"Just like that?" Jude questioned.

"No. I was gonna ask one of you before I sent for my squaw and papoose. I don't want my kid raised on no damn reservation. I was coming east to look for work when my horse went lame over by your soddy yesterday. When I saw this layout, I decided to stay. I'm a good man with horses and you both know it."

"Okay. You've got a job here," Jude promised, "but for now Jules and I have to talk, so make yourself scarce."

"Jules just said he couldn't help you, so this will be my chance to repay you, white man."

"What can you possibly do?"

"Why, I can put on war paint and stage a one-man Indian uprising. I'll seize the unwanted woman and carry her off. She'll be so frightened by this heathen country she'll never come back. I'll abandon her—within walking distance of a train depot, of course—just in time to catch the 8:30 eastbound."

All three men guffawed, but soon returned to sobriety.

Jude said, "That's a hell of an idea, Rance, and I wish I could say, do it! There is one thing you could do, if you can tolerate that grizzly's presence. Come up to the house for meals instead of eating in the bunkhouse for the next couple of days. An Indian at her table may take her off her high horse."

"Or put her on one to ride out of here," Jules added caustically. "For your sake, I hope your schemes work, little brother, even if you don't deserve them to."

Annie had just stepped from the tub and tied her wrapper around her when Daphne opened the door and walked in without knocking.

"At least I see my edicts are starting to be obeyed: they brought the tub up to your room. Last night they tried to tell me baths were taken on Saturday nights in the middle of the kitchen floor here, for it was too much of a chore to carry enough water for a bath up and down the steps."

"I never thought of that!" Annie admitted guiltily. "Why, that's probably true."

"Your few weeks of marriage to the wealthy rancher have obviously not elevated you from your plebian level, Annie. I thought you would carry the whole thing off with more aplomb. Instead, you come riding in here astride a horse in that awful divided skirt, looking as if you might have been digging ditches."

"Laying sod," Annie corrected, but did not wait for Daphne to answer. "Why are you here, Daphne? Where is Mr. Beaumont?"

"Geoffrey!! That low-life worm! I don't know where he is, nor do I care. He vowed we would marry in New York, but he never found the time to make arrangements, although he found plenty of time to pawn my jewels and cash the wedding draft. He left me alone constantly until the money was gone. Then he came crawling to me, begging me to marry him in a shabby little ceremony and return to Chicago with him, where he hopes to become a schoolteacher. A teacher! He says he never wants to think of gambling or traveling again. The teaching profession appeals to him now. Imagine! Why, we'd be as poor as church mice!

"But I'll get even. I'll find those incriminating papers of Papa's the first time I get to Chicago and turn them over to the authorities myself!"

"Then you're just visiting here on your way to Chicago?"

"Of course not, silly goose. I can't go there, Papa thinks I am here. There is nothing for me to do but accept my fate. Perhaps if I had known that Jude Eastman was so handsome and that his father owns a bank, I would have come in the first place. Well, no matter. I'm here now!"

"But Daphne—you assured me what was on the paper meant nothing. That it was taking the vows and living with the man that made it a marriage."

"You were so naive, Annie; it was always easy to deceive you. The names on record in the courthouse are what make it legal. You are out of luck, for I have come to claim what is rightly mine. Papa arranged it all for me! Although I did not appreciate his gesture at the time, it is fortunate he did so; I find myself in need of a husband and this stupid cowboy will serve my purposes. Perhaps you'll want to return to being my lady's maid?"

"No!" She would not stay anywhere in the proximity of the perfidious Mr. Jude Eastman nor his hateful wife. It would be more than she could bear.

"Then what's to become of you? You have nowhere to go, poor thing!" Daphne mocked.

"Get out of this room and don't come into it again," Annie warned.

Daphne just shook her head, saying, "My, my, would you listen to who is giving orders! In two days I shall give the order having you evicted from here as an imposter and a thief. Perhaps I shall send for a sheriff and file charges against you!"

"I said get out! For two more days *I* am Mrs. Jude Eastman and you had better remember it, Miss Armstrong. *Get out!*"

The door slammed on Daphne's angry exit.

All six leaves had to be put in the claw-footed round oak pedestal table to provide room for the group that assembled for lunch. Gil asked Tex and his wife Elmira to join them so he could discuss some business with his foreman afterward. There was also Mrs. Danvers and her son, Annie and Daphne, Jude and Jules—and Rance Whitebear.

At the sight of the Indian, both Daphne and

Annie stopped in the wide arched doorway of the dining room. Annie's fright of yesterday returned at the sight of the big, reddish-skinned man, but when he smiled at her it eased her fears and reminded her he was an old friend of Jude's. Shyly she returned his smile and continued on into the room. Jude quickly pulled out the chair beside him and she sat down before anyone could see she was shaking slightly.

"What is that heathen doing in this house?!?" Daphne exploded.

Both Jude and Jules started to speak, but it was Gil Eastman's gruff voice that loudly rebuked, "At the present time you are a guest at this table, just as he is, and I'll thank you to remember it. I'll not have our friends insulted. Not by *anyone*. You will soon become accustomed to our ways, I am sure. No man is measured by the color of his skin on my ranch."

Annie watched Daphne's expression. She was not used to being rebuked, and she was most upset because the only vacant place left at the table was next to Rance. Her eyes were flashing daggers when she flounced over and seated herself. Rance just stood there with his arms crossed on his chest.

Jules remembered to make the introductions before he sat down. First he introduced Annie to Elmira, then he said, "Daphne Armstrong, this is—"

"Eastman," Daphne corrected.

"As I was saying," Jules drawled, "this is Rance Whitebear. Jude and I went to school with him. Rance, meet Miss Armstrong. I believe you met Jude's wife, Anne, yesterday."

Annie started to acknowledge the introduction but Daphne interrupted, "Papa Eastman, make your son stop suggesting that my maid is my own husband's wife. It is too ludicrous to be believed. There is legal proof that it was I, Daphne Armstrong, who wed your son Jude. The certificate will prove it."

"I've said we'll get the letter as soon as possible—in the meantime, well, it's only natural for all of us to think of Annie as Jude's wife. Why don't you just consider the circumstances and try to overlook it."

"It upsets me too much. I can't ignore it."

"We shall all try not to make an issue of it— one way or the other. Now let's eat. Rance, why are you still standing like that?"

"No sit by old squaw who insults chief of tribe," Rance growled.

"These Indians are a proud breed," Jude hurried to explain to a thunderstruck Daphne. "The white man may possess their land, but they can't take away their fierce pride. Rance became chief of his tribe when his father died and he is used to receiving respect and being paid homage. Why, in his camp the squaws—women—are not even permitted at the same table. Try apologizing to him; maybe he can be persuaded to forget your outburst and sit by you."

Gil, Dannie, and Shawn could not believe their ears. First Rance acting high and mighty, and then Jude defending his ridiculous charade.

It was true Rance was a chief, but he had always come to the ranch just as a family friend and had been treated accordingly. His tribe had been broken up and sent to two or three different reservations.

Daphne glared maliciously at Jude and then at the Indian. Finally she said, "Oh, for heaven's sake, sit down. I'm sorry I insulted you. How was I to know you were a chief?"

Rance scowled menacingly at her for a moment longer. Then he barely opened his mouth and grunted, "Ugh!" before gingerly sitting on the chair, pulling it as far away from her as possible.

Gil decided he'd better put an end to this, even though it was amusing. "Annie," he asked to change the subject, "how did you happen to meet Rance yesterday? I thought he was here."

"He stopped at our—over at the sod house first."

"She thought I was stealing her horse," Rance explained.

"You must admit, it looked like it. You took his bridle and walked toward him," Annie defended herself.

"If I'd seen you, I'd have asked to borrow him. I didn't know there was anyone hiding out."

"Where were you hiding, Mrs. Eastman?" Shawn asked exuberantly.

Annie corrected him before Daphne could. "Please call me Annie."

"Okay. Where'd ja hide?"

Annie blushed. Jude raised his eyebrows questioningly at her, then glanced at Rance, who only shrugged his shoulders.

Annie admitted in embarrassment, "I was hiding in our—in the outhouse."

"So that's where you came from!" Rance acted pleased to learn this information. "I didn't see a sign of nobody till you yelled 'stop, thief!' and when I looked up, there she stood with an arrow from my own pack fitted to the bow and pointed right at my heart."

"Do you really know how to shoot a bow, ma'am?" Shawn wanted to know.

"You had him at your mercy, Anne?" Jules asked. "I never heard of anyone sneaking up on you, Rance, and with your own bow, too!"

"Where were you, Jude?" Gil sounded rather cross.

Rance interrupted, "I'll bet you can't really hit the broad side of a barn with an arrow, can you?"

"I most certainly can, and I'll prove it to you sometime," Annie promised.

"Wow!" was Shawn's verdict.

While everyone else started talking of other things, Jude quietly asked her, "Can you really shoot a bow?"

"I have many times before. It was a popular sport in England."

Jude gave her a searching glance and returned to his meal. Annie looked closely at him for the first time since they rode in. She wished she could read what was in his eyes, for she'd never seen this look before.

This exchange had not escaped Daphne's notice, and it did not please her at all. After lunch, she hustled up to Jude and possessively put both hands on his arm as she reminded him sweetly, "You forget yourself, Jude Eastman. I suppose it has become natural to whisper sweet nothings to my maid in public, but you must cease at once. I will not be humiliated. Do I make myself clear? I'll not tolerate it."

Jude distastefully removed Daphne's hands from his arm and warned her in a low voice, "I warned you once about insulting Annie. If you ever do it again, I'm going to forget you are a lady. I'm going to assume you are a spoiled, ill-bred child and turn you over my knee and spank you. Do I make *myself* clear?"

"Jude!" she whimpered and reached her arms out to stop him, but he was walking rapidly away. Pouting, she called after him, "Please come back. We must talk," but he just kept walking.

Annie missed the words between Jude and Daphne, but did see Daphne with her hands possessively on Jude's arm. She ran straight to her room and threw herself down on the bed. She was furious with herself—furious that it bothered her to see Daphne touch Jude and even more furious at herself for remembering what his touch did to her. She knew that Daphne had a wife's right to be possessive. It *had* been naive to sign the papers with Daphne's name, and besides she knew for a fact that Jude hated her. He had told her and shown her that over and over again.

How haughtily she had told Jude that he had

bought a wife but that he would never have her love, for it was not for sale. For sale? Heavens no! She had absurdly given it to him and received nothing in return. She had given her love to a despicable, mistress-loving rogue who hated her with a vengeance. In spite of knowing this, her insides had done somersaults when he'd looked at her with that special glance this noon. Wistfully she started to walk back and forth across the floor, pondering her predicament.

It was while she was nervously pacing that she saw the letter addressed to her on top of the tall chest-on-chest. She tore it open, wondering who could possibly have written a letter to Annie Ellis and sent it in care of Twin Trails, Cottonwood, Nebraska.

She sank down onto the edge of the bed to read it. It might be from the kindly Mrs. Barrister, she thought as she broke the seal.

The letter was from Carter.

My dearest Annie,

It is with heavy heart I send you this letter of sincere best wishes for your future happiness. There are no words to express the anguish Daphne's news caused me, for I honestly believed you were learning to care for me as I cared for you. When she wrote that you had married one of the cowhands who works for her husband, Jude, I could not believe it.

However, her letter convinced me that I would be wasting my time to come west to bring

*you back with me as I had planned. I can only
hope you find all the happiness you deserve—the
happiness I was hoping to give you as my wife.*

*I recalled your words about how you would
not marry me because it would hurt Maybelle.
Since I hadn't seen her in months I could only
believe this was some of Daf's mischief. Yet out
of loneliness and distress I did call on her one day
and I believe what you told me is true. She does
love me. I am now sincerely trying to return her
affections. It is most difficult when my heart is
still with you. Perhaps in time I may be able to
give her a mended one.*

*Sincerely yours,
Carter*

*P.S. Daphne's letter came to me from New
York, so she and Eastman must be taking an
extended wedding trip. I don't know why they
don't return to the ranch; she sounded disillusioned with New York.*

Annie read the letter once and then tried to
reread it a second time through her tears. Carter
had loved her! He had wanted to *marry* her. It
was Daphne's mischief which had caused Annie
to believe otherwise. She threw herself face
down on the bed, weeping from despair. She lay
there sobbing brokenly until she fell asleep from
exhaustion.

*   *   *

Jude tossed and turned on his bed at the far end of the bunkhouse. After the crude beds in the soddy this one was sheer comfort, but he still couldn't sleep. Instead, he lay there remembering over and over again the night Annie had told him that someday there would be something he would want that he could not buy. Love, for instance. It was not for sale. Love had to be earned, she had warned him. God above! Why hadn't he listened? He would give everything he'd ever hoped to possess just to have that true love of hers she had talked about.

Daphne had tried to talk to him alone several times today. The grizzly had even gone so far as to imply that Annie had been her brother's mistress, but Jude didn't believe it for a minute. Annie had too much pride. Besides, a man would be insane to make a woman like Annie his mistress instead of his wife.

It might well be that rejection by this stuffed shirt Carter caused her to come here. If he was anything like his sister, he probably would be fool enough to want only a highbrow wife. Jude knew down inside that Annie *had* taken sacred vows to be a wife to him. She had heatedly told him so too often for him to doubt it. If only she had come out of her room today so he could have talked to her!

Jules had ridden out early this morning so he could be back tomorrow. There was no longer any hope of being alone with Annie to apologize and try to convince her he loved her or to persuade her to tell him the truth of this drama.

Jude refused to even think of a marriage to

Daphne Armstrong, a woman who was a carbon copy of his mother. No matter what Pa wanted or how binding the legal statutes were, Jude would have no part of it. He'd give up Twin Trails if he had to and find a way to get out of any such tangle, for he was going to spend the rest of his life trying to win Annie's love.

Chapter Seventeen

✦ ✦ ✦ ✦ ✦

ANNIE STAYED IN her room until she saw Jules ride into the yard the next afternoon. She had accepted the trays of food Mrs. Danvers had brought up to her, but she had refused to see anyone else who knocked at her door. There was nothing to say.

Critically she took a last look at herself in the mirror before going downstairs. She was wearing the red and black chintz dress she had purchased in Chicago; it was much too warm for this weather, but she could not bring herself to wear one of Daphne's gowns. She'd considered wearing one of the split-skirted riding ensembles she had made for herself, then she could just mount Pegasus and leave after the truth was revealed. Would they even allow her to keep the beautiful stallion?

Jude had waited at the foot of the stairs since

Pa had informed everyone that Jules was coming up the lane. He needed to see Annie to be sure she was all right. Hiding in her room this way was not like her. Something more than this marriage thing must have happened.

As he watched her come down the stairs, he was sure of it. His wife looked beautiful in her stylish, brightly colored gown, but she also looked lost and forlorn. Once more he wished he had the right to take her in his arms and promise her everything would be all right, but he had lost that privilege, forfeited it that first night when he had rejected her. He prayed she'd let him make it up to her. Jude did not touch her when she reached the bottom step, although he wanted to. He could not even get her to meet his eyes.

Annie politely greeted everyone and assured them she was fine. Then she went and stood looking out the window at the Sandhills, the land she loved. The land she would soon be leaving.

"Papa Eastman." Daphne's shrill voice could easily be heard above the others. "Let us dispense with any trite conversation and get on to the letter. You did find the communication from his lawyer, didn't you?" she asked Jules. As he nodded, she ordered, "Read it, for it will put an end to this nonsense once and for all!"

"Yes, it will, won't it," Gil commented. "This certificate Hank mailed to me should stamp finish to it."

No one moved or spoke as Gil tore open the

seal and scanned the enclosed document. Slowly he admitted, "This is my son's signature, I can vouch for that, and there's not a doubt in my mind it isn't Henry Fellman's, for I've seen his often enough. Was the pastor a Reverend Tolliver?"

Daphne did not answer but looked at Annie for confirmation. Annie verified in a near whisper, "Yes, it was Reverend Tolliver who officiated at the ceremony."

"Then everything is right and tight. It's all here. Legal and binding. The identical copy to the one on record in the Chicago courthouse lists the bride's name as—Annie Ellis."

Jude let out his long-held breath and mumbled, "Thank God." It was impossible to read any expression on Gil's face.

Daphne and Annie were both stricken speechless for a moment, but Daphne recovered within seconds and screeched, "You lie! That says Daphne Armstrong on there. Let me see it." She nearly grabbed it from Gil's hands, then proclaimed, "It's a fake!"

"You told me the certificate was the legal proof, Daphne," Gil reminded her. "Now you're telling me it isn't?"

"It's not. Jules must have changed the name!" she accused.

"Well," Gil said, pondering the matter, "the signature doesn't appear to be altered, nor would Jules do such a thing. If you doubt me, I suppose we'll have to have Hank get that preacher and bring him all the way out here. The two of them can undoubtedly identify the girl who took the vows.''

The color drained from Daphne's face but she refused to be bested. ''They would probably lie, too!''

''Lie?'' Jules asked. ''Pa's trusted attorney and a man of God? I doubt that, Miss Armstrong. However, I disagree with Pa. We don't need their word; I'll settle for Anne's word any day. Did you take those proxy vows, little sister?''

Annie looked at him so honestly that he knew she had before she replied, ''Yes, I did. It was I who took the vows, Jules.''

Jude informed everyone, ''The subject is closed. Annie Ellis Eastman is my wife, for better or for worse, till death do us part, and that's the end of it.''

Annie was shocked at Jude's outburst, yet she sensed Jude would hate being married to Daphne even more than he hated being married to her. What she couldn't understand was how her name had gotten on the document when she had signed Daphne's name to it.

Daphne had turned her venom on Annie now, swearing, ''You scheming little bitch. I don't know how your name got there, but I'll see you repaid for this dastardly trick. Papa will straighten it out for me.'' Gil, Jude, and Jules all started to protest at once but it was Annie who responded.

''No! You are the schemer, Daphne. The word dastardly does not even begin to describe the foul tricks you perpetrated on me—and on your own brother. You are lower than the lowest snake, and I'm glad Geoffrey Beaumont didn't give you the glamorous life he promised. You deserve whatever befalls you. Selling the beautiful jewels you inherited from your mother was despicable, and when your father and Carter find out what you did, I'm glad I won't be in your shoes.

"Incidentally, I had a letter from Carter—oh, don't look so downcast. Your malicious letter reached him. It hurt him as you knew it would, since he cared for me and was planning to *marry* me, but there was one thing you didn't count on; he is going to marry your friend Maybelle now."

"Not Maybelle Meyers! I can't stand that goody-two-shoes! I loathe her . . . look, Annie, I will telegraph Carter and confess that I lied. He'll want you back, I know he will—and you can tell everyone here that the proxy wedding was really mine. Couldn't you? Please, Annie! You have to do this for me! There are things you don't understand. I must remain in this proxy marriage, but—you—why, you can go back and live in our mansion in Chicago as Carter's wife—," she wheedled.

The two women had forgotten anyone else was in the room until a firm masculine voice interrupted, "No. Annie is not leaving here. She is my wife." Both of the women turned at once to look at Jude.

Gil offered, "Is that how you want it, Annie girl? To stay here in the Sandhills where you belong?"

Annie did not hesitate. "Yes!"

"Then, Daphne, I shall take you back to North Platte tomorrow," Gil declared, "and put you on the train. I'll telegraph your father to expect you and that he can count on my backing for at least another year or two. That should get him out of the red. Perhaps you can contrive a story about your adventures, but if you cast any aspersions on any of the Eastmans, including my daughter-in-law, my agreement to support your father's plant will be revoked. Do we understand each other?" He didn't wait for a reply but went on, "Jules, help your brother carry his things from the bunkhouse back to his and Annie's room. Everything has been cleared up here now."

Not everything, Annie thought. How was Jude going to sneak out of a second-story window to go back to the bunkhouse? Well, one thing was certain: she had a home at last. A forever kind of home.

Annie found herself pacing her bedroom floor as she waited for Jude to come upstairs that night. She had dressed for bed thinking she would pretend to be asleep when he sneaked through her room, but then she recalled she would undoubtedly have to help him climb down to the ground, so she tied her wrapper over her nightgown and impatiently awaited his arrival.

As soon as he stepped in the door she asked, "Where is your rope?"

"What rope?" he pretended not to understand

what she was talking about. He had been lucky enough to get another chance with Annie, and this time he would not play the fool.

"You know," she explained as if to a child, "the rope to tie to the balcony railing for you to climb down."

"Annie. Those little posts on the balcony would not hold my weight. They would break in two."

"Oh!" She bit her lip as she looked around for an alternative. "We'll just have to tie it to the bed headboard and you can climb through the window as you did at Double Tree. We will brace the bed against a wall and I'll hold tight and pull against it with my weight. You know I'm strong."

"I'll vouch for that, honey, but we have no rope."

"Don't call me that. There is no one here to impress with your falseness."

"And if I told you it was not a falsehood?"

"I should merely consider the source and ignore such a lie," she firmly informed him. "I know—we will knot sheets together into a rope."

Annie had no reason to trust him, Jude was well aware of that. He had to give her time. "You must know there are not enough sheets in this room to make a rope long enough. No, there is nothing for it, Annie. I have to stay here. I'm sure Pa contrived something to make my marriage to you legal, and I don't want him to think his efforts weren't appreciated.

"Even if I were to find a way to climb down, he would be bound to hear the speculations from the bunkhouse. I don't want that. As I said, I'm grateful for whatever he did to rid me of that Chicago grizzly."

"Yes, for she might not have been so agreeable to allowing you to keep your mistress as I."

"I gave you my word about that, Annie. Can't you trust anything I say?"

"Trust that your father had hallucinations and imagined this ranch? Trust that my home here was to be a soddy? Exactly what does this word 'trust' mean to you? The only thing I trust is that you will recall the vow you swore to me the day we met, and get out of this bedroom."

"That's one vow I made that I will keep until you release me from it. I don't plan to sleep in your bed, Annie, just here on the floor, if you will permit me to." He knew he could give her no believable reason for his earlier lies and abuse.

"On the floor? In here?"

"It is no different than in the soddy, is it? Except that you will have a more comfortable bed, while I have one even less comfortable. Please."

Annie had never heard Jude use the word 'please' with such humility. This was his own house. His own room, in fact. She hated to concede to him after the lies he had told her about everything because he hated her so much. However, he was right about his father's interference and it had benefited her even more than it had Jude. She had no choice. He must not either, or he wouldn't be here. Reluctantly, she agreed.

"It will be all right, I suppose, but I don't think there are any comforters in here since it's summer. Perhaps tomorrow I can find the linen closet and get you two or three."

"The floor will be fine for me, Annie, if you'll just give me a pillow. Turn back your covers now while I snuff out the lamp."

Annie carefully pulled down the lovely quilt and folded it over the footboard of the bed. The lamp was out now but enough moonlight filtered through the window for her to pull down the sheets and remove her wrapper. She could tell Jude was trying to fit his heel into the bootjack without being able to see it properly. He must have succeeded, for first one boot hit the floor and then the other.

"Here is your pillow," Annie offered in a husky voice as she walked toward him in the moonlit room. Up close she could see that he was now unbuttoning his shirt. Even from the distance that separated them she could sense his virility, and it stirred something deep within her. The slight male scent of him overwhelmed her and she found herself heatedly remembering the sight of him without his shirt on, cutting down the cottonwood tree. Disgusted with herself, she shoved the pillow in his direction.

Jude reached out to take the pillow from her, but accidentally grasped her arm instead. He could feel the warmth of her pulsating body through the worn fabric of her nightgown. He knew he should let go of her, but he couldn't. She was not struggling to pull free, yet he felt a tenseness in the way she stood, offering him the pillow.

Casually he took it and dropped it to the floor with one hand, gently pulling her up against his bare chest with the other. Soon she was flat against him and he was enfolding her with both arms as he hoarsely whispered, "Annie. Annie girl," and then he was kissing her. He lifted her slightly off the floor to nestle her closer to him. Her lips were soft and sweet and responding. His heart thudded harder. His lips released her, and he raised his face a few inches to try to read her eyes. It was too dark. He turned his face at a slight angle to keep hers where he could savor her mouth more fully with his craving kisses.

He kissed her until both were breathless. This time he only lifted his lips an inch above hers, inhaled deeply, and then their lips were pressed ravenously together again. Jude lowered his hands from her waist to her buttocks to snuggle her more tightly against him.

The feel of her firm breasts against his chest excited Jude tremendously. He pried her lips apart with his tongue and gently used it to probe the sweetness within her mouth.

Annie had not expected Jude's kiss when she handed him his pillow. She had herself completely convinced that he did not love nor want her. Since she was not prepared for the kiss, she was not prepared to resist. At the first touch of his lips, her body betrayed her. It revelled in being held so close to him that it could easily feel the heat of his bare chest against her breasts. They immediately joined the mutiny by puckering their tips into hard tight knots that pulled forward to encounter the erratic feel of his heartbeat. Her own double-crossing heart was matching his, beat for rapid beat. Even her legs were perfidious, for Annie knew if Jude were to put her down they would not hold her. Her insurgent body encouraged her arms to steal around his neck and her hands to move up into his thick, curly hair, then down to his shoulders, on to the inviting soft springy mass of hair on his chest, his bulging arm muscles, back up to his cheeks to hold his face firmly against hers, then return to swirl through his hair again.

Annie had never known such hard, deep, demanding kisses. Jude's body had conquered the revolution of her own and was making it do as he willed it to. It was offering him total capitulation and Annie was sure he knew he had won, for his body had engulfed hers completely as they lay across the bed. She had not even realized it when her disobedient limbs walked with him to the edge of the bed, nor sunk down upon it.

His hands were everywhere, demanding her complete surrender. He had untied her nightie and was tenderly inciting her riotous breasts. She was turning, spinning, whirling. There was no end to this mutiny. She didn't want it to end until it had satiated the havoc of her passionate needs, for they had become real and urgent.

Jude had known women intimately since he was in his teens, but never had he been so completely ensnared as he was tonight. He had been mistaken about Annie; she was not a prudish, cold spinster, but instead the most warm and loving woman he had ever known. As she met his passion and needs with passion and needs of her own, his body twisted him into such a furor of torment he thought he could not wait another minute to take her completely. He knew he had brought her desire to a peak where it matched his own.

He did not want just Annie's body, he fiercely reminded himself. Bodies could be bought. Young, inexperienced girls could be seduced—and this was exactly what he had done. She was no twenty-six-year-old spinster but an innocent eighteen-year-old girl. Tonight she would permit him to take her body, but what about tomorrow? Would she hate him for breaking the last of his vows to her? Would there be any trust left to base a marriage on? Could love be built on such a foundation? Not true love. Not the kind of love and marriage he wanted to share with her.

Jude kissed Annie very softly now, only a whisper of a kiss as his fingers continued to slowly and tenderly brush across the nipple of her alluring breast. One more thing he had been wrong about. They were not small at all, but generous round globes which had always been well hidden under the fullness of the dresses she wore.

Jude pleaded, breaking their wordless lovemaking, "Release me from my vow, Annie, my love, tell me I can continue to show my love for you, sweetheart. That I may share your bed. I was wrong to ever swear such nonsense as that I would not want you. Tonight has proved me a liar once again, for I want you, woman. I want you in every way a man can want his wife. Say you release me, please. Say it and mean it with all your heart."

If Jude had not spoken, Annie's mind would have remained in the state of destruction where her mutinous body had placed it. She would have reveled in the consummation of this love-making. Her body needed the fulfillment she sensed Jude could give it. But his words brought coherent thought to her mind. She began to wonder what tonight was all about. Another humiliation? Lust because he had been away from his mistress for so long? An act he felt he owed as repayment to his father? Was it possible for a man to hold a woman and want to kiss her this way and not love her—even a little? She just did not know.

"I don't know," she finally whispered. "I don't understand you. I don't understand anything, not even myself."

How could she understand, Jude thought sadly, when he had given her only reasons to misunderstand.

He began to retie her gown, for he wanted her too much to take her when there was any doubt left in her mind. Tonight had told him everything he needed to know. He had a passionate, loving wife, and he was confident that he could make her fall in love with him. For this he could wait as long as it took.

"We'll talk about this again, my precious. Right now I want you to get some sleep. I suspect you didn't get much the last couple of nights, from the circles under your eyes today."

"I *was* worried about what was to become of me, Jude, for I did sign that certificate with Daphne's name. She wished to run away with her—with Mr. Beaumont. He was a gambler, so her father would not give his consent. They went to New York. So that she would not be missed, she persuaded me to marry you and come here in her place. Her father and her brother thought she kept the bargain. They were not part of the deceit. I wanted to leave Chicago, for I thought I was going to have to work in a manufactory. I had to work in the mills back in England, in Birmingham, and I hated it. I hate being shut up indoors. I grew up on my Grandfather Ellis' farm and I loved it there . . . but he is dead now. I had nowhere to go, so I went along with her plans out of desperation . . . no, I confess I wasn't that desperate, I entered the scheme hoping for a better life for myself, but I was afraid when it was Daphne's name on the certificate, I would be sent away from here. Then there was Carter's letter, which was waiting here for me. It upset me, too."

"Then you loved him a great deal?" This was a question Jude Eastman had wanted to ask all day.

"It was not love, but I cared for him. Perhaps one day it might have turned into love, but Daphne convinced me he wanted me only as a—a—mistress. This I could not accept. That what I had mistaken for caring was something so demeaning. I am glad I received his letter, for it makes me feel better about myself, that I am not always a poor judge of character.

"The only good part of it was that Daphne's efforts to convince me Carter had a fiancée backfired. I found her friend Maybelle was so in love with him that her world would have ended had she lost him. Carter has now discovered Maybelle's love and is beginning to return it. I think they will find lasting happiness with one another."

Jude could not hide his relief. *How very much she had been through!* No wonder she had stood in his room that first night looking like a sad and forlorn little waif.

"You have had to bear a lifetime's troubles in only a few short years, and one day soon I shall spend the entire day convincing you how glad I am that they all happened—because they led you to me. Now you sleep. May I just hold you in my arms so you'll know you are safe and secure now?"

For her answer, Annie snuggled down into the crook of his arm up against his side. Cozily she lay there and thought of how differently Jude had acted from Dev when she ended their lovemaking. Jude had not acted angry nor cast her from his arms. He had continued to hold her until their passion was bearable. If only she could believe it was because he loved her more than Dev had. If only she could believe he loved her at all!

Jude gathered Annie more tightly into his arms when he heard the soft, even breathing of her sleep. God, how he loved this feisty little bride of his. Tonight he had hopes that his passion-filled thoughts of the last three days might become realities. He vowed he would go very slowly with her until he gained her trust—and her love.

Chapter Eighteen

✦✦✦✦

WHEN OLD BERT had the audacity to drive his freight wagon right up to the lane of the Twin Trails ranch loaded with cedar posts and rolls of barbed wire, the ranch hands expected all hell to break loose. The recently invented wire with its sharp points every few inches was a menace to the cattlemen. It meant homesteaders could fence off their plowed-up acreage with only one or two strands of wire, not four or five as they'd needed before, with posts close together to make it strong enough to resist a determined cow.

Bert cracked his whip. "Whoa, you damnable

mangy relatives of a mule. Whoa, I say, cuss your miser'ble hides." Once more he cracked the whip as the wagon stopped with some final clangs and thuds and a few last rattles of the six-horse chain hitch. The cowhands didn't know what Bert was doing so far off his regular freight run, but they did know he was going to be ordered off this place for being a traitor. He'd be lucky if no one took a shot at his own miserable hide. All activity stopped as everyone watched Jude stride purposefully out to the loaded wagon, but he didn't yell or even brandish his six-shooter. He only motioned on beyond the barn, and Bert proceeded to drive the wagon down that way.

There were a lot of mystified looks among the men nearby. Rance and Tex didn't wait for answers, but went to Jude's side. Jules had also come out of the house to join the group around his brother. He asked, "What are you thinkin' of, lettin' that slimy nester-lover on the place, little brother? Run him off no matter what excuse he gives you for needing a place to stop off on his run!"

"He's stopping to unload my order."

"You're kidding! Jude, your old man is gonna disown you sure. I've ramrodded for him enough years, I know he'd never put up a fence 'cept like the wooden one around the house, never barbed wire," Tex warned.

All three men were flabbergasted when Jude announced, "Pa's not. I am. That was only one of my reasons for wanting to run this place.

Another is cutting and stacking prairie hay for winter feeding. Pa never went for that, either, but it has to be done. The past few mild winters aren't going to last forever, and while the hills here will be some protection from blizzards, we still need feed. A blizzard can wipe out half a herd, and you all know it."

"But stringing wire?"

"I don't intend to feed all the damn cattle in the countryside over the winter, only my own. You must see that I can keep from overgrazing if I put up fence. I know how much pasture and water I have, and I'll put cows on it accordingly."

"I hate to admit it, but you're even making sense to a fence-hating Indian," Rance remarked. "I thought fences were invented for reservations and army posts—to keep Indians in or out according to the whim of the day."

Tex was still shaking his head as he claimed, "I can't be a part of doing this to your pa, boy. He's gonna be back today or tomorrow from takin' that critter to North Platte and he's gonna be upset as hell. Barbed wire!" He shook his head again.

"Pa knows I bought it, Tex. I'm putting crews to work today installing it. I've held the herd stationary and had riders out since we got here to turn back anybody else's herds that wandered this way. Strangely enough, there's only been a couple to turn back. It seems I'm not the only rancher up here who feels this way. Ramsey's Bar D to the south of us even volunteered to pay for half the fence between our places and to furnish a posthole digging crew. I suspect our other neighbors will do likewise."

Every available man was put to work to get the ranch lands fenced. Gil had sent a message he had to return to Double Tree on business, but he'd be back soon to see how the consarned fence was coming along. They all knew this was as close to consent to a barbed-wire fence they'd ever hear from an old range cattleman like Gil Eastman! Two other adjoining ranches had agreed to help pay for the fence and to send crews to help install it.

Annie was busy working on a wall of her own. She had gathered all the rocks she could find and was using them to enclose Mrs. Danvers' carefully planted flowers in an attempt to keep the dogs and chickens out. Jude asked her teasingly one night as she lay in bed beside him, if she missed building walls so much that she had found a substitute! He had never again tried to make love to her, but each night they shared the double bed. When he pulled her beside him, Annie's traitorous body wanted him to do more, but he'd only kiss her hair and whisper, "Good night, honey." Within minutes he'd be slightly snoring. Either digging postholes was as tiring as plowing sod, Annie thought, or else he had accepted her refusal and was relieved by it.

She could no longer keep from loving her husband. Even remembering his past behavior didn't deter her; she knew if it still mattered, she wouldn't love so much to cuddle close to his warm bare chest when she went to sleep each night.

"The rock walls remind me of England," Annie told him, "and it pleases Mrs. Danvers to have someone care about her flowers. She loves pretty things and I fear she has had few in her lifetime. When I accused her of working too hard crocheting or embroidering every spare minute she has, she told me I didn't know what a luxury it was just to have the threads to work with."

"She has had a rather bleak existence. Her husband seemed plagued with misfortune; he tried ranching and was burned out by a big prairie fire, so he moved east and went into farming, but the drought hit three years in a row and ended that venture. Finally he worked for a blacksmith in Omaha for a meager wage until his death. Dannie has told us often enough how much it means for her and Shawn just to have food to eat.

"You weren't ever that poor, were you, honey? You said you had to work in the mills in England. A drifter who wintered over at the Double Tree a couple of years ago told us that was a miserable existence."

"Oh, it was, Jude!" Annie no longer reprimanded him when he called her "honey." She had grown used to it. Deep inside she even admitted she liked the possessive way he said it. "It was the long hours in such a dark and gloomy place that I hated the most. I never saw the sunlight except on Sundays, and then only through overhanging smoke. It was bad, but at least I didn't have to go hungry. I lived at my aunt's lodging house. The food was not very tasty as a rule, but it was edible."

"I hate to even think of you having to live that way. You were born to be riding free. I love watching you ride Pegasus. Maybe tomorrow we could meet for a gallop. I'll quit early. Ride south to the corner of the fencing, and I'll meet you there about four. You will meet me, won't you?"

"I'd like that. I only hope I can slow Pegasus down so Rocky can keep up!" she teased.

"Sure of yourself, aren't you? In a race Rocky would leave your Pegasus in the dust."

"Is that a challenge?"

"It is—just as you are."

Annie did not quite know how to interpret this, so she just moved a little closer and sleepily vowed, "Pegasus will win."

"And what's the winner's prize going to be, sweetheart? I'll take a kiss from you for mine."

"That's agreeable with me, too," she mumbled and she felt his arm close a little tighter about her as she drifted off to sleep.

Work stopped on the construction of the rock wall several times the next afternoon as Annie went to check on the time, or sent Shawn in to check it for her. She wanted to quit early enough to put on her favorite riding skirt and the pale yellow blouse Daphne had given her with ruffles at the neck and on the sleeves, for today she was going to resume her role of seductress. She was going to take her hair down from the braids she had wrapped around her head and pin the front up into a pompadour, letting the back flow free. Jude had once commented on how much he liked her hair long and loose. Yearningly she thought of the prize of a kiss and the possibility that Jude might twist his fingers in her long hair as he held her to kiss her. Just the thought sent shivers running up and down her spine. "Jude Eastman," she thought, "this is the day your royal highness is going to be felled, the day I move a mountain!"

Hoping she hadn't arrived too early, Annie slowed Pegasus to a walk when she came into view of the corner fence post. Jude wasn't in sight. She was sure she was safe this close to the house, but since her encounter with Rance she had never ventured very far away.

Eagerly anticipating Jude's arrival, she stopped and permitted Pegasus to nibble some grass as she waited by the end post for her arrogant husband. They were working west of here today, he'd said.

Annie would never have ridden the few feet farther to the top of the hill if she had not heard Rocky whinny. It was a riderless, impatient sound, and she concluded Jude had stopped off to inspect the new fence. Before she reached the crest of the hill, she could see across the tall

grass to the rim of a low canyon made by a
washout where Jude was standing—with his
mistress! That beautiful red hair of hers was
impossible to mistake. It was Mrs. O'Mara,
proprietress of Cattleman's Haven in Cattle
Creek. He had brought her to the Sandhills to be
with him again!

Annie felt the thud of her heart as it dropped
into the pit of her stomach. Shooting pains flew
into every part of her as she watched the woman's arms go up around Jude's neck so seduc-
tively. So this was why he had asked her to meet
him here—so she could witness one more humiliation! Had he sensed she was becoming
complacent, beginning to care for him? Had he
wanted to remind her of how things really were
between them? Well! She needed no reminder!
Angrily she whirled Pegasus around and headed
back to the ranch.

The rapid movement caught Jude's eye; he
glanced toward the rise of the hill just in time to
see Annie's raven hair flying out of sight. He
roughly pushed Rosie away from him and ran
toward his horse, calling back over his shoulder,
"Accept it, Rosie. I won't be coming back!" He
swiftly mounted Rocky and lashed him lightly
with the reins to give the command for the
horse's fastest gait.

Damn!

Damn Rosie! Whatever possessed her to come
out here today? When she had written him,
telling him she was waiting for him in Cottonwood, he had let her know in no uncertain terms

that he would never be coming to visit her again. Unfortunately, she hadn't accepted it; she was trying to ruin everything.

Annie was riding like the wind to keep him from catching her and explaining. He applied his seldom-used spurs to the horse's flanks, hoping to overtake her before she reached the house. He had to make her listen to him, and, more important, to believe him.

He knew exactly what that little firebrand was thinking right now. She was thinking he'd sent for Rosie to move up here, and that he had planned for her to see him today. *Damn* Rosie! All the progress he had made with Annie would be lost!

Annie urged Pegasus to go his fastest, but Jude was gaining on her. Rocky was a bigger stallion with an extra long gait. The jubilantly challenged race had become one for her very life. She didn't ever want to see Jude Eastman again as long as she lived. If she could just get to the house before he overtook her, she would run upstairs to their room and lock herself in. Annie did not think beyond that, for her mind was too filled with what she had just witnessed. Jude must be an abbreviation for Judas. Yes, he was a Judas! A two-timing, word-breaking, lying traitor! The ranch house was close now, but not close enough.

Someone had shut the split-rail gate at the end of the lane. If she stopped to undo the latch, Jude would have more than enough time to catch up with her. In the training ring she had not worked on high hurdles with Pegasus, yet she was confident he could make it. Quickly she flapped the reins from one side to the other, then leaned forward so she and the horse would be as one when they vaulted the gate. Pegasus easily made the jump and continued to gallop up the lane.

Jude's horse was a quick-cutting, stop-and-start cow pony, not a jumper, so it took only seconds to lift the loop that held the gate closed and open it enough to let Rocky through. Then Jude was demanding the most the horse could give with a nip from his spurs. He, too, was leaning far forward in the saddle to give Rocky speed.

Finally he was beside Annie and planned to waylay her when she jumped off her horse. He suspected his fiery wife intended to run inside and lock their bedroom door, and he wanted a chance to explain to her without a confrontation in the house where they might be overheard. Even Jules would misinterpret Rosie's showing up at the house today.

Neither of the riders noticed Gil's buckboard or the group assembled on the steps to watch the end of this race until a cacophony of cheering broke out. Annie was forced to act jovial as she stood on the porch steps, accepting congratulations from the family. Everyone was talking at once.

She nearly missed Gil's quiet comment. "Annie girl, I sold the Double Tree. One of the buyers was a friend of yours—Devbridge Rossington? He was acting on behalf of his family, an earl or something, he said. They were part of a group of foreign investors trying to take advantage of the supposed forty percent profit the cattle industry is paying."

"Dev—? Dev's here? In America? In *Nebraska?*"

"Yes, and he knows you're here. He very much wants to see you. Guess you know what I told him! Never to show his face around here! 'Course, he's in North Platte; if you want to see him, I can't stop you, for he tells me you are his in every way."

"Well, I'm *not!*" Annie swore vehemently and turned toward the front door. She hadn't seen Jude come up onto the steps after giving their horses to Rance to rub down. At the sight of him, the realization that he had overheard the conversation hit her, and she knew her face flushed a violent red. However, she owed this traitor no explanations, so she merely hurried on into the house to help with supper preparations. Devbridge Rossington was blocked from her mind by Jude's betrayal today, and she thought the evening would never end so she could get away from him.

While Annie had blocked Dev from her thoughts, the Englishman was all Jude could think of. Over and over again Pa's words rang, "You are his in every way." When he saw Annie start up the steps at bedtime, he thought of that skeleton key in their door lock and was right behind her, taking the steps three at a time.

Annie opened the door to their room and was trying to push it closed, but Jude managed to get one hand inside the frame and the other on the knob. It was easy to force his way in.

She was visibly trembling and as white as the lace curtains on the window. "Get out of here. Get out or I'll scream!"

"You won't scream, Annie, for you know it might cause Pa to have another heart attack."

She answered with controlled fury. "What are you doing here? Until today I thought we might have a marriage; I have learned we do not. You have made a mockery of it once too often. The whole thing was a sham, and that sham has ended."

"I assure, Annie, our marriage is no sham and I did not mock it. I give you my word on that."

She stared at him. His word meant nothing; he would swear anything to cushion his conscience! "I swore the day I gave my love to the man I was to marry in England, I would never be humiliated again, but you—"

Jude did not hear the rest of her words; he suddenly felt as if the floor had given way beneath him. All his frustration, his anger at Rosie and at himself, suddenly focused on Annie. She had deceived him all along. She had had a lover in England!

Women! They were all alike, just as he'd known long ago, except that this one's innocent act was more contemptible than either Ma's or Rosie's, for it had trapped him. She'd made a damned fool of him! How she must be laughing at him! No wonder she had been agreeable to his mistress—she had already been the mistress of another man. His innocent little wife, whom he had been nurturing so gently because he thought she was a youthful virgin, had in truth been eager to keep him from finding out she had already belonged to another man!

"I have been an ignorant ass, haven't I, for not taking what is mine when others have gone before me."

"What are you saying?"

"Not what am *I* saying. It's what *you're* saying. It was that earl's kid, wasn't it?"

Annie did not know what Jude was talking about, but he sounded jealous. She thought of him and his redheaded mistress and wanted to hurt him, so she replied, "Yes, it was!"

"You bitch! You admit it!"

Jude grabbed for her, pulled her roughly up against him, and kissed her violently. His teeth almost sank into her soft lips as he crushed his mouth hard against hers. Barely giving her time to trap a breath of air, he forced her mouth open and plunged his tongue inside. It was plundering into every corner of her mouth with such hard, pulsating thrusts that Annie feared she might faint both from lack of air and from her boiling indignation at Jude's attack.

For it was an attack, not a kiss. He had pulled her inches off the floor as he always did, but this time his hands held her buttocks firmly while he rotated his own hips and began to grind the hardness of his manhood against her. She felt only revulsion and tried to thrash her arms and beat him on the back and shoulders, wherever she could land a blow. She was flushed with anger and indignant hurt and wished he would stop these savage kisses so she could tell him so. He did not release her, but continued the onslaught as they slowly sank to the floor, both too weak from lack of breath to remain standing. When she tried to kick and push free, he only put a booted foot across her legs to hold them and held her hands above her head while his other hand and his lips continued the aggression.

As soon as he immobilized her he took his hand and easily ripped first her blouse and then her chemise to the waist. How she hated him! And yet, in the midst of this abhorrent attack her body was getting hotter and hotter, like the raging fires of hell. As he began to use his mouth and teeth to nip and draw turbulently at her breasts, she discovered this repugnant act was making her throb somewhere deep inside and it enraged her all the more.

She tried to turn her head when his mouth returned to hers, but he would not allow it. Firm fingers took hold of her face and turned it so he could resume crushing her tender, sore lips. The nipples on her breasts traitorously stood in peaks, as if to entreat him to return his attentions to them. Every inch of her was ablaze and she hated both him and herself for this final, demeaning degradation.

Jude was surely through shaming her now, for

he was breathing heavily and his kisses had stopped again. No, not stopped, for now he was kissing her eyes, her ears, her nose, her chin, her neck, the valley between her breasts, then her navel, each kiss searing her body just a little more than the one before. She felt all the button loops on her best riding skirt ripped from their anchors and the skirt as well as her ruffled undies were pushed down, then pulled off over her feet. She tried to use her now-free hands to cover herself, but instead she found herself covered by Jude's body. At some time he had pulled down his own trousers, for she felt the hardness of him bare against her own inflamed skin. He was going to inflict the most demeaning humiliation upon her—break the vow he had made to her, and she loathed him for it, but her rebellious body was pounding with quivering vibrations and would welcome anything which could quell the inferno inside.

She tried to remind him of his vow, but his lips were passionately upon hers again and his hands rapidly seduced her body. When he guided his hardened staff to the blaze between her legs, she tried to prevent his entry by moving from one side to the other. This only incited him more and he stabbed into the burning coals with such a scorching pain that she cried out in spite of his attempt to silence her with kisses. It hurt so much she could not hold back her tears.

Even as it hurt, it began to ease some of the torture. Jude had suddenly slowed down and seemed to be treating her with a gentle tenderness. He murmured desolately, "Annie, Annie, why do I always have to be so wrong about you? Oh, my god! My beloved virgin bride! What have I done to you?" He continued to stroke her gently as he entangled his fingers in her hair and give her soft, intimate kisses everywhere. A little more of the pain subsided with each stroke and at last Annie felt a tremor quaking inside which magnificently released the pent-up inferno.

When Jude felt Annie relax in his arms he permitted his own climax, but it was not the vanquishing one he had planned, nor a jubilant release as he had hoped it would be for his first time with Annie. Instead, it was only the end of a devastating pillage. He had raped his own beautiful, loving wife.

Of course she had been no man's mistress. Not his Annie! He suspected she had run from the mere suggestion of it in England, as she had in Chicago, and run to—what? A depraved husband who brutally ravished her body in a manner no man would use with the lowest whore.

She was still lying there, crying softly from humiliation, pain, and debauchment. He stood up, pulling up and buttoning his trousers as he did so. She did not move. Did not say a word. He had even broken that fiery spirit of hers that should have been lashing out at him now with every despicable word she knew.

Gently he picked her up and carried her to the bed. Holding her cradled in one arm with a knee up under her for support, he pulled back the quilt and sheet, then lay her down on the pillow. She remained unmoving, still sobbing soundlessly. He removed the remnants of her pretty blouse and skirt, ones she must have put on special for him today, for he had not recognized them. He found the linen face cloth on the towel rack attached to one end of the commode and poured water from the pitcher into the wash basin. It was still light enough out to see the white ironstone pitcher with its matching bowl. Taking the wash basin to the bed, he carefully washed Annie from head to toe. Washed the filth of himself off her, then dried her with his own shirt.

He knew he should sleep on the floor, but could not resist slipping into bed and trying to pull her consolingly into his arms. "Dear God, I'm sorry, Annie. Oh, honey, I''m so sorry! Please, please, try to forgive me."

At last she moved. She pulled to the farthest edge of the bed, as far away from him as she could get, and said, "Not only the word of an Eastman mocked, but the final vow broken!" Then she began to sob as if her heart would break.

Once again Jude tried to pull her into his arms to comfort her, begging, "Please, Annie, let me hold you. Please don't cry."

She shrugged his arms away, saying vehemently, "Don't ever touch me again!"

He knew he had no right.

Both of them lay awake long hours into the

night, Jude filled with recriminations, Annie with a too-often-mended heart. This time it had been shredded, torn asunder, and she feared it might never become whole again.

Chapter Nineteen

+ + + +

AT DAYBREAK JUDE saw the full impact of his brutality. Annie's lips were swollen, and her lower lip had an obvious cut made by a tooth. Her beautiful body had small bruises here and there, even on her lovely breasts. Where he had kissed her neck, the valley between her breasts, and even on her abdomen there were purple marks from the pressure of those searing kisses. Her eyes had dark circles under them and even though they were still closed, the red puffiness around them was obvious. He wanted to grab her in his arms and hold her and rock her as one would a battered child. Rock her and promise she would soon be all well again. But would she ever be well again? Well enough to trust any man? He hated himself as much as he grieved for what he had lost, and he grieved for her unhappiness.

He made no effort to stem the tears that rolled down his cheeks as he thought of the first night they had shared this room, this bed. The warm, loving girl who had matched his wants and needs with wants and needs of her own. He recalled what she had said about Daphne's brother, that she was glad, for it meant she was not always such a poor judge of character. She must have trusted that English bastard at one time. Reluctantly Jude recalled she had almost trusted him—at least, she had seemed to begin to, and maybe even to care for him. She had obviously worn a special outfit yesterday and left her hair down to please him.

How cute and cocky she'd been, challenging him to a race and how readily she had agreed to a kiss as a prize.

Damn Rosie O'Mara.

Jude had planned for the two of them to race to the little soddy. There he had hoped to promote love and trust between them by recalling all they had shared while they worked there together. He had the words all arranged in his mind to explain how wrong he had been. He was going to tell her how, deep inside, he'd loved her since that first night in the bedroom at Double Tree. He had hoped that the kiss he won for winning the race would seal their future.

Instead, he had lost. Lost the race. Lost everything. If he could have explained to her, and kissed her and brought her back here yesterday reconciled with him, he might have stood a chance. The rape had smashed any hope there might have been.

It was even his fault about Rosie. He should

never have told her he'd send Annie away and things would be as they had always been. Pa hadn't raised him that way. How could he ever explain all this to Annie? The thought of her leaving here was painful, but the knowledge that she would be sure she had only been used was worse.

Somebody was rattling the milk pails and Shawn must have turned the chickens out of the coop, for two roosters were having a duel to see which could crow the loudest this morning. There were going to be enough questions to answer when Annie did not come down to set the table for breakfast; he could not cause more by not putting in an appearance himself. He covered her with the thin muslin sheet, threw her a butterfly kiss, and left the room.

Neglecting his morning shaving routine, he completely forgot to wipe the tears off his face. He used his shirtsleeve to do so as he went down the steps.

Everyone was waiting at the table. Briefly Jude explained Annie was tired this morning and would remain in bed today. The looks his pa and his twin gave him added fuel to his already guilty conscience. Dannie and Shawn were both sympathetic, saying Annie had been working too hard building stone walls lately.

Stone walls, Jude thought. How he wished the walls between him and Annie were made of stone so he could tear them down one by one with his bare hands. He had built an insurmountable barrier between them. He finished his meal in silence and then went to join the fencing crew.

Bright sunlight was streaming into her bedroom windows when Annie awoke. Her aches and pains were mild compared to the pounding memories in her mind and the ache in her heart. She still did not understand why Jude had done what he had last night. Wasn't humiliating her with his mistress enough? Why had he committed the final act of debasement? She tried to block out the memories as she painfully crawled out of bed. She was shocked and sickened by the look of her own nude body in the commode mirror. No one must see her this way. She could not stand the thought of having anyone witness her shame.

She pulled an old nightgown from the drawer and put it on, then tried to straighten the room. She shoved all her torn clothing into the bottom of the big wardrobe.

Leaving here would be the hardest thing she had ever had to do, but now she would go. She began to wonder where her pigskin holdall had been put after it was unpacked. It would be all she'd need to pack the few things she wished to take with her, for she wanted none of the clothes Daphne had given her, nor the skirts she wore for riding. Only the serviceable gowns cut down from Mum's old ones would be necessary.

She started to fold them into a pile on the foot of her still unmade bed. Beside them lay her small beaded bag with the coins in it Jude had tossed at her the first night she had met him.

She tried not to think beyond packing clothes, yet images of Jude kept coming to her mind: laughing, calling her "honey," scowling, masterfully astride Rocky—and beyond him were always vistas of her much-loved Sandhills. Then his perfidy banished the images. She clenched her fists so tightly her own fingernails made the palms of her hands bleed. Grandfather's words echoed: "Annie, you're a born fighter." "No," she whispered to the echo, "I am a born loser, Grandfather, a born loser, and even all your love cannot save me from this!"

Tears trickled down her eyes when she thought of her grandfather. The last few days she had been thinking how happy he would be to know she had found a wonderful home in America, a beautifully trained stallion, and a handsome husband, just as he had predicted. It seemed her grandfather's dreams for her had come true.

Then yesterday they had splintered into a million fragments with no way to pick up the pieces and put them together again. She added a warm coat and muffler to her fast-growing stack of things on the bed. Not everything would fit in the suitcase; she would have to carry the coat over her arm, for winter would be coming before long and she would need it—wherever she was.

The brisk knock on the door startled her out of her reverie. She wished she had thought to turn the key in the lock, for she did not wish to have Dannie bring her in a tray of food. She did not want anyone to see her, for even in her gown

and wrapper some of her bruises were notice-
able, especially her swollen, cut lip, and her
dark-circled puffy eyes.

Gil's voice asked, "May I come in, Annie
girl?"

"I'm—I'm not dressed, Father. Perhaps later
today, or better still, tomorrow. I'm sure I shall
feel better by then."

"Put on a wrapper, child, for I must have
words with you. It won't take long."

"Come in, then," she answered despondently. What did it matter if he saw her this way,
or her clothes ready for packing? He would
know soon enough, for she had to ask to have
someone drive her to a train depot and Gil
would have to give the order. She wanted to be
gone before Jude returned tonight.

The stack of clothing appalled Gil, but not
nearly as much as the sight of her did. He began
to tremble so violently that he had to hastily sit
down on the edge of the bed. Had Jude actually
hit the girl? Why would he do such a thing?

Gil's heavy rasping breaths frightened Annie
and she quickly sat beside him, putting her arm
around his shoulder to try to calm his dismay.
But it was not dismay that rocked Gil's equilib-
rium; it was pure, unadulterated anger. Anger at
his own son.

"He'll pay for doing this to you, Annie girl.
He'll pay dearly. To think it was all my doing
that caused this to happen to you! My stupid
dreams and selfish demands and tampering
with other people's lives."

"Oh, no, Father," Annie assured him. "It was no more your fault than mine, for I willingly fell in with Daphne's plan for me to come here and . . . when I had the opportunity, I did not leave."

"Do you wish now you had gone back to Willy Armstrong's son?"

"No, not at all. How did my name get on that paper, anyway?"

"The minute you walked into my house I knew you weren't an Armstrong and I was inordinately pleased. I wired Hank and told him to discreetly find out who you were and if you were as you seemed, to see that the name was changed before the certificate was filed. He's a good attorney, but luckily he's always putting off the paperwork. Just as I'd assumed, he'd already secretly uncovered who you were and after my telegram he carefully recopied all the names before recording it."

"Then you knew all along I wasn't Daphne. How awful for you when you had wanted someone refined and elegant."

"*Thought* I wanted someone like that, Annie. Thought. It took only a few minutes to realize how wrong I had been. When I first met the boys' ma, she was a young carefree girl, the daughter of a banker. I was the happiest man alive when she agreed to marry me . . . but Annie, I never made her happy. She was never carefree again and I blamed myself for what I'd done to her. She left me, not died, just packed up and left. Even the boys don't know that, for

I moved from East Texas within the week. God, what that does to a man's pride! To have a woman swear he'll never make it, never provide her with a decent life!

"Then and there I swore to build a house and furnish it so even she would have been satisfied. Not to win her back, for I'd never have wanted her back. I just had to prove things to myself.

"You proved what an ignorant old cuss I was, girl. You showed me everything I should have looked for in a wife. You far surpassed her in beauty, and you have so much more to give. Spirit. Grit. Willingness to accept life as you meet it. No, you not only meet it, you go forward and challenge it. Most of all, you're filled with love, girl. All those years I thought what my house needed was the fancy trimmings, but I didn't stop to realize it was already filled with all it needed. Love. Maudie's. The boys'. Mine.

"Then along came that Daphne and put a seal on what I'd already learned. She was exactly like my woman and all the things in the world would never have made her happy. I was glad both boys got a taste of her.

"I'm about as stupid and stubborn as that worthless son of mine. Dear Lord, I can't believe he actually beat you."

"Beat me? Jude would never hit me!"

"But your lip—"

"It's not as it looks. We did quarrel and I do wish to leave, but I bumped my own mouth on the chifforobe door. That is how it came to be cut."

Gil did not argue, but continued to look skeptical as he asked, "You're going to leave with your Englishman, then? That earl's son who wants to take you back to England with him when he finishes his business here?"

"Dev? Goodness no! I don't want any part of him."

"Yet, you're leaving us one way or another, aren't you, child? If not with this Englishman, then where are you going?"

"I don't know yet. I'd like to have some time alone to think things over. Maybe I can find work as a maid or in a lodging house or something."

Gil could tell how desperate she was by her voice, but he had to know something before he gave any thought to her future. He knew he could secure one for her, but the answer to his question would determine its course. "I will see that you are well provided for, child, but first tell me, is there any chance you might be carrying my grandchild?"

Annie had not even thought of this possibility. She had only thought of the pain of the last vow finally broken and his word as an Eastman to not cause her embarrassment by his liaison with his mistress shattered. Lord of mercy! She *could* be pregnant!

Gil was still waiting for her answer.

At last she murmured, "Yes," her voice almost inaudible.

Gil knew he could not deny that this made him happy. A child of Jude and Annie's! How often these past weeks he had dreamed of just such a happening. That son of his had a lot to answer for. As he recalled that haunted look in Jude's eyes, he suspected he might already be answering for a lot of it.

"I have no right to ask this of you, Annie girl, but if I give you my word that Jude will stay out with the fence crew, will you stay here until you know? You won't have to see Jude. Will you stay, child?"

This time her "yes" was even less audible.

"You can't ask this of me!" Jude swore incredulously. He and Gil had eaten a silent supper and were sitting perched on the porch railing watching the sunset.

"I'm not asking, boy. I'm telling you. I had to promise Annie to get her to stay. She was packing—"

"Packing!" Jude remembered how often he'd encouraged her to do this very thing, and now the word shot through him like a sharp-honed knife.

"Yes. She was going to leave here today until I told her she wouldn't have to see you. She must stay. She could be carrying your child, you know."

Jude looked quickly at his pa, more quickly away again. Had Annie told him of the rape? Undoubtedly not, or Pa would be much angrier than he was. Would she stay at the ranch if she was pregnant? A thin wave of hope went through him. This was not the basis on which he wished Annie to stay, yet it would be better than nothing. It would give him time.

All day he had been afraid he would come home and find her gone. She had kept the vows "for better, for worse, til death do us part" until he had nearly killed her. Not in body, of course, but in heart and spirit. "Pa. I have to see her, talk to her. I can't just go away as you ask. There are things you don't know. I'll go if she wishes it, but first I have to have just a few minutes with her—if she will agree to it."

"Only if she agrees to it, Jude. There will be no force, and only for a few minutes!"

"I know, Pa."

Jude went slowly up the stairs wondering if the words had ever been composed with which to ask for another chance after everything he had done. Was there any way on earth to apologize?

The door was locked, as he had known it would be, so he rapped lightly with his knuckles.

"Annie. May I come in and pack a few things?"

She was so long in answering he thought she was either asleep or going to refuse him, but then the key in the lock clicked and she opened the door.

He had never seen her look more beautiful than she did standing there in the candlelight. Beautiful and brave, for she stood there defiantly, even though he could read in her eyes her fright of him. Her eyes were no longer red and puffy, and most of the swelling had receded from her lip.

"Don't be frightened, Annie girl. I swear I won't touch you."

Her eyes told him what she thought of his worthless vows, but still she said nothing.

He went to a drawer to get some shirts out, wishing he knew what to say her. All he could think to tell her was the truth. "I'm glad you're staying."

The statement surprised Annie from her silence. "You are. Why?"

"I want you to stay."

"But last night and yesterday afternoon? All those ploys of yours to force me to leave after all else failed?"

"You thought *that?*"

"What else was I to think? I don't know another reason why you would plan such vile humiliations."

"Oh, honey! It wasn't that way at all. Not at all!" He could hardly keep his hands off her as he beseeched her to believe him. "I did not invite Rosie here. She may have wanted me and touched me, but you watched—you saw that I did not want her. Did not touch her. Ask Jules. I have spurned her since she came to Cottonwood . . . and last night. I was jealous as hell. I thought the Englishman had been your lover and I used you brutally in my anger. I was so wrong—but I wanted you to be mine! Just mine! That he'd had your love tore me up. Today I've come to realize that even if he had been your lover, it wouldn't matter. You are my wife now, but last night—all I can say, Annie, is I went insane with my jealousy."

"Jealousy, Jude?"

"Yes. Strange, isn't it? I never had a wife before. I never knew I would be so possessive. If a child results from last night . . . don't leave, Annie. Don't take my child away. At least talk to me—"

When she didn't say anything, Jude knew he had to keep his word this one last time. He finished gathering up his clothes while she stood and watched him. He wished he knew what she was thinking, but her eyes gave him no clue. She just stood there, watching his every move.

Gil called from the foot of the stairs, "Jude, you coming down now?"

"In a minute, Pa."

He drew another breath, then continued, "After fencing it will be time to mow hay, Annie, and then there is the fall roundup. I could stay away for a long time, if you wished it. If only you will stay here where I know you are safe. Will you stay?"

How could she answer this question? She had nowhere to go and no reason to stay. He'd said his intentions were not to force her to leave. Gil had made him say it because she might be pregnant. If she were not, would she stay? Beyond fencing? Beyond haying? Beyond roundup? If only she could believe he had not sent for Mrs. O'Mara to come to Cottonwood to live, or to visit him at Twin Trails yesterday!

Knowing the proud, arrogant man he was, she could almost believe his story of jealousy. Jude Eastman would not want a wife who had belonged to another. That he did not love her would make no difference. And if there was a child? Yes, he'd want that child even if he did not love or want its mother.

After long moments of hesitation she came to her own acceptable solution. "I'll stay until the first snowfall, Jude, for there is nothing I want more than to see the beauty snow will bring to these hills, but my staying isn't contingent on not seeing you. This is your home—but this is *my* room!"

There was a spark of the old fire flashing in her eyes as she stated her terms. Jude wanted to grab her up and whirl her around and kiss her for what she had agreed to, for what was in her eyes, but Pa's heavy footsteps were on the stairs so he could only say, "As you wish—honey," and then he left the room for the bunkhouse. The boys would have a month of laughs over this. Undoubtedly they'd claim it was exactly what he deserved, and Jude resented falling prey to their criticism. If he rode out to join the fence crew tonight, someone might suspect he went into Cottonwood. He was damned if he did—and damned if he didn't.

"Pa," he asked, "how's the floor in your room?"

"There's a rag rug on it, Jude, and I expect I can spare a quilt for you." Gil's eyes had a knowing twinkle. "Too bad I only have one pillow."

The door of the big front bedroom opened within seconds. *Swish!* A pillow was tossed out into the hall.

Jude and his pa both looked questioningly at one another, then at the closed door.

Only three rocks had been put into place on the wall the next morning, when not only Shawn but two other Double T ranchhands came to the front yard to assist Annie. Gil Eastman was going to take no chances Annie might work too hard and risk any danger to his hoped-for grandchild. Caring for a child's welfare was one thing, but this was ridiculous, Annie determined as she went to the barn to search for Gil to get him to rescind his orders. The chances she was carrying a child were small, but Father did not know that. He was sure to think that since she and Jude had been sharing first a soddy, then a room with a double bed, there were strong possibilities she might be pregnant. Annie did not believe pregnancy would result from the assault Jude had inflicted upon her body, but it was possible, she supposed.

If she shared the love of a child with Jude, would that be enough? No. She refused to even think of life with him chained to her by such a bond. Mrs. O'Mara was here now and Annie felt a little guilty that she had insisted on staying until the first snowfall. Jude was undoubtedly wishing she would go long before that so he could resume his affair with his *chère amie*. *So what?* He did not deserve any cooperation from her to make him happy! In fact, she hoped he was miserable. *Damn miserable!*

Chapter Twenty

✦ ✦ ✦ ✦ ✦

JUDE *WAS* MISERABLE. Damn miserable! The reasons were far from those Annie envisioned, however. The days working on the fence were not bad. It was hot, hard work, and time was of the essence now. All the fields in which he was going to have stacks of mown prairie hay had to be fenced before winter to keep other herds out. Concentrating on the work, bantering with the men, and making plans to keep the supplies coming and the crews progressing as fast as necessary filled his days.

It was Jude's nights that were sheer hell. First, it was nearly impossible to get to sleep in spite of his dog-tired body. Visions of Annie ran rampant in his mind—Annie laughing, blushing, teasing, laying sod, riding horseback—and then the images of her sobbing, frightened, misunderstanding, and angry. God, what a mishmash he had made of her life! Jules had told him a few days ago that Annie told Pa she was not going to have a child. She had also told him she wanted to leave late this fall after it snowed, and she would not agree to Pa's suggestion she live in

Cottonwood with him and Maudie in the new house he was building there near his bank.

Only until snowfall. The thought echoed over and over again in Jude's mind. That was all the time he had, and what good was the time doing him when he was here and Annie was back at the house? She was a strong-willed girl and she had made up her mind to leave him. It would take strong measures to change her, and he wasn't even there to try.

When he did fall asleep at night, he did not stay asleep. Several times each night he'd wake up to pull Annie closer into the crook of his arm, against his side where he liked to have her sleep—only to find he was not in their double bed. Roundup would be a relief. Then at least he could get up and ride night herd for awhile instead of lying here in agony, hating his own guts for being such an ignorant, hot-tempered fool.

The hell of it was, he'd hardly see Annie before she left, if it snowed early this year. He planned to mow in pastures near the barn and put the herds there for winter so they could get a few of the expensive crossbred heifers inside while they were calving. That meant he'd be eating at the house, but with a table full of people there would be no chance to persuade Annie he was not the foul, gutless bastard she believed him to be. He'd given her every reason to think it, he cursed with self-recrimination. If only there was some reason to see her alone, to talk with her alone.

Along with exhaustion one night came the

perfect ploy, a scheme that would give him some much-needed time alone with his wife. He reminded himself it was his own plots and schemes that had landed him where he was, but this time it was different. He admitted to himself now that his plots had been halfhearted. He'd enjoyed the battle, and she had challenged him as often as he'd challenged her. If she met the challenge this time, he knew he would put his whole heart into making it work.

The following morning he didn't wait for daybreak before nudging Jules awake and telling him to take charge for a few days as he had business to take care of in North Platte. Then he saddled Rocky and rode hard toward the ranch house.

Annie sat at the oak dining room table, chin cupped in hands, thinking. She hoped she would like the home Gil had found for her. A friend of his had been chosen to serve on a government agency in Washington, D.C., but he didn't want to leave his invalid wife for long periods of time without a companion. They had been very agreeable to hiring Annie to stay with them this fall.

Gil had set aside a large sum in a personal account for Annie, but she had told him she'd not touch it. He believed her; the girl was stubborn as a mule and determined to be independent. By placing her with a friend, she could be self-sufficient while he could keep track of her. He still prayed that someday she and Jude would work things out.

Annie hoped from now on life would be peaceful: no surprises, no foolish infatuations. She had to remind herself she did not want any love at all—especially not Jude's. Once again her traitorous body disagreed. Demeaning as his attack had been, it had fulfilled needs deep inside of her. Why? Because she loved him? Even though he did not love her? An inner rebellion kept those indescribable feelings from that night fresh in her memories. She wished she had reached that plateau out of love, for in spite of all her reasoning, she wanted to experience that release again—but only with Jude! Tightly clenching her fist, she vowed to rule her heart and her emotions, not let them rule her.

Annie almost jumped up and ran out the back door when she recognized Rocky's unusual gait galloping up the driveway and into the barnyard. Just in time she recalled herself and sat back down to finish her letter to Mrs. Barrister. Jules had ridden in several times to order food and fencing supplies, but Jude had not returned once. She wondered if he had heard that she was not pregnant. She decided he probably had; Gil would have sent him the message.

"Annie girl," Jude began as if he'd just seen her five minutes ago, "where's one of those mail-order catalogs? Do you know?"

"In the parlor on the lower shelf of the library table, as always."

"You forget, I haven't lived in this house as

much as you have. I don't know where things are."

"That is no fault of mine. I did not say you could not stay in your own home." Annie was beginning to get her dander up.

"No, that's right. It was only my room you evicted me from, wasn't it?" Jude asked, purposely trying to rile her temper. If she got disgusted at him, she would fall in with his plans without thinking.

"That situation won't be true for much longer. Your father has found a place for me near Omaha."

Jude was taken aback. "When do you leave?" He tried to make it sound disinterested.

"Don't get your hopes too high, Mr. Eastman, for I said I will not leave until after the first snowfall, and I won't. Unlike you, I keep my word!"

That tongue of hers was as sharp as ever, Jude noted. Thank God he hadn't broken her spirit.

"Sometimes in Nebraska one is snowed in by a big drifting snowfall that doesn't thaw until spring, just more snow and more snow piles on top of it."

"You may as well save your breath, for I am not leaving until I see the hills covered with snow. I'm looking forward to seeing this beauty all around us here—"

"And I'm looking forward to being snowed in until spring!"

Annie was not quite sure how he meant this, so she quickly changed the subject, offering, "I'll

get you the catalog. Which one do you want?"
she called back over her shoulder.

"Any that have horse-drawn scythes in
them."

"You don't have a scythe yet?"

"No. That's why I came in. I think I should
order one."

"Jude!" her voice was full of asperity. "The
things in the catalogs come from a long ways
away. Sometimes it takes five or six weeks to get
them here."

"That's all right. I don't need it for several
weeks. I won't be done fencing for another
month, then there's the roundup. I may have to
wait until I'm through with that to put up hay."

"Jude!"

"What?" he asked, raising his eyebrows innocently.

"You cannot wait much longer to mow. From
the look of the fields, it is haying time now!"

"It is?"

"Yes, it is!"

"Are you sure? How do you know?"

"I told you, Jude. Remember when I was
laying rocks, and I told you I had often helped
cut and stack hay for winter use?"

"Oh, yes, I do remember that, now that you
mention it. So you think it is time to cut it now
. . . but we have no way to cut it."

"Can't you get a scythe anywhere else? Perhaps borrow one?"

"I told you, honey, cutting hay for winter
feeding is innovative around here. As far as I

know, no one else has done it before. No, I couldn't borrow one." Pointedly pondering aloud, he remarked, "I suppose they have them for sale in North Platte, now that there are so many homesteaders."

"North Platte is not too far; you can go there and get one."

Jude could tell by the tone in Annie's voice she was glad there was a solution. He hoped she was as glad as she sounded.

"The thing is, Annie, I can't spare a single man from the ranch right now and I'd need one of them to go along and spell me occasionally on driving if I were to make it there in one day and back the next. It would be easy on horseback, but not with a wagon. No, I'll just have to give up my idea of haying until next year," he said despondently.

"You give up on everything, don't you? Is nothing worth your effort? This haying meant a great deal to you at one time. Now you are ready to forget it!"

"Annie, please. It grieves me enough that I have to give up the idea, without you lashing out at me. Believe it or not, I am fighting for my entire future right now!" He quickly added a stipulation to disguise his meaning, "getting the fence in and all." He tried to sound as if his spirits were low. "I'd give anything not to give up haying, but as you must see, I have to."

"No you don't, Jude. I can drive well enough to spell you."

"You'd do that for me?"

Annie did not even realize what she had offered until after she said it, but Jude was not going to give her a chance to change her mind. He picked her up and whirled her around gleefully, saying, "Thanks, honey. You'll never know how much this means to me." Then he set her down, kissed the top of her hair, and practically ran from the room, calling back, "We'll leave at dawn tomorrow, so be ready. I'll be working around here today, so tell Dannie to count on me for lunch and supper."

All Annie could do was try one position and then another in the big double bed that night. None of them were comfortable. She knew it was because Jude was using his pa's room just down the hall from hers. Knowing he was lying there in his drawers with no shirt on, her out-of-control body craved being pulled against that solid chest into the crook of his arm. She tried to recall his public exhibitions with his mistress, his broken vows and ploys to be rid of her, but she could not stop the desires that flooded her.

She flipped over onto her stomach, reminding herself it would soon be dawn and time to leave for North Platte. Perhaps she could plan to leave the Sandhills before snowfall if Jude was going to be staying in the house often. Yes. She would help with the haying first, then leave. They would need all the help they could get after such a late start.

* * *

All day as they rode through the golden countryside Jude and Annie constantly found things to talk about. First they talked of the Sandhills and the ranch, then of Jude's life as a child in Texas and later at Double Tree, and of Annie's life in England. They ate the basket of food Annie had brought along sitting under the shade of one of the few trees along the trail. It was quite late when they arrived in North Platte, but fortunately Jude knew the way to a hotel.

The little man from the train depot was now a hotel clerk. Annie wondered if he had two jobs or if he had gotten fired at the depot. He was certainly looking her over in a strange way as Jude stepped up to the desk and asked, "Is one of your best rooms still open tonight? If so, I'd like to reserve it for my wife and myself. As soon as we register, we are going to get a bite to eat, so please see that our cases are sent to the room."

The little man looked down at the two small cases and seemed relieved that Annie was no longer traveling with the pile of luggage she had arrived with last spring.

Annie had been so busy observing the depot-manager-now-hotel-clerk that she failed to notice Jude asked for only one room. She was jolted into awareness when the man handed Jude one key, saying, "That will be Number Sixteen. It's our nicest room. Newly painted this summer and clean linens yesterday—and nobody quartered there last night, neither, so they're still fresh."

"Fine, then. We'll take it."

"Jude," Annie started to correct him, but stopped when the clerk began to stare suspiciously at her. He'd be sure to think they weren't married if she asked for a separate room. She would discuss it with Jude while they ate. Perhaps he could help her think of a reason why they needed two rooms. Instead, he scotched the idea.

"A separate room here, honey? A woman alone? This isn't Ogallala, but it's still not safe for you. There are far too many drunks and traveling men or lonely cowhands. The clerk looks like a blabbermouth.

"No, I'll just have to sleep on the floor in your room—if you'd rather I didn't share your bed. I must say, after the long trip I was looking forward to a good bed, but I'm tired enough I'm sure I'll be able to sleep just fine on the floor."

He had never been less tired in his life and he knew he'd be lucky if he got five minutes' sleep in the same room with her, let alone in the same bed. It had been hard enough being in the same house last night. All day today his insides had been churning with desire. He'd started to put his arm around her several times and then hastily pulled it back. Everything depended on tonight. All of his plans had gone well so far; he hoped his luck would continue.

Annie could hardly swallow the food the waiter served them because her mind had already surged forward to Room 16. Could she trust herself alone with Jude? He'd said he was tired and she knew that meant he probably would be asleep a few minutes after they went to bed. It was only her idiot self who would lie there wide awake, her mutinous body tautly coiled. Maybe she should give him the bed and lie on the floor herself, for she wouldn't sleep anyway.

Room 16 was quite clean, as promised. It was a corner room with windows in two directions, the curtains billowing ghostlike out into the room. Annie's pigskin holdall sat suggestively side by side with Jude's black leather valise on the floor inside the door.

Seeing how nervous Annie was, Jude decided he should give her time to undress and take care of her personal needs without him in the room, so he remembered aloud, "I'd like to check on the team, if you don't mind, honey. I'll run over to the livery stable and be right back, if you're sure it's okay, that is."

She could hardly tell him she did not mind in the least. What she did mind was the idea that he would soon be back, and the way he kept calling her "honey" all the time . . . it was only habit, she knew, but the way he said it still bothered her tremendously.

"That will be fine, Jude. Take your time," she finally replied.

Jude was not going to take his time. He'd not risk having Annie fall asleep before he got back.

*   *   *

Hastily Annie poured water from the enamel-ware pitcher into the washbasin and tried to sponge off all the dust from the dry dirt road. After she brushed her hair she laid her clean dress over the chair so some of the wrinkles would fall out before morning. Then she stuffed her soiled gown in the bag and tied the ribbons at the neck of her nightie. She had to run to make it to the bed when she heard Jude's footsteps in the hall.

As he opened the door, she noticed he must have washed up at the pump in the back yard and dried off with his denim shirt, for it was now slung carelessly over his shoulder and his wet hair was curling riotously. She heard him turn the key in the lock and then he started to sit in the chair to pull his boots off. When he saw her dress laid out neatly, he came and sat on the edge of the bed instead. After he pulled off his boots and socks, he stood up and undid his belt, then unbuttoned his trousers and pulled them off. He laid them over his valise, then turned back to the bed again, asking, "Are you awfully tired, honey, or could we just sit and talk for awhile? A man gets damned lonely sleeping out under the stars every night, listening to a bunch of other men snore. It would mean a lot just to hear a soft voice for a change."

"I suppose that would be all right." She knew she wouldn't sleep a wink anyway, especially not after seeing him standing there nearly naked!

Jude took one of the pillows from the bed, moved it to the foot and propped it up against the brass rail, saying, "I'll just sit down here, if that's okay."

Annie propped her own pillow against the headrail, questioning, "Why are you being so considerate, Jude? I don't know this meek, timid side of you at all, and I'm not sure I want to spend the night with a stranger."

Jude laughed, then reminded her, "You told me when you first came to Cattle Creek—that first day in the general store, in fact—that you wanted a meek, docile old fellow whom you could keep under the cat's paw."

Annie chuckled softly at his misquote but hurried to explain, "It was only what I expected, not what I wanted."

"And what did you hope for when you signed those papers, Annie?"

He had slid into a more reclining position and the elbow he had propped up on the bed to hold his chin with his hand was rubbing against the bare calf of her leg. The hairs on his forearm were tickling her leg and causing erotic sensations to pulse up to her thighs and beyond.

She tried to keep her voice casual. "I suppose I hoped for an upright, hard-working man who would be kind to me. I got the impression he'd be shy because he was over thirty and not married. I didn't mind; shyness I could have accepted."

"So you were disappointed, then, when you met me?"

"Not completely," Annie admitted honestly. "You were handsomer than I expected."

"Do you think I'm handsome then, Annie girl?"

Now Jude's fingers were tiptoeing up and down her leg. He was hardly aware of what he was doing, Annie was sure, so she didn't say anything, but she wished he would stop because the fingers were doing much more damage to her poise than the rustling hairs had.

"I hate to admit it, for it will only make you more arrogant than you already are, but you *are* handsome."

"I don't mind in the least admitting you are beautiful, honey, and that I was shocked as hell when I first saw you. I had expected a sour prune old maid. I liked what I saw."

"Then why did you treat me so abominably?"

"Because you acted like a highbrow snob."

"I was trying to be Daphne," Annie giggled. "I thought that was what you wanted."

"God, no! That was the last thing I wanted— and Annie, I have to admit, that was part of why I was afraid of you."

"You—afraid of me?"

"Yes. I was afraid Pa had arranged a replica of Ma for me. He had this penchant, you see, to make a woman like her happy just to satisfy himself that he could do it, I guess. Yet he did not wish to marry again, so I felt he foisted his demands on me and I resented it, but I wanted the Sandhills ranch bad enough to agree. I didn't think you'd stay."

Jude had moved considerably closer now. Annie could see the silver splashes shining in his ice-gray eyes, he was so close, his fingers still doing their sensual little tattoo, but on her thigh, now. It was as if her nightie was not even covering her. It was getting difficult to keep her voice steady.

"So you set about to make sure I didn't. First one plot and then another. I still cannot believe some of your schemes! That soddy was awful."

Her voice indicated how hurt she had been when she found out he'd lied to her, so he risked moving closer still, hoping to distract her. He was now turned around, lying on his side up by her shoulder, head still propped on hand, as he told her, "I was a fool!"

"Yes, you were. You should never have signed vows you did not intend to keep. However, you have won after all, for I am soon to leave as you wished."

"No, darling!" Jude pulled himself up so he was sitting in front of her as he put his hands on her shoulders and looked deep into her eyes. "I mean I was a fool because I ever tried to persuade you to leave. Please, Annie, don't look away. Look at me, for you must hear this. I was not used to being wrong and you made me wrong every time I turned around, but I could not admit it, not even to myself. Not until the day Rance came to the soddy. It was that day I finally admitted to myself that I loved you. It was just as you prophesied that first night—I wanted not only your love, but your heart and soul and respect. By then I knew I had thrown away any chance I might ever have had, and I was a desperate man, believe me!

"I was going to tell you about everything then, but I had hoped to have a few more days alone before confronting you with it. I wanted so damned bad to make you fall in love with me first, then take you over to the big house."

"But Jude, by then I *did* love you. I hoped you might come to love me, too."

"Jesus! You once loved me and I threw it away?" Somehow Annie was in his arms and his head was on her shoulder as he continued, "I have no right to ask this, Annie, but is there a chance in the world you could ever love me again?"

Annie's double-crossing heart and body cried "yes!" but she forced her mouth to say, "I don't know how to answer that, for I don't know what this is all about. My heart wants to believe you but there is Mrs. O'Mara—"

"There is not, nor has there been since the day you came to Cattle Creek, a Rosie O'Mara in my life, Annie, not once. Believe me, in spite of myself I'm afraid I was thinking of you."

"You were?" She sounded incredulous.

"Yes, love, I was. I can guarantee you a very, very faithful husband, Annie girl, if you will only give me a chance to prove it."

Annie looked sideways to Jude's head on her shoulder to try to detect the truth of this in his eyes. She wanted so badly to believe him.

Jude had turned his face toward hers and his eyes were filled with honesty—and love. She was sure he read it in hers, too, because for a second, an eternity, they just looked deeply into the hearts reflected in each other's eyes. Then slowly their lips came together. Softly at first, hesitantly, but there was too much turbulence built up in both of them for this kiss to remain a gentle one. Eagerly their lips demanded more and more still. They had slid down into the bed, lying side by side facing each other. Jude's hands were still holding her shoulders tightly, and Annie had slipped hers through the space between them to entwine around his neck. He did not have to pry her lips apart; they opened for him with sweet anticipation. He thrust his tongue into her mouth to assuage the hunger he had known for so long now. He feasted on the enthusiasm she was sharing with him.

When he started to rotate his tongue within her mouth, he found her own tongue thrusting to meet his, trying to join in the rhythmic rotation, and when his tongue receded, hers carefully followed the path and she timidly began to appease her own seeking appetite. Jude felt a sensation he had never known before and he moaned with pleasure.

His hands were no longer on her shoulders, but now carefully untying the bows of her gown. One hand tunneled inside the folds of her nightie to find a warm, pulsating breast, and he cupped it into the palm of his hand as he allowed a thumb to run up and down, up and down across the hardening nipple. Gradually he moved his lips downward to taste of this tempting delight. His lips were velvety soft, and they feathered the edges and then began to draw on the center of this prize he was softly kneading in his hand.

Annie loved the things Jude was doing to her. Pressed so close together this way, she could feel the hardness of Jude against her own softness and began to squirm in anticipation.

Jude tenderly put her breast back within her gown and raised up above her as he turned her onto her back. Looking down into her eyes, he vowed, "Annie, I have to have that answer to my question now, because if I have you tonight, I'll never give you up. Is there any chance you can learn to love me again, for I won't allow you to leave if there is."

Annie was insulted. Couldn't he tell she loved him? "Jude Eastman," she exploded, "I've told you often enough that I took those proxy vows with every intention of being true to them. It was only when you seemed willing to go to any measure to be rid of me that they faltered. Unfortunately, you managed to bruise my body and break my heart but in spite of this they would not stop loving and wanting you. I must confess, my mind has been very out of sorts with such perfidy—but even it has now joined their ranks, I fear, for I seem to love you with every part of me. You had better be prepared to spend the rest of your days with me now, for I'm afraid you will find such a united me impossible to be rid of."

Jude's heart sang louder with each word. How could he have been so lucky as to have someone like Annie come into his world? She was everything a man's dreams were made of. Beautiful beyond compare, but her loveliness went far beyond the devastating vision that she mirrored. It radiated from inside her as well.

"Oh, my love," he proclaimed as he came down over her to kiss her once again, "I swear to God I will never give you reason to leave me. You will undoubtedly get angry at me and retaliate with that sharp tongue of yours to put me in my place, but there will never be anything we can't work out together—for together we will always be, Annie girl. I just need one more proclamation from you, my sweet. Say you release me from my ridiculous vow, for this time I want us both to feel only shared love."

Annie's voice was soft. "Yes, I release you. It was a ridiculous vow, made and accepted by two people who didn't know what they were saying. For heaven's sake, will you stop being ridiculous now and kiss me?"

This kiss was different than any they had ever shared. It was longer, deeper, more. It rocked both of them by its intensity, for it solidified every word that had been said and formed them into a bond that would never be broken. It left no room for any doubt, and when it ended, both of them were trembling slightly from its fervor.

Jude was cautious as he removed Annie's gown, for every instinct wanted to tear it off her and begin adoring her bare body; but he knew this time he had to go slow and make it beautiful for her. He unbraided her hair and twisted his fingers in it as he had longed to do so often. He held it twisted tightly as they shared another kiss, this one filled with rising excitement as their tongues joined one another in a throbbing titillation. His hands were cupping both breasts now, giving special attention to the one which had been cheated earlier as his hands kneaded and his thumbs rubbed provocatively over the hardened tips.

As his mouth left her lips, it was with feather-light kisses that it seared her neck, her shoulders, the valley between his teasing hands. Then he took one of the hardened tips into his mouth as he tried to remember to suckle it sensitively, but she was yielding to him so rapidly it escalated his ardor.

Annie's fingers ran through Jude's hair. The palms of her hands roamed lovingly over every inch of his back, his neck, his shoulders, and now they were reaching to slip under the top of his drawers. They were tentatively creeping down to experience the roundness of his buttocks.

As his suckling began to escalate and excite her beyond endurance, she came down hard and firm on his buttocks with the flat of her palms, pushing him down onto her as hard as she could. She was wiggling her own hips up to meet her enforced pressure and it was more than Jude could bear. He quickly slipped out of his drawers and came down to her, his staff potently between them. Her body was eager for him. She slightly spread her legs as his hand surged between them, seeking her readiness. With the welcoming groan of a long-denied lover, Jude probed within her, still trying to recall all his determination to go slow and easy.

She made it impossible for him to remember,

for after her slight initial pain her body began to remember that beautiful plateau and it started to surge to meet Jude's every thrust. They began to float higher and higher, far beyond any elevation either of them had dreamed could be achieved by two people, and when the explosions came within them they found the world of togetherness they had both wanted and needed for so long. All the love and release in the world was waiting there for the two of them.

Afterward they lay unbelieving in each other's arms, completely sated.

At last Jude rolled over and pulled Annie into the niche of his arm where she fit so perfectly and murmured, "Oh, Annie girl! When you spouted about 'for better, for worse,' why oh why didn't you tell me how much better the 'better' would be? You made tonight the best night of my life, honey!"

"Jude," she answered disgustedly, sleepily, "how could I know some arrogant cowboy was going to propel me far beyond my wildest dreams and most erotic fantasies?"

It had been impossible once again for Jude to sleep straight through the night, for this time when he awoke to pull Annie closer to his side he found her adorable body there beside him, and when she so sleepily, affectionately, responded to him, he could not just settle for kissing her hair and going back to sleep as he used to, for now his body refused to endure the agony it had then, and demanded the sweetness of fulfillment it knew awaited.

It was much too late to start back to Twin Trails by the time they awoke the next morning. Jude told Annie it was just as well, for he was afraid the way he felt today he would have to stop along the route more than once to fulfill all his long-denied desire for her. He made her blush, but it was a blush of pleasant anticipation.

They dressed and went to buy the scythe and hay rake but found few other things they wanted to shop for; as soon as their wagon was loaded they ate a large breakfast in the hotel dining room, then hurried back to their room. The hotel clerk looked suspiciously at them when they said they would be staying a second night. He looked at them even more suspiciously when he saw them cross the lobby again very, very late in the evening to go to the dining room for supper. They only smiled at him, then looked at one another and smiled the secret, knowing smiles of lovers everywhere, each possessively gripping the other's hand more tightly.

Annie suspected Jude had not really needed another man to help drive, for he drove most of the way home the following day, holding the reins in one hand with the other arm about her, often turning his head to give her a quick kiss or to nuzzle her neck. He was right, too, about not being able to make it all the way home, for in the early dusk of evening they stopped and made love in a cozy hideaway of tall rippling grass where they were surrounded by the beauty of their beloved Sandhills.

It was not even a total shock when they rode into the ranch yard and Tex strolled out to meet them, looking quizzically at the items in their wagon as he said, "Old Bert delivered that scythe you'd ordered from Omaha yesterday, so I put two men on the cutting today, like you ordered."

Jude looked quickly at his wife, hating to have his double-crossing found out this way. He had planned to tell her, but he had become so wrapped up in his newfound happiness he had completely forgotten. Would she hate him once again? Would this new scheme undo everything? He hoped to God it didn't. Even the thought was beyond endurance.

His wife looked at him vexedly, but then she began to smirk as she said saucily, "Do your plots never end, Mr. Eastman? First I must ride drag and then lay sod. Now I must handle the team pulling our second, *much needed* scythe. Well, let me assure you, sir, I can and I will do it."

High up into the air went that cute tilted nose Jude adored, and she swished toward the house with smug assuredness while her little fanny flipped the slight train of her dress one way and then the other.

The broad smile on Jude's face told Tex all he needed to know. He was delighted to think of how excited Gil was going to be by this reconciliation. Tex even remembered something he had to send a man into Cottonwood for the first thing tomorrow so he could give Gil a message. On second thought, Tex decided to go in himself. He wanted to see the expression on his boss's face when he told of his son's latest shenanigans.

About the Author

The local university was as far away from home as Jan Lesoing ever got, but her vivid imagination knows no boundaries! While she has spent most of her adult years raising children—hers, his, and even "theirs"—Jan decided to realize a lifetime dream and write a novel, for which readers of romantic fiction are more than grateful! Jan's characters come alive through their passions to challenge their destinies, and it is through courage and determination that their lives blossom and grow. This universal theme makes her romances both compelling and compassionate. Currently Jan makes her home in Nebraska where she lives with her husband and celebrates her children and grandchildren. Look for her next novel, *Destiny's Interlude*, to be published by Pageant Books in 1989.

Reading—
For The
Fun Of It

Ask a teacher to define the most important skill for success and inevitably she will reply, "the ability to read."

But millions of young people never acquire that skill for the simple reason that they've never discovered the pleasures books bring.

That's why there's RIF—Reading is Fundamental. The nation's largest reading motivation program, RIF works with community groups to get youngsters into books and reading. RIF makes it possible for young people to have books that interest them, books they can choose and keep. And RIF involves young people in activities that make them want to read—**for the fun of it.**

The more children read, the more they learn, and the more they **want** to learn.

There are children in your community—maybe in your own home—who need RIF. For more information, write to:

RIF
Dept. BK-3
Box 23444
Washington, D.C.
20026

Founded in 1966, RIF is a national, nonprofit organization with local projects run by volunteers in every state of the union.

OUR HISTORICAL ROMANCES LEAD THE FIELD!

LOOK FOR THESE SUPER-SELLERS FROM PAGEANT BOOKS!

LEGACY OF SECRETS

She couldn't run from the past—or from his promise of breathtaking love—but Ellis Pennington is determined to uncover the haunting murder that has kept her ancestral home vacant for over twenty years. Set in historic San Francisco before the 1906 earthquake, this passionate love story ignites more than flames of desire in its hungry heroine. But will her legacy of secrets threaten her future happiness?

By Pamela Pacotti
ISBN: 0-517-00036-9   Price: $3.95

SURRENDER SWEET STRANGER

A brazen, flame-haired rancher's daughter is forced into marriage to protect her father's honor. The unlikely groom is an aristocratic bullfighter, now languishing in a Mexican jail after his attempt to assassinate the emperor Maximilian! Yet from their first encounter at the altar, their passion set off sparks so fierce, so complete, that their fate changed the destiny of a nation!

By DeWanna Pace

First-Prize Winner in the Southwest Writers Workshop

ISBN: 0-517-00652-9   Price: $3.95

AVAILABLE AT BOOKSTORES NOW!